Where

the

Nights

Smell Like

Bread

GLEN PETERS

RATTLING GOOD YARNS
PRESS

Rattling Good Yarns Press
33490 Date Palm Drive 3065
Cathedral City CA 92235
USA
www.rattlinggoodyarns.com

Cover Photo: Glen Peters
Cover Design: Rattling Good Yarns Press

Library of Congress Control Number: 2024950029
ISBN: 978-1-955826-79-2

First Edition

For Paolo, who started this whole mess.

Praise for
WHERE THE NIGHTS SMELL LIKE BREAD

"If you think Henry James had the last word in American-European relationships, you've not read Glen Peters' sweepingly romantic and realistically detailed *Where the Nights Smell Like Bread*. This propulsive, superbly written first novel is an exciting tour guide and a daunting gay romance primer on the varieties of Old World disturbia, where first impressions are anything but true."

— Felice Picano, *author of Ambidextrous: The Secret Lives of Children*

"This sexy, sad, life-affirming story of love, friends, and family found when you least intend, will make you nostalgic for lost love, hungry for sensual pleasures, yet glad you're old and out of the game...but not necessarily in that order."

— Sara Marchant, author of Becoming *Delilah and Essential Planner for my Mother's Huge Cult Following*

"*Where the Nights Smell Like Bread* sweeps us along with narrative power. Glen Peters' vividly drawn characters discover that they can't escape the twists and turns of modern life whether they're in Los Angeles, Madrid, or a small Italian mountain village. At the same time, they also experience the joys of family, whether born into, made, or found. Touching, compelling, and true, this book —and especially the narrator Mark—who will come alive and linger in your heart and mind."

— Georgia Hughes, editorial director,New World Library

"A moving story of love lost and found, unfolding during adventures in Europe and under the encroaching shadow of the pandemic. Glen Peters' writing is lyrical and haunting, as he explores one man's journey to create a meaningful life."

— Emily Dwass, author of Diagnosis Female: How
    Medical Bias Endangers Women's Health

"A classic verse by Hafez translates, "The story of love is all but one, yet each time I hear one, it sounds unrepeated!" Glen Peters' new novel, *Where the Nights Smell Like Bread*, is indeed a fresh story of love as it opens new doors that the reader may not even know existed. I finished it in just a few days and found it unlike any story I have ever read. The narrator remains objective throughout, but tender emotions are palpable on every page."

— Zoe Ghahremani, author of *Sky of Red Poppies* (San
    Diego Book-of-the-Month)

"Glen Peters invites us to be passengers on a compelling journey of one gay man's winding path of self-discovery and acceptance. Surprising twists and turns, crisp dialogue, vivid descriptions and distinct observations reveal a kind and caring narrator who is willing to explore the yearnings of his heart near and far, as well as the joys and struggles of his family, friends and lovers. This is a satisfying ride well worth taking. Bravo!"

— Patrick McMahon, author of Becoming Patrick, a
    Memoir of Adoption

"*Where The Nights Smell Like Bread* is a luminous debut novel from an extraordinarily gifted author with a promising future."

— Eduardo Santiago, author of *Tomorrow They Will Kiss*
    (Edmund White Debut Fiction Award finalist)

"There's a painterly quality to the way Glen Peters writes which, while using seemingly everyday language, transcends to a luminous veracity of flesh and bone, love, credibility, and all when you least expect it. Details enhance the otherwise page-turning narrative with the eye of a connoisseur. An engaging, deliciously crafted novel."
— Craig Martin Getz, poet, *The Gold Rush, 2021*

"Who is Mark Anello? Glen Peters' protagonist is a man on a quest, an eternal, age-old quest. Mark is looking for love. This sweeping novel encompasses friendship, family, food, art and addiction; but, above all, the beguiling and treacherous waters of queer love. We follow Mark across two continents against the backdrop of the recent pandemic, accompanied by an engaging and often surprising cast of characters. "A toast to Mark, who's never lonely when he's with friends who feed him." And this novel feeds us too, with a rich and rewarding feast of words."
— Sue Burge, poet, The Artificial Parisienne

"Glen Peters' protagonist experiences the warmth and hospitality of Italian and Spanish locals, who embrace him with open arms. His characters are drawn with authenticity and affection, even with their flaws. His journey is a transformative experience that leaves him with a richer understanding of life's possibilities for a gay American seeking love. It's a well-told story by an accomplished writer."
— Joseph McCormick, author of Until the End is
    Known, a Bisexual Memoir

"If American expat writer Henry James had been freed from the social and sexual constrains of his era, he might have written an intriguing international romp like Glen Peters' *Where the Nights Smell Like Bread*. Facing his own vulnerability, Mark Anello, a dissatisfied California math teacher, pursues relationships from Hollywood to Italy, Spain, and Switzerland while striving to "live and give" amid an assortment of lovers and friends whose own foibles throw up obstacles. Daniel Defoe's classic 1665 A Journal of the Plague Year cannot compete with the unfolding wit, intrigue, and frustrations that Peters conjures in this modern version of a world turned upside-down during the COVID pandemic and its aftermath. Insights into Europe's beauty and art add to the novel's allure."
— Donata Lewandowski Guerra, playwright

"After reading only the first few pages of Glen Peters' *Where the Nights Smell Like Bread*, I was hooked. The dialog engages immediately and characters leap from the pages full-blown and ready to take on the world. Mark Anello, the narrator, is, by turn, funny and tragic, and his romantic interest, the enigmatic Alessandro is charming, long-suffering, but ultimately lovable. Intrigue abounds in a landscape rich with the imagery of a master storyteller."
— Patrice La Mariana L.P., psychoanalyst

Dilige eos quo fides te constringit
et ex toto corde fac.

Love those with whom fate brings you
together, but do so with all your heart.

~Marcus Aurelius, *Diaries*

1
Two Rings

We sit at a café in Ischia forking our poached fish. "It's bland," I say, pushing a piece towards Alessandro, who swirls his wine glass with one hand and pinches a cigarette in the other.

He takes a short sip and a long drag. "So, take out your American gun and shoot the cook. Americans like to murder Italian food, anyways."

The late afternoon sky blooms in cauliflower clouds. To the west, the Tyrrhenian Sea flashes the way everything flashes when you know you're headed for trouble.

"Excuse me," I say. "Americans don't necessarily murder Italian food. No more than Italians do, judging from this place."

He looks at me, twists his mouth into something that's both a smile and a frown, then shuts his eyes as if to show infinite patience. "Mark, my dear. This is the natural taste and how we like. Not American fish burger."

I'm reminded to watch what I say to Alessandro. In recent weeks, my comments about Italian cuisine seem to annoy him, as does small talk in general. Still, we've traveled together for three summers now and got on well before something began to change. He's still the eccentric provincial from the village of Pivonnia I met in San Francisco, and I'm still the native New Yorker dislocated to Los Angeles. He still clerks in the Ministry of Education, and I'm still stuck teaching middle school math in Glendale. Two middle-aged men on the fair (and fairer) side of thirty-five who met on separate vacations and fell into each other's easy company, soon spending entire summers together, which were as much about seeing each other as seeing the world—the world of Italy, that is, as Alessandro proclaims it to be not only the birthplace of great art but culinary magnificence. Clearly, on this last point, we disagree. He lives for *prosciutto crudo*. I crave chicken quesadillas. Especially now. In Ischia. At a café that serves bland fish.

But the sex keeps me hooked. When our bodies brushed against each other that first night in Rome, something came alive in me. Alessandro, short and thick-framed, is not a beautiful man, in clothes or out of them, and not a particularly attentive lover. But the glide of his skin against mine still holds an astonishing power, the power to reel me back to him every year.

"Are we going back to the flat, or do you want your sweet?" he asks a little later as we stand before a fruit stall. "I read about a solar eclipse tonight we see from over the roof."

"That would be a lunar eclipse."

"Really? Because of the sun shining on top of the moon?"

"Because of the Earth's shadow on the moon."

"Complicata," he says, tapping his phone.

This much I've learned: when you're involved with a man but stumble through his language, conversation is filled with hazardous extrapolations. We find the car and lurch back onto the palm-shrouded road to our hotel, Alessandro at the wheel. He drives cautiously as we ascend the foothills of Mount Epomeo through a yellow froth of bougainvillea. We converse in fractions. Alessandro makes me laugh with his malapropisms, and he winces in pain at my shredded Italian. Worse still, he rolls his eyes in boredom at my slow and precise Italian.

"So, we have been to many places this time," he declares. "Urbino, Senegalia, San Severino, Civitavecchia for the spa..."

"Yes, we have."

"Not to mention the islands: Sicily, Levanzo, Favignano, Pantelleria, even. And now Ischia."

"All amazing."

"We got naked in Cavascura and painted each other with muds."

"Sure did."

He glances down and checks his phone. "Did I make a nice tour?"

"Brilliant."

Alessandro sighs. "But we hardly see anything of Pivonnia, my hometown, and now not much time."

"True. I would still like to see the museum in the Palazzo."

"Palazzo Buovogenario. *Eh*, but no museum. Private house."

"Hard to imagine."

"Sì, sì…" he observes, reverently. "La Principessa Pellagrina Buovogenario di Rovare, a descendent of Papa Leone the Nine."

"Pope Leo the Ninth?"

"No one goes inside. The Principessa is a rich hag who murders young men."

"She—*what*?"

"Murders young men! Your hearing no good, now?"

I stare at Alessandro. "You're making this up."

"Sì, I make it all up. I make a fairytale for you."

By now, late in our third summer, you'd think I'd be accustomed to these off-center conversations, but they still throw me, and I try to assess the veracity of this one. Which leads me to another puzzlement: physical attraction aside, who is Alessandro, really? Is he ironic and clever? Insightful and sensitive? What makes him laugh? How has he suffered? With his English rough and my comprehension of his northern dialect rougher, I can't know. Is he *kind*? That's the greater mystery, even after spending so much time with him. But this summer, I decide finally, that he is not. This isn't to say that he's unkind, either, but I've come to settle on the idea that Alessandro is simply an unreflective and impatient man driven by an appetite for adventure and discovery. I suspend concluding that this is a superficial way to move through the world, and once again, resolve to follow him into this energetic empty space in pursuit of something new. Once again, I become his sidekick in an improvisatory narrative, the possible outcome of which neither of us discusses with the other.

We met in the summer of 2016, three years before this current adventure, in the dining room of a B&B on Castro Street. Always late to rise in the morning, I tumbled downstairs just as the kitchen staff started to remove the breakfast chafers. Alessandro, thinner then and with fewer lines on his face, wore a turtle-green shirt and sat across from someone whom I assumed was his partner, a gaunt Australian with rosacea. They were arguing, and maybe because I was the only other one in the room, made no attempt to conceal it.

"I don't want you to be upset with me, love," said the Australian. "You knew I'd planned to meet this mate before the end of the week."

"But we were going to the Tea Garden with the red bridge. My friends are waiting."

"You go on along and I'll meet everyone later. Then we'll all have a nice dinner."

"You forgot about the Tea Garden?"

"Yes, I—well, no, I didn't forget. It's just that the fellow texted me this morning to say that this afternoon was convenient for him."

"He comes to our room?"

"He would prefer it, but if not, I can go to him."

"And then?"

"Oh, please, stop acting like a child. We're both on holiday."

"And *then?* What do you do in our room?"

"We discussed this before, and I'd assumed resolved it. Now go meet your friends, and I'll join you in just a bit."

The Australian, his phone chirping, leapt from his chair, knocking a saucer from the table. He didn't stop to clean it up, and he didn't look back as he flew through the door and galloped upstairs. Two Hispanic women entered and began to noisily disassemble the juice station.

I made eye contact.

"Alessandro," he offered, gloomily.

"*Mi scusi*, but your boyfriend is a *stronzo*."

His eyes brightened. "You speak Italian?"

"*Un po,' ma non perfettamente,*" I stammered.

"You speak Italian like an Irish," he said, looking in the direction of the stairs. "Braxton, my partner, likes freedom." I know him many years, so I'm a bit used to."

"The devil you know is better than the devil you don't."

"You know a devil?" His eyes popped.

"Quite a few, actually."

This seemed to amuse him. His broad face stretched into a toothy smile as he threw back his head and laughed. "Quite a few, actually!"

I offered my hand. "*Mi chiamo Marco. O Mark.*"

He reached out and squeezed the tips of my fingers, avoiding the hand. "Nice to meet you, Marco. O Mark."

"You're traveling with your partner?"

"*Sì.* Today our last day, then to Seattle. We are seven years."

"Congratulations," I said, feeling unsure it was the right thing to say.

Alessandro looked towards the stair again. He swatted a hook of dark hair from his wide forehead. "*Eh,* Braxton says I should be more like him and not so serious."

I waited for more, but he was quiet. "So, are you?" I asked.

"We are very different."

"I got that."

"As for your devils, in Italy, we say, *ma, é così che va.*"

I tried to repeat, "*Ma, é cos...*"

"*É così che VA,*" he hammered.

"Meaning?"

"But that is the way it goes."

"Got it. In America we'd say, *that's the way the cookie crumbles.*"

"Oh my god, cookies and devils!"

He stood abruptly and saluted. "Well, I go to meet my friends now. Goodbye." He turned to walk away, then stopped to face me. "Thank you for the good laughing."

By chance the following afternoon, I met Alessandro and Braxton as they dragged their luggage to the curb while waiting for their cab. Braxton gave me a curt smile and turned away to light a cigarette. He spoke to me in profile.

"He hates it when I smoke in taxicabs, so I puff away like a mad dragon now." Taking a last draw, he turned and looked at me with an expression more curious than hostile. "The two of you made a spark, I hear."

I laughed. "We hardly said ten words to each other."

"That's quite a long run for Aldo, as he's not the loquacious sort." He fumbled with another cigarette but didn't light it. "Pity we're not staying longer."

"Yes. It would've been nice to get to know both of you."

"What do you do?"

"I teach middle school math to bored kids in California."

"How dreary," Braxton sniffed.

A taxi pulled up with a broken dome light. The driver popped the trunk but didn't get out.

"Aldo," said Braxton, "give your American friend an email or Twitter or something. He'd like to keep in touch."

Alessandro reached into his pocket and pulled out the neatly folder paper, something he'd obviously prepared beforehand.

Alessandro Pugliacci
Via Gemma Galgani 9d 62011
Pivonnia, L'Aquila (AQ), Italia
acapado@hotmail.com

"We don't live together, you see," Braxton offered, hoisting a suitcase. "I'm in Sydney, and Aldo lives in a little mountain town east of Rome. But we travel annually, don't you know."

An hour after they'd left, I sent Alessandro a short *buon viaggio* message. A week later, I received his response, a blank email with an attached photo of Alessandro in Seattle stirring some smoking red concoction in a pot. Intent on his work, he hardly notices Braxton mugging grotesquely behind him. Behind Braxton, several other men appear to laugh uproariously. The following week, another email with a belated caption: *Sauce amatriciana with slice pork and fresh carot.* And a month after that, a detailed recipe with the note, *You are a maths teacher, please check my mesurements for ingrediendi.* More photographs, recipes, and notes followed until, in June of 2019, I accepted his invitation to visit, booked a flight to Italy, and shared a bed with Alessandro Pugliacci in Rome.

By then, I hardly remembered the sound of his voice. Braxton was out of the picture, and Alessandro had landed hard. He'd put on more weight. He'd started to smoke. We'd lie in bed together in the dark. And in the rising light of morning. And in the heat of the late afternoon. Then we'd go out for pizza at Café Dei Tre Fratelli.

"Are you coming up to see the eclipse?" I ask. "It's almost nine o'clock."

"In a moment, *caro*," he calls out in a singsong.

Alessandro sits at a small table in the lounge area of our hotel, talking to a young Argentinian named Valentino, who cleaned our flat. Lately, he's taken to disappearing when we return to the hotel after touring, or immediately after we finish our *terza portata* in the hotel café. Last night, he left me to eat dessert alone, until a British couple at the next table invited me to join them. Tonight, it's this housecleaner, half his age. I linger for a moment, watch Alessandro lean back and laugh at Valentino's jokes as they share a *digestivo*. Then I climb the iron stairs to the roof noisily in the hope that Alessandro will hear me and follow. But he doesn't.

Couples stand in silhouette against the lambent Tyrrhenian that begins to take on the tinge of the reddening moon. Light glances in every direction as scooters turn the corner and sweep their beams across the roof. Soon, the moon becomes splendid: a marrow-colored ball that blackens at the center until it's a hoop of fire. A golden ring with one blazing carnelian.

On the way back down, I bump into the British couple.

"Where's your chap?" says the wife. "Gone off again, has he?"

An hour later, I'm in bed waiting for Alessandro to emerge from the bathroom. Finally, he does, still in his underwear. He climbs into bed and turns his back to me. On the terrace below, I hear laughing and the wails of some Italian pop star. Somebody shouts to keep quiet. Somebody shouts back.

As I drift off to sleep to the distant hiss of the sea, a twilight dream takes me back to the apartment on East 84th Street.

I'm five years old and sit in my pajamas under the kitchen table as rain ticks the window. My father walks to the table where my mother stands, his black shoes shining like giant beetles. I hear my mother crying above me, so I reach for one of my father's shoes to keep it from moving away before he bends down to lift me to his rough face, kisses me, then hands me off to my mother, who buries my face in her soft shoulder. After my father leaves, the rooms of our apartment seem changed. They're larger and have a different sound as my mother grows smaller. She's very small by the time I meet Ibrahim, at nineteen, who takes me to Colorado and abandons me eight months later. Those rooms had a different sound, too.

I'm awakened by the chirp of Alessandro's phone. He leaps up, naked now, and stumbles towards the dresser. A moment of silence and then another chirp. And another. I roll over and fall back to sleep.

In the morning, I write to Marina, Alessandro's oldest friend and, for the past few months, my confidante. *I think this might be my last summer here, I'm afraid,* I tap into my phone while Alessandro lingers in the shower. *My friendship with Alessandro seems to have run its course.* I think of saying more but decide not to. *Anyway, I hope to see you again when we return to Pivonnia on September 10 because I leave for California the following day.*

Marina knows a little about California because she lived in Santa Barbara for two years while studying the American murals of the WPA artists. Her English is good, but this time her only response is a weeping emoji. I know she'll want the details later.

At noon, we fill the car at the *benzinaio* and arrive at the Ischia pier late in the afternoon, the car queue for the rust-bucket ferry returning to Naples overnight already very long. An hour later, we find our parking slot and enter our small cabin mid-deck. It's squeezed between even smaller cabins containing large families and screaming babies.

We tuck away our suitcases, Alessandro's phone chirping several times. He scrolls through a message, then places the phone on the small table beside the bed. We undress and make love without showering. Two hours later, a dinner horn wakes us from a nap, but neither of us stirs. I turn on my side and look at Alessandro.

"A fantastic island, Ischia. Thanks."

"So, I am a good travel agent?"

"*Ma certamente.*"

He stumbles to the head, talks above the racket of his pee. "You are spoilt to have someone like me take care of all the details for you. I could charge a lot of money."

"As I said before, I appreciate it," I answer. But Alessandro either doesn't hear me or pretends to not understand.

"Very lucky you, relaxing while I do all the work."

"Are you joking?" I prop myself up, stifling my annoyance.

"Yes," he says, smiling and sitting on the edge of the bed. "I make a little joke."

"Ridi, ridi," I say, Italian for *yuck, yuck*.

"Bravo. So, I have a nice surprise for you, now. When we return to Pivonnia on Thursday, you will meet an important lady."

"Who?"

"I wrote her cousin and secured the invitation."

I shrug.

"She lives in a very nice house that you wanted to see inside of."

"The Palazzo Buovo—?"

"Buovo*genario*," he says, overpronouncing it. "A tour from the Principessa herself, at four-thirty in the evening. Are you happy finally, for god's sake?"

We spend the next thirty minutes on deck chairs where the breeze cools, and the retreating vista of Ischia flashes across the rose gloom of dusk. Alessandro reaches out and caresses my hand, strokes the tender spaces between my fingers.

"I have a smoke now," he says suddenly, as I'm nodding off. He slips his hand from mine and gathers his tobacco paraphernalia.

"I'll come with you," I reply. "Let's explore the lower decks."

"I'm just smoking."

"Fine. I'll explore the lower deck while you have your smoke, and then I'll join you, and we can walk around a bit."

"We will lose our chairs, *caro*."

"We will find another pair of chairs," I say, not yet realizing what the conversation is really all about.

But soon, it becomes clearer. On a hidden stretch of side deck below, several young crewmen assemble to have their smoking break. We step off the stairway and see them just as one squeezes another's backside. When we enter their smoking area and Alessandro lights up, all eyes are on us.

"Buonasera," Alessandro says offhandedly.

They return the greeting in chorus, and within seconds, Alessandro and the smoking crewmen are engaged in a lively and raucous conversation that I can barely follow. It goes on for a very long time, so I finally excuse myself and stroll away to explore.

Forty minutes later, I return to find the deck empty. The sea hisses below and the sky is crazy with stars. Ischia, distant now, glimmers like a phantom ship. I text Alessandro and receive no reply, so I return to our cabin. I text him again. And again. Then I phone. The call goes right through to voicemail which means that his phone is probably turned off. I pace, trying to calm myself. Then I pick up the phone and call Marina.

Luciano answers gruffly, and when he finally understands who I am, barks something to Marina. After a moment, she answers, but her voice is so soft that I can hardly hear her above the drum of the engines. It's clear that this is the wrong time to chat, so I ask her if this is the wrong time to chat. "Yes, Mark, she says. I'm sorry."

I undress, take a sleeping pill, and after a fitful bout of tossing, finally fall asleep.

Five hours later, our car clatters down the ramp to Naples' Mergellina pier.

"Carissimo," Alessandro says, "I am a lucky man to have you in my life. Because you have passion with me."

I catch the flub in his pronunciation: *passion*. He means to say "patience," and yes, I agree, I have patience with him, this morning pushed to the limit.

I stare through the windshield as we drive past slapdash Neapolitan apartment houses on our way back to Pivonnia.

"So, what were you doing all night with the crewmen, and why didn't you at least text me?" I ask, but Alessandro counters with a story that many of them were from a village close to Pivonnia and knew some of the people he grew up with.

"When I hear the dialogue of the mountains, I become very *sentimentale*," he tells me, glancing into his rearview mirror, "So, I spend an evening with two of them smoking and having a bit of wine in the bar. If you spoke Italian, you could have joined us. But they wanted very much to meet you, anyhow."

"They'd met me already."

"Yes, but you were a bit rude to walk away like that. I could've made a translation for you."

I ruminate over this table-turning.

"And Valentino the housekeeper, the night of the eclipse?"

"*Mamma mia*, caro, so jealous. Look at you, so healthy with the nice skin and curly brown hairs, with the delicate face of *un intellettuale*." He reaches out and squeezes my crotch. "And *bel cazzo, eh?* Why such a handsome man as you so jealous of an ugly man like me? You know what they call me as a schoolboy? Quasimodo! Can you believe? Because of my big square head."

There. I've said the wrong thing again. I apologize.

We turn onto the autostrada. Alessandro turns his big square head to stare at me while driving, something he's never done before.

"Mark, you expect me to go with no one else when we're apart?" He stares until a driver honks him to attention.

"Hardly, since you go with everyone when we're together."

"No, you are wrong about that."

I look beyond him. The words come slowly. "For three summers, I've come all the way from California at your invitation. But when I go back to the States, I hear nothing from you all year. You don't even answer my letters. So, here I am again, and now every five minutes you disappear somewhere."

He says nothing and fumbles nervously to roll a cigarette, the car lurching.

"I want to be with you, Alessandro—don't you get that?" I say. "And if you really feel you're lucky to have me, you'd want to be with me, too. You'd invite me to make a life with you here. I have the money, I'm learning the language, and I found a lawyer who can do the residency paperwork."

He takes a twitchy drag and breathes it out. I hear him mutter, not quite to himself, *Oh my god* as he cranks down the window. Another drag, then: "What do you do in America when you're away from me?" The words come out in puffs of bitter smoke.

"Nothing. I wait to come back," I answer. "Look, I'm sorry if this sounds like the argument you had with your Australian boyfriend in San Francisco."

"Braxton. No argument. We had an arrangement."

"An arrangement you didn't seem to like very much, as I recall."

We turn a corner, and the green valley of Campania appears, the musky scent of grapes in the air.

"You are a romantic man," Alessandro says, not unkindly, "and Italy is a very romantic country. Here you feel the emotions *intensamente*."

"My feelings are real."

"Maybe, but now you also make up a romantic story in your head. Your American fairytale. Happily ever afterwards. We Italians are puzzled by it. Here, we are born into our stories and make the best of them. We get old but carry our bread up the stairs."

A motorcycle roars past us.

"Explain it to me, Mark. What is this strange American loneliness?

"No idea what you're talking about."

He looks at me quickly, his eyes glistening. "I am the first man you make love to?"

"Of course not."

"When we first meet, you are alone. Why?"

"Because something ended without even a fucking goodbye. Just ended. Eight years of something." Now, my eyes glisten.

The valley dulls to brown as we head west to Rome.

"*Eh*, your heart is broken, and you feel angry and lost. So, in your fairytale book, you look for a prince to save you. But I am a grass*hooper*."

"A what?"

He makes a springing motion with his fingers.

"You mean, 'frog.'"

"Whatever. *Froag.*" He glances at his wristwatch. "So, I try to make you feel better now and tell you what happened with Valentino at the hotel that night. I express my deepest feelings for you."

He goes on to explain that the housekeeper needed advice because he wrote songs and planned to visit Rome to meet a producer. He wanted Alessandro to hear some tracks he'd mixed on the office computer. While listening to the music and gazing through the window, Alessandro thought of me on the roof as he watched the eclipse.

Now, he places his hand on my knee.

"I saw the moon make a ring as you predicted with a ruby stone," he says. "I wanted to take that ring from the sky and give it you with 'Alessandro' scratched inside so you will always remember me in America."

Thursday afternoon, we're back in Pivonnia, and I decide to buy a ring. A pair of them, actually, in silver. It's the day we tour Palazzo Buovogenario. While Alessandro naps, I call Marina and ask her to join me in the piazza to translate for the jeweler. She shows up at three o'clock, an attractive and spirited young woman dressed stylishly as usual, but looking tired today, her platinum hair pulled into a careless ponytail. She seems confused about the ring business as I pay the clerk and place the ribboned box in my pocket, so I try to explain. Maybe it's cruel, but I buy the rings because I want, when I leave Italy forever, for Alessandro to look back and remember that someone once gave him a ring—someone believed in him, risked heartbreak and disappointment and asked for his love in return. I'm compelled to plant this seed, to set up this drama of future regret in my cavalier seducer and betrayer.

Marina raises her hand to interrupt me.

"That's worse than anything Alessandro has done to you," The words tumble from her. "If you make this grand gesture and return home, you will easily move on and find someone else. But you must know that he will not easily find another."

A church bell peals the half-hour.

"Do you want to marry Alessandro? In America, will be possible soon."

"He doesn't like America. He's happy with me part-time."

"Then, for what reason, these rings?"

"Because I want his heart to break with mine when it's over."

"When what is over?"

"What might have been. A life together."

She closes her eyes and looks down. Then, she opens them. "It's cruel to make someone regret something that only might have been. You must accept what is now. You must be honest and break whatever holds you to Alessandro—that holds each of you to the other. You must break it completely!"

We enter Piazza Buovogenario from a side street, startling a flock of rock pigeons that takes to the air in a flurry. Marina stops to look at me, touching my shoulder.

"Dear Mark, take with you the best of your friendship with Alessandro. You have all of Italy to come back to, and you will return soon."

"Return soon," I repeat. "Do you really think so, Marina?"

"Of course. You have your journeys and memories with Alessandro, and you have his friends who are now also your friends."

Maybe she sees the doubt in my eyes. She touches my face.

"And Luciano?" I ask, "why do you stay with him when he clearly hurts you?"

She hardly seems to think about it. "Because he is the father of my children and loves them. It's better that he loves his children more than his wife, because this way, I make a bargain with my conscience and do as I please."

We arrive in front of the Palazzo and wait for Alessandro, Luciano, and the cousin of the Principessa to join us. The pair of silver rings, tucked in their box and secure in my pocket, press against my skin.

"*Ciao, ragazzi!*" Alessandro calls out as he approaches with the others. The cousin of the Principessa is quite something with her high bubble of silver hair. She's as solid as a tree. When we meet, she noisily offers me her hand.

"*Piacere mio,*" I mumble, kissing what little flesh I can find behind a filigree of jewels.

Alessandro beams. He drapes his arm across my shoulders and announces, "We must thank Signora Buovogenario di Rovare because she has talked to the grand lady inside." With his free hand, he lifts his phone to check a message that came in silently.

By now the palace, with its overbite of balconies, swallows us in its shadow. Signora Buovogenario clankily removes her baubled phone from a satin handbag and makes the call. Soon, I expect the grand iron gates to open and admit us into what is, no doubt, a gorgeous stone loggia, but instead, a small door opens at a grimy edge of the palace where a uniformed maid beckons us to enter. We walk through a narrow corridor that leads to a small, scissor-gate elevator that can barely contain the six of us, but it lurches to the floor above, and we exit into a tiny foyer with a single door. Then, after a soft tap to announce our arrival, the maid pushes open the door and we follow.

The Principessa sits at a card table slurping soup. A black and white television set flickers in the corner, and a small electric fan nods back and forth on top of the refrigerator. Peacock feathers, in a tall vase, stir gently in the breeze.

One by one, we stoop to kiss the trembling hand of the Principessa, who still grips her soup spoon. She beckons us to sit and a kitchen helper brings wine in a crystal flagon and a silver plate of biscuits. No one talks very much because it's understood that the Principessa is hard of hearing and finds conversation tiresome. The television blares, bright with dancers. The Principessa finds this amusing, beaming at us and pointing to the screen so that we might laugh, too. And we do.

The cousin is the first to speak up. Addressing the Principessa elaborately but receiving only her scant attention, she announces that we are waiting for the *siniscalco*, or "keeper of keys" to appear who will unlock the palace. But he's also a bus driver on alternate Thursdays and may not yet be off his shift. A few biscuits later, a clattering of the elevator announces him, and in walks a tall, tired-looking man wearing a stiff red jacket. He carries a glass-topped box of keys near his chest, ceremonially, as if in a procession. He bows lightly to no one in particular.

The Principessa motions for her maid to switch off the television and the box is placed before her. Clearly, this is serious business. She studies the keys—there must be nearly fifty of them—and carefully selects three.

She gestures to the key-keeper who bows again, and places the chosen keys on an iron ring. The Principessa grunts something to her maid, who, knowing the routine, has already placed the four-pronged cane before the grand lady. With a great groan, she rises and waves for us to follow, the siniscalco at her side.

"The tour of the palace shall begin now," announces cousin Signora Buovogenario and makes an elaborate bow to the Principessa, which we are obliged to follow. And then, in a lumbering parade led by the *Nobile Signora* and her key-keeper, we enter a narrow hallway (one that I'd assumed led to the toilet) and emerge in Wonderland.

The chamber is colossal. Huge mirrors edged in an eruption of gilt, appear one after the other against a wall of red silk shot with stars. On the opposite wall, mullioned windows let in the light from a loggia below, floored with spiraling marble. The furniture—gold-crusted sofas, cabinets, and tables—is pushed to the side to highlight the scale of the room. And everywhere, *everywhere* art: sculpture, paintings, tapestries; urns of all sizes in malachite; a huge bronze of a serpentine monster looms from a corner, wrestling with its saintly nemesis.

"*Guardate lassù!*" calls the Principessa, pointing above without looking up, her voice now clear and strong. We slow our pace, raise our heads to the vaulted ceiling, and take in a riotous swarm of angels and demons circling the eye of a Baroque hurricane. Drapery billows, lightning flashes, and putii grip the muscled calves of haloed supermen as they alight and tumble in divine battle.

Alessandro pokes my side. "You like? Maybe you can marry the Principessa."

The next room, or grand salon, contains no furniture. But it's a corridor of masterworks. Marble figures obscure marble figures before walls congested with paintings large and small. The Principessa, now hitting her stride, marches forward. She sweeps her hand from side to side nonchalantly, indicating this and that, without looking at any of it.

"Tintoretto..." she announces with a sweep left. "Ghirlani..." with a sweep right. She marches farther down the corridor and slows, apparently looking for something. She finds it and commands us to stop. With a grand gesture, she directs our attention to a luminous, sensuous, velvet-hued oil painting of the Madonna with a lamb, the unmistakable work of a master.

"Raffaello Sanzio da Urbino," she trumpets, studying the painting. A moment passes. *"L'assicuratore mi dice il mio più grande tesoro."*

Alessandro translates. "Raphael of Urbino. The insurance man says her most valuable treasure."

We observe a few seconds of reverential silence before letting out a collective sigh of admiration. Then, abruptly, the parade resumes.

On a roll now, the Principessa smacks her cane rhythmically as the side-to-side hand business continues.

"Vasari... Guercino... Maratta..." she calls, motoring along, *"Tanti, tanti. E così tanto!"*

Again, Alessandro clarifies. "So many, so many, and so much."

She pauses before an equestrian tapestry, draped above a porphyry mantelpiece.

"Pietro Coecke van Aelst..." She turns to us, flashing a crone's smile. *"Anche mio. Tutto è mio."*

"Also mine." Alessandro's breath rasps in my ear. *"Everything is mine."*

The Principessa turns and winces. We follow her to the far end of the corridor. Beyond it, a never-ending series of opulent rooms appear, but she appears tired. Two young men enter from a side corridor, one pushing a wheelchair, and the Principessa is secured and wheeled away. We send her off with light applause.

Cousin Signora Buovogenario resumes her self-assigned role as proxy tour guide. "The tour of the palace is now ended," she announces, to no one's surprise.

We applaud again.

"Thanks, Alessandro," I whisper, "Nice place. Would she consider a time-share?"

"You are crazy, " he replies, checking his phone.

The key keeper, now looking a bit disheveled, bows to us unnecessarily, makes a motion to follow him, and we wind our way back through a series of service hallways that were used by wood carriers to fuel the elaborate porcelain radiators. I walk beside Marina now, who, I'd noticed earlier, had begun to argue with Luciano and broke away from him. In the dim immensity of the corridor, her voice is small.

"Everything is hers, but she has nothing."

"Why, Marina?"

"Because she's a spoiled old woman who suffers as much as we do but hides it with pride. I've heard she tells the servants to bring her young men at night, just to 'pass the time.'" She glances sideways at me.

Now, she takes my hand and squeezes it.

"You okay, Marina?"

"No. I feel very lonely in this place."

When we emerge in front of the Principessa's apartment, her maid comes out and insists we come inside again. We oblige, and find the Principessa happily recovered, sipping a cognac. We take our seats and the Principessa stammers something to her cousin.

"The Principessa has enjoyed our company as she receives very few visitors," Signora Buovogenario announces.

Marina looks away.

We mutter our gratitude as the kitchen helper brings out an elaborate tray of spirits. It's clear that we're expected to drink. In fact, it's clear that we're expected to get toasted with the Principessa, who's now, it's become clear, a bit over-fond of the sauce. But the others, including the hyper-aristocratic Signora cousin, reluctantly follow. All but Alessandro, who looks worried.

"Alessandro," I call out to him. "Ask the Principessa if she gives out party favors."

Marina giggles and translates. *"Regalini."*

"Party favors? No, I forbid you to ask that," Alessandro gruffs.

"Come on. Ask her if I can take something with me back to America. A painting or statue or something."

"You are crazy!"

Marina tips her glass and takes a last swallow. "Ask. You might get it."

"I will not allow!" Alessandro's eyes shoot daggers.

The cousin, three-sheets-to-the-wind by now, asks what's going on. Marina leans over and translates.

I persist. "Look, Alessandro, if you won't ask, then perhaps the Signora will do me the favor."

The cousin beams. Surprisingly, she's in. She puts down her glass, rises from the table, and addresses the Principessa formally.

"*Cara Principessa, il nostro amico Americano vorrebbe avere un piccolo ricordo della sua collezione.*"

"Oh my God," Alessandro says, covering his face.

An ominous silence follows, but the cousin continues to smile and winks at me. I suspect she knows the game, but I'm not so sure about the Principessa, who regards me, raising her head imperiously and leaning backward. She smiles thinly, her eyes locked to mine in a stare down.

"*Americano,* eh?"

"Sì, I answer. "*Dalla California.*"

She nods and looks away. Then she rises, studies her audience, and begins to recite something, solemnly. The cousin provides the running translation.

"She says that the American soldiers occupied this palace at the end of the war and helped defeat the fascists in Italy. And for that, she offers America her heart…"

The Principessa waves the cousin to silence. Then she smiles at me warmly. She struggles to get the words out in English.

"But as for my treasures, Signore … eh, *no.*"

I pretend disappointment, then rise to leave, feeling uneasy that this silly jest might've been lost on the Principessa. The cousin strides towards me, still smiling.

"Don't worry," she reassures. "I understood your joke so I play the game with you."

"And the grand lady?"

"She plays the game better than any of us."

Alessandro fumes and seems unconvinced by the cousin's reassuring smile. He's suddenly in my face.

"You've humiliated me, Mark. You make ignorant American comments and she will never invite us back."

"I make a little joke, Alessandro. Like you."

But he storms off ahead of everyone and bolts from the elevator when we reach the ground floor. In the piazza, he rolls a cigarette and puffs.

His phone chirps.

It's dark now, and we finish off the evening with some prosecco at a local bar. The pair of silver rings, in their little box, dig into my hip. Alessandro has cooled down but avoids looking at me. His phone chirps a text, but he doesn't respond. It chirps again. This time, he gets up from the table holding the phone, and walks to the far side of the room. But even from here I can see that he's making a call. And even from here, I can see, in the movement of his mouth, the shape of a name: *Braxton*. He stops his free ear with his finger. Then, discovering that I'm watching him, goes outside where he's still visible through the window. Marina looks at me with soft eyes, but eyes that encourage me to finish what I've started.

Alessandro pockets his phone and rolls a cigarette. I get up to join him. I approach, his back turned to me, and startle him with a tap. He turns, caught in a smile that instantly dissolves.

"What, Mark, you spy on me now?"

"Tell me something."

"Something."

"All summer, you've been slinking off to read phone messages when we're together."

"What does it mean, 'slinking?'"

"What are you hiding, Alessandro?"

"Nothing. Not hiding."

I wait.

"Well, I text Braxton in Australia sometimes."

I take a deep breath. "How long have you been texting Braxton?"

"Why?"

"I want to know."

"One year. A bit longer, maybe." His face changes, his eyes growing dark again. "But I speak to him for the first time only just now." He flicks a large ember towards me, "After what happened inside when you embarrass me in front of the Principessa."

He calms down, draws on the stub, and looks up at the palace, now half-lit by streetlights. "Anyways, I go to see Braxton next spring in Budapest. Our favorite season for flowers there."

Marina and the others quietly exit the bar. They appear prepared to leave without us if we're engaged in some important conversation, which I decide we are not. I take Alessandro's arm and we walk towards our friends. The café lights of the piazza dim and blink out.

I find the courage. "Braxton seemed like a good man. Clever. Educated. And, like me, has *passion* with you."

"Too bad you don't get to know him better," Alessandro sighs.

We look at each other quietly.

"*Ma, é così che va,*" I finally say, speaking it carefully. "That's just the way it goes."

"You remember. Bravo."

He pulls me closer and thumbs a tear from my cheek. "Or as they might say in America, 'That is the way of the cookie, which has crumbled.'"

2
Who is Mark Anello?

The night before I leave for Los Angeles, Marina invites me to dinner. Over a good Nebbiolo, she asks about my plans. I tell her I have nothing much planned other than preparing myself to meet my new students in September. She brushes that aside and recommends I do something nice for myself.

I've spent the last six days living with Marina and Luciano after I left Alessandro standing in his hallway looking hurt when I refused his gift of two seashells. The teacup-size scallops, tossed on a shelf, were nominal keepsakes from a walk we took along the beach in Trapani, Sicily, three years ago. "Something from our first summer together," he'd said, cradling them in his hands, "Now you take home to remember Alessandro and good times." After I declined a third time, he offered me fruit, which I also declined, as well as a prosciutto sandwich. Finally, he asked for eighteen euros and reminded me that he did all the food shopping for the previous week and we hadn't yet settled. I took out my billfold, paid him, and looked one last time at the vestibule of the house we'd shared for three summers, the old-style house with long corridors and frosted glass doors that opened shuttered rooms. I thought for a moment that I'd run next door and say goodbye to Alessandro's mamma, whom I'd met only once, but a honking horn signaled Luciano's rescue.

Over another glass of Nebbiolo, Marina admits that Luciano isn't thrilled to have me living in their apartment, although the kids, Angelina and Fabbio, their six- and eight-year-old, enjoy laughing at my bad Italian. But Luciano isn't fond of men who sleep with men, she tells me unapologetically. He asks why so many of her friends are *finocchi* and especially why so many American tourists are of that persuasion. Marina relates that she explained to her idiot husband that maybe Americans are just more open about these things than Italians, and that Luciano might be quite surprised to learn how many of his coworkers at the garage were also of that persuasion. She laughs when she describes the horror on his face. Emboldened by the wine, I puzzle aloud how such an educated and attractive woman finds herself married to—but Marina anticipates the question and swats it away. "You would miss your flight if I began to explain," she says, spooning her gelato.

We take the long path home through Pivonnia's Centrale, Marina confessing that tomorrow, the day of my departure, will be her thirtieth birthday and, three days later, her anniversary. This is news to me, and I scold her for not telling me sooner. She shrugs it off as unimportant and says how relieved she feels that the kids have finally learned to adjust to their father's mercurial temperament and are doing well in school.

"They are bright and sensitive children," she says, "And they see what's going on."

I want to ask Marina to elaborate, but sadness seems to settle on her, so we walk in silence. The weather has turned cooler now and *Ferragosto*, the festival of the Assumption and three-week holiday, will end soon. Fewer people stroll about the piazza as shops chain down their canopies. Back in the apartment, Fabbio and Angelina greet me exuberantly and exhort me to say something funny as I make my way to the bedroom to gather my suitcases. But I see that Marina has already placed them in the hallway and secured their zippers. The kids get their wish when I thank Luciano for his hospitality in Italian, which seems to have already begun to deteriorate. He grabs my shoulders, squeezes them in a gesture that feels like he's both pushing me away and keeping me close, then slams me into his chest for a tight hug. Everyone tears up.

At 10 p.m., Marina drives me to Ancona and drops me off at the budget Flixbus station, where I'll catch my all-night shuttle to Fiumicino Airport in Rome for my 5 a.m. morning flight. I'm one of only six backpacking tourists on this enormous, broad-windowed bus that whines and chuffs through the darkness of the autostrada. I doze, then wake up to see the majestic Gran Sasso mountains backlit in a pre-dawn blue. The bus downshifts as we enter a labyrinth of parking lots and snorts to a stop in front of the terminal. In the warming light, I gather my stuff, find my flight, and settle into my seat as the sun begins to rise.

For the next twelve hours, we follow the rising sun, first over Eastern Long Island and then above the San Gabriel mountains of Los Angeles. I'm home.

As the Uber pulls up to my house on Montrose Street, I experience what by now is a familiar deflation at the sight of the neighborhood with its Mediterranean concoctions of architecture corralled by gas stations and nail salons. My neighbor, Mrs. Sandoval, who's taken in my mail for the past few months and paid bills with the stack of blank checks I've left her, is already outside pruning her hibiscus bushes. She peers from under her wilted garden hat, sunglasses a-tilt. "You're back," she says, neutrally. "I put your mail in a box on the kitchen table." Mrs. Sandoval, in all my years of travel, has never expressed even the slightest curiosity about my trips, although she sometimes refers to them indirectly by reminding me that she doesn't eat Italian food because of acid reflux.

I shower and, against sensible advice, go to bed and sleep for three hours. The buzz of my phone startles me. The I.D. photo of the caller makes me wish I'd remembered to turn it off.

"Hello, Allen."

"Hey! Loren told me you'd be back early this week."

"Just got in. You sure don't waste time."

"So, how was your third honeymoon in fair Italia?"

"A magical dream come true, as usual. What's up?"

"Big changes for me. I thought you should be the first to know."

"Good, I hope."

"I'm the featured comedy act at the Highliner on Sunset next Saturday. Jody pulled me from the opening lineups and put me center stage on their busiest night of the week. *Magnifico*, right? Is that how you say it?"

"*Mazeltov.*"

"Wait—were you in Italy or on Fairfax?"

"Haha."

"Anyway, you're invited."

I don't answer. I'm hungry.

"Come on," he wheedles.

"Jet lag," I plead.

"This is Monday. The gig is Saturday. You could recover from a vacation to Jupiter by then."

"Then, just no."

"Look, before you decide, listen to some of this great new material I've put together... *Folks, have you ever thought: what's with all these weird new colors for cars? Some new niche market, like, designer getaway cars? Describe the bank robber's vehicle, sir. Well, officer, it was a teal bluish-green with oyster grey trim around the door handles ...*" Allen stops as if waiting for a torrent of praise. He fishes.

"What do you think?"

"Funny. I like it."

"So, will you come?"

"No. How's Lawrence?"

"Still sexy, still rich. But he doesn't get any of my jokes. You always did." Allen waits again, and I know what's coming. "Maybe I married the wrong man," he delivers, deadpan.

"Maybe you did."

"Please come."

"This conversation is going nowhere, Allen. I just got back, I'm hungry, and I'm hanging up." And I do.

At the waffle place down the street, I ruminate under a shedding palm tree. Allen. Alessandro. Men whose names begin with the letter A, as in—*assholes*. But at least my eight years with Allen had been a wild ride through L.A.'s underground club scene with its wannabe superstars, YouTube influencers, boy toys, and cheap drugs. Allen was way more into that stuff than I was. Allen was also way more into messing around with just about anyone he thought could do something for him, and early on, Allen made that clear. It seemed like everyone was doing that sort of thing in this kind of town in those days—West Hollywood, that is (or was)—and who was I to complain if Allen played the devoted partner at home, making dinner, remembering birthdays, providing a long, after-bath massage almost every time I wanted one? "Mark, my schoolteacher boyfriend," I'd once overheard him describe me to friends, "my bookish sweetheart who brings home a steady, if modest paycheck." Allen, the "natural talent and his sidekick Mark," I'd overheard him say to other friends, "a man on the rise who'll hit it big and make his partner proud."

There were complications. Allen's inheritance, for one, had obliterated his ability to keep a job so that by now, at forty-three, he was incapable of even looking for one. But the money would run out one day, and Allen had put all of his eggs into one basket, and these things often turned out badly, and this one had begun to. But *who was Mark Anello*, for Christ's sake, son of an abandoned mother from a line of Brooklyn grocers, to give advice to Allen Riesler of the now defunct but once-prestigious Rieslers Quality Footwear chain? Allen, with his big Jewish family taking everyone in on Rosh Hashanah and even putting up a little evergreen tree one year to please their son with his *shegetz* boyfriend. Allen, with his predatory realtor cousins who advised these *faigelahs* to buy foreclosures in Provincetown. Finally, Allen, *non plus ultima*: who'd learned to glad-hand, suck-up, and play rich, but wasn't.

Enter Lawrence *superbus maxima*, with his Lamborghini and house in Malibu. Lawrence, who was fifty-two when Allen met him, but with a personal trainer, flaunted the body of Poseidon when he climbed, sans swim trunks, out of his infinity pool. At first, they were invited as a couple to Lawrence's home for cocktails and dinner. And then Allen went alone. And then Allen went alone, and his furniture followed. And then Allen's family left Mark alone, believing, Mark surmised, that Allen had made Mark out to be the dumper instead of the dumped. So typical. So... *Allen*. And such a gut punch to hear, six months after the breakup during a reproachment dinner with ex-partner and new husband, "But Mark, we'll always be family."

Choking on a last swallow of coffee, I shake myself out of this third-person dramatization of my life-story and resolve to put the past behind me. I start swimming at the community plunge the following day and commit to three times a week once my school schedule settles. I keep up my Italian at the local Extension class at Glendale High, and why not? I still love the language, although I'm much better at reading and writing than speaking and understanding. Alessandro had been scant help in improving my conversational fluency. Alessandro's impatience. Good riddance to Alessandro's impatience.

This year, my students at Glendale's Robert Cavendar Middle School (or "cadaver school," as they call it) seem more enthusiastic than students of the previous year. In my Algebra class, an interesting mix of faces looks up to me from their desks: more young women than men (we never say "girls" and "boys" anymore), twelve Cambodians, nine Bangladeshis, and five Salvadorans reflect the changing demographics of the district. Of the 137 students I teach over three periods each day, eight students clearly identify as LGBTQ with no apparent socialization or bullying issues. I'm reminded of how good it is to be a teacher in California.

After one of our weekly staff meetings, I ask Principal John Lavosso to consider adding one non-math course my regular courses to take advantage of the state's new interdisciplinary approach to education, an initiative from Sacramento to show how diverse fields of study are related. John can be a short-tempered boss, a bit of a loose cannon in his mid-sixties who's short timing until he retires, but we get along. I think he'll support the governor's encouraging a more holistic model of learning by having the same teachers take on something outside of their specialties, master it, and so inspire students to do the same. Next to algebra, astronomy is my passion; astronomy and mathematics go hand-in-hand. But Lavosso, true to his stripe, dismisses my interest because, he reminds me, the number of students increases every year while the pool of STEM teachers dwindles.

Dwindles is a good word for October. The days shrink and the nights turn cool. The sunsets at 6:15 make me sad. At home one evening, I think about getting a dog. I imagine the wagging and wiggling and jumping around when I come home late afternoons and picture long walks through the neighborhood when I might relax, gather my thoughts, and try, once again, to settle back into my life and be happy here. But the truth is, I'm unhappy here and unsettled. I spend more time in my car than in bed, it seems, and live in an area where the stars are bleached out by the billboards of car dealers.

My neighbors come and go. My morning coffee splashes in its cup holder when somebody cuts me off—like, *every day*. Teaching holds possibilities, but I'm frustrated by the curriculum constraints and fear of offending parents. The truth is, I want to travel. And the truth is, I miss Alessandro. Although Marina and I keep in touch with *WhatsApp* and occasional emails, she offers no news about him. This means that either she knows something and doesn't want to tell me or knows nothing at all. Both possibilities make me uneasy. I wonder if Braxton joined Alessandro in Pivonnia and shares his bed, or if they've stolen some holiday time. I wonder if they'll really hook up in Budapest to see the flowers. And weirdly, I also wonder if Alessandro feels okay or if he's just sitting around brooding like I am.

My curiosity finally gets the best of me, and I tap out an *Any news about Alessandro?* message late one night, at about the time I know Marina has gotten the kids off to school and settles down with a cappuccino. She responds immediately: *I see Alessandro walking alone at the usual times, so nothing different here. How are you?* I resist prying further and leave it with *All good on this end!* But she seems chatty, having just finished her chores, and texts me about how cold the weather turned with an early snow expected that night. She envies my living in a place like Southern California and especially Los Angeles, where she nurtures the fantasy of movie stars on every street corner and starlets sipping root beer in drug stores. Then, she goes quiet. The little green "online" light on *WhatsApp* blinks out.

Two weeks before Thanksgiving, I call my mother in Glendale who pretends not to know me, her familiar guilt-inducing joke when weeks go by without my phoning her.

"How's your friend in Italy?" The second thing she says.

"That's over."

Silence, then, "Sorry, Mark. Find somebody closer. Like in the same country?"

"Noted, Mom. Thank you."

"Did you gain weight out there?"

"A little, I guess."

"I'm not cooking this year. Loren said he'll take me out or order a turkey from Whole Foods. Will you be joining us?"

"I want to lose weight."

"You don't lose weight when you go to Italy and then come back for the holidays. That's why Julius Caesar invented January."

"I'll be there. Remind Loren that I hate cranberries."

Holiday froufrou begins to erupt in store windows. Here we go again: Christmas coming on like a six-wheeler that's lost its brakes and I'm balls-to-the-wall miserable weeks before I'm supposed to be. I half-remember an Italian phrase for that, "balls-to-the-wall," but can't bring it up because what little headway I've made with Italian has begun to fall away unless I read the Italian newspaper online, which I don't much, anymore. Because I'm goddamn lonely and don't like Christmas. Because I'm goddamn single on Christmas. Because I'm goddamn single when it isn't Christmas.

To take the edge off, I join a dating site, one that claims to offer real connection and not just a hookup. But many of these guys blur the lines. A doctor "favorites" me and drops a note. We talk on the phone, and I like his voice and what he says. He listens to Shostakovich and reads James Baldwin. He loves to wrestle with his dog. But when we finally meet, his ears and nose flash a bit too much hardware, and his opened shirt terrifies with tattoos of flaming unicorns. Over Boba tea (his preference), he wants to know what kind of animal I see myself as and confides that he possesses the *animus* of a wild Palomino. This surprises me because, not to be unkind, he looks more like a Clydesdale—a bit too thick in all the places a human body is supposed to bend. I'm out the door when he insists that I'm an otter and inter-special lovemaking is his particular area of expertise. Out of curiosity, I check his profile a few days later and notice that he's changed his profession from doctor to veterinarian.

But the next fellow seems, at first, like the real thing. This gentleman claims to be a geothermal engineer and an expert in tunnel drilling, something I can work with. He's also very handsome in a tatty Bradley Cooper kind of way. He laughs at my jokes and enthralls me with his account of how the E.U.'s Chunnel was designed and *pulled off* between Kent and Calais—his way of putting it. Best of all, he leans over the table seductively and asks what I do with my time, so I make a fake flub and describe my profession as "sex worker," quickly fake correcting it to "math worker." This puts a naughty grin on his face. Good. We share a sense of humor. We enjoy flirting and dig each other's bones. But eventually, I get serious and talk about my classes in Algebra and Geometry. He listens quietly, frowns, then wants to know if I really believe in geometry which strikes me as pretty strange since he claims to be an engineer, for fuck's sake. He goes on to say that he doesn't believe geometry provides an accurate description of the physical universe and, in fact, fills people's heads with misleading and dangerous untruths. I see where this is going: Mr. Tunnel-Driller thinks the Earth is a gigantic pizza surrounded by Pringles and the solar system a jumbo stack of pancakes. I'm out of there right after I respectfully disagree and before he has the chance to describe how Jesus talked to dinosaurs.

After a few more weirdos reach out with requests for photographs and measurements, I eighty-six my profile and cozy up with my imaginary dog to reflect on where I'd like the rest of my life to go. All right. I thought I'd found a new life in a new place with a new man, but I hadn't. Being single means you get to think about *you*. So, I think about me. *Poor me.*

I make the mistake of whining to my mother over our Thanksgiving dinner, but she huffs and tells me she's been goddamn single on Christmas for over forty-six years and can't imagine it any other way. "But you have your family," I remind her. "So do you, she reminds back."

In the middle of this cesspool of self-pity, it's a relief to get a 7 a.m. *Whatsapp* video call from Marina the following day. I fumble with the connection and broadcast an image of my boxer shorts for ten seconds before I get the angle right. Marina looks good: her platinum hair stylishly wedge-cut now, her eyes bright behind red-framed eyeglasses; the sexy librarian look.

"*Ciao bella,*" I say. "You look fantastic!"

"Mark dear, I decide to make plans for the holiday and ask now if you wish to join me in *Spagna*."

I notice her English isn't quite up to par, probably because she has no one to practice with.

"Spain? What's in Spain?" I say.

"Madrid. Everything is beautiful there. Then maybe we go north to Toledo, Zaragoza, and Barcellona. My old colleague owns a flat she makes available for free. Four bedrooms!"

"With Luciano and the kids?"

"Just me, and maybe I meet a friend. We stay a bit and relax together. You have been to *Spagna*?"

"I have never been to Spain, Marina." I say it as if in a trance.

"Bravo, you come then. I arrive December 1st and stay a month, perhaps a bit longer. Flat is available through January."

"That's this Sunday, Marina. I couldn't—I mean, I'd love to, but it has to work with my Christmas break."

"Whatever. You will figure out and buy tickets. An opportunity to see Madrid for almost nothing."

"You've thrown me a challenge here, Marina."

"Yes. So write me your dates and I wait for you. Ciao, bello!—" and she's gone.

My mind does some quick calculations. At Cavendar, we break for the winter holiday from December 19th to January 2nd, fifteen days, a Thursday through Thursday. How can I possibly show up on Monday, December 2nd, and ask Lovasso for a month off starting the following day? *How can I possibly...* goes through my head until it's interrupted by Marina's enticement, *an opportunity to see Madrid for almost nothing*.

I tap in Lovasso's personal cellphone number knowing that it's 10 a.m. in Miami, where he's been vacationing for the past two weeks, as he has for the past three Thanksgivings. He vacations in Miami to visit his girlfriend, who works as a Hilton Hospitality manager. It's a stretch, but I'll leverage my "Exceptional Teacher" status and remind him that I worked extra holiday hours during his three years of pleasure trysts and ask for a big payback: an entire month of vacation time starting the first week of December. Maybe I'll even turn on the guilt to ask for a few extra days in January by bringing up my disappointment at his turn-down of my request to teach Astronomy, *ignoring* the governor's recommendations—I'll put it that way. Finally, I'll cap off my argument by playing into Lovasso's sense of gender entitlement and point out that female teachers score these holiday add-ons all the time. Married people also use "family time" as an excuse whenever they can. Lovasso's divorced and enjoying his second adolescence. Hardworking single guys like us also need a break now and then!

He's grumpy, makes a big fuss about my bad timing, reminds me that *he* makes the rules. Then I hear a woman's voice slide in sideways and he vanishes for a moment only to come back all sweetness and light to say that, against his better judgement, he'll allow it on the condition that I never ask for such a thing again. I thank him and promise slavish devotion for the rest of my career.

I jump in the shower to focus, then set about finding the cheapest forty-eight hour "walk-up" fares to Madrid on Skyscanner, aiming for a departure the first week of December and a return the first week of January. I score with a thirteen-hour Iberia flight from LAX on December 3rd for nine hundred dollars and a return flight on the morning of January 8th for the same price. By noon, I've messaged Marina on *WhatsApp* to give her my itinerary: leave at 11 p.m. from LAX on Tuesday, December 3rd, and arrive, after a short layover at Heathrow, at Madrid's Adolfo Suarez airport at 8 p.m. on Wednesday, December 4th. Marina peppers her *bravo* response with happy faces and red hearts.

That evening, I call the family and deliver the news that I'll be spending Christmas and New Years in Spain. My mother responds with her usual irony, honed and perfected over the years to soothe the disappointment that still knocks around from that long-ago day in New York when my father walked out. But ultimately, she commends my free-spiritedness and encourages me to enjoy myself.

As December 3rd approaches, Marina calls several times to provide the address of the apartment and directions for taking the metro from the airport to a station in the Plaza de Chueca or "Crooked Square," of Madrid. I get online and learn that this neighborhood is one of the epicenters of Gay Pride and wonder if that was the reason Marina invited me—or at least the reason she didn't invite Luciano. Little by little, another idea dawns that reveals both Marina's abandon and her caution: Crooked Square provides a cover. Luciano won't be jealous because he can rest assured that his wife will be safe in this white-wine-and-tapas paradise for *finocchi.*

3
Plaza de Chueca

Three days and thirteen hours later, I phone Marina from the platform as I wait for the metro to Centro de Madrid, my legs stiff from sitting, arms sore from lifting, and eyes bleary from Googling. But I'm happy to learn that our flat is just a few blocks northwest from Parque del Retiro, the neighborhood of The Prado and Reina Sofia museums.

After a twenty-minute ride, I climb a long run of stairs to the Plaza de Chueca, suitcase banging behind, and emerge into a crowd of Wednesday night revelers. Christmas lanterns crisscross overhead, beautiful couples drift about holding tall drinks, music collides from different directions, and the spill-out from the cafes makes it hard to find my address. I clatter in the general direction of a building that looks like an apartment house and see Marina emerge from a throng of people clustered nearby.

She grabs my arm and kisses me on each cheek. "December begins the Christmas season here and people celebrate," she shouts over the scrapes of an over-amped speaker. She takes my shoulder bag and leads the way into the building. As the elevator grinds to the top floor, she apologizes for the commotion and assures me that the flat is quiet because it faces a back garden. She hugs me and says how happy she is that I've come. We walk down a long hall, turn a corner, and step into an apartment that's elegant and enormous, although some of its best details—the wainscotting, the crown molding—show the familiar scars of carelessly installed electrical conduits. I'm shown to my bedroom. Wine and small sandwiches of *jamón* await on the kitchen table.

"*Allora*," she says, settling down. "You made it. I would take you downstairs for tapas, but there are too many people now. Maybe we see a bit later. Or, tomorrow, a nice café for coffee and *roscón de reyes* cakes for Christmas."

"Fine. I'm worn out," I answer.

"You eat something now and then you go straightaway to bed," she says, a bit bossy. "Tomorrow, I take you around and show you Madrid. And we talk."

"Not so fast," I say, as she starts to clear plates. "Who's this friend you're meeting?" She stops and turns to me, holding a plate. Then, she puts it back on the table, sits down, and lights a cigarette—something I've never seen her do before.

"Jesus, Marina, when did you start smoking?"

She blows a long plume and looks up. "Not my friend, Mark. My lover."

"Thought so."

"I wanted to tell you after I introduce him tomorrow so you like him as I think you will. But now you hold my secret."

"Your secret is safe with me."

"Of course," she says, waving away her smoke, "but I don't want you to judge me for this."

"I don't judge you. It's your life."

"You think I make a bad decision?"

"What decision? To have an affair? You said you had an arrangement with Luciano, didn't you?"

"Yes, but now I wish to make a divorce."

This complicates things. I rub the bridge of my nose, too tired to engage but feeling I should know more.

"An Italian, I presume?"

"No, a Spaniard. But he doesn't live on the peninsula. He lives over two thousand kilometers in Gran Canaria, several hours by Ryanair to Madrid."

"A Spaniard who lives in the Canary Islands." I turn this over. "So, why do you meet your Spaniard here instead of in the Canary Islands? Is he married?"

"No, he is *un vedovo*, a widower. And he comes to Madrid now for an important Council meeting with the Spanish Ministry of Culture related to his work."

"Interesting."

"And when my colleague tells me her place in Madrid is available and suggests you, my 'American friend' for company, I also see an opportunity to join Carlos but, of course, think of you as well. I will see Carlos quite a bit while you visit."

"Complicated."

She stubs out her cigarette and continues clearing. "You get some sleep and we talk tomorrow. It's beautiful here and you will love it. And then I have something planned for you that makes you happy, I think—maybe as happy as I am sitting with you right now."

The bed is soft, and the apartment is quiet, even with the long window open. The cool night air seems richer here than in Los Angeles; there's a smoky sweetness to it that reminds me of baking bread. How lucky I am to be in a city where the nights smell like bread! In a bright window across the alley, a man strolls nude smoking a cigarette and talking into his phone, his free hand splayed across his chest as if caressing himself. Right. *Crooked Square*. Epicenter. I draw the scratchy blanket over me and wish I'd showered. Tomorrow. Many things start tomorrow. Marina and more of her confessions start tomorrow.

Commotion in the hall outside my bedroom startles me: Marina's voice on the phone, the up-and-down and the loud-and-soft of it. She's arguing, but with whom I don't know, nor do I recognize the language. The argument, or whatever it was, eventually dies down, so I roll onto my side and drop off with a prayer that this visit doesn't turn into an opera.

The following morning, Thursday, we buy two tickets for a 9 a.m. bus tour. Holding our paper-wrapped *roscóns* and cups of coffee, we sprint to Parque del Retiro to board the luxury bus and claim our open-air seats at the top level. Perched high, I take in this city of monuments—warrior angels that stand atop the Beaux-Arts Metropolis building, frothy figures prancing about the roof of the Royal Palace, Francoist supermen who peer down from the basilica of the Valley of the Fallen—a restless, fractioned architecture that captures the spirit of the *Caudillo Generalissimo* and the smoldering frictions of political conflicts here. But Madrid is also a beautiful city, with a skyline of licorice-colored domes that stretch before us from the roof terrace of Doña Luz, a tony bar high above the Gran Via where we find ourselves in the early evening. Marina thinks she has me fooled with this apparently arbitrary venue for cocktails. Sitting here, at this conspicuous table at precisely this hour, means that I'm about to meet a particular person: Carlos.

"We've known each other for two years," Marina says," as we settle down with *Aperols*. "I met him in an online group for people with grief issues."

"What's a grief issue?"

"People who carry too long the grief."

I say nothing, but begin to understand what informed Marina's advice, months ago, to break off whatever held me to Alessandro. She was advising both of us.

"Exactly," she says, as if reading my mind. "Anyway, at the time, Carlos was struggling with the sudden death of his wife. We talked on my private phone for many hours each day while Luciano worked and the kids were at school." She takes a short sip of her Aperol, her eyes focused somewhere else. "I have met Carlos only once before, when he came to Italy. He is an archeologist."

I say nothing, taking in the view. Then: "What happened to his wife, Marina?"

"Burned in a fire. Six years ago."

"Jesus, I'm sorry. Well, I look forward to meeting Carlos."

"Maybe you still wonder why you're here?"

"Am I misguided to think you wanted my company?"

"When I met Carlos in Sorrento for a conference, it was very difficult because Luciano wanted to follow with the children. That was unusual for him."

"He suspected?"

"I don't know. But this time, when I tell him I wish to get away from the children for a bit and go to Madrid, he tells me he wishes it wasn't Madrid because he hates Spain. He calls it a poor imitation of Italy with bad food."

"So, you're off the hook."

"No. He wants to come anyway. He's suspicious."

"He has reason to be suspicious, Marina."

"Do not judge me, Mark."

"I didn't mean—"

"So, I tell him the flat will be very noisy and that I've invited you to come because you've never seen Madrid and you want to see it. I tell him about Chueca, the gay people who go there, and then he says he won't go there."

"So, I'm your cover. Does Luciano own a firearm? In America, we'd change our names and go undercover."

"Of course not."

"Then, it's not about my company. I'm your alibi."

"Of course it's about your company. It's always about your company, Mark. But it's also about seeing Carlos, whom I love very much. This is why I tell you to come and stay for long because I have something for you, someone I want you to meet. I hope we can both go home with new excitements in our lives."

The sun has dropped below the skyline and the air turns chilly up here on the terrace. I excuse myself to look for a toilet and return just in time to see a tall, slender man approach Marina from behind and place a wrap around her shoulders.

"You left this in my room he says," bending down to kiss the nape of her neck."

"Sweetheart," Marina says, glowing like a bath candle. She gestures towards me. "I present my dear friend Mark from America. California, no less!"

Carlos looks up to smile, then approaches with an outstretched hand.

"So very pleased to meet you, *Señor!*" he says, with only a trace of an accent. His eyes are dark and his face stubbled.

Already, I can sense their restlessness as they sit close to one another and opposite me. Carlos orders a gin and tonic and asks me vague questions about California—have I hiked up to the Hollywood sign, have I snorkeled in the Pacific Ocean—while stroking the back of Marina's neck. He seems to have a thing about necks. From a first impression, he doesn't strike me as quite up to Marina's level. He's about my age, I'd guess, or maybe a bit older, but very beautiful. His rich dark hair and sharp features complement Marina's soft fairness. Carlos takes a last sip of his gin and turns to her, tapping the tip of her nose with his long finger.

"Shall we go, my princess?"

"Yes," Marina says, gathering herself. "I'll give you the keys to the flat, Mark, and we'll see you in the morning."

"Wait—you're leaving with Carlos?"

Carlos answers, his voice overloud. "We'll be going to my small pensione near Puerta de Toledo tonight, before my colleagues arrive there tomorrow, for some much-needed rest and privacy." Carlos tries to placate.

"I think it's you who needs the privacy," I shoot back. "We have four bedrooms at Chueca and you'd have plenty of privacy there and—"

"Mark," Marina interrupts, "tomorrow Friday evening, Carlos will stay in our flat for a while. Tomorrow morning, I have ten o'clock reservations for us at the Reina Sofia museum where you will see the Picasso *Guernica*."

"Whatever. I guess I can find my way back."

"Quite simple," says Carlos. "You take the N20 bus south from the corner, then get off at Banco De España, beside the square. Or it's also a lovely walk from here. You have the euros?"

"I have the euros," I assure him, shaking his hand and squeezing Marina's.

Back at street level, I wave goodbye to the love-struck couple and decide to take the so-called lovely walk from here. It's Thursday night, December 5th, and many of the party people have decamped Gran Via for livelier neighborhoods. Families hobble by wheeling carts of groceries, their kids munching crown cakes. Pedestrian traffic dwindles as I continue west and approach Chueca via Calle de Hortaleza, a narrow street with shuttered storefronts. Men stand in the dark alcoves, smoking and leering, some stroking themselves. Here and there, a glimpse of activity as the young and the old, the beautiful and the plain, seek pleasure. Boys step out to prowl and pace: looking, turning away, then looking again. A beautiful one, save for his harelip, approaches me. He smiles, bends over, and slaps his own ass. Allen would enjoy this.

Back at the flat, I surrender to jet lag and turn in early. But I sleep poorly, unsettled about an evening that's turned strange. I start to drift off to the sound of a distant bell pealing in the direction of Puerta del Sol, Madrid's great oval-shaped plaza. It's not to mark the hour, but to announce a time of prayer for Camilo Sesto, the popular Madrid singer and composer of love songs, who's been hospitalized after a heart attack. I know this because I saw the curbside headline in an English-language newspaper on my way back.

At 7:15 Friday morning the phone rings, waking me up. Marina asks how I've slept. I remind her that it's after midnight in Los Angeles and I'd like to sleep a little longer. She says, "Of course, but in Europe, we don't often think about what time it is in Los Angeles."

Marina and Carlos plan to arrive at 8:30 a.m. and take me to breakfast at a favorite café across the Plaza. Then we'll catch the bus to Parque del Retiro and walk to the Reina. We'll wait in what's sure to be a long line until our admission time at 10 a.m. Carlos is a bit more genial at breakfast, which consists mostly of toasted tomato bread and *pincho de tortillas*, or pastries. The cappuccino is dark and rough. He initiates genuine conversation by asking if I have a list of things I would like to see in Madrid. I mention that, besides *Guernica*, I'd love to see the Hieronymus Bosch triptych *Garden of Earthly Delights* at the Prado. He tells me that Prado is even closer than the Reina, and maybe we can even get inside later in the afternoon. Marina suggests the Palace Mayor and Royal Palace. I remember something about an outdoor promenade of booksellers near the south entrance of Retiro Park. Carlos says he knows it and loves it and makes a point of visiting there himself when he's in Madrid. "But Mark, you must read Spanish to enjoy such books, unless you collect them only for their beautiful covers," he says. "But if you do, I forgive you!"

As expected, the admission queue for Reina Sofia is long and there's no place to sit while we wait in the morning chill. I hear many languages. Groups of Chinese tourists cluster around their tour guides who hold little flags. Germans stand dourly, reading pamphlets. "So many people,"

Marina says, taking my arm. She brightens when a man approaches us, a tall, light-skinned black man who walks with a slightly dropped foot.

"Dario!" Marina gushes, "You came!"

"Never too proud to accept a last-minute invitation," the man, clearly an American, says, pecking Marina on each cheek. "I'd live at this museum if they gave me a key."

Marina introduces Carlos first, who not only shakes the hand of this intriguing stranger but bows his head to him. "I respect all artists of exceptional talent, Señor Soole," says Carlos. "And Marina tells me you are one of them."

"Too kind," the man replies.

Marina nudges me forward, "Dario," she says, "This is my dear American friend of three summers in Italy who now joins us in Spain. I present to you Mark." I note how she's turned things around: Carlos introduced to Dario, and Dario introduced to Mark.

"Where in the States?" Dario asks.

"California. Los Angeles. And you?"

"Des Moines, Iowa, but a long time ago. I've lived in Italy for the past thirty-two years."

"Dario now lives in Poreta, a few hours from Pivonnia," Marina volunteers. "He doesn't like to travel but sometimes comes to Madrid to deliver a painting when he makes a big sale."

"Don't tell my secrets, Marina," Dario chuckles. "Anyway—" he extends his hand to me, "Hello."

"Hello," I say, noticing his eyes—a soft and striking green.

"Dario Soole," he says, squeezing my hand before releasing it. "An Iowan who's here in Spain to revive the New York School of Expressionism and lives in Poreta, Italy. And I've just sold a painting for sixty-eight thousand euros."

"Congratulations," I say with the others.

Dario smiles, looks at me. "I'm sorry, your name again—?"

"Mark. Mark Anello."

"As you can see, Mark, and your friends already know, I have a slight impediment in locomotion. A late case of polio as a child, luckily mild. But nonetheless, it does slow me down a little, although the occasional tremors in my hand add an interesting unpredictability to my brushwork."

"Dario is becoming famous," Carlos interjects. "We see him in many magazines, even the ones you buy in the Canaries."

"Too kind," Dario says, then turns back to me. "You'll have to come visit my studio in Poreta sometime. I would love to sketch you."

I can't contain the titter that erupts and I look Marina with an expression of *is this guy for real?* but she looks away.

Once inside the Reina, we're swept along by the stampede of people who head for the second floor, Gallery 6, where *Guernica* lives. It's almost impossible to break out, so strong is the torrent of bodies that pushes through the corridors. Tiny flags tremble above a sea of heads as tour guides shout out to keep their charges in the fold. The smell of sweat and spray of perspiration is everywhere.

"This is hideously epic," says Dario, grabbing one of my shoulders to steady himself. I notice his difficulty keeping up, so I slow down and allow Marina and Carlos to move ahead of us.

I take Dario's arm and squeeze it. "Maybe this isn't a good idea."

When we reach Gallery 6, we're among the last viewers to enter. So many tourists pack the space that it's impossible to see the lower third of Picasso's great painting with all the jockeying to press forward and take selfies. Marina and Carlos have disappeared.

Dario tugs my arm. "Let's change our plans. How about we have a coffee in the park and relax a bit? There's a wonderful avenue of bookstalls where I always manage to find something interesting. Are you familiar with the work of Giovanni Boccaccio?"

"Sure, the medieval writer who wrote the *Decameron*."

"Yes, but Boccaccio is mostly known for his poetry. Some call him Italy's Chaucer."

"I loved the Pasolino's version of *Decameron*. Some twisted shit, for sure."

"Oh, dear," Dario says.

This guy is beginning to make me feel stupid. For me, when you're just getting to know someone, a little erudition goes a long way. I don't know quite what to make of this Dario Soole as we stroll together. He's like an English aristocrat who speaks American English with dash of Parisian haughtiness'—a bit of a fop, maybe. But he's certainly good-looking enough, and I'm drawn to the puzzle of him. He walks unaided now, and I notice his firm chest under his cotton shirt, a sweater draped over his shoulders. His face is round and coffee-colored, his green eyes intelligent, and a dusting of grey stubbles his face, although his chin is clean-shaven in a careful line.

"I'm fifty-four," he suddenly announces, as if he senses I'm sizing him up. "Not a young man, but not yet a terribly old one, either."

"Certainly not."

"As Marina mentioned, I'm here to deliver a painting, which I've already done, and just yesterday wired the payment to my account in Italy. I've taken an inexpensive room in Vallecas and brought along some art supplies, so the rest of my time in Madrid is mostly leisure until I return on the ninth of January. If you see a stumbling, not-terribly-old man sitting on a park bench sketching, it's me."

This is much better. I take his arm and speak without thinking: "And if I saw that man, I'd think him fine-looking, intelligent, and not terribly old because I'd want to know more about him."

"Too kind."

An hour later, we sit on a bench drinking sour cappuccinos while he flips through the Boccaccio he bought at one of the stalls. He sees something and presses his finger on the gutter between pages to mark the place.

"This is one of several poems Boccaccio wrote that celebrate romantic love amid the beauty of the Tuscan countryside." He holds the book before us so he can read while I follow.

> *Lieti fiori e felici, fioritura notturna*
> *Che circondano it mio amante, sotto la luna*
> *Piaggia ch'ascolti sua dolci mormorii,*
> *mentre dormiamo sotto le stelle.*

"Very nice," I say. "But it's weird Italian."

Dario flips the page. "It's fourteenth-century Italian, but here's an English translation by someone named Percival Plounce. I don't recognize the name, do you?"

"I don't believe I do."

"Read it aloud for me, please."

I steel myself for the humiliation but play the good sport.

O, joyful blossoms, night-blooming flowers
that surround my lover beneath the moon;
Let me listen to his sweet murmurings
as we sleep under the stars.

I hesitate, then look up. "It's better in fourteenth-century Italian."

Dario laughs and checks his watch. "Of course it is. So, I think we should find our friends and join them or find them and not join them."

"They do like their privacy, it seems."

Dario hands the book to me and gets up. He stretches his arms behind him, highlighting square, muscular shoulders. "*Amor est dolor et amor est,* as allegedly Cicero penned. 'To love is to suffer and to suffer is to love.'"

"I'd agree with you there," I say, unpocketing my phone which immediately blazes to life with an unknown number. I answer and it's Carlos. "*Ragazzi!*" he shouts, "We lost you in that zoo of museum and decided to return to the flat so you might better enjoy each other's company."

"We had a nice afternoon and I'm sorry not to call you, Carlos. What's happening this evening?"

"I believe our beautiful princess Marina cooks for us tonight. I bought two bottles of a nice Rioja Alta which, when consumed liberally, will make us foolish."

I drop the phone away from my ear and look at Dario. "Marina's making dinner for us. Will you come? I mean, unless you have other plans..."

"I do have other plans," Dario replies, "But I can accommodate dinner tonight."

"Count us in, Carlos. And thank Marina."

"Excellent," he says, "and I'm so delighted the two of you have hit it off."

4
After Hours

The flat is bright and warm on a Friday evening that turns cold. The kitchen smells of fish because Marina spent hours de-veining shrimp for the paella, a dish she's never tried before. Carlos hovers around her and guides her hand as she pours white wine into the steaming rice, and for the first time, I see a genuine affection between them. Carlos pivots and fills four glasses with the Rioja, and we take our seats at a table set before two large windows. A light rain begins and taps the trees outside.

I look at the faces surrounding the bright dinner setting. It's hard to believe that I've been in Madrid for only forty-eight hours. Time moves differently here, and every moment is vivid.

Carlos raises his glass, and we follow.

"*Un brindis a los nuevos amigos,*" he cheers. "A toast to new friends."

The Riojas tastes rich and sweet and bitter all at once. Marina's paella fills the room with the smell of onions, sausage, and shellfish.

"My goodness," she says after her first sip of wine, "In less than a month, it will be New Year's Eve for twenty-twenty. I feel so old!"

Carlos places his hand over hers.

"How do people celebrate here?" I ask, "Besides eat those strange custard cakes?"

Carlos talks while chewing. "I have never been to the Puerta del Sol for the big... New Years celebration. I suggest we go to the Puerta del Sol and stand beneath the tower... and eat a grape each time the bell tolls." He swallows, daubs his mouth. "At the twelfth toll, we cheer and dance and get fucking drunk with all the crazy Spanish bastards."

"I think that's a lovely plan," Marina says.

"I'm in," I add, looking over to Dario, who says nothing.

"Yes, it's wise to plan early," Carlos beams. "When the time comes, I suggest we meet here at ten o'clock, have some champagne, then take our cups of twelve green grapes to the square. Party time, eh, Americano Mark?"

"Except for the grapes, yes."

The rains stops and a fat moon appears. It floats just over the rooftops of neighboring houses.

After some serious eating and drinking with compliments to the cook, Dario kicks off the first serious topic of conversation. "So, tell me, Señor Carlos, what brings you to Madrid, and what do you do for a living?"

"I'm an archaeologist, Señor Soole. I created an organization that works with the Ministry of Culture to discover and preserve sites of early cultures on the Canaries. The Ministry then submits documentation to protect these sites. That is my purpose in Madrid at present. These meetings, which include officials from UNESCO, are now finished and I believe have been very successful." He raises his glass. "A toast to me!"

"Bravo," says Marina, raising her glass.

"Interesting," Dario says. "Do tell me more."

Carlos takes a long sip of Riojas, then pushes the glass away.

"After many centuries of study, two speculations emerged of Canaries' ancestry. One believed Celts inhabited the islands while the other claimed Indo-Europeans. But new archeological discoveries tell us that the first inhabitants of the Canaries were the Amazigh, a people who lived in North Africa more than three thousand years ago."

"Even more interesting," Dario says. "But how do we, or shall I say *you*, know this?"

"I cannot take all the credit, Señor Soole," Carlos protests, "as several members of our team discovered new clusters of Punic hieroglyphs in the Gáldar cave of Gran Canaria, hieroglyphs that use the only partly deciphered consonantal alphabet, similar to what we find in caves of the Amazigh of Libya."

"They came over in pretty little boats," Marina volunteers, a bit tipsy, "And now we must protect their secrets."

"Yes, dear Marina," Carlos says patiently, "*secrets* lie at the heart of this excavation. We know that in regions where Punic hieroglyphs were found, great social upheavals followed—the destruction of the Berbers and the rise of the pharaohs for example, the collapse of democratic Athens for the Macedonian oligarchy, the Roman Empire… a great consolidation of power.”

“Quite fascinating,” says Dario.

“So, what does it all mean?” says Marina.

Carlos leans across the table, his eyes blazing. “It means that we have possibly discovered, in the Gáldar cave and nearby, a set of instructions for an entirely new world order that seems to have been carried out successfully, first in the ancient world, and then in Europe. A body of writing as influential to Western Civilization as Plato's Republic or the Pauline epistles of Christianity—and all of it now threatened by fucking condominiums!

“Impossible! Outrageous!”—in chorus from the table.

Carlos looks directly at Dario. “The new discoveries lie six hundred meters beyond the perimeter of the protected area, Señor Soole, so we must apply for annexation to stop the proposed groundbreaking directly over them.”

“Yes, you must,” Dario says, “and call me *Dario*, please. I admire you, Carlos, for taking up such an important field of work.”

“Thank you, Dario. I might add that to be successful in this work one must cultivate contacts throughout Europe. One must know lawyers and apply the most delicate strategies; many, many lawyers, all of whom communicate and share similar concerns. But above all, one must have energy to do battle!” He reaches into his shirt pocket and draws out a vial of blue pills, swallows one, then shakes the vial to draw attention to it. “My *energy*, Dario.”

“I appreciate your explanation and admire your courage and dedication.”

I push my chair away from the table and get up to use the toilet. “I'm sure knowing a lot of good lawyers helps you take on these greedy motherfuckers,” I say on my way out, feeling pressured to apologize for the greedy motherfuckers whom it's inferred are American.

“This is why I can appreciate art, *Dario*,” Carlos continues, ignoring me, “Because I am a lover of beauty and protector of secrets, as you are.”

"Well—" Dario says, changing his tone, "We all have our pikes and windmills, do we not?"

When I return, Dario flashes me a rascal's smile as if picking up my wish to change the subject. "So," he says, looking around genially, "as you all know, Mark and I are Americans. But I've been out of the States for thirty-two years and have no idea what's going on there. The few American friends with whom I keep in touch seem terrified by their current government."

"We are all terrified," Carlos says. "I would not wish to bring children into this world, especially American children."

"What an odd thing to say, Carlos," Marina says, surprise in her voice. "America is still the future, although many Americans seem very lonely and confused," she continues. Her comment triggers a memory of our secret conversation at the palace of the Principessa last summer.

"Are you lonely and confused, Mark of Los Angeles?" Carlos blurts out, now also tipsy from the Riojas.

"No, not particularly. Not when I'm with friends who feed me."

Carlos raises his glass. "A toast to our American friend Mark, who's never lonely when he's with friends who feed him!"

We halfheartedly toast again, although I'm unsure of the intent of Carlos' remark. But he winks at me across the table, which makes the remark friendlier if friendliness was intended.

After we finish our flan, Dario leans forward and pushes back his chair. "Well, my dears, time to go as I have another appointment."

We all rise to embrace him and see him out, busses on each cheek the usual formality. When it's my turn, I extend my hand. "Thanks for coming and spending time with me."

"Oh no," he answers. "This is an appointment for both of us."

I turn to the others and shrug. "So, I guess I'm going somewhere." I turn back to Dario. "Where am I going? Care to say, so I can tell my hosts when I'll be back?"

"It's a surprise," says Dario, putting on his sweater and handing me mine. "You'll tell them all about it later."

After the recent rain, the streets smell fresh and shine bluish in the clear, winter moonlight. We set out in the direction of the park again. I notice Dario making an effort to walk quickly, glancing at his wristwatch. Soon, we turn onto the familiar avenue leading to the museums. The ground is slick with the fallen leaves of chestnut trees.

"We're walking where, to the park?" I ask, breaking the silence between us.

"Not quite," he says, a bit winded. "We're going to see something we didn't quite see this morning."

"It's almost nine o'clock, Dario. The museum is closed."

"I've made arrangements."

He takes my arm as we approach the two glass towers of the Reina Sofia, now dark. We walk past the wide edifice and take a path along the side that leads to a pair of glass doors. Dario visors his eyes against the dark glass, then knocks. A light comes on and the shadow of a man appears. The doors open.

"Hello, Brindo," says Dario.

"Hallo, Signor Soole."

"*Grazie mille per il favore, stassera.*"

"*Prego. Sempre a disposizione.*"

"Christ," I say as we ascend the steps to Gallery 6."

"Picasso," replies Dario.

After a short walk through an empty corridor that echoes our footsteps, we pass under an archway and enter the enormous Gallery 6 again, this time, all by ourselves. And there, before us: Picasso's masterpiece, softly radiant.

"*Vuoi più luce?*" asks Brindo, quietly stepping in behind us.

"Do we want more light?" Dario looks at me. Without waiting for an answer, he calls, "*Si, un po di più,*" and suddenly *Guernica* blazes.

"Wow," I say.

"Wow," Dario repeats, in assent.

I'm astonished by the size of it—more mural than painting—the chaos of figures, standing and prone, reaching to the sky, cowering beneath a bare lightbulb; figures crushed indoors or immolated by fire, everything happening everywhere and at once in a freeze-frame of horror.

"It's so much better to see it without people tittering behind their cell phones, wouldn't you agree?" Dario says, his voice soft, eyes fixed forward.

"Thank you," is all I can muster up.

He doesn't stir. "Do you see how Picasso removed all the color? It's like a photograph from a newspaper. It's believed his inspiration came from a photo in the French newspaper *L'Humanité*, one of the first to report the German bombing of the Basques in 1937."

"Yes, I see a photograph."

"The Basques were a very gentle people," Dario says, his voice soft as a prayer. "Their town, called Guernica, was burned to the ground."

"I'm not that familiar with their history. Sorry."

Dario doesn't move. He studies *Guernica* as if in a trance.

"Apart from its politics, the painting is very beautiful. Notice how your eye is led around, first to the raised arm of the woman, then to her prone body. This is Cubism; the time is 'always' and the place 'everywhere.'"

"Like Duchamps? The nude breaking into pieces when she comes down the stairs?"

Dario glances sideways at me and smiles warmly. "Yes, something like that."

He moves closer to me and places his hand on my shoulder, turning me gently to direct my view.

"But here before us is *eternity*—an eternity of hope and an eternity of terror. An eternity of love and an eternity of—not hate, but something far worse than hate, indifference."

He pulls me closer to him. After several moments of silence, during which we just stand there and I enjoy standing there encircled, as I am, by Dario's thick arm, he breaks the spell.

"Well, shall we let our kind friend downstairs close up and continue his nap?"

"Poor guy. We should give him a gift."

"Oh, I have. A small painting that's already increased in value. He could sell it tomorrow if he wanted. But if he's smart, he won't."

We leave the museum for the cool night air and walk towards the intersection. "When did you arrange all this?" I ask.

"A few days before you arrived. Marina said that she wanted to introduce me to someone and her description of you was inspiring. I knew currying some future favor from my old friend Brindo might come in useful. A secret telephone call right before dinner sealed the deal, my inspirational friend."

"You're a gentleman and scholar, mister Soole, and I look forward to seeing your work, now that we've talked about Picasso's."

"Of course, and I'm so glad you said that. My hotel is only a short tram ride from here, and that's where I keep slides of all my recent paintings. I also have some fine grass secreted away. If you indulge."

"Should I call the others and let them know I'll be late?"

"They already know," he says, stopping, looking at me, touching my face. "They already know," he repeats, kissing me lightly. Then, deeply.

"Dario," I say, stepping back, "this was brilliant, and I'm touched and excited and attracted and all the rest, considering I'm still jet-lagged and getting used to a new place and new people, not to mention getting over someone I probably shouldn't have been with in the first place—"

"Stop," he says, not unkindly. "There are no rules to this. If our friendship seems wrongly timed, I'll take you home."

"I'm here for a whole month."

"As am I, and I have work to do. But the chemistry for me was immediate, and the moment seems right. I want to show you how I've spent my life, Mark. I want you to know how I've spent my life up until this very moment."

"I want to know."

"Then there's nothing more I can say. There are no rules to this."

The hotel, in the Vallecas neighborhood south of the city, squats in a dark corner above a shuttered café. Dario rents a small room that occupies a corner of the top floor. A single long window looks over the café courtyard where chairs have been flipped onto tables, never to be righted. He opens a tin box and rolls two joints—fat, crooked ones that look like they might collapse under the weight of their payloads—and hands me one. We light up and puff a bit, then sit together at his desk under a bright lamp while he removes sheets of slides from their leather sleeves and directs me to hold a magnifying glass over several of them.

"These are a few that were displayed at an exhibition in Milan last year," he taps, "And this one," he taps again, sold to a Cincinnati millionaire, whose name I promised never to reveal: Roland Schneinzle, the laundromat king."

Dario's work is dense—difficult and edgy—large canvases covered with precise glyph-like figures that suggest they might say something, but assertedly do not. I sense their originality and even their brilliance, but he's clearly beyond me. I resist his guided tour and begin moving the glass among slides at will. A few nudes, men and women, men and women together and with each other, less abstract. Soon, I discover a still life of odd-shaped bowls filled with unusual objects: a camera, a rose, a condom packet. Behind them, an orange scene of Tuscan hills shimmers.

"I love this orange one," I say.

He brushes me off. "Old work. Too decorous. Something I don't do anymore, although still life paintings always sell." He seems to sense my embarrassment. "But I'm very happy it pleases you."

"I guess I have a lot to learn."

"Not so much, really. Did you enjoy the nudes?"

"Very, very nice."

He exhales a cloud of smoke and stubs out his joint. "*Playse*, sir ..." he begins in Oliver Twist cockney, "May oye render your likeness tonight?"

"My likeness? How?"

"Nude, of course," his voice returned. "Completely and purely naked—the entire bare glory of you exposed under a lamp that I'll shade with a bit of cloth."

"I don't see any paints or brushes—"

"A sketch. A cartoon, maybe, before I begin the actual painting which, if I choose to finish it, will be beautiful and my gift to you."

He clears the bed of debris and smooths out the sheet, propping it up, here and there, with pillows. He places a thick folded blanket at the foot of the bed should we need to take a break and I grow cold. I undress and he studies me, guides me down, positioning a leg here, an arm there, raising my chest higher, then lower. His hands feel warm and rough against my skin, the careworn hands of a working artist. He tucks a pillow into the small of my back so that I roll slightly towards him. He backs up, takes in the view, then approaches and adjusts the lamp, first socking it over with a light blue scarf. He assembles his materials: a tray of charcoal, two rubber erasers, and a large spiralbound sketchbook. Then, he positions his chair at the far side of the small room and sits very still, staring at me, his pad and charcoal poised. Almost immediately, I grow hard. I'm rock-solid within ten seconds and don't know what to do about it.

"Now, now," he says. "I don't want that because it hides the contours of your belly. Just relax and trust that I'm serious about drawing you."

"I will. I am, I say," and for the next hour or so, I hardly move, transfixed by watching Dario as he works and a full moon that rises in the window behind. His drawing hand, the left, is slightly crabbed, and he drops the charcoal several times. But I see a whole new expression on his face: focused, intense with a kind of fury, even; the struggle to control his body and direct his talent towards a new challenge—me.

"Every man I draw is fundamentally different," he says, breaking the silence. "The body is merely a container for something else. And what takes form beneath *your* skin, Mark, concerns me and perhaps even startles me."

"You're scaring me. What?"

He pauses for a moment, the tip of his charcoal poised in the air. "I see a deep well of longing, of sadness—a dark tunnel winding through a mountain. I see a man who carries enormous disappointment and heartbreak. A man who wishes for love and deserves love but fails to love himself." He turns the finished drawing to me so I may see it. He's right—it's all there. I don't know how he captured it, but it's there.

"You really got me," I say. The tears well up and I shudder.

Dario throws down his sketchbook and rushes to me. He holds me tight and rocks me. "There, there, sweet Mark. Let this happen, now. You're safe. You're with a new friend, someone who may even love you. Empty this sadness from your heart so you can fill it with joy."

He kisses me, pulls back the covers, then tucks them over me. The storm inside passes and I take a deep breath. He unfolds the blanket and draws it up. Then, he dims the light, removes his clothes, and joins me.

The next morning, when I push the buzzer at Chueca, Marina comes down in her bathrobe and opens the door. "The god damned elevator is broken," she says, pulling the rail as we climb the stairs. Inside the flat, I look around.

"Carlos gone?"

"He left late last night."

Marina looks tired and drawn.

"Everything okay?"

She reaches for a cigarette, something she does thoughtlessly when she's upset.

"Luciano called late last night and demands I come home. He says the children miss me and Fabbio is fighting at school. *Mamma Mia*, I've only been gone a week!"

"Shit."

"So, Carlos, who was undressing for bed, hears my side of the conversation with Luciano — not understanding all the words but seeing my emotions — and becomes very *agitato* himself. He says he must leave, immediately."

"Then Carlos is a coward."

"Stop."

But I don't. "If Carlos really loves you, you'll face this together."

She takes a long draw from her cigarette, her fingers trembling. "You don't understand. I have children. Italy is not America where the women can say 'fuck you' to the men and fight for their kids. Italy in not that way at all. Besides, you are homosexual, so you know nothing of the complications and responsibilities that come with marriage. Look at you—you come home so cheerful from a night of lovemaking with this artist friend of mine. A friend of *mine*, I say again."

I'm stunned speechless by this tirade. I reach out and touch Marina's hand. She doesn't pull it away.

"My beautiful Marina, I'm sorry you feel I betrayed you by spending the night with Dario, but I thought you wanted us to meet, no?"

"*Certo*, she says, wiping a tear from her cheek. "But it happened so fast."

"I guess there are no rules to this."

"I would like each of us to be with someone who loves us. It seems you have found it and I have not."

"He's an interesting man and I like him, that's all." I take her hand in both of mine. "This is about you and Carlos. I worry that the longer you hide the truth from Luciano, the more dangerous this becomes."

She wipes her face and composes herself. "Yes, you are right."

"Yes."

"You are right because men are always right about these things. You are right because men always tell women to do the *right* thing and that they are in danger, which is another way of telling women that they must obey their husbands or even men who are not their husbands. Do men say this to each other? Of course not. I see how men laugh about their conquests, unconcerned about who might overhear. But if a woman confesses that she's unfaithful to a man, she's punished, because she's unfaithful to *men*, not just to her confessor. You know this Mark, because you, with all of your complications, are still a man."

"Marina, you're right. But so am I. Please talk to Carlos so he understands what's at stake for you. I'm sorry if it hurts you to hear that I might have my doubts about Carlos."

We sit quietly for a while, exhausted by the intensity of our conversation. I try to cheer her up—both of us, really—and suggest coffee and pastries downstairs tomorrow morning, after which we can walk and enjoy a beautiful and crisp Sunday. I tell her I've made no other plans to see Dario, so she and I can spend the next few weeks together, or together with Carlos, if she wishes. Of course, I want to call Dario but hold off. What's happening between us is happening too fast.

The week beginning Sunday, December 8th, begins quietly, and Marina seems better. On Tuesday, we visit the local market where she buys bread, marmalade, and cocoa for our breakfasts and jamón for our lunch. Midweek mornings, we stroll about the neighborhood, then return to the flat and relax all afternoon. Later in the week, we continue our tour of Madrid and visit the Bellas Artes Longoria Palace, designed, Marina tells me, by Gaudi's under-recognized contemporary José Grases Riera.

Late Sunday afternoon, we walk through Retiro, where we view the Crystal Palace in the deep, green heart of the park, its monstrous dome of strutwork and glass rising above the trees. That evening, we discover a strange little restaurant where Marina challenges me to order *Anguilla*, tiny whole eels resembling bean sprouts, sautéed alive in olive oil.

As we walk back to Chueca, Marina tells me that, earlier in the day, Carlos called to say that he looked forward to celebrating Christmas Eve with her and the "American fellows" and wished to know what kind of wine we preferred. He seemed completely recovered from his agitation and suggested, as an apology, cooking dinner for us. The storm appears to have passed, at least for now.

Settling into the flat with a glass of wine, I have my excuse to call Dario, hoping he'll be free. He picks up the phone but sounds distracted.

"Yes? Who is this?"

"It's Mark, Dario."

"Ah, hello, Mark. I didn't recognize the number. You caught me sketching."

"Sorry to interrupt. Should I call back?"

"No, no, of course not..." I hear a shuffling about in the background. "Just let me get more comfortable here—there! So, how are you, my beautiful subject? Your drawing sits on my dressing table."

"I'm... extremely well." I struggle to contain my delight at hearing his voice. "I wanted to ask..."

"Yes?"

"Are you alone, Dario? Should I call back?"

"Of course I'm alone. The room is just a tumbling mess, and I have to sweep things off the bed to sit down."

"We were wondering if you had plans for Christmas Eve. Carlos is making dinner for us here and suggests I invite you." That comes out wrong.

"Suggests, does he? Well, tell him I possibly agree. But only on the condition that I get to spend some time with you before Christmas Eve, young man."

"I think that will be fine."

"How about tomorrow, Monday? I have no social obligations and I'd love us to spend at least a few days together."

"Tomorrow? Well, I've been helping Marina through a bit of a crisis."

"I know something about this crisis. Be careful how you advise her."

"But maybe we can visit the Prado tomorrow. I'd love to see the *Garden of Earthly Delights* with you."

"Ah, yes, the sixteenth-century eroticism of Hieronymus Bosch would be an interesting viewing experience together, I venture to say."

"We'll have a bite after."

"A bite afterward would be delightful. If not several bites across your paradisical skin."

I blink hard. "Excuse me?"

"Never mind. I'll prepare a cheeseburger dinner for us. I'm the master chef of hotplate cuisine."

"I was thinking more in the neighborhood."

"Oh, I see."

Marina appears in the kitchen doorway holding two cups of expresso.

"Thanks, Dario. I'll make reservations online for tomorrow morning and call you. *Ciao*," I say, disconnecting.

"Is Dario coming for Christmas Eve?" she asks breezily.

"Yes. Would you mind if I spent some time with him this week?"

"No. Go and resume your friendship with Dario. I'll tell Carlos he will be joining us," she says, placing my coffee before me before she walks away humming a tune.

I get up early Monday morning and book two tickets online for 10 a.m. Then I call Dario to say that I'll meet him in an hour at the Puerta de los Jerónimos gate on the eastern side of the Prado. I choose this gate because it steps down into the museum rather than up, mindful of Dario's difficulty with stairs.

The sun shines mildly on this mid-December day, and I enjoy my now familiar walk to Retiro Park. I'm both happy and nervous to see Dario again, whom I spot immediately in a green leather jacket. We embrace and he kisses me lightly on the side of my neck.

"So good of you to be mindful of your crip friend in the selection of an entrance. There are four others, you know, completely oblivious to the existence of disabled people."

"Yes, I'm well aware. You look terrific in that jacket, by the way. It brings out the green of your eyes."

"An ancient cloak from a long-dead friend. It resists my occupancy these days having seemingly shrunk to half its original size. Shall we go in?"

The corridor leading to Hall 56, where the *Garden* hangs, is surprisingly empty compared to the crowds that crushed towards *Guernica* at the Reina only two weeks ago. Dario takes my arm as we walk.

"Do you wish to see only the Bosch or are there other works that interest you? The etchings of Goya are wonderful."

"I'd like to see them, but it's such a beautiful day. It might be nice to sit in the park again."

"You're reading my mind, dear man. The Goyas can wait for another day as this reassures me that they'll be another day."

"They'll be another day," I say, squeezing his arm. "Already, a very pleasant start to this one."

"Too kind," he says as we turn a corner and enter the great white hall, the far wall of which blazes with the three-paneled Bosch masterpiece in all of its dreamlike spectacle. We approach the painting slowly as if walking towards an altar, stop close enough to marvel at its intricacies, but far enough away to reassure the guards we intend no harm. Dario straightens his slight stoop and stands tall beside me, looks straight ahead as if taking the whole of it in, but the look on his face shows none of the rapture I remember when we viewed *Guernica* together.

"I will say little about this work, Mark, as I don't wish to provoke you with what some might call a controversial analysis... but here, in contrast to the Picasso, we see an eccentric sensualist torn between the temptations of the flesh and the promise of eternal salvation."

"Right. That's what it says on the description card below."

"Yes, but here's my departure: the torment of Bosch was personal, whereas Picasso's was universal."

"I'm listening."

He turns to me, frames the air between his two hands as if to make a picture. "Stay with me here, Mark. You're a fifteenth-century artist struggling with forbidden impulses. Yet, in this pre-psychoanalytical world, the creative expression of your work reveals precisely what you seek to hide. It's clear to me that through this masterpiece, Bosch's unconscious confesses both an erotic attraction to men and a terror of them. At the same time, there's the promise of purification in the baptismal waters of the fountain."

"I guess... when you put it that way."

"Three panels. Three choices. Three consequences," Dario continues. "For every day Bosch remained alive this work admonished him to choose carefully."

"And what did he choose? Does anyone know?"

Dario takes my arm, and we move closer to the painting while a guard moves closer to watch us. Dario discretely points to the lower right corner of the central panel.

"See here. A man inserts flowers into another man's anus in paradise. The other men watch with pleasant curiosity as if waiting in line. What do you think?"

I study the odd group of figures and try to see what he sees, but say nothing.

Dario turns away and motions to leave. "I'll say no more. The work confounds me as well, to tell you the truth."

We walk through the corridors silently and exit the museum from the west, Dario taking my arm again. Behind the trees and just beyond the racing cars of the avenues, the whole of Madrid stretches before us in scalloped limestone. But we turn away from it and walk deep into Retiro along leaf-strewn paths that lead us to the bookstalls, most of them shuttered until the first of the year. We pass a puppeteer presenting the journey of the three kings to a group of children who fidget and laugh when the kings pummel each other with clubs. The shadows grow long under the trees and the air cools. We find a vendor selling cocoa and sit on a stone bench facing north towards the great splashing Fuente de Neptuno, where cars wheel around to all points of the city.

Dario sips his cocoa quietly. "A strange city, Madrid," he says, "lovely and cruel."

"In a way, yes."

He rubs the corner of his eye with his finger. "So, Mark, are you torn between sensualism and the fear of eternal damnation?"

"Aren't we all?"

"Exactly right. And I was quite happy to see you grow annoyed with my rather facile analysis. I see that I no longer enchant you, a very good thing."

"You're blind if you think you don't enchant me."

"Am I? Should I worry that our friendship is already burdensome?"

"Not yet. There aren't many people in my life who open new doors. But you do. So did Alessandro, in his odd way." The name doesn't seem to register with him.

"I'm glad to hear that. You open new doors for me, as well. But I'm quite tired now," he says, unfolding a piece of tissue and placing a small blue pill in his mouth. "These vitamins help, but do I fear that I'm slowing down."

"You have a fire inside, Dario. You have to tend to it."

"Very wise advice, my friend. So. Would you mind if we sat here for just a moment longer, then called it a day? It's been quite perfect, and I would like to return holding that feeling until the next time."

"I feel exactly the same," I say, and I do. In the soft moments that pass, neither of us speaks. Dario seems to have recognized the "American Loneliness" in me as I have in him; it's something that both draws us together and throws up storm signals as we navigate our growing mutual attraction.

"Until the next time, then?" Dario says.

"Until the next time," I whisper, leaning into him across the small space on the bench to press my face against the side of his neck. His leather jacket squeaks. We hold each other's face at the smallest distance so that our eyes lock and kiss deeply—a kiss that tastes like cocoa and cream.

"See you on Christmas Eve," he says, rising noisily.

"See you."

And with a small wave, he turns and walks brusquely down the path, startling a family of finches into fluttering from their roost on a derelict drinking fountain.

When I return, Marina is busy sweeping the flat, her silver hair tied in a knot. A pile of sheets, towels, and colored tablecloths clutters the center of the room. "You've come back?" she says, looking up. "Why?"

"You want me to leave?"

"Of course not. This is good because I will need your help with some of the preparations. Below lives a woman who takes in laundry. You can help me carry the linens and pillows down to her."

"This is how you prepare for Christmas Eve? With linens?"

"Carlos is coming to spend the night tomorrow."

"Oh."

"You won't mind?"

"If you don't mind my staying here."

"You won't go to Dario?"

"We'll see each other Christmas Eve."

She looks down and tends to her sweeping again. "Very strange this way of courting you Americans have. I thought you would be buying roses by now."

The following morning, I lay in bed until I hear the door close and know Marina and Carlos have left. I rise and go to the window to see another beautiful day unfold—a week of beautiful days following.

On Christmas Eve morning, the air is raw with the pealing of bells. Marina fusses about the flat, dusting tables, sweeping floors, and plumping pillows. She acts like a new bride. She tells me Carlo plans to bring fresh fish from the market that evening—traditional for Christmas Eve—and then a fat capon for Christmas Day.

I'm happy to see her bustling about, but risk interrupting her high spirits with a question I need to ask: "Have you and Carlos talked about what needs to be talked about?"

"Not yet," she says breezily. "But we had a lovely time on Tuesday and have talked every day since then. Carlos admits that we have something important to discuss and wants to discuss it." She looks up as if sensing I'm not entirely pleased by her answer. "After Christmas, Mark, I will put this situation before him directly."

"Good."

"I'm not worried, now, because Carlos is very apologetic and sweet to me. He will sleep here again tonight. Do you mind?"

"No, of course not."

"And you join Dario."

"I don't want Dario to assume—"

"Of course he assumes. Are you blind? You're lucky to have such a fine man desire you so much. Now, I give you my best advice: *Love* Dario."

5
Feliz 2020

Spanish families celebrate Christmas Eve quietly in Madrid, as we will tonight. But for next week's Epiphany festivities, they'll pour out into the streets to watch the grand parade for *El día de los Reyes Magos* or "Day of the Three Kings."

Each January 5th at 7 p.m., the procession of kings, transformed into Godzilla-sized puppets, ambles south along Paseo de la Castellana towards the great traffic circle at Plaza de Cibeles. Marina and Carlos will miss the parade since they'll leave Madrid less than forty-eight hours into the new year. But at least tonight, we'll all be here to celebrate Christmas Eve together—this ramshackle family of ours—raising our glasses to toast amid the clanging of church bells.

At five o'clock, Carlos blusters in with two wrapped parcels of bream and mullet and a plastic sack of tiny octopuses. Immediately, he sets to work making a green pepper and onion-tomato sauce for the fish stew. For the first time, I hear Carlos sing in a high, clear tenor voice as Marina stands beside him. I watch him wheel around, fish on his fingers, to kiss her. A raucous buzz announces Dario, who doesn't know about the still inoperable elevator because I forgot to warn him. I rush downstairs, just as he starts to rattle the cage.

His annoyance fades when he looks up and sees me.

"Hello, sweetheart. It appears I'll have some climbing to do, the challenge compounded by this ridiculous torta."

"Sorry. Give me the cake. Put your arm around my waist, hold the banister, and we'll climb together."

And up we go, stumbling awkwardly for the first run of stairs and then finding our rhythm for the remaining ones.

"You're an amazing dance partner," Dario says when we reach the final landing.

Inside, kisses are offered and wine is poured and we're all quite merry when we sit at the table. Carlos ladles stew into each bowl and cuts the bread. Dario sits beside me. I place my hand on his leg and gently rub it. He puts his hand over mine and then, quite unexpectedly, lifts both of our hands and places them on the table.

"Ah," says Carlos, not missing a beat. "We have two men in love at our table. I should've made a pot of oysters to improve their stamina tonight!"

The evening continues in this lighthearted spirit as Marina and her guests tell jokes and share unusual encounters they've had in Madrid. For a moment, I think about sharing my stumble onto the cruisy Hortaleza street, but hold back. Carlos explains how differently the Spaniards live in the Canary Islands compared to those on the mainland and tells us that the cost of living there is well worth the inconvenience of isolation and the invasion of tourists every year. Dario seems to enjoy himself, but says little. He's genial, but I suspect the banter bores him. I don't think he would've come if it weren't for me and his hope that I'd go back to the hotel with him tonight.

After the torta with expresso, everyone settles down. Marina pours a cordial for each of us and takes her place beside Carlos on a oversized couch. "Ah," Carlos says, curling his arm around her, "All good things must come to an end. Marina leaves the day after *Nochevieja*, January 1st, and I the following day. He nuzzles Marina deeply, and soon they grow passionate. Dario, sitting on a second couch, watches them, then bids me sit beside him, but I'm uncomfortable with the increasing heat in the room.

"Listen, you two," I finally say, startling them from an entanglement, "Let me help you clear things away before we leave."

Marina turns to me, her hair a-fright, her face flushed. "You are leaving together?"

"They are leaving together," Carlos repeats.

"Very well," she says, getting up. "Tomorrow at four o'clock, we have the capon. A special recipe from Carlos."

"A special recipe from Carlos," he slurs.

We find our wraps and stand by the door. Marina hugs us good night and a happy Christmas; Carlos waves, too lazy and drunk to move. When she steps out into the hall with us, Marina takes me aside and says she appreciates my friendship and promises she'll find out what she needs to know from Carlos before New Year's. "I must know if he is serious about our relationship by then," she affirms. "Before I return to Italy and my family."

The room in Vallecas seems smaller this time, probably because art materials are scattered everywhere, the bed covered with drawings. They're beautiful, these drawings, some in color pastels—a view from the window of the sad tables below but transformed into a composition of languid dancers; a meticulous portrait of Dario's right foot, geometric studies of cubes and rhomboids and all sorts of topological shapes, made beautiful and sensual. I also catch a whiff of turpentine, although I see no brushes around.

"I'm sorry, Mark, I wasn't sure of your company tonight." Dario rushes to the bed to gather his drawings and stacks them on the desk, stepping on an opened box of pastels that splinter under his foot."

"Fuck," he mutters, overconcerned about it all.

"The garret of a working artist, like in *La Bohème*."

"Shall I be Mimi, or shall you?"

"Stop. We'll take turns."

He pours me a Christmas brandy recommended by a clerk in one of the art supply stores he'd found. "It's called *Pacharán*," he says, "Made from blackthorn berries, anise, and coffee. An exhilarating if enigmatic concoction, I should say."

He's right.

The room has no shower, so we bathe in the ample porcelain tub, our clothes and hair stinking of fish from Marina's kitchen. The small lamp above the desk provides the only illumination until Dario steps out, slick with bathwater, to switch it off. Now, the only light comes through a window opposite the tub, the yellow glow of a wall lantern soiled by a compost of leaves. The water feels soft against our skin and we relax. For the first time, I enter Dario and, in turn, he enters me. The light on the water shudders, and the rocking of our bodies makes gentle splashes that chime like bells. With few words exchanged, we step out and slowly towel each other dry. Then, we climb into bed and fall into a warm, deep sleep.

"Marina's ill," Dario calls to me from the doorway, holding the phone."

"What's wrong?" I stammer, half asleep.

"Carlos says it's nothing serious, but she has a slight fever and a headache, and she's coughing quite a bit. He puts the phone back to his ear. "Do you want to talk to Mark, Carlos?"

"Tell her to rest up," I call out, assuming our plans are off.

Dario listens and nods, repeats, "Carlos will make her a nice soup with the capon and they'll rest."

"Probably just a winter nasty," I say as Dario ends the call. He picks through scattered clothes looking for something to put on. His body is beautiful in the morning light: solid, golden; a fine mat of white on his chest, broad at the top and narrowing to a "V" at the groin. "A cold day, today, sweetheart—" he says, still picking, "A very cold day today: Christmas Day, *Anno Domini Nostri Iesu Christi,* two thousand nineteen," he chants, like a Gregorian monk, sleeving into his robe.

Despite the cold, we decide to go out. Vallecas is a neighborhood of working-class Spaniards, and the streets are lively during these early hours of Navidad. Pastry shops bustle as customers crowd in to select sweets for the afternoon dinner. A street vendor hawks roasted chestnuts and hot chocolate, and kids race around their stumbling parents, who scold affectionately. The day begins to warm.

Dario takes my arm and suggests cappuccino and cake at a place he'd discovered called El Agujero del Ratón, the "Mouse Hole." It's precisely that: a hole-in-the-wall on a sketchy street that runs alongside El Parque del Payaso Fofó (Park of the Flabby Clown), where street people hang about, rattling their cups. I pull Dario along, wishing to pass quickly, but Dario stops me. A woman looks up, trembles, raises her cup: "*Unas monedas para Navidad, Señor?*"

Dario disengages and plunges his hand into his coat pocket. "Mark, I've worked very hard during our week apart and have been fortunate to sell a painting for more money than I ever expected, to Señor Munas, who'll put it in his home where I hope it attracts other commissions. So now I give back on Christmas, if only a little."

As he pulls out his billfold and draws a note, two young men approach, one on each side, "*Dario!*— " I call out, but one lunges for the billfold and grabs it while the other knocks him down and gives him a kick in the side. "*Maricones! Comedores de culo,*" they scream: *Faggots! Ass-eaters!*" People stop to gawk, but no one moves to help as the thugs, from a safe distance, repeat their slur and spit on the pavement in contempt. An old woman appears and scolds them like a ferocious grandmother. They look at each other, then remove the cash and toss the billfold on the ground. I approach to pick it up.

A heavyset woman with flour on her apron rushes out of the The Mouse Hole and helps me help Dario back on his feet. She motions forward and leads us towards the café. We pass another street person, who looks up and leers, "*Deberías darle a la mujer todo tú dinero. Al menos es una mujer honesta y no una ladrona!*" Dario gets the meaning: "I should have given the beggar woman all my money because at least she's honest and not a thief." The woman seats us at a table in the café. All eyes are upon us. The children seem transfixed by the bruise on Dario's forehead and creep towards our table to gape and stare. But our kind lady rescuer, the baker here, shoos them away as she warns Dario in halting Italian to be very careful in this neighborhood where violence against homosexual men has increased. She attributes it, amusingly, to the high spirits of the season, a season that honors children and family and the church and the divinity of the innocent infant Jesus—none of this mixes well with two men strolling about looking like a couple in love. She brings us two large Christmas cakes and cappuccinos and asks for nothing in payment.

Back in our room, Dario sketches quietly having mostly recovered from the pain of the kick in his side. He sleeps, and I sift through his drawings most of the afternoon, developing a better understanding and appreciation of them. At about four o'clock, I take the phone into the toilet and call Marina to see how she's doing. Carlos answers.

"She's better and enjoys a bowl of my delicious soup now. If you were here, you could partake."

Carlos's voice sounds warm and reassuring. Protective. I believe Marina is well cared for. I begin to feel more optimistic about their future as a couple.

At seven o'clock, Dario wakes and suggests a simple dinner of pasta, butter and cinnamon, a Christmas concoction he'd perfected during the lean times and grew to love. It's delicious, and we revisit our bottle of Pacharán. I think to call my mother but it's still not late enough in Spain for it not to be too early in Los Angeles. Tomorrow, then. The winter dark descends, and to keep warm, we get cozy in bed. Church bells peel into the night—soft bells, raucous bells, bells near and far. But the city is quietly alive. Even the windows above the sullen courtyard burn bright tonight, people moving about their rooms.

Christmas, 2019. And I'm in Madrid with a man I never expected to meet and I'm clearly falling for. The date of my return, January 8th, looms like an execution. When I share this awkward simile with Dario, he laughs—"You are indeed one for drama, my handsome hero. Let's do our best to enjoy what remains of our time together," he says, wrapping his arm around me sleepily and pulling me close, the soft puffs of his breath against my neck.

New Year's Eve draws closer. The stretch of days leading to it pass calmly as we find an easy rhythm with one another, our lovemaking frequent, but never routine, our talks—art, poetry, psychology—expansive and thrilling. Marina recovered from her mysterious malady but wished to remain alone with Carlos to enjoy their last few days together. Tonight, *Nochevieja*, they're excited to join us at Puerta de Sol, the magnificent half-oval at the center of Madrid, where we'll all watch the bright clock rachet to midnight atop the tower of La Real Casa de Correos.

As we walk to the metro, Dario stops at a fruit vendor and buys four paper cones, each containing twelve green grapes that we must eat, one by one, at each peal of the bell. We get off at Chueca, ascend to street level, and ring the buzzer. Carlos appears first, galloping down the stairs and pointing to the now taped-over elevator. Marina follows, stepping carefully.

She looks stunning in a black sequin jacket and stylish pantsuit, her silver hair piled into a high ponytail. Carlos struts his stuff in a brown leather jacket, tight jeans, and a bright red cashmere scarf. Dario and I regard each other's shabbiness and break into laughter. "Guess who won't be dancing tonight!" Dario says, handing out grapes.

"My god, man! What happened to your head?" Carlos asks, sticking his finger into Dario's scab.

"Some hooligans assaulted then robbed us," Dario replies, pushing Carlos' finger away. "Their reason unclear."

"When did this happen?" asks Marina.

"Yesterday, in Vallecas," I say. "Near the park."

"A very dangerous neighborhood for fellows like you," says Carlos offhandedly, and we speak no more of it.

It's nine o'clock and already a great migration drifts towards the Puerta. We follow the throng south on Hortenza, then west on Gran Via to the Art Deco Schweppes tower at Plaza del Callao, then head south again to the limestone canyon of Calle de la Montera, a promenade that leads straight into the Puerta. During the long walk, we couple and uncouple in conversation: Carlos, quite buoyant, tells me how much he's enjoyed my visit and looks forward to seeing me again. Dario and Marina, two old friends, talk heart-to-heart and, no doubt, compare notes about me; then Carlos and Dario, who appear to resume their discussion about archeology and a mutual appreciation of beauty. Finally, Marina finds me. We fall slightly behind the others so she can share some important news. She takes my arm, reminding me again of our tour through the palace of the Principessa so many months ago.

"Carlos loves me and wishes to marry me. He says he will do anything he can to assist me in breaking away from Luciano and even telephoned a lawyer in Rome he knows who has been successful with divorce cases involving custody."

"I'm so glad to hear this, Marina. I'm so happy for you."

She squeezes my arm. "He tells me I am the answer to his loneliness, the cure for the emptiness he still feels after losing his wife. He also describes circumstances of her death I've never heard before."

"Tell me."

"She burned herself in a fire because she believed he was seeing other women. Poured the *benzina* all over herself to make *un suicidio* in their own house. He denies all and tells me she was a very sick woman who was pregnant with their first child and wished to punish him. I believe him."

"That's horrible, Marina. My heart breaks for Carlos. I hope you both find happiness and healing together."

I reach into my pocket, glad that I remembered to take them with me before leaving for Spain, glad that I remembered to bring them along this evening.

"What is it, Mark?" She accepts the small velvet box.

"Something you might find more useful than I did."

She flips open the box and recoils. "The two rings you offered to Alessandro? No, it's bad luck!"

"I never offered the rings to Alessandro, thanks to you. He never even knew about them."

"Ah," she says, not entirely convinced. "All right, then."

"I mean, if things are moving along with Carlos now, a couple of rings might come in handy."

"You are funny. Perhaps so, yes. Anyway, when I return to Italy, I will see this lawyer who helps me plan. I believe Luciano abuses the children, especially Angelina. One day, I will take them shopping to buy school clothes and then stay away until Luciano receives the petition."

"You'll need to plan this all very carefully. It won't be easy."

"It will be very easy, Mark. Everything is easy when you're in love."

Puerta del Sol is brilliant with splashing fountains and festive lights, and already people are dancing to a live band in front of the blue Navidad tree with its star of fanning lasers. The air is cold, but nearby, a vendor sells hot rum and chocolate. On the broad face of the Casa de Correos, under the clock tower, brilliant and intricate images of the Three Kings dance with angels and comets. The four of us huddle together, abandoning the idea of exploring to look for warming refreshments. By 11 p.m., the crowd has grown so huge that it's difficult to move anywhere. But we've found a clear view of the bright clock, and we stake our territory, keeping close.

Carlos raises his cone of grapes. "Soon, at midnight, you know what to do," he shouts, vapor bursting from his mouth. "When the clock chimes the midnight hour, you eat a green grape and continue eating one grape for each chime, twelve chimes in all, one for each hour. You must not miss a chime or forget to eat your grape, for this is bad luck. Or at least, not good luck."

"Spanish fatalism," Dario observes.

The crowd prickles with excitement as the music winds down and the *maestra de ceremonia,* a young sequined *caribeña* woman with improbably blonde hair, steps to the microphone. She first whips up a final scream of enthusiasm from us, then announces—first in Spanish and then in English—that the midnight hour draws near, and we should prepare our grapes. Floodlights illuminate the great clockface, and a digital counter appears directly below it to tick off the seconds of the final minute.

And now it begins, the final countdown in one great human chorus:

Diez

Nueve

Ocho,

Siete

Seis

CINCO

CUATRO

TRES

DOS

UNO—

FELIZ 2020! blazes in neon pink to the screams of the crowd that drown out the first chime, but we laugh and do our best; the second chime is only slightly clearer, and so on, as we munch our grapes, unconcerned about their synchronicity. Only Carlos appears troubled that his timing might've been off. We hug each other as others hug around us when the first volley of fireworks explodes behind the tower in percussive cracks. White fountains launch their comets moonward and burst into confetti that sparkles downward like shrapnel. Huge, phosphorescent flowers bloom and sizzle, sea anemones and jellyfish wheel their false constellations across midnight's pitch—and then something goes wrong: an errant missile and its twin burst directly overhead. Yellow smoke sifts down like mustard gas as cinders and shards follow in flaming spirals so that the revelers cover their heads, duck, and laugh nervously. The sulfurous haze dims the neon *FELIZ 2020* to an illegible cipher as black ashes sleet down, poisoning the air.

"Es como la guerra, las bombas!" A grandmother yells, her trembling hands making a roof above her head. Celebrants echo her cry like a clarion call but transform it into screams of delight, joy, and madness. *"It's the end of the world!—Madrid is Pompeii!"*— they shout as if conjuring a vision of Vesuvius and its suffocating ash. *"Dónde está la policía para protegernos?"*—an old man calls out, staggering through the crowd with a young boy... *"Where are the police to protect us?"*

But the chaos subsides, the beacon of *FELIZ 2020!* gathers back its light, and a nervous smattering of applause rises up, grows louder, turns into a roar of cheers as the music starts again as if to banish this sinister angel and her unwelcome visit to our celebration of the New Year. But now, a new madness: the relieved, besotted, and "crazy Spanish bastards" begin to kiss each other with abandon—polite kissing, drunken kissing, passionate kissing, strangers kissing strangers who've kissed strangers and who'll carry their kisses to other strangers. The musicians launch into a techno-rock rendition of *Marcha Real,* the Spanish National Anthem, followed by a lyrical tribute to the love songs of the recently departed Camilo Sesto, which seem, after some minutes, to tamp down the high-spiritedness of the partiers and signals them to move on or go home, the sanitation scooters with their yellow lights already positioned along the perimeter of the square.

But the Puerta empties slowly, and, still corralled by the crowd, we wait for an opportunity to find the exit.

"I have never seen such a thing before," Carlos shutters, wrapping his red scarf around his neck. "Do you think a problem with the pyrotechnical design?"

A wild-eyed man stops before us on his way out, waves his finger and shouts in broken English, "A very bad omen tonight! The year ahead will bring catastrophe."

"Away with you!" Carlos shouts, and the man flees.

"Carlos, I am very tired and have much to do before I fly back to Rome," Marina says, "As you do, darling."

I hug Marina and ask if we can join her for a cappuccino before her flight tomorrow.

"Oh no," Marina and Carlos chime together. Marina continues: "I removed my bags and closed up the flat three days ago to stay with Carlos in San Fermin. He will come with me to the Aeroporto at 6 a.m. this morning. We only returned to Chueca to meet you last night." She opens her purse and withdraws the large key on its ribbon.

"You've moved out? What about the rest of my things?"

"You stay at the flat, Mark, and enjoy," she says, handing me the key. "You take Dario and have this beautiful place alone together and show him our neighborhood."

"The time ahead in Madrid will be fun," Carlos adds. "On January the five, the parade of the Three Kings. Unfortunately, I leave tomorrow, one day after Marina and will miss it entirely."

"I leave the eighth," I say.

"And I, the following day," Dario adds.

"A mass exodus," Carlos sighs, "Our band of rascals broken up and scattered to the four winds."

Marina takes his arm, smiles at me. "When you leave, Mark, put the key on the dinner table and close the door behind you."

We all stand together silently for a moment.

"So, this is farewell, then," I say, hugging her. "And also to you, Carlos." I extend my hand.

"Such an opera!" Carlos cries, squeezing my hand. "We see each other very soon. We see each other at the wedding of Carlos and Marina!"

Marina looks at me, a look that says *You see?*

And with a wave, they're gone.

6
Bloody Bastard

Dario seems tired. His limp is more noticeable as we walk through the ash-covered Puerta to the street. I take his arm to steady him.

"Plaza Chueca is much closer than Vallecas," I say. "Why don't we take the metro back and sleep a few hours? We can shower, eat something, then go back to your hotel."

"Sleep is just what I need, sweetheart. This evening has been a strange and exciting adventure, but now I'm weary of it."

As we enter the building's hallway, I remember: "Shit, I forgot about the busted elevator."

"Ah yes," he says patiently, just as a shadow appears inside the cage and a man exits, carrying a toolbox.

"*Ahora funciona*," the man announces, his voice thick with drink. And then follows with English. "You and the cripple can go up now."

We wake up late in the afternoon and shower together, enjoying the luxury of hot water with just a turn of the tap. As I dry Dario's back, I whisper over his shoulder: "Would you like to stay with me the whole week? It's safer here, and we can take a hot shower five times a day if we want."

"That sounds lovely. I pay for my room weekly and, other than the evenings spent there with you, I won't be sorry to go. But I'll need to work. I have other commissions to plan."

We fall into a comfortable rhythm during our days together in the sunny flat. One night, over an impromptu dinner, this:

"Tell me your story, Mark."

"Tell me *your* story, Dario. Are you still feeling tired?"

"A bit."

"Do the little blue vitamin pills still help?"

"I am essentially a very healthy man, Mark."

"I'm sure. But maybe we shouldn't drag around so much."

"Whatever plague I suffer, your company is the best tonic for it."

We sit at the table beside each other so we can enjoy the view through the window. Grey pigeons strut across the rooftops. I reach around and rub the small of Dario's back.

"Tell me about your polio. Weren't you vaccinated like every other American kid in the nineteen-fifties?"

Dario turns and looks at me with feigned outrage. "The nineteen-*sixties*, if you please. Yes, I was vaccinated, but with the Sabin sugar vaccine. It came out twenty years after the Salk." He places his hand over my hand. "Kids preferred sweets to needles, you know."

"The Sabin sugar vaccine," I repeat, half-remembering something terrible about it. And then it all comes back. "Oh, God."

"My mother dragged me to Cincinnati. We were among the first, and we were the unfortunate."

"The early untested release," I say. I guess it was all over the news in those days."

"Such a pretty little thing in its dainty white cup. Too bad Mr. Sabin hadn't figured out that swallowing the virus didn't kill it. Forty-eight hours after sucking on my little pink gumdrop, I couldn't stand on my feet."

"Jesus."

"I was one of the lucky ones. With physical therapy, most of my mobility came back. And years later, I joined a community of volunteers who reached out to some of the less fortunate ones. But they're all dead now."

"I'm so sorry, Dario."

"And this is why, Mark, a vaccine will never again enter my body—" He twists his body to look at me, his green eyes flashing, "*A vaccine will never again enter my body.* Just so you know, my beautiful friend." He tops off his wineglass, sips. "Your turn." He waits. "No? Well then, next question on your list, please."

"Is somebody waiting for you back in Poreta?"

"Yes, the love of my life: my black Schnauzer Trixie. She's well cared for at a shelter owned by a lady-friend in the neighboring commune. I adore her. You mustn't be jealous."

He takes another sip, looks at me, and raises his eyebrows to show he's ready for the next question.

"Have you been with many other men?"

"All in the past. I remind you, Mark, that I'm fifty-four years old. My last was a fellow I met while still a student at Pratt. Swedish-descent and a Hawkeye—that means 'Iowan'—like myself." He swirls his wine delicately, then raises it to his lips, but doesn't sip. After that, nothing to speak of." He looks at me. "Same question, Señor."

"Yes, a guy in Hollywood for eight years. Failed comedian, now happily married. End of story."

Dario studies me, not uncomfortably, but with an intense curiosity I can't read. "Have you ever been with a man of color, Mark?"

"No..." I say, and consider leaving it there, but don't. "Have you?"

"Give me a time frame."

"Time frame?"

"Weeks, days, hours...? I haven't stepped out today, so certainly no one in the past twenty minutes." He pops his eyes and covers his mouth in cartoonish outrage. "A little joke." His face relaxes. "Yes, of course, I've been with men of color. All men have color in the eyes of an artist."

"*A little joke*. Exactly what Alessandro used to say."

"Who's Alessandro?"

"An Italian from Pivonnia I was involved with last summer. I thought maybe Marina told you."

"Ah, Alessandro Pugliacci. Yes, I've met him. An odd cat. Goes by 'Aldo,' I think."

"Tell me more about your Swede."

"Liam was an Italophile who borrowed money from his family to buy our house in Poreta after our first Italian vacation. We became permanent residents, but eventually, Italy proved too much for him while I took to it. Now, with our sinister president and all the violence in America, not to mention its atrocious medical system, I'm so thankful I decamped."

"Is Liam still alive?"

"No, dead of AIDS at twenty-nine, a few years after our time together. After his passing, I acquired the green leather jacket you admired." He looks at me, clearly woozy from the wine. "End of story," he says, rubbing his foot against mine under the table. He gets up, removes his shoes and socks, then carries them into the bedroom. I clear the table but stop to watch through the open door as he removes the rest of his clothes and stretches his splendid body on the bed, his sex at full attention.

He cranes his head in my direction. "I am essentially a very healthy man," he calls out, as if reminding me.

Madrid turns warm this first week of January and even grows hot in the afternoons. We open windows and go about naked most of the day. Dario stops every few hours to sketch me, then pesters me to sketch him. The results seem to please him.

One evening, after hours of creative lovemaking, we dress and go out. It's January 5th, the night of the Three Kings parade, which we avoid because of the crowds. Instead, we explore the perimeter of the Plaza, hold hands, and enjoy drinking in a lively *taberna* in the company of others like ourselves. Sitting at a Bistro table under a canopy, Dario leans forward and kisses me—a long, deep kiss where all the flavors of his body converge into a sweetness on my tongue. The night air hums with strains of the parade as we stroll among the throngs on Gran Via. Through the silhouettes of rooftops, I watch a huge harlequin puppet float forward and gaze down at his invisible puppeteers. Soon, we pass Marina's rooftop café Doña Luz, where I first met Carlos, then follow the strains of a saxophone to discover "Billy's Tempo Club," American jazz tumbling out from an open door. A crowd of young people fills the place—wannabe Bohemians, Amy Winehouse lookalikes, poets in docker beanies—who clump over the tapas bar to touch the food and scream in each other's faces. The music comes from a spare ensemble—sax, trumpet, and electric guitar—right next to the table selected for us. But the players take a break and disappear just as we sit down. Except for one, an older black guy who blows spittle from the beak of his sax, then plops down to join us.

"Either of you guys play?" He looks at Dario. "How 'bout you, blood?"

"No, I don't, sorry."

"Americans, right?"

"We are," Dario responds coolly.

"My name's Joey Huggins. My piano man's got sick and I need my foundation."

"Sorry, can't help you," says Dario, still cool.

"Something's goin' around, man. I had to cancel three gigs last week 'cause my boys can't blow. Me—? I feel like shit myself tonight, but a man's gotta eat."

He reaches out and shakes our hands without asking our names, and then stands.

"Anyway, nice to meet a coupla Americano brothers. Listen, I shouldn't tell you this, but don't eat the shit they serve here."

"Well, we plan to eat the shit they serve here," Dario says. "Is it not good?"

"Oh, it's fine. Just the same old Spanish shit."

He slaps Dario's shoulder, and then he's gone.

We eat because we're famished. The tapas offerings taste delicious, breathed-over or not, and the white Alberino wine, superb.

It's very late now, and outside, the air turns damp. I walk us back towards Chueca, taking the familiar way I remember from my stroll along the Gran Via weeks ago when Marina and Carlos sent me on my way. I look down at my feet, the pleasant buzz of the wine turning to melancholy.

"Our friends are gone, Dario, and in four days, I leave."

"As do I, the day after you."

"What happens to us after—"

"I don't know. I've considered this."

We walk in silence, not touching.

"For me, I see us—" I begin.

"Me, too," he interrupts.

We turn north in a lazy stroll, me leading the way now to whatever street seems familiar. But a sudden chill runs through me, followed by a stab in my head. A wave of dizziness gathers, crests, and passes over. My saliva tastes strange, and an odd odor fills my nose. I slow down and miss a step.

Dario seems to notice. "Everything all right, Mark?"

"I think so. I just feel a little off. Probably the wine."

"Our soft bed awaits us," he says, as we amble on carelessly. But I soon realize that I've wandered onto the dark and narrow Calle de Hortaleza. In a flash, I connect the name to what I'd seen there weeks before.

"Shit, Dario, I forgot that this is a busy cruising street. You cool with that?"

"Not at all a problem. Perhaps we can find an attractive third for our erotic adventures." He seems to sense my discomfort and places his arm across my shoulders. "A little joke," he says—bringing up the memory of Alessandro again. I make a small effort to pull away, but he tightens his grip around me. "Sorry, that sounded careless," he adds. "Truth is, I'm far from considering such a thing, my sensitive friend. Time is not on my side."

"Don't be ridiculous."

"But even if it were, the answer would be the same: I'm interested only in you, Mark. My sweet surprise. My companion. My *lover*."

I feel a swelling in my heart that takes away my breath and makes me want to stop and kiss him. But the setting is hardly romantic. We just keep walking.

"My house in Poreta sits on a ridge with a view of the Umbrian countryside. A stone house, four hundred years old, with an orchard for apples and persimmons. I hope you'll come there. I hope you'll someday live with me in Poreta..."

He trails off, distracted by what surrounds us. Shadows change shape. Faces and the furtive movement of bodies emerge from the thin light, then withdraw. I can see that this still fascinates Dario, who twists his head from side to side to see what can be seen while I look straight ahead towards the end of the street, eager to return to the flat for what I hope will be a long night of lovemaking.

Suddenly, Dario stiffens, snaps his head forward, stumbles a bit, then grips my arm and quickens the pace. He looks straight ahead with a fierce intensity.

"Oh, Jesus. Oh, JESUS, *MOTHER FUCKER!*"

I've never heard him swear like this before.

"Fucking *HELL!* Fucking bloody *HELL...*" he says again and again, the anger in his voice undiminished.

"Dario, what's wrong—?"

He stops. I feel him trembling. The words come out soft and slow. "Look to my left side, just slightly behind us... the *bloody bastard.*"

I turn to look, and now I see what he saw. It goes on in a shaft of light near the intersection. A man wearing a bright red scarf and brown leather jacket. A man with his jeans pulled down to his ankles. A man being serviced by another man until he's spun around and returns the favor to yet another man. A man who looks up and sees me, then jumps to his feet and leaps into the shadows. *Carlos.*

I feel the blood drain from my face. "My god!—didn't he leave five days ago?"

Dario grabs my arm again and we hurry to the end of the street, three blocks from Plaza Chueca. Neither of us says anything, until I do.

"I just don't get it."

"I've been suspicious for a while," Dario says, his voice tight. "How did Carlos know Vallecas was dangerous unless he'd checked it out for himself? And he made a pass at me once."

"When?"

"During our walk on New Year's Eve. Some nonsense about the beauty of the damaged male body and his fascination with disease... *che stronzo pervertito!*"

I glance back to look. So does he. We continue to walk for several minutes, neither of us saying a word. Finally, "Was that really him, Dario? Was it Carlos?"

"Yes," he answers, at the same moment I answer myself.

In the dim light of the flat, we sit opposite each other. Dario gets up and pours two glasses of wine. I sip, then put mine aside.

"He knows he's busted," I say. "Now what?"

"We'll decide who to talk to, and when—"

"And *soon*," I interrupt. "Marina's about to divorce her husband because Carlos is full of shit. Plain and simple. He'll ruin her life."

"Only if she's already served Luciano papers, and I'm sure that hasn't happened."

That night, I toss and turn, unable to sleep. Dario throws off the thin sheet, stretches me out, and begins massaging my upper back and shoulders with long, deep strokes. His touch is loving and sensuous, but he avoids arousing me. Arousal is impossible tonight, anyway. I'm agitated about Marina. I wonder if I advised her poorly. I wonder if I was complicit in this disaster.

"You decidedly were *not*," Dario says, pulling the sheet over us and rolling me onto my side. I feel his strong arm around me, the warm friction of his chest hair against my back. Comfortable and safe at last, I sleep.

Hours later, in the deep of night, the chills I felt while walking return and then the stabbing in my head. I groan softly. Dario tightens his arm and murmurs, *"It's all right, it's all right."* But the chills grow stronger until I'm wracked with them, violent spasms that shake the bed as if we were in the throes of rough lovemaking. Then, sweat pours from me, soaking Dario, soaking the bed, turning our top sheet into a damp slush.

"What's happening, Mark?" Dario stammers as he rouses himself. He sits up, climbs out of bed and stares down at me. "Mark, are you having some kind of attack? Do I need to call a doctor? *Mark?*" But I can't get the words out because my teeth are chattering uncontrollably. Still, I try to speak, and in one last effort, I bite down on my outstretched tongue. Blood fills my mouth and pours over my bottom lip.

"Oh my god!" Dario screams. "We need a fucking doctor!" He switches on the lights and tears through the flat, looking for the number of an emergency contact. Finding nothing, he shouts, "A neighbor, I'll wake a neighbor!" But he's nude and scrambles for clothes. While this happens, the shakes and chatters subside, and as soon as I'm able, I call out: "It's over. I'm okay, I'm better now."

He comes in wearing only a T-shirt, backwards and inside out. He walks to the bed and stands over me, terror and love in his face.

"You're all right?"

"I'm better. Just let me rest a minute."

But I'm not better. I'm burning up and the room begins to swim. And I'm nauseous. And some hideous, rotten smell pollutes my nose.

"I saw something above the toilet," Dario says, rushing away. "I think you have a fever."

When he removes the thermometer, it's confirmed: 39 degrees Centigrade or 103 degrees Fahrenheit. Still, I reassure Dario I'll be okay if I can just rest through what remains of the night.

"It's just a sudden flu," I say. "Some new bug I've picked up."

"Or food poisoning," Dario adds, brighter. "That musician warned us about it last night."

"I don't think so. Get back in bed with me."

As the early morning light comes up, the ache in my head makes me nauseous. Dario brings his bathrobe and helps me get up. I stand, bracing myself against the back of the chair, while he strips the sheet, a brown oval of sweat at its center. My temperature has dropped two degrees, but the headache pain increases until I beg for some relief. He rushes to the toilet and returns with a plastic box filled with pills and picks through them in the dim light. His hand shaking, he places one of his blue vitamins in my hand and examines the box again. But as I lift the pill to my mouth—

"No!" he yells, grabbing my hand and knocking the pill from it. "I made a mistake. You want the ibuprofen here," he says, dropping a larger pill into my palm. He brings a glass of tangerine juice and instructs me to swallow it.

"This tastes like vinegar," I say. "What is it?"

"Tangerine. You've had it before and liked it."

"No, I've never had this before."

He puts me back to bed with clean sheets, stays close to me the rest of the day, and alternates pacing with sketching. From time to time, I wake up from the blear of the ibuprofen and notice a growing pile of drawings he's torn from his pad and discarded on the floor. Sometime in the late afternoon, I see him on the phone with somebody and hope it's Marina. I ask if it's Marina, and he says no, it's a call to his doctor back in Italy for some advice.

"Most likely a virus," Dario reports to me. "Exactly as you've explained it. He says to eat just a little, drink liquids, and rest as much as possible."

"How much resting do you think I can get in before I leave tomorrow morning?'

"You're not leaving tomorrow morning."

"Yes I am, Dario. I have to leave. I have work to do, bills to pay, and responsibilities at home I have to meet."

"Stop being such an American, Mark. Your health—"

"Stop lecturing me, Dario. I have a job I like with a salary I need. Unlike you, I haven't sold a painting for sixty thousand euros. My flight from Adolfo Suarez leaves tomorrow morning at nine-twenty. Will you help me get there, or not?"

Dario jumps up from his chair and kicks the drawings at his feet. He paces like a wild puma, glares at something through the window. "Yes, of course. But you're an utter imbecile."

We spend a difficult last night together. Dario wants to touch me, but even the lightest brush against my skin causes pain, my entire body an exposed nerve. Throughout the night, I swallow what seem like palmfuls of ibuprofen, which make me dizzy and rip my stomach but take the edge off the migraine and bring my fever down to 101. When the alarm rings the next morning, he guides me into the shower, then follows and washes me. He helps me dress. It's humiliating, I tell him, a glimpse of the chronic infirmities that lie ahead in old age.

An express car picks us up with another couple inside going to Canada by way of the U.K. After only a few moments, the air in the car closes in on me, and I struggle to breathe. By the time we're let off at the shuttle-to-terminal platform, I'm gasping. "This is something new," I tell Dario. He pushes another ibuprofen into my mouth and forces me to swallow, having already tucked two boxes into my carry-on bag for the flight home. The shuttle bus pulls up, and it's clear that we're the last pick-up because it's crammed with standing passengers.

So, it's here I bid farewell to Dario, tears in his eyes and in mine. It's here I promise to see him again, soon, in Poreta, to sleep in the comfortable bed of his beautiful house filled with his brilliant—as I've come to see them—paintings. I climb aboard the bus and strain to see him through the smudged window, his face clear one moment and clouded the next. And I keep that image of Dario Soole standing outside, straining to see me through the same window, for a long time.

7
Old Wounds

When I'd sat with my family at Thanksgiving only days before I left for Spain, I wouldn't have imagined that today, April 11th, 2020, I'd be setting out on a cross-country road trip with my mother. Our destination: Chicago, a memorial service for my father. And I wouldn't have imagined that I'd first hear of this memorial in a phone call from my brother while I sat at my kitchen table teaching first-year algebra to ninth graders.

The beneficiary notification arrived in March from an attorney-executor in Calumet City, Illinois. It was stamped with a filing date three weeks prior, along with the attorney's address and contact information. Joining my mom later that day, I read the letter aloud to her. From what I could make of it, my father had left us some money and property, which included his instructions, *And to Frances Anello, my former wife of twelve years and mother to my two sons, Mark Anello and Lorenzo Anello, who has special needs, I leave the entirety of my estate inclusive of the Highland Park home at 487 Cypress Lane and all furnishings therein....* The letter also mentioned a substantial cash amount without details. "Do you know anything about this house in Highland Park?" I'd asked my mom, who stood backed into a corner of the kitchen with one hand on her chest and the other over her mouth. "I don't know anything about it or about him. I haven't talked to Victor in decades. Have you?"

This news of my father came as yet another shock during those early months of chaos when the world, as we'd known it, began to plummet into darkness. When surgical masks, rubber gloves, and even face shields became macabre accessories for stepping outside. When apples and heads of lettuce were soaked in vinegar-water, and ordinary pedestrians looked like hazmat personnel and crossed the street to avoid one other—if they went out at all.

And then the emptying of classrooms when Los Angeles County Supervisor Vivian Ekchian ordered a complete shutdown of schools for the remainder of the academic year. A hodgepodge system of remote instruction replaced classroom learning. I struggled to adjust. So did the students.

When my mother recovered from a second reading of the letter, I handed her the phone and encouraged her to call the attorney. Over a speakerphone set too loud, Attorney Samuel Derwitz's voice crackled and expressed relief that she'd received the notification. He explained that he would be sending paperwork attendant to the bequest, including inventory lists, valuation reports, settlements paid, mechanics of the disbursement, and title-transfer documents. Mom asked if there would be a reading of the will. He chuckled, "No such thing, Ms. Anello, readings of the will are Hollywood inventions, something from your neck of the woods. Besides, this is a Trust, not a will. Mr. Anello saw to it that there would be no intra-state complications or ancillary probate requirements in the transfer of his property."

"I see."

"Once all title transfers are completed and taxes paid, your former husband instructed immediate distribution of his liquid assets to you and your sons. There have been no contesters, so far. You are his sole heirs."

"I feel so strange about this," my mother said to this stranger at the other end, tears welling up in her eyes.

"Were you in touch with your former husband, Ms. Anello?"

"Not since the divorce, many years ago."

"Well, if you should find yourself in this part of the country, which I'm certainly not suggesting with times being as they are, there'll be a small memorial service for Victor at Holy Name Cathedral on Thursday, April 16th, with all commensurate precautions, of course. I can leave all paperwork in my office for you to pick up and review, sign, and then return to me at the memorial if you choose to go."

"That's very kind," my mother responded, daubing her eyes.

"You and your sons will have to make a decision about whether you'd like me to have the Highland Park property appraised and sold or if you'd like to take immediate possession."

"I understand." More daubing.

A pause, then: "I hope you'll go, Frances, if I may call you that. I'd like to say hello. I knew Victor for many years, and he talked about you and the two boys."

"I think we should go," I'd said to my mother after she ended the call. "Some closure for you, for me, and maybe even for Loren, too."

"This is all so unreal. We should see what Loren thinks."

"Loren won't care about the details. He'll want to figure out how to outsmart the tax man and where to park his share."

About Loren—or more precisely, about Loren and my father—the circumstances of which we rarely discussed because the details were so embedded within our family history that we had no need to pick them out in conversation. My brother's birth name is actually "Lorenzo" in honor of Lorenzo de Medici, the Florentine prince whom my father admired and claimed as a distant relative. Loren soon disappointed him by showing signs of cerebral palsy at eight months, the result, later determined, by a viral infection my mom had during the first trimester. But Loren turned out to be a beautiful boy who's since grown into a handsome and intelligent man, although burdened with increasing ambulatory difficulties. The benztropine and oxybutynin lessened the tremors and helped him walk unaided, but with the plague upon us, the delivery of medications became unreliable, so the amounts he needed he mostly no longer received. My mother loves my younger brother fiercely, and so do I, but that love made her hate my father even more for abandoning his sickly second son, and her hate was contagious. We rarely spoke of Victor to Loren as he grew older, and having no memory of his birth father, Loren seemed uninterested. But it still puzzles me why I never mentioned Loren to anyone in Italy or Spain, even when asked about my relatives. Even when Dario once said that he'd sensed in me a "complicated filial affection" for another male in my family, but couldn't make out the details.

We plan our trip. Flying to Chicago is out of the question. Air travel risked infection, as did travel in general, or so-called "non-essential travel." So we pack up the car and drive, taking all precautions along the way and anticipating the complications, inconveniences, and even the possibly higher risks of such a journey during this era of "shelter-in-place" and "social distancing"—two new descriptives that enter the American *Lingua Franca* and make themselves at home.

"How far is Chicago from home, Mark?" my mother asks, waking up from a long snooze as we wind through the southern Mojave Desert.

"Two thousand miles and about twenty-eight hours, two hours and almost three hundred miles of amazing scenery that you slept through."

"I was dreaming about home," she says. "Probably because I'm a little worried about Loren. Should I call?"

"He's a grown and capable man, Mom, and I'm sure he'll call when he needs to call."

"You'd make a very poor mother," she says.

"Do you want to go home? I can turn around right now."

"Don't be a smartass. I can probably still best you in verbal sparring. No, I do not want to go home, you homo."

"I appreciate that."

"No offense. That's what we used to say in the old days and meant no harm by it. That's what Auden called himself. And of course, Ginsberg."

"People used lots of words in those days that meant no harm but were very harmful."

"This is going to be a long drive," she says turning on the radio.

Dreaming of home—where's home? I wonder, hypnotized by the scrolling road and its blinking dashes—*dreaming of Italy and Spain,* which seem by now, only a dream, but a dream that also brings back the nightmare of my fourteen-hour return flight to Los Angeles and my near-collapse at the customs gate as the fever raged. They'd seated me next to an infant-harnessed young woman who immediately grew alarmed by my obvious distress and asked to be moved. But the flight crew couldn't accommodate her for hours, so we were forced to keep uncomfortable company until I fell asleep. I woke up when the flight attendant asked if I'd like something to eat and found the two seats next to me empty. God knows what I said to her, but in the blear of a hallucination, I saw what looked like a tight-jacketed blonde nurse standing over me alongside a doctor in a white coat who seemed to hold a scalpel and clamps as if to cut me open. When I blinked, they were gone.

Flight over and cleared through Customs, I wobbled to the exit door and propped myself against a pylon at the Arrivals Platform to wait for my Uber, then gasped for air during the thirty-minute ride, the driver several times turning to ask if I needed to go to the hospital. Somehow, I'd mustered up the strength to say, "Just a bad cold," and downplay something I knew was pretty serious, although—*who knew anything then?* When I woke up in a slush of sheets the next morning, I barely had the strength to phone Principal Lovasso but felt relieved when he seemed confused about my return date then started grumbling about some new strain of bird flu breaking out in China and Northern France and how the staff was worried that "You'd bring something back with you, and I don't mean souvenir."

I called my mother, an inveterate newshound.

"Yes, I've heard all about it, but you weren't in those places, Mark. You were in Spain."

"I was in Spain with about a million other tourists, Mom. The museums in Madrid were crammed. On New Year's Eve, there must've been three thousand people packed together in the Plaza."

"Don't obsess. When do we get to see you?"

"Not yet. I don't want you or Loren to catch this thing."

As my strength and attention improved, I began to follow the news, including a story about a man in Snohomish County, just north of Seattle, who'd recently returned from Wuhan China. The man, a healthy American tourist in his thirties, complained of acute breathing problems, a loss of taste and smell, and severe chills accompanying a high fever. Bloodwork revealed infection by a mysterious new agent, given the eponymous title "Coronavirus" by the Centers for Disease Control, because it resembled the barbed crown of the more familiar rhinoviruses. But in a sinister digital rendering, the germ looked more like a medieval mace, spiked and deadly.

In late January, I returned to school part-time and began my transition back. By then, the news channels blazed with reports that the virus had spread to nine European countries, including Spain. By early February, a deadly cluster of infections appeared in Codogno, Lombardy, a region north of Pivonnia, Alessandro's hometown, and began to creep south. The plague, or *pandemic* as the media branded it, became a topic of conversation among the school staff, teachers, aids, and office workers alike. The news sensationalized clusters of contagion—without knowing exactly how they happened—and *who might be infected and who not* became part of everyday conversation. As February tucked up to March with its dark, cold evenings, I settled into my couch and flipped through channels, once stumbling on—god help me—a clip of my ex, Allen Riesler, on a local station running his routine in an empty club:

Hey, have you heard about this new thing they're calling the Coronavirus? Scientists discovered you catch it from drinking one too many Coronas with your chips during the playoffs!

By the middle of the month, I felt strong enough to restart my evening swims at the Y. The locker room talk all about the Snohomish County guy, now called "Patient X," and how he was probably the first to *bring this shit home from that shithole, China*—a sentiment similarly expressed by our diplomatically challenged president, who continued to confuse everyone with contradictory pronouncements. But I wouldn't have dared share my locker room thoughts with these men and their buddies, their sons, and their coworkers—*that here, rinsing in the shower just across from you, stands someone who'd traveled in an airplane that discharged 522 passengers into the Los Angeles night just hours before they went to work the next day; who coughed into the faces of hundreds of other Americans at the Customs gate; who gasped for air then forced it from his lungs in a taxi that went on to carry thousands of passengers to their destinations... that here, showering ten feet away, might stand the true "Patient X"*—who survived this disease but left enough of it behind to infect everyone else.

The phone chirps, interrupting my doom-scrolling. My mother jolts and looks down. "It's Loren," she says, fumbling to connect. "Hello, sweetheart! We're driving through Nevada to Las Vegas, where we'll spend the night."

Loren hates the speakerphone because he feels it draws attention to his mild speech impediment, so I only hear my mother's side of the conversation. She's quiet for a moment.

"Good!" she says, holding the phone away from her ear and turning to me. "Loren said he talked to his colleague, an estate attorney, about the tax liabilities we'll have to figure out with Victor's bequest, depending on how we get it." Without waiting for my response, she says, "That's great, Loren. After all, you're the numbers guy in the family."

"So am I," I mutter, mostly to myself.

Turns to me again, "Loren says this estate fellow wants to meet as soon as we get back."

"What? Nobody's meeting anyone these days! We're not walking into a strange office and sitting across from someone we don't even know!" I think about how my mom thinks about it. "Do you mean *Zoom*?"

She nods vigorously, half in one conversation and half in the other, says goodbye to Loren and puts down the phone. "Yes, Zoom, whatever that is. It's something a car does. That's what it is."

I drive without talking, still steamed about her numbers guy compliment. Finally: "By the way, you have two number guys in the family."

"Of course," she says. "But Loren has a complex because he's only a stay-at-home accountant while you have a degree and a teaching certificate."

"I went to college to get my degree. Loren wasn't interested."

`We drive for a while. My mom looks out of the window. "I worry about Loren," she says.

"I worry about everyone."

"What's happening to the world, Mark?"

"Nobody has an answer. Certainly not Trump."

"They say it should be over soon." She smooths out an imaginary wrinkle in her dress. "I think it will be over soon."

We'd settled on Las Vegas for our overnight stay because of the availability of accommodations there and the lack of them everywhere else. As the virus began to spread east, Nevada followed California and ordered a statewide shutdown of all non-essential businesses. But the Las

Vegas mayor successfully opposed the governor's mandate, so after ten days of closure, adjustments were made for disinfecting and social distancing, and casinos and their hotels reopened. In the safe space of my car, I keep two bottles of hand disinfectants in the cup holders and a box of N95 masks stuffed into the glove compartment. Like astronauts, we'll do a mutual suit-check before exiting our capsule into the Hostile Outer. Our luggage contains similar precautionary supplies.

As we enter the lobby of our hotel, a doorman in a bright floral cloth mask stops us for temperature taking—a little gun resembling a supermarket scanner tapped against our foreheads. The dozen or so people in line before the check-in desk all wear masks and stand, socially distanced, on smiley-faced yellow circles spaced six feet apart. Everyone seems cheerful; everyone mutters unintelligibly behind their masks and cocks an ear to understand.

We roll our luggage to the nearest elevator lobby and wait among impatient others to ascend to our room. Finally, we join a small group in the elevator. As the doors shut, off come their masks so they can chitchat and laugh. I'm about to say something when the door opens and they're pulled away by alcohol-fueled friends in similar high spirits, also de-masked. I shoot an alarmed look at my mother, who shoots back, but follow with a wink of assurance that we're protected by our N95s, although the news is mixed about their effectiveness. Truth is, the news is mixed about *everything,* and I know that there'll be other moments of anxiety during our stay which I'll do my best to get through.

But the room looks clean although the air bites, strong with the odor of disinfectant. Our pillows shine, shrink-wrapped in plastic, and laminated signage informs us that no housekeeping services will be provided during active occupancy. We decide to have a light dinner in the café, taking the five flights of stairs downstairs instead of the elevator. We're greeted by a masked hostess and seated at a corner table, far removed from the other occupied tables in the room. She removes the folded table card that says "Disinfected" and places it in her pocket. From the same pocket, she pulls out two sets of cellophane-wrapped utensils: fork, knife, spoon, and small napkin, and places one set before each of us. Not a single condiment appears on the table, nor is water served. When our burgers arrive, wrapped in waxed paper on an unadorned plate, we slicken our hands with sanitizer, unwrap the burgers, and use a fork and knife to eat them quickly and without speaking. We return to our room in an empty elevator.

Lying on the bed, I look at the map while my mother carefully unpacks her slacks, blouses, and dresses and hangs them in the closet. Anticipating my question, she says, "I realize we're only staying a few nights, but any wrinkle I can avoid, I'll avoid. Who knows who we'll meet at this memorial? I'm nervous."

I smile and go back to my map. "I wish we could make Chicago by the fifteenth, Mom, but that's too many hours of driving each day. I'm thinking Moab, Utah tomorrow night and then Omaha after that."

"It's fine, we're fine, and everything is just lovely," she says, unfolding her pajamas. "But I'd advise young couples to put off their honeymoon until it's safe to step into a bathtub." She stops her unpacking before she's finished and looks up at me, serious-faced. I know something's coming when she walks over and sits at the edge of my bed.

"What is it?" I say, not looking up.

"Mark, you never shared very much about your friend out there— Darian, was it?"

"Dario."

"Dario. Well?"

"He's taken up with some young Egyptian. A guy who does landscape work in his garden."

"Taken up?"

"He says the guy is safe company. Goes from the garden into the house and back again. No fears of contagion." I meet her eyes. "I don't ask questions, Mom. With things as they are, this isn't the time to pry."

"That's a very adult point of view. I just had high hopes—"

"I know."

She sighs. "I'm afraid maybe you just don't have luck with men. Just as I never had luck with men."

I toss the open map over the bedside, watch it float to the floor. "Mom, do you know how weird and embarrassing it is for me to hear that you never had luck with men? You're my mother, for god's sake, not my fag hag."

"I appreciate that."

"I'm sorry. It's just that… well, you're sixty-eight years old."

"Oh, I see."

"Let's get some rest," I say, switching off my tiny lamp on its tiny table beside my enormous bed in a room of this ridiculously enormous and eerily quiet hotel. But as I lie there in the dark, enfolded in bleach-acrid sheets, my thoughts now drift to Marina. In the chaos of my return, the urgency to call and warn her about Carlos faded, probably because I'd never figured out, either independently or with Dario's help, exactly what to say and how to say it. After those few early phone calls with Dario where he'd asked about my health and expressed relief in my recovery, communication dropped off quickly, probably, in part, because Dario hated texting and wasn't too fond of phone calls, either. Dario liked to look at people; he loved looking at me. He brought something out of me, looking back at him, that pushed away the clutter of words and cleared the way for emotions far more powerful to move between us.

Still, I wonder if Dario called Marina. I wonder if Marina called the lawyer. I wonder if Marina is in danger and I cursed myself for never finding out.

At around eight o'clock the following evening, we pull into Moab to find a funky little motel at the perimeter of Arches National Monument. The pickings are slim in this vast swath of badlands, but as darkness approaches, a silver sphere winks out to us over a sign that reads *Satellite Inn*. The room features framed headlines of the first moon landing and, as if manifesting mom's karmic observation, the bathtub is filthy and clogged with hair. We go to bed early in the shadow of a mountain and wake up at 5 a.m. for the long drive to Omaha.

The next day, we cross into Nebraska by early evening and pull into a McDonald's along a long prairie road. Distant telephone poles line the horizon like gibbets. Mom looks tired, but she's a trooper. The McDonald's is drive-through only, of course, and after the sliding drawer delivers our food, we step out of the car, stretch, and sit at one of the concrete tables, first covering the surface with napkins. Several other cars pull in behind us and also take meals to their tables. A thin, naked-faced man with a small boy seat themselves at a table right next to us, the man coughing and spitting as he unwraps his burger. The boy, eating while running, hacks the air as he circles our table and points a playful finger at us. Two unmasked women in flip-flops and sparkly sunglasses share a large container of fries while screaming at their brood running havoc with food falling out of their mouths. When another car pulls up, a van with MAGA and gun stickers plastering its windows, we wrap up our half-eaten burgers, toss them, and an hour later, pull into the weed-riddled parking lot of a hotel outside Omaha. It's there, lying on the bed and scrolling my phone, that I find my father's obituary.

"I've found it, Mom. Victor's obit. It's in the *Calumet Sentinel*."

She stretches on her bed and turns to me, her smile tight. "Well, let's find out how he spent the rest of his life, shall we?"

I read aloud:

Victor ("Vince") Eugene Anello, 70, a resident of Highland Park, Illinois, died peacefully at St. Anthony Hospital of heart failure. Born in Brooklyn, New York, he was the only son of Rose and Eugene Anello, also of Brooklyn. Vince spent many hours—

"*Vince?*" My mother interrupts. "Who's *Vince*? Nobody ever called him that. How do you even *get* Vince out of Victor?"

I continue:

—spent many hours in New York City where he attended Toscanini concerts and Italian operas with his father. In 1969, after receiving his B.S.E. in engineering from New York University, he worked as a construction foreman and married Frances Cirrone, with whom he remained for twelve years. Moving to Chicago and finding great success in real estate investing, Vince retired from engineering and worked at the University of Chicago, helping to develop entrance exams for advanced degree engineering students. He met his second wife there, Lorraine Hopkins, and enjoyed 18 years of marriage before her death in 2007. Vince was preceded in death by his

parents, his sister Mary-Veronica, and his daughter Annalese-Hopkins Anello. He is survived by his first wife Frances Cirrone Anello and their two sons Mark Anello and Lorenzo Anello, all of Los Angeles, California.

I look up to find my mother staring at me. We say it together: "Great success career in real estate investing?" and burst out laughing.

She gets up from bed and walks to her suitcase, fussing. "I guess that's why the checks got bigger as you boys grew older," she says, half to herself, "I never asked for it."

"Maybe, Mom."

"I made very few demands of your father."

"I know, Mom."

"And now a daughter with this woman. I wonder what happened."

It's a relief when we reach Chicago late afternoon on April 16th and check in to a suburban hotel where we're greeted courteously and shown to a room that's clean without smelling toxic. Our appointment at the attorney's office to pick up paperwork is set for five o'clock that evening and the memorial for twelve noon tomorrow. After the memorial, I'd like to check out the Highland Park property, at least in a drive-by, and then get us back on the road by early evening.

After quick showers and a change of clothes, we set out for Calumet City, a suburb just south of downtown. Attorney Samuel Derwitz's office occupies the ground floor of a brick mansion set in an old neighborhood of oak trees and jug-shaped lampposts. We buzz, the great door clicks, and we push in. Through the slotted receptionist window, a woman appears, asks our names, then points down left to a large manila envelope on a table. We pick up the envelope and look up to thank her, but she's gone.

Outside, I wonder out loud if the Highland Park house is close by. My mother nods, looking down. She's somewhere else.

I say, "If it's in anything like the houses in this neighborhood, I'd sure like to see what we own, wouldn't you?"

"I suppose," she answers, holding the envelope against her chest. I can see there's a lot going on inside her.

"Okay, you're tired," I say. "We'll just go back and rest."

"He had no one," she says as we cruise back to the hotel under giant trees with tattered winter leaves. "I wonder what happened to him that he had no one."

"He did all right, married again, and had a daughter."

"Or inherited one," she says.

"I wonder if she knew about us, Mom. Maybe we'll find out more tomorrow. I'm nervous too, but I want to know more about 'Vince,' the real estate tycoon who wrote college exams."

"Now I see where you got your bug for teaching."

"Funny, that, right?" I reply, "If teaching is what I do these days."

After another sterilized dinner, we return to our room and sit facing one another for what seems like a long time, the envelope on the desk beside my opened suitcase. We stare at the envelope together, then look at each other.

"Well," my mother says, "Should we see what's inside?"

I toss the envelope on the bed and pull our chairs alongside it. Mom does the tearing. A formidable bundle of photocopies and maps and letters and forms and documents spill out, clipped together in twos, or threes, or fives, the grouping of which only further obscures their purpose.

"Jesus, we need a lawyer to make sense of all this," I say.

"Just a moment," my mother answers with sudden and surprising focus. "Let's figure out what deserves our immediate attention and push the rest aside for now. The key to understanding all of it is understanding just a few documents, I think."

I'm impressed.

She teases out a six-page, five-columned list with the enticing double-heading of *Inventory and Appraisal of Real Property / Inventory and Appraisal of Personal Property.* She lifts the paper up to her face at an angle so I can't see the figures. Through the paper, I see the shadow of her finger run down, across, then down again and stop. The pointing finger folds back into her hand, her hand half-covers her mouth. Her mouth quivers.

"The last appraisal of the Cypress property was in 2016 with a returned valuation of three million, eight hundred and sixty-four thousand dollars."

"Oh my god! Do you—"

She stops me, turning over the page, her pointer finger moving again.

"The valuation of inventoried possessions, including art, antiques, personal items—my god, the list is long—comes to two million, four hundred and twenty-eight thousand dollars."

She puts down the paper, tears in her eyes. We're both very quiet.

"Thank you, Vic," she whispers.

I leap up and hug her so tightly I'm afraid I'll break her ribs. "That's over six million dollars, Mom! Do you realize—I mean, do you *realize*?"

"It's all a dream," she says, collecting herself and picking up the paperwork again. "There's a form here I need to sign if I want the house reappraised for sale rather than take possession. And another form for what's inside the house." She looks up at me, a strange expression on her face. "I say we let it all go and never see it. I say we accept your father's gift, thank him in our prayers, and shoo away the past, don't you agree?" But her tone is more decision than question because she signs off on the title before I even have a chance to respond.

It's nearly midnight before we discover an additional cash bequest of six hundred and forty-five thousand dollars, disbursable immediately when the release of trust form is signed and settled. An hour later, still awake in the dark, I call across to her in the other bed.

"Do you want me to consult Loren about all of this before we see Samuel?"

"I'll call Loren first thing tomorrow morning. If I can get any sleep."

She makes the call at 10 a.m. on our way to Holy Name Cathedral on East Superior Street. From her half of the conversation, it doesn't take long to figure out that Loren's excitement is dampened by his disappointment that the estate doesn't include a car. "Jesus Christ, Loren," I call over my mother's emoluments, "you can buy yourself a new car with the cash you're getting." Mom holds the phone away from her face and mouths, *he's got a bit of growing up to do.* We turn the corner onto East Superior, pull into a parking lot across from the cathedral's Gothic quarry, and follow pedestrian signs to a modern building at the edge of a concrete courtyard. A glassed-in marquee displays "VICTOR ANELLO MEMORIAL" beside double doors flanked by flowers.

I take my mother's arm, or maybe she takes mine, and we step inside to the smell of cupcakes, wafting from a refreshments table pushed against a near wall. A tabled guest book invites our signatures before a wall of photographs: Victor, as I almost remember him, leaning out from the driver's side of what looks to be a Chrysler Imperial; Victor, sporting a very '70s mustache, shaking hands with another mustache. He and his presumed wife dancing; he and their presumed daughter laughing around a Christmas tree. My mother takes it all in quickly and then faces the room. Only twelve people occupy the space, nine sitting and three standing in conversation. Everyone wears a mask, so we take out ours and put them on. An Asian lady wearing a corsage hands each of us a memorial program, my father's toothy mug on the front.

A tall, silver-haired man approaches, his eyes smiling. "Frances and Mark, is it?"

"Hello," Mom replies.

"Sam Derwitz. So, so glad you could come. Please sit as close to me as you can, and if you'd like, I'll announce you both, in case you would like to share a memory."

"That's very kind, but no thank you," says my mother."

"Of course," Sam says warmly. "In any case, I'm right over there beside the lady in dark grey, my wife, who was also very fond of Vince."

We take our seats in proximity to Attorney Derwitz, who twists around and looks at us, his eyes bright and curious. I study the others and overhear bits of conversation that lead me to believe that most in attendance are either coworkers of my father's or grad students from the University of Chicago he might've mentored. The memorial begins with soft music: Puccini's *Nessun Dorma*, from the opera *Turandot*, the program informs, which soon fades to silence as a young man stands at the podium and announces my father's name, then reads aloud his obituary. When he reaches the "first wife Frances Cirrone part," a few heads turn in our direction, already wondering, I suppose, if Mom is she. Mom steadies her gaze ahead, unreactive.

My hunch delivers. A parade of young grad students appears, each young man or woman praising "Vince" for his encouragement with their careers, his sage advice, his story-telling—all aspects of this stranger I never knew but feel, after a while, I would like to have known. An emotion rises up in me, not for what I knew and lost, but for what I didn't know and would never find out. I feel a sadness and, at the same time, an emptiness. I feel it for my mother and for Loren, and also for my adopted family in Europe—Marina, Dario, and even Alessandro. I feel it grow big enough to swallow the whole world as it struggles to heal itself.

A stout-legged and smartly dressed woman steps up behind the microphone. She identifies herself, with a slight German accent, as my father's neighbor on Cypress Lane and talks fondly of their neighborly gatherings outdoors. "Even on days just like this one," she says, opening her hands in a kind of benediction. "And his wonderful wife Lorraine, who sang for us and the beautiful little Annalese, so talented with the dancings and paintings. Such a perfect and happy family and so hard for him when he lost them. But today, he goes to join them," again the hands spread out, "And they all sing and dance in God's backyard on a beautiful day that will never end!"

There's not a dry eye in the house, except for ours. My mother and I look at each other and decide to flee as soon as we can. We feel like intruders and voyeurs—marginalized intimates forced to endure memories that aren't ours but still feel stolen from us. Right after the announcement for cupcakes and coffee, we make our way to the door. Attorney Derwitz intercepts us, his mask off.

"I'm sorry if this was difficult for you. Would it help me to say that Vince, who was my dear friend before I became his attorney, talked at length about his former family and how much—and this is confidential—he wanted to see you all again."

"No," my mother says. "Please say no more about it."

"Understood," Derwitz replies. His tone changes, "So, have you completed the paperwork, Ms. Anello? Can you return it to me?"

"Yes, it's in the car. We'll bring it out."

"And what did you think of the house?"

"We didn't see it."

"No? Wasn't the key included in the envelope?"

"No."

"Well, I—" Derwitz stammers, "The key should certainly have—"

"It doesn't matter. I've signed myself off title. Sell it."

Derwitz turns to me, almost imploringly.

"Mom, I begin..."

"Ms. Anello—" he interrupts. "*Frances*. And *Mark*. Please visit the property before you sign off. I'm going to call someone to meet you there with the key. If you still wish me to sell after you've gone in and looked around, I'll happily take your completed documents. But in the meantime, keep everything. I won't accept them today."

My mother nods in agreement, wearily, and extends her small hand to Derwitz, who takes it in both of his. I take her arm, which feels stiff, and we walk outside, faces following us as we step down to cross the street, faces following us as we turn slowly out of the parking lot, faces following us even as we turn back onto Superior Avenue and turn east to North Michigan Avenue to join Highway 41. She sits quietly as I navigate the highway for the twenty-minute drive to the affluent suburb where my father, Vince Eugene Anello, spent presumably the happiest years of his life—or at least he had everyone fooled into thinking so.

During my idle hours in our hotel, I'd learned that Highland Park is a neighborhood for music lovers. The Ravinia Festival happens there, and the Chicago Symphony makes Highland Park its home during the summer months. As we drive, I mention this to Mom to see if I can kindle some interest and enthusiasm. She says, "He loved his classical music, your dad. When we were first married, he'd sing opera for me when he made tomato gravy." She looks through the window as we cruise through a neighborhood of row houses. "I'm sure it wasn't easy for him, working early mornings at construction sites when he had so many..." she struggles with the word, "*Creative* ideas about things."

"What kind of ideas?"

"Oh, I don't know. He seemed to live in another world, sometimes."

We exit the highway and turn east on Central Avenue into a shaded downtown, a wide boulevard separated by a grassy island, artisanal businesses on both sides, all shuttered. Dry leaves from maples accumulate in the vestibules of these shops, and cafes wave tattered tablecloths from tables strung together and haphazardly locked with bicycle cable. Here and there, a cyclist weaves along the curb; here and there, a dog-walker. But we're the only car on the street. We turn north on Dale Avenue and catch a glimpse of Lake Michigan before Cypress Lane appears, the start of it ranged by huge, naked elms. Just halfway through our turn, Victor's enormous house mid-block leaps out from the large houses, not only for its cream-white color within a row of red brick, but for the eruption of turrets and towers that spring from its roof. A small blue car sits in front. The masked woman who steps out to greet us, the one behind the window in Derwitz's office, introduces herself as Stephanie, a paralegal. She bids us follow her up the wide front stairs to a four-column porch that makes me think, I guess because of the neighborhood's musical associations, of an overture before the grand opera.

"The house was built in 1903," Stephanie recites. "It's one of the original model homes for Highland Park, which had been incorporated thirty-five years before. It's Italianate in style, unusual for the neighborhood, which featured mostly Tudor and Queen Anne."

"Very fancy," my mother says, looking up and visoring her eyes.

"Mr. Anello added on a bit within the constraints of the city's historic preservation plan, which is doing its best to keep developers from buying these homes to tear them down. Do you see the rotunda on the northeast corner? Mr. Anello added that to take advantage of the views over Lake Michigan."

We follow her pointing finger, keys jangling beneath it.

"Come on!" she says playfully as she snaps open the lockbox that hangs from the brass handle then turns the key in the door latch. "Let me just step inside to turn off the alarm, then you can follow me and start your exploring. Take your time. This is your home and Mr. Derwitz very much wanted you to see it. I'll wait outside to lock up again."

The door closes behind her, and we wait. Then, it swings open to admit us. "Remember, everything inside is also your property," Stephanie says as we enter, "So feel free to examine and make note of anything that particularly interests you, although nothing may be removed at this time."

"Thank you," my mother says, her eyes darting around.

"And don't miss the greenhouse in the back," Stephanie calls from the porch. "It was designed by Vince along with the swimming pool, which, unfortunately, hasn't been cleaned in a while."

We thank her again and walk deeper into the entrance hall, where glittering things surround us—a white marble fireplace, a tiered chandelier on a velvet-sleeved chain, and a sconce-lit staircase twisting into an arch above. Oriental vases of every shape and size surround us; paintings of questionable taste, offset by their impressive dimensions, lean from the walls: an entryway made to impress.

"Well, *la-dee-dah*," my mom croons.

"Nice, but it looks completely staged," I say. "A 'look what I have' house."

"Maybe that's what your father wanted. To be a 'look what I have' person before he had the courage to be himself."

We leave the hall for one of several large rooms that open to the side. The first is a pleasant and airy space with comfortable and casual furniture. A grand piano sits in a far corner before a row of French doors with a peek of the garden beyond. Bookshelves stretch floor to ceiling and display leatherbound volumes with gold lettering on the spines. A long, low table in front of a sofa spreads a collection of oversized architecture books, among them, *New York City of the Sixties in Photographs*. All very interesting. Things get even more interesting as we enter a second room that appears to be a gallery. Modern art stuns the eyes with slashes of red and yellow, stuff I think I've seen before and assume is valuable. But here again, a mishmash: a schmaltzy bronze of leaping dolphins, a glass cabinet of African masks, and something else that attracts my mother's attention on a wall above a potted plant: an arrangement of framed photographs of an attractive, middle-aged woman in riding gear, sitting on a horse.

"Are you fucking kidding me? A horse? She rode a *fucking horse?*"

I glance over her shoulder. "Looks like it, Mom."

"He hated animals and complained for the two days we took his sister's dog into the apartment. And then he marries a woman who rides horses?"

"I don't know. Looks like she might've had money. Only rich people ride horses."

As if evoked by some spell, other framed photographs emerge from the clutter of the room, some placed beside knickknacks, others scattered across tabletops, and still others tucked into the vacant hollows of bookshelves. One by one, we examine them.

My mother approaches a tabletop photo in a fancy frame. Stares down at it.

"I guess this was the daughter," she says, picking it up to look closer. "Your half-sister, Annabelle, or whatever her name was."

"Annalese, I think," I say, coming up behind.

The photo shows a young girl, maybe fourteen, straddled on her bicycle and smiling, with a view of the big house beyond.

"Cute," Mom mutters, then hands me the photo and walks away. Two smaller photos flutter out, tucked into the back, the same young girl in an oversized armchair and the girl again, thinner now, smiling from a hospital bed with a large bandage wrapped around her head. A woman, by now I'm certain my father's wife, sits beside her holding a balloon.

"Did you see these others, Mom?" I ask, not sure if I should ask.

She studies them in my hand. "Obviously some problem with this child, considerably more serious than Loren's problem. Must've been quite a disappointment for him."

We leave this room and walk with less interest through the other rooms, all similarly outfitted with comfortable furniture and bric-a-brac. We continue to the kitchen: large, yellow, wallpapered. Country charm collides with 1980s stainless steel. We peek outside to the greenhouse— a Victorian concoction worthy of *Harry Potter*—with a huge algoid plunge beside it.

"Do you want to take a look upstairs, Mom?"

"Why not?" she says, turning sharply to face me. "I wonder what kind of taxes he paid for a place this big."

"I'm sure Derwitz has all that information. But remember, the house was last appraised in 2016. It's probably gone up in value, and with the pandemic, taxes are slightly down."

Eight bedrooms occupy three entire floors of the rotunda, with the two largest bedrooms on the highest floor, where we wind up. Lake Michigan shines blue-grey through a curved and curtainless window, an expanse of glass so enormous the room seems to end and suspend us in mid-air. A row of photos of Annalese in a tutu hang in a separate sitting area off this main bedroom—which I assume my father and his wife shared—until I come upon an adjoining second bedroom, similarly sized and luxurious, but with the distinct masculinity of the man my father has become in my imagination. I mention this discovery to my mother who's already entered the closet of the first bedroom and stands before racks of fancy clothes.

"I want to see what she wore," she says, sweeping clumps of hangers. "All too big for me, as if I'd wear any of this ugly stuff anyway." She stoops and looks under a bureau. "I wonder where she hid her jewelry."

"Mom, it looks like Victor had his own closet in a completely separate bedroom."

"Serves him right," she snaps. "Go in there and see if there's something you can use."

I do. The closet holds the faint smell of what I imagine to be my father's body. I push through suits and garish sports shirts, very 70s and awful. But the shoes! A high shelf contains dozens of them, the stitching along their backs suggesting Italian-made and very expensive. I stretch my arm and sweep my hand across to pull a few pairs down, but it bangs against something hard and un-shoe-like. I wiggle the mystery object closer to the edge and lift it down. A metal box, mottled and pocked with rust. Inside, I find Kodachrome photos of a four-year-old me, baby Loren, and my beautiful mother—photos taken in the long-ago kitchen of our Upper East Side apartment in New York City. In one, my father forks a steaming blob of spaghetti from a pot. In another, my mom mugs with the same fork by her face. And then, the *letters*, at least twenty of them bundled together. I recognize my mother's handwriting on the envelopes and note the cancel date of the stamps—all letters she'd written to my father in the months after he left. Finally, buried in the deepest place possible in such a box, a single unopened letter that post-dates all the others, addressed to my mother, I assume from my father. A red stamped REFUSED stretches across the front of it.

I just can't keep this to myself. "Mom!" I call out. She hurries in, seeming to sense something in my voice. I hold up the box. "Letters. Letters from you to Dad. One from Dad to you. I guess you refused it."

She's matter of fact. "He never answered any of my letters, until, out of the blue, I finally got one. But I was over him, and by then, I just wanted to forget him. I told the postman to take it back if that's the letter you're talking about."

"It might be, and it's here."

"Well, read it if you want. I don't care to."

"But Mom—"

"I don't care to, Mark, do you understand me? *I don't care to read it.* If your curiosity about your father extends to some maudlin letter he sent six fucking years after he walked out on us, then be my guest."

"That was thirty-one years ago, Mom! *Mom!* I think he wanted us here. I think he wanted us to find just what I've found."

My mother stares at me, her mouth half-open as if to say something. A shudder passes through her before she bends forward and breaks into wracked sobs so convulsive that her legs begin to fold under her. I rush forward to catch her, hug her.

"It's okay, we did fine. We're family and we're happy. You made a good home for us."

She pulls herself together and sweeps away a strand of grey, sweeps the emotion from her face. "Have you noticed that there's not a single picture of your father and his wife together? And now separate bedrooms. How *perfect*."

We walk outside to a spot by the greenhouse, find a stone bench under a bare elm that clatters in the breeze. The ground surrounding us is dappled with its shadow. I carefully open the envelope and draw out two sheets inside, read to her slowly.

Calumet City, Illinois. April 9th, 1988

My Dearest Fran,

I know I've already made you angry by writing this letter after so many years of no word from me. But please let me try to open a small door between us if you can find it in your heart to do so which I sincerely hope you might. I have struggled painfully with the realization of what I have done and not found happiness in the years following. I know this also upsets you, as you see me as selfish and self-absorbed as I now see myself. But we were so young when we married and from traditional families who did not encourage us to find out who we were and what we really wanted but only what they wanted—healthy children, which I didn't provide and so made me a failure in their eyes. What saved me was my new dream to follow my life's calling to bring me the success I felt I deserved, which I would surely have shared with you and the boys should that dream come true. And now it has, dear Fran. In only five years, I have established myself as a restorer of homes here, in Chicago, a city that no one seems to appreciate as much as I do, having lived in New York where even the newspapers are more expensive, ha-ha. I have made my success and reach out hoping that maybe you'll forgive me for our divorce which seemed best as it would force me to support you and the boys with no alternative but to do so. My way, and I know it seems a strange way to prove my dedication and my hope for forgiveness. But I find myself a very lonely man now, today in particular for some reason, and then I remembered it was the day we first took the place on E. 84th and began our young lives together. Oh my sweet Fran don't hate me for saying these things to you now as I realize they may hurt you terribly. I ask only for your patience and will wait as long as I must for your response, praying that one day, near or distant, we might talk once again.

With love, Victor

I look at my mom, afraid of what I might see. She's composed, thumbs a small tear from her cheek.

"Keep the letter," she says. "I want you to have it."

"But—"

"Keep it. And let's go home."

As we leave the house, I catch a glimpse of Stephanie looking at her watch, mask off. She sees us, waves, then rushes back inside to set the alarm and comes out smiling.

"All done already?" she asks.

"We are," Mom replies. "Thank you."

"Any decisions?"

Mom hands her the key. "Sell the house and everything inside. And thank Mr. Derwitz for his kindness."

She takes my arm as we walk back to the car to retrieve the envelope and hands it to paralegal Stephanie, who nods and receives it quietly.

8

News From Italy

We didn't see any money from the sale of my father's house until October 2020, and by then, much of it had been scraped by taxes. As Sam Derwitz warned us, Mom paid dearly for listing 487 Cyprus Lane. Even with the help of an ace Chicago accounting team to tally the costs of renovations for a distressed property, the capital gains on the house and everything inside were huge, as were the high commission fees paid to the corporate-owned reality that bought the mansion as a tear-down. But, all monies withheld and accounted for, the trust was finally closed on September 21st. We parked our more modest fortunes where Sam recommended we park them, in high-yield certificates of deposit, putting aside 10% cash for emergencies. By now, Dad's executor had proved himself to be a reliable and honest contact, if not a family friend.

As the stay-at-home season ambled towards the holidays, a new normal emerged. The web came alive with virtual celebrations and sing-alongs. Zoom parties in make-believe Caribbean resorts offset the gloom of isolation and boosted the will to make merry. The internet became a window to the world. Italians approached the season with a new YouTube post every day of Advent showing neighbors singing and raising glasses to one another across balconies. But Italy was hit hard by the plague, which had moved steadily south from the central *Regione* of the peninsula to the more rural areas of Puglia and Calabria in the south. *Regione Le Marche*, which included Pivonnia—Alessandro, Marina, and Luciano's hometown—struggled to survive as the virus raced through nursing homes, schools, and other vulnerable populations, stealing *nonne e nonni* from their grandchildren and children from their young parents almost overnight. The nurses and nuns who administered to the sick were also stricken, as were the prelates, laundry workers, kitchen helpers, and even the visiting priests who wore their masks but removed them during prayers—all dead within weeks of exposure, their lungs bleeding in under-equipped *Pronto Soccorso* wards of hospitals. So devastating were Pivonnia's losses, that the small mountain town emerged from obscurity to become one of the featured stories in the international media's coverage of Covid's ferociousness.

Every evening, I would drill through data on *Il Istituto Superiore di Sanità* where I found only a few epidemiologic statistics for Poreta, where Dario lived, and an analysis suggesting that *Regione* Umbria had seen fewer infections because of its lower population density. But I'm only a troll in all this information-gathering because I haven't talked to any of my Italian friends in almost a year. So, on Monday, December 7th, the day of the first available Covid test, I vow to take the test and share the results, positive or negative, with my friends overseas.

On December 14th, nurse Sandra Lindsay of Long Island Jewish Hospital receives the first Covid-19 vaccination to the clatter of cameras. When she is done, she faces the photographers and pleads for other healthcare workers to follow her lead. Later that same day, California Governor Gavin Newsom watches healthcare workers at Kaiser Permanente Medical Center receive their inoculations, cheered by their colleagues.

The news reports stress that the Pfizer and BioNTech companies are the initial developers and front-line suppliers of what's being called the "mRNA Solution." Their vaccine contains no traces of the Covid virus but creates a harmless imposter protein that fools the body into producing antibodies to destroy the actual virus should it enter the bloodstream. A second company, Moderna, soon releases its own versions of this technology. Behind them, other companies wait to jump into the distribution pipeline—AstraZeneca, Johnson & Johnson, Sanofi-GSK, Novavax, and Valneva—but none of them contain the Solution.

This breakthrough cheers just about everyone, although vaccination availability for the general public is scarcely mentioned. Still, Covid testing sites continue to roll out piecemeal throughout Los Angeles zip codes. Ours is among the first. However, scheduling a test proves challenging, with appointment times on the CDC's over-trafficked website filling up within five minutes of their posting. When I finally connect to a calendar at 3 a.m. for a same day appointment at 9 a.m., I message Principal Lovasso to find a sub for my morning class and race to the Montrose Community Center.

The long line outside dampens my hope for a speedy in-and-out. Stragglers pace along the sides, looking to join friends and cut in front of strangers. Social distancing facilitates this cheating, and arguments break out. By nine-fifteen, the line stretches from the building's gated patio to the sidewalk and halfway down the block to the corner. Individuals file one at a time through the gate, and as I get closer, I see a row of swap-meet-style tents with long folding tables: this tent is a "station" for verifying appointment time and address, that one is for administering the nose swab, and a third one contains computers so that each patient can set up a personal portal for receiving results online, an unwelcome and frustrating procedure for most. After two hours, I pass through, get swabbed and jabbed, and then I'm released to resume my day. And after three days of "results pending" messages on my phone, I'm informed that my test information may be viewed on the CDC website by logging in. This, of course, is impossible. Nearly a week later, at 5 a.m., I finally connect. Negative.

I'm relieved but not convinced. The nurse at my swabbing station warned me that the swab or "antigen test" would only detect active infections within a six-week window. An infection that might've occurred further back could only be identified by finding remnants of the virus' DNA through a "polymerase chain reaction test," which was expensive and involved a blood draw. Such tests were not widely available in the United States, although much of Europe and the U.K. had them— my excuse, finally, to call Dario and ask about his health after months of silence.

At 2 a.m. on a Saturday morning, I get up to make the call. It's noon in Poreta and Dario might be working. It's not the best time to interrupt him, but I want to follow through before I lose my nerve. I tighten the grip on the phone as I punch in the odd sequence of numbers, then wait for the distinctly musical ring of Italy. The phone purrs for about ten seconds before Dario's voice wobbles in with an amusing, snarky message:

Soole here. I'm in the studio mornings from seven to ten and from thirteen to sixteen. Speak to me between, not during.

He repeats the message in Italian, which sounds considerably friendlier.

"Dario," I stammer, clearing a frog in my throat, "Mark, your long-lost California friend, puts his tail between his legs as he calls you with a simple 'hello.' I'm assuming you're fine, as I am…" I pause, at a loss. "Anyway, I'm thinking of you, which is a stupid thing to say because I haven't called, but you haven't, either. So, let's fix it. *Ciao*."

A week later, Christmas Eve, still no response.

On Christmas Day, Loren shows off his new car, an Audi sedan with calf-leather seats and Bluetooth connectivity to every device he either owns or will soon buy. It's a pity he has nowhere to go. None of us does. For most Californians, the holidays of 2020 are shelter-in-place occasions where even intimate family members, nursing a sniffle or two, feel spooked into wearing masks as they serve themselves dinners from covered pans left on the stovetop. Crisp-skinned roasts are quarantined to the hinterlands of dining rooms or stay entombed in ovens for haphazard carving. Empty chairs are placed between brother and sister, husband and wife, and grandma's exiled to the end of the table where no one sits opposite her.

The four members of our family haven't shared a meal in months, so masks go on and come off because none of us has ventured outside recently. Even Loren, against his misgivings, buys his Audi online, its refreshing "new car" smell replaced by the antiseptic mist of alcohol.

But my mother feels cheerful and energetic, she says. She believes the pandemic will be over soon and looks forward to new adventures. When life returns to normal, she'd like to do some traveling. She's also kept in touch with Sam in Chicago and calls him after dinner to wish him and his wife Sarah, a lovely holiday. An invitation is extended on both sides to "visit sometime."

Loren asks about my plans and boasts that he's taken on fewer clients because he doesn't need the work. I warn him, as my mom looks on quietly. I tell him it's dumb to burn through too much money at this point in his life because he's older and has physical issues while, at the same time, the job market is shrinking with layoffs. Loren gets up from the table and leaves the room.

"You shouldn't lecture him," my mother says, not looking at me. "And calling him 'dumb' doesn't help your argument."

"I wasn't lecturing. I just want him to slow down and think about his future."

"That's lecturing. Have you thought about yours?"

"I'm *working*, mother. I've never stopped working, and now, not only do I take my work home, but my work has *moved in*. Do you know what it's like to be *on call* all day and half the night?"

"You mean the remote teaching thing?"

"Yes, the remote teaching thing."

"Well, Loren feels inferior to you and has a need to compensate."

"Loren just spent seventy-three thousand dollars on a new car. I'd say he's well-compensated."

"That's none of our business," she says, looking away again, "And especially none of your business."

As if the previous conversation never happened, she suddenly changes her tone and throws out a few ideas she has for New Year's Eve. "It's on a Friday," she says brightly, "So you have two more days to relax." I tell her that's just what I plan to do. Already, I worry that I won't get enough sleep the Sunday night before Monday morning when the new year kicks in. Already, I worry that my students have forgotten half of what they've learned.

On Friday, New Year's Eve, I call my mother and Loren, then spend the rest of the evening watching Turner Classic Movies in a Sci-Fi marathon. The Leslie Nielsen classic "Forbidden Planet" takes me through the midnight hour with hardly any awareness of it—it's all so different from the spectacle in the Puerta del Sol last year.

On the first Saturday night of 2021, I keep myself company with guacamole and an airplane bottle of Scotch with sprays of soda, the old-fashioned soda in the blue bottle with a squeeze cap. I find these in the deepest recess of my pantry and remember that I'd bought them in a bodega near Olvera Street years ago. It's after midnight on Sunday before I drag myself to bed, too tired to wash up or brush my teeth.

I'm dreaming about getting a haircut when the phone, buzzing and blazing from my bedside, wakes me. A *FaceTime* call. Dario. I pick up and struggle to focus, seeing that Dario's beard has grown longer and his face rounder. Those green eyes—I'd forgotten them.

"*Ciao*, sweetheart," he begins. "Did I wake you?"

"S'okay, Dario—I mean, it's great. *Stai bene?*"

"*Sì sì, più or meno, ò tu?*"

"Why are we speaking Italian?"

"Sorry I haven't called. We snuck off to Pisa, just to get away."

"To Pisa? What's in Pisa?"

"A leaning tower. Maybe you've heard of it. Still leaning."

"Who's 'we,' if I might ask."

"Jabari, my landscaper."

"So, you call in the middle of the night to tell me this? Congratulations," I deadpan, "I hope you're both very happy."

"I called because I miss you and wanted to talk. Maybe we should try another time."

"I'd love to talk, but I start school in about three hours and need my sleep."

He's silent for a moment and I can hear him breathing. "Remember our time together last year?"

"How could I forget Plaza de Chueca? And you still look great, you bastard."

"Why do you have the covers pulled up to your chin like that?"

"Because I'm in bed and it's cold."

"Pull 'em down. Let me see."

"Not enough light to see anything."

"Sure, there is. You're embarrassed."

"How do you know I'm not wearing scuba gear?"

"Because I know how you sleep. I remember how you felt against me, and I know you remember how I felt against you."

"You're a pain in the ass," I say, as I kick off the bedcovers.

"Move it around a little for me. Can you make it grow?"

I comply, and it does.

"Very nice, sweetheart," he says. "Now tuck up and go back to sleep." And *blink*, he's gone.

At 6 a.m. on Monday, January 4th, I log in to the Robert Cavendar instructors' portal and check email. I've kept on top of things during most of the winter break, answering notes from students, parents, and other teachers, which sometimes meant looping a taciturn Principal Lovasso into the conversation. But I stopped checking over the weekend, and now, 236 emails crowd my inbox. I select the last ten and delete the rest. At 7 a.m., I review my 8th-Grade syllabus and lesson plan for the next month; surely half that time will be taken up in a review of material taught before the break. Few students bother to keep up. The ones who do are impatient and vent their frustration to anyone who'll listen— usually me.

At 7:45 a.m., Nafia appears, closely followed by her best friend Tulia, both from Bangladesh. Tulia is already on her phone. They wear colorful scarves around their heads.

"Good morning, ladies. Did you have a good holiday?"

"Good morning, Mr. Anello," Nafia says. "Yes, we have, although not really a holiday for us."

"That would be Ramadan, correct?"

"No, Eid al-Fitr, when we break the fast. Ramadan is an invention of Americanized Muslims and not authentic to our culture."

"Ah, thank you," I say, unable to keep it all straight.

Other students appear in clusters, none muted, so my virtual classroom soon becomes a cacophony of chatter and laughter. I see we'll have the usual amount of ADD this year.

"Welcome back, everyone," I announce after muting all of them and wait for them to settle down. When the smirks disappear and they look attentive—already bored, but at least listening—I open up the room.

"So, what do we remember from last year's study of numerical operations? Can someone review what we've learned?"

"Two and two makes four," Silvo from Guatemala cracks.

"No, five," says Joseph from Santa Barbara.

"Okay, okay. Let's review. Who can name the basic rule of divisibility?" A gallery of blank faces appears. Phones lifted to several of them.

"Excuse me people, and that means *you,* Mr. Sturbil and Ms. Cindee Li Liu, but if you can't turn off your phones for one hour, I'm going to remove you from class today. One warning you get, and you just got it."

They obey, putting down their phones and looking away in embarrassment. Already, I have a headache. Maybe that was harsh. I'll probably hear from a parent.

"Now, the rule of divisibility. Anyone?"

Andy Prento waves his hand.

"Yes. Andy."

"The rule of divisibility helps us figure out if a number can be divided by another number without going through long division and all that other bullshit."

Titters from the others.

"Language, please. So, it's a kind of shortcut. Can anyone give me the divisibility rule for, say, prime numbers three, five, and seven?" If this were a real classroom, I'd pace back and forth in front of my whiteboard.

Andy jumps in again. "If number A can be divided by number B so that the remainder is zero, we know that number A can be divided by three. If A divided by B results in five or zero, A is divisible by five. To figure out if A can be divided by seven, take the last digit of A, double it, and subtract it from A, without the number you just doubled. If the difference is divisible by seven, then the original number can be divided by seven."

"Fine job, Mr. Prento," I say.

"Fine job Mr. Prento," someone mimics.

Andy lifts his middle finger at the heckler. "Wash your dad's car, dumbass."

"*Enough.* Now, how about the divisibility rule for the ordinary number nine? Any of the ladies?"

Nafia half-raises her hand.

"Yes, Nafia!—but wait. Excuse me, *Christy Foswell* with the interesting shade of hair, would you do me the favor of putting your real name under your face instead of 'Mandalorian Space Goddess?'" This takes a moment. "Thank you. So, Nafia."

"May I take a phone call? It's my father from Amsterdam."

And so, the school year begins with this class and five others struggling through Proportional Relationships, Percent Calculations using Proportional Relationships, Multi-Step Computations using Percent Calculations, and I'll finish up the term—if I ever get there—with Measurements and Graphs. They struggle with all of it, even my brighter classes; they struggle because they either find it hard to pay attention or just don't care to pay attention. Often, I hear myself talking only to myself and slip in a joke or two to see if anyone is tuned in. Almost no one ever is. It's useless to assign homework because few students bother with it, so I take the easy way out and hope it survives the scrutiny of my higher-ups. Tonight's assignment, for example, is to play an online game using the Rule of Division to destroy an evil army of zombies that sweeps across the Earth. "Bring me your highest five scores," I say, doing my best to make the assignment sound serious. Andy Prento messages me that he's played the game before and thinks it's an allegory about Covid. I don't think he's wrong. I'm sure this will set some parent off.

Although it's still months away, I look forward to Easter Spring Break, although I'm sure it will do little to lift the lingering gloom of isolation during the pandemic. As 2021 strains on, gone are the virtual parties and entertainments online. Everyone seems tired and sad. A revolt among some who refuse to wear masks makes public outings uncomfortable again. The revolt grows into a political movement, stoked by governors and senators, all the way up to the so-called president, who ridicules the precautions. Shout-downs and even physical altercations occur between the masked and the maskless. It's ugly.

On March 28th, a week before an early April 4th Easter, Loren and my mother make swab appointments, and both test negative. My mother states her intention to food shop for a leg of lamb this Easter and asks if I'll come with her. But it seems my workload may stretch into my free time this year, so I defer to Loren, who's glad to do it because it's an opportunity to chauffeur Mom around in his Audi. Already, I'm buried in final assignments and test results, and my kitchen table becomes a desk for organizing the necessary paperwork as the school year enters its final quarter. The stacks of paperwork include numerous forms requiring even more numerous codes, which, in turn, plug into computations for assigning a student grade. As usual, the "I" code for "Incomplete" goes to the top of the list since many students blow off the required coursework with excused absences. This once meant summer school if the student wanted to advance a grade level. But with the pandemic upon us, standards are relaxed because parents would scream if their kids were held back. I'm forced to graduate many students from middle school into their first year of high school knowing they may fall even further behind and maybe even drop out. The whole system is broken, and there's nothing I can do about it.

I need to remind myself that there's another life waiting for me, that once I walked the streets of Madrid with a brilliant and sophisticated man who slipped us into museums after-hours, then took me home to his bed; a man I shared a flat with while pigeons preened outside our window and music rose up and the nights smelled like bread. It's time to enjoy that life again. Soon, a vaccine will be available for anyone who wants one, we're promised, and our lives will pick up where we've left them. It's time to call Dario and Marina and pick up the pieces.

I plan to phone Dario at midnight, the Thursday before Easter weekend. A hunch says I'll reach him, since it'll be nine in the morning in Italy, the hour when he sips his green tea and plans his day's work. I dial and he picks up immediately.

"This is too miraculous," he says.

"Dario? It's Mark—"

"Yes! Yes, I know it's Mark. We've communicated telepathically across the miles because at this *precise moment*, I was about to call you."

"No..."

"Yes, yes! So, you see, the stars, once again, align in our favor. How are you, and how are you, and why haven't we spoken sooner?—never mind, we're speaking now."

"I'm okay. Busy as ever. We have the tests now. I'm negative and so is everyone in my family."

"Good, good. We also have them. But I haven't partaken. Ah, well."

"I miss you."

"And I, you." A moment of silence, then: "Some news about me: I plan to sell the house. It's become a demanding mistress with an unforgiving garden and too much for me now."

"Moving in with your young Tutankhamen?"

"Jabari? He's gone. Never was, really."

"He lived in your house."

"It's a large house."

"You shared a hotel room."

He sighs. "Do you *not* remember our lovely conversation during that unfortunate walk back to the flat on that unfortunate street?"

"Hortaleza Street. Of course I remember."

"Do you still love me?"

"Do I—?"

"As I thought! You've forgotten how to love me. Now, I'll have to remind you. Such a bother you are!"

I try to collect my thoughts to phrase the next question. "Dario, I'm confused. Why did you tell me about Jabari to begin with?"

"A test, and one you failed miserably. You are a hopelessly jealous creature."

"That I am."

"It's sweet, but so annoying. Especially at my age when the rose begins to lose its blush, and one feels decrepit. I've done my best to dispel it from my assortment of unhelpful emotions."

"I'm sure your rose still blushes."

"God, it's good to hear your voice."

"Same here."

"And how I miss you. But it wouldn't bother me in the least if you saw others while we're apart, which I assume you do."

"Sorry to disappoint. Tell me what's going on with Marina."

"I'll give you the short version, but you should call her. Call at eleven p.m. your time on Friday, because on Saturday morning Luciano goes to his gymnasium to run about like a rabbit. So, to give you the quick story, Marina is back with Luciano and the children. The Carlos fiasco seems to have ended quietly."

"Quietly? I expected disaster."

"We've spoken several times, and each time, she asks about you. She feels embarrassed that she didn't listen to your concerns about Carlos and even attacked you over them. This, I didn't know."

"It was nothing. I'm glad she's okay."

"Well, there are still complications. You'll talk to her."

"Are you painting?"

"Indeed I am. My recent work is very good, I think. You'll have to come soon and see it. You'll have to come soon and enjoy my beautiful house before it's gone. I hope, with the developments in the States, that's possible soon."

"I should tell you. My father died. I've come into some money."

"Sorry to hear about your father. Delighted for your good fortune. Plan a trip."

"I shall. *Ciao*, and love to you."

The next day, at eleven o'clock, I call Marina. I've just finished tapping when I realize I'm on the wrong end of the day. It's evening there.

The phone rings for a long time and I'm about to disconnect when a man answers. *"Pronto?"*

Shit. I'd hoped to avoid who I assume is Luciano. Try my best to speak clearly.

"Questo è Mark dalla California. Marina è libera di parlare?"

"Marina è un po' occupata adesso... chi è?"

"Mark. Marco, *dalla Cali—*"

"Oh my god. You."

"Me?"

"Sì. You. The stealer of paintings."

That voice. Alessandro.

"Yes, Alessandro," he says. "So, how are you? Marina very busy in the kitchen preparing me for my party."

"Your birthday?"

"I move to Basel Switzerland next week for a new position. *Marina-a-a-a!*" he calls out, "*Vieni qui subito, è Mark dalla California*—your thieving friend."

She takes the phone, breathlessly. "My goodness, such a surprise, but I'm so glad you have called me, finally."

"Not a good time, it seems."

"Unfortunately, no. We are preparing a celebration at my house for Alessando, as you can hear. I don't know why he answered my phone. I'm very sorry."

"It's fine," I say. "I'll call you late Easter Sunday here, early Monday for you."

"Please. I look forward. *Ciao*." and she's gone.

At least they're all alive and doing okay, I think, stepping into the shower. For now, that's enough.

In a conversation with my mother early Easter Sunday, she tells me that Sam Derwitz's wife Sarah has fallen ill—not with Covid, but with a reoccurrence of Hodgkin's Lymphoma which for the past five years, had been in remission. Sam has checked her into St. Joseph's hospital and visits every day, usually finding his children there also.

"For the first time, our conversation became very personal and touching," my mother confesses. "I wanted to be there for Sam during this difficult time. Sarah's a lovely woman from what little I know of her."

"I'm glad you can be supportive. Please give Sam my best."

"Loren offered to do some research on herbal remedies for cancer, but I don't think Sam is receptive."

"I wouldn't go there."

"But he's only trying to help."

"What time do you want me over for dinner?"

"Loren would like to eat early, so come at two. Would you like to come earlier and help color Easter eggs? You always loved doing that when you were a little boy."

"No thanks, Mom. I have stuff to do and some phone calls to make before school starts up again Monday."

"Always busy, you."

And she's right. I'm busy because I'm busy, and I'm busy because I need space from my family where, probably because of the isolation, this co-dependency between my mother and my brother has amped up. When I'm with them, I feel like the third wheel of a couple. I hope as the pandemic winds down, Loren will start looking for a woman other than my mother, simple as that.

I get home by midnight on Sunday, settle in with a glass of wine, and make my call to Marina. She answers on the first ring.

"Hello, Mark. Now we have privacy!"

"Hi, Marina. You sound wonderful. Everything good?"

"Yes, Perfetto. I am alone today. Luciano takes Fabbio and Angelina to their nonna's." She laughs. "Hilarious that you speak to Alessandro! So, tell me, you are well? Dario described the awful sickness when you left. Did you have the Covid?"

"I don't know. By the time we had tests here, it was too late."

"All of us tested quickly and all showed antibodies," she says. "Maybe I brought it back to Italy from Madrid from the time got sick on Christmas Day. The children are fine, but Luciano was positive, and so was your dear friend Alessandro."

"Oh, no."

"Yes, but we are all fine now."

"What does it mean 'having the antibodies?' We don't have a test for them here."

"It is unknown. The doctor says maybe having them means we are entirely recovered. Or perhaps the virus is still inside and will come back in a different way. But we are the lucky ones, so I don't think about it and live my life as before."

"Brava, Marina."

"Unfortunately, Alessandro lost his brother Simone and his mother, who you remember, lived next door."

"My god! I'm so sorry for Alessandro!"

"He didn't show much emotion about it. He's very strange that way, as you know."

An image of Simone flashes before me, tending to his vegetable garden beside the house.

"And Braxton?" I ask, "Has he come back from Australia to stay with Alessandro again?"

She's quiet for a moment, then: "Honestly, I don't know. Alessandro doesn't mention Braxton and I see nothing of him, even as Alessandro prepares to leave for Basel which seems a very strange thing to do right now."

"It's so good to hear your voice, Marina, and so sorry we've been out of touch. It doesn't mean I haven't thought of you and our beautiful times together."

"Non importante, caro. The world changes and we change, too."

"I'm afraid to ask, but—"

"Carlos? I thought perhaps Dario told you. Carlos has disappeared. As you can see, I am back here with Luciano, not entirely happy, of course, but who is?"

"I'm glad it's all behind you and you're settled."

"You want to know about the lawyer now, I'm sure. When I returned to Italy and called him, he changes his mind and tells me I have no good reason to ask for a divorce from Luciano and very likely will lose my children if I go forward. I am very surprised to hear this since I thought this lawyer, as Carlos promised, would support my situation."

"That's strange," I say, while thinking that it isn't strange at all. This is Carlos' doing, the cowardly escape he set up to avoid exposure.

"Yes, it's very strange," Marina continues. "I consulted with another lawyer whom the first one suggested after turning me down, but that lawyer said exactly the same, as did another one, and then a lady lawyer in Florence. They all explained it almost exactly in the same words as Carlos' lawyer. So now, I try to forget Carlos who never answered my calls and who was never at work when I tried to reach him." Her voice breaks a little. "He hurt me very deeply. You were quite right to have doubts, I was too ashamed to speak to you after I attacked at you."

"You are very dear to me, Marina."

"Now, tell me. You and Dario?"

"I don't know where things are with us. He's been keeping company with someone. We still have feelings."

"Of course you do. He loves you. You will be patient with each other."

I wake up the next morning to the chittering of mockingbirds and a cloudless blue sky that fills my bedroom window. The weather turns mild these late days of April, and I sometimes take short strolls through the neighborhood before starting work. More and more, people seem to venture out now, and I notice fewer masks. Maybe it's because the news of Nurse Sandra Lindsay's second Covid vaccination has begun to sink in, and she becomes the poster-woman of optimism and a symbol of America's pharmaceutical genius. Or maybe it's because vaccine distribution accelerates, although availability is prioritized among essential workers and the most vulnerable. But as the spring of 2021 turns to summer, warnings sound that impatient Americans will relax their guard and bring on a new spike of infections.

On May 25th, the open-air community pool in Glendale reopens with limited hours and requires online scheduling. To prevent time hoarding, schedules open up at 5 a.m. each day. Within minutes, slots are full. When I finally manage to make an appointment for 11 a.m. on Memorial Day, the rigamarole is ridiculous: I check in at the appointed time fully suited since locker rooms are closed. I wait on a pool bench until my appointment time. When called, I go to my assigned lane, separated from another swimmer by an empty lane, so that an eight-lane pool is reduced to four lanes. And, if that isn't frustrating enough, I'm given the signal to begin laps only when the swimmer adjacent to me is at the far end of the pool to avoid our swimming side-by-side, empty lane between notwithstanding. Of course, this system falls apart more often than it holds together, and swimmers who repeatedly fall out of sync without correcting themselves are called out and made to vacate.

As I walk to my car, wet and aggravated, a guy ambles up beside me, similarly pissed off.

"Was that fucked up, or was that fucked up?" he says.

"Pretty bad. I'm done with this."

"Do you know anybody with a pool?"

"If I did, I wouldn't be here."

I get a good look at this dude as I click open my car. A bit younger than me. Nice looking. Sexy smile. A dusty blond with stubble and a swimmer's build gone a little soft."

"My name's Jim Hollander," he says.

9
Meteor Shower

I'm in an R.E.I. outlet on Melrose Avenue talking to a six-foot clerk about sub-zero sleeping bags. He looks about eighteen, if that, in jeans so tight they look like dance leotards. "It'll be cold where you're going," he warns, "At least at night." He reaches deep into the rack and pulls out a bag shaped like the giant chrysalis of a monarch butterfly. "Two of these can be zipped together and made into a single bag for you and your camping buddy," he says, reading my mind.

Jim likes to visit the Mohave Desert in early November to observe his favorite meteor shower, the Leonids. This year, they'll peak on Friday, November 5th. I'd warned him from the beginning that I knew next to nothing about roughing it, but all through the summer and early fall, I've come to enjoy, in his company, the mountains and high deserts from the comfort of his soft-top camper. The outdoors provides, as he puts it, a "detox" from his heady work as a technical writer for a large Simi Valley telecommunications company. In our four months together, I've begun to see Jim as an unlikely graft between geek and Nature Boy, a reader of "Wired" magazine and lover of Thomas Pynchon novels. He drives a motorcycle on the alternate days he reports to the office and never takes elevators. He's good in bed.

I've never been one for sex outdoors, but Jim has it down. On our first trip to Pacheco Canyon, a palmy enclave in the northeastern Mohave, we'd camped near a rock pool refreshed by a waterfall. We made love in and out of the waterfall, then lay across a flat boulder, the heat of the sun on our chilled skin.

So, this time, it's November and the Leonids.

"You know, I've never left the U.S.," he says as we turn onto the Interstate to begin this latest meteor-spotting trip.

"Why not?"

"I don't know. My mom always said there was enough to see right here."

"Not an unusual American point-of-view," I say. "So, neither of your parents ever went to Europe?"

"Not that I know of. My mom had pancreatic cancer when I was a kid and died when I was only nine."

"Sorry. You never told me that. Is your dad still around?"

"I wouldn't know," Jim shoots back.

"You weren't close, I take it."

"No."

"Well, Italy and Spain are cool. You should go."

"Will you take me?"

"Might be complicated."

"You have some kind of long-distance boyfriend over there, right?"

"Some kind of boyfriend, yes."

"Fuck. Why does everybody I date have *some kind of boyfriend?*"

"It's very long-distance. He's in Italy, six thousand miles away," I say, surprising myself that I've said it.

"That's like... *so reassuring,*" Jim quips back, being Jim.

At around four o'clock, we enter the desert and find a high, level spot near the Cima Dome, the Mohave's ancient, cinder-black, and perfectly symmetrical volcano. It's the kind of late afternoon when everything turns purple in the low light of shorter days, and bats spook about overhead. Jim is a good cook: carne asada tonight with fire-roasted corn and baked zucchini. For dessert, he serves apple cake baked at home with a confectionary sugar glaze. Delicious. After we sponge-dry the dishes, he lights two joints and offers me one. A soft wind comes up and rattles the tent, cranked high and taut.

"The peak viewing time for the Leonids is around two in the morning," Jim instructs, "so maybe we should take a snooze so we're not too tired later. After all, you old guys need your rest."

"Is that right? Remind me of how old you are."

"Thirty-four."

"Well, I'm thirty-seven. Not quite a generation gap."

"What's that?" he says, honestly having no idea what it is.

I'm good with the nap idea. We zip our bags together and nest inside. He falls asleep quickly and snores. I don't mind. We wake up about an hour later, warm and sticky. We mess around. Jim is versatile and very good at both. He's smooth as silk inside and grips me tight. He likes me to look into his eyes when I'm in deep, but it's dark now, and all I can see is their soft reflections. We clean up and pull on our jeans, parkas, and wool caps for when the air turns cold. At two o'clock, we sit in pitch darkness, half in the tent and half out of it. We peer out into the nighttime desert stretching before us, vast and mysterious. The sky above glows softly with stars.

A brilliant slash traces down against the glow.

"Did you catch that one—the green? That's cuprite, a volatile form of copper."

Another streak, blueish, followed by a cascade of them, a few disappearing over a low ridge.

"The blue is probably cobalt or potassium. The bright white, magnesium."

"Listen to you."

"Shit, a whole cluster made it all the way down. They're probably sitting in the sand just over that ridge. We should go looking for them tomorrow."

"Fuck, yes."

"Fuckity-fuck, yes."

An hour later, the streaks dwindling, we huddle side-by-side in the cold, our breaths steaming. Yawning together, we zip up the tent and crawl back into our cocoon.

"As far as I'm concerned, being here together right now is all anyone ever needs," Jim says, lying on his back in the dark.

"You might be right about that," I answer in the dark.

"You're damn right I'm right."

"I miss Madrid, though. When it's winter over there, the nights smell like bread."

"That sounds weird. Here, the nights smell like night."

The next morning, I wake up to see Jim through the opened flap. He's already dressed and drinking coffee, the sun barely up.

"Good, you're finally conscious," he says as I stagger out. "Have some cowboy coffee."

I sit across from him in the clear but nippy air, drinking a slush of grounds added to boiling water and only partially strained out.

He resumes poking his battered iPad.

"What I thought was a distant ridge is just a little over a mile from here. The trail is marked out clearly on this USGS map. Before the sun gets too strong, I want to hike out there and find us a piece of meteorite."

"I thought they were meteors."

No, now they're meteo*rites*. Because they failed to burn up before they hit the Earth."

"So, they're failed meteors," I say. "They disappointed their meteor colleagues."

"I've got my safety hatchet here in my pack. I'm going to use it if you ever say that again."

He fries some eggs and bacon and swallows another cup of sludge. We lace our shoes tight and wear our floppiest hats, check for adequate water, and tighten each other's pack so there's no bouncing or friction against our spines. We do a few squats to loosen up, then set out in the pink of early morning. Chuparosa and bitter-bush glitter in the early light, slick from the dewpoint. A jack-rabbit lopes. We fall into a rhythm, Jim's hiking style more measured and efficient than mine.

Glancing at me, he advises: "Never hook your hands through your straps. Always allow your arms to swing freely for momentum and balance, especially when climbing, which we'll have to do to get over that ridge."

I improve my gait and walk alongside him. "Tell me more about your dad, Jim."

"Tell me more about your boyfriend, Mark."

I back off and think about his question. "I'm not sure how to describe Dario. He's mysterious and sexy, but I'm not sure we're a good match. He lives in another world I can barely relate to."

"How long did you guys stay busy?"

"Don't laugh, about a month. We met in Spain right before the pandemic, and then I came home. But we've kept in touch. Sort of."

"Just a month? Good."

"Before Covid, I was going to Italy every summer, and I got really hung up on this other guy."

"You're into the long-distance thing."

"Not necessarily. Before that, eight years with a narcissistic stand-up comic in Hollywood who dumped me for someone much older. How's that for a put-down?"

"You're into the difficult guys thing."

"I guess the challenge is a turn-on. Not sure why." I glance sideways at him. "And not sure I should've told you that."

Jim looks down. "Thanks for being honest," he says, then looks up again. "Actually, I don't like to talk too much when I hike. Let's just relax and take in everything around you. This is a time to appreciate the world and our place in it."

So, he's got me thinking now—what is my place in the world? And what's this all about, this knocking around with Jim? Should I mention him to Dario, or is this what Dario expects? Or is this what *I* should expect from now on?—partly with one, partly with another, not entirely with anyone? Where does my life go from here once it's okay to return to Italy? And why, lately, do I have such a strange feeling of dread about Alessandro?

"Excuse me, scoutmaster," I say. "Is talking allowed if I have to pee?"

We stop, turn in opposite directions to relieve ourselves. A strange modesty.

"Another fifteen minutes or so and we'll be over," Jim says, wiping water from his chin. "Looks like the trail turns west to the lowest pass, so we won't have to climb much. But I put a location pin on the spot where I think the meteorites fell, so we'll have to double back to get there."

After twenty more minutes of hiking, the shrubs begin to thin out. We pass over the crest and start down the opposite side, and I notice the flat bottom changes color from a gravelly ochre to an almost pure white where nothing grows.

"The wind piles sand against the base of the ridge, and the sand can cover stuff," Jim calls out. "But we haven't had any wind since last night, so any rock from, say, the Kuiper belt should stand out. Know what that is?"

"Something they carry at *Nautica for Men*?"

"An asteroid cloud. Start scouting, eagle-eyes."

But I see nothing but white when we reach level ground. Same for Jim. We toe through the sand and sift through small dunes that look like they might cover something. Nothing. White uncovers more white.

"How wide an area do we need to search?" I call out, on my hands and knees.

"Not sure. I'm thinking if anything made it down, it would be here or very close. Maybe we can walk a square, you in one direction and me in another."

We stand back-to-back, then pace off one hundred steps at a right angle to each other. At the end, we turn ninety degrees and walk forward another hundred paces in a zigzag pattern so that our footpaths make an intersecting grid where each of us can check and cross-check a small area for anything unusual. But after ten minutes of this, I get sloppy and begin to wander off. Jim appears farther and farther away and starts to yell out to me, then shrugs in a *what the fuck?* gesture. So, I've screwed up this grid thing and I'm tired. By now, this seems silly, and I'm pretty much over searching for meteorites. Besides, I have to pee again and maybe even do the other thing. The heat of the sun blasts down, so I hike even farther from Jim towards a nest of boulders that makes a kind of peninsula and offers small shade. I crawl over the first boulder and start to slide down when, suddenly, I see them: five rounded chunks of what looks like crumpled aluminum foil, but in colors that range from deep blue to bright yellow-green. They're scattered over a wide wash, some in the shade and some out of it. The two in full sunlight catch my attention first. As I come closer, I notice their shallow craters: perfectly formed ovals suggesting a similar angle of impact, possibly pieces of something larger that broke up before it hit the Earth. I drop to my knees to study one carefully, then carefully lift it out, half-expecting it'll burn me. But it's strangely cool and heavy—*heavy,* with perforations like a sponge. It's like nothing I've ever encountered before in my life—other-worldly, in fact: a meteorite.

When Jim arrives, he lets out a *whoop,* then tackles me down. He picks up fistfuls of sand and tosses it over both of us.

"You bastard!" He laughs, "You fucking found them! I fucking love you, Mark!" he screams, twirling around and doubling over as if he has cramps. We dump half the water we're carrying and divide the meteorites between our backpacks. Their weight bogs us down. It takes much longer to hike back to camp and we're winded when we get there. But the night comes on fast, and we need to collect our gear to pack out.

Driving on the Interstate, Jim is almost in tears.

"Do you know what we've got here? These are stony chondrites with traces of iron ore, one of the oldest things in the universe."

"How old is that?"

"Maybe two billion years."

"Damn. Worth money?"

"Depends. If any one of them contains crystals of iron-nickel, that means it's riddled with olivine-peridot, a precious stone. I have high hopes with that yellow-green color."

"How do we find out? Or do we?"

"Bring 'em to the metallurgy department of some college and hope we'll get 'em back."

"Jesus. Maybe we should just live with the mystery."

We drive for a while, the lights of Los Angeles appear over the pass.

"You're an amazing fella," Jim says, glancing at me."

"Thanks."

"And guess what? We're not long-distance. Do you copy me, Spock?"

"Roger," I say, and nothing else.

10

The Line Begins Here

America continues to cheer as vaccination sites appear all over the country. Five days before Christmas, the shops glitter. Fewer shoppers wear masks and happily stroll in groups of threes or fours. Outdoor tables appear at restaurants with outdoor people gathered around them.

Availability and access to vaccinations remain unclear this last month of 2021, and Jim and I hang onto every shred of news. We learn that the highest priority still remains with healthcare workers and medical personnel. Next, people over the age of seventy-four. Both Loren and my mother find themselves in the third category: people sixty-five to seventy-four and people sixteen to seventy-four with medical conditions. Loren's Cerebral Palsy wins him a blue ribbon, so they access the CDC website easily and schedule their drive-throughs. On Christmas Eve morning, one day after the release of the Pfizer locally, Loren and Mom pull into the parking lot of the Montrose Library and get their jabs.

For all the optimism and enthusiasm in the air, for me, the holiday season is still a remote affair. My visits to family have dwindled since meeting Jim, who I haven't even mentioned to Loren or my mother.

Today, two weeks into the hopeful new year of 2022, I slouch on my sofa with my bare feet up on the coffee table and watch my latest stream. I'm three-quarters vertical and the TV is low to the floor, so I have to look through my bowl of cereal, my feet, and my pair of yellow-green meteorites to see the bottom half of the screen.

The vaccination stories continue to scroll with clips of smiling people in their cars, sleeves rolled up, thumbs jabbing. I'm curious to know how these vaccinations will find their way to Europe. In a brief conversation with Marina, she tells me that distribution is chaotic in Pivonnia, and their priority groups are, as expected, quite different from ours. Nonetheless, she's already had her shots, along with Luciano, and the kids will soon follow. She isn't familiar with the situation in Switzerland. She hasn't heard from Alessandro but assumes he knows where to go and how to take care of himself. With some uneasiness, I recall my conversation with Dario and his vow to never allow a vaccine to enter his body. I wonder if he still feels that way. I want to call and find out, but the *Jim thing* makes me nervous because—despite Jim's professed indifference—I feel guilty that I'm regularly getting busy with someone new and know Dario will sense it. How can he not sense it? Jim is the best thing that's happened to me in over a year.

Weeks go by. Public demonstrations against the vaccine begin to appear. One group makes the news by blocking traffic on the road to one of the biggest inoculation sites. But among the happily vaccinated, sex makes a comeback as 2022 lurches forward. People form "safe-pods" and play catch-up in Jacuzzis or suburban living rooms. The world has gone crazy, and I'm beginning to feel like an outsider watching a party from the curb. But I'm not really interested in parties; I just want to relax when visiting my mother and Loren without any concerns of infecting them.

On Valentine's Day, a Monday this year, I dismiss my students early so I can jump on the portal and schedule my appointment. But by 2:30 p.m., it's already too late to get through. Two hours later, six new openings appear a week from today, and I scramble to nab one of them and fill out the required fields. But at the end of the process, when I click the "Schedule Now" button, the screen throws a "No longer available" message. I'm determined to beat this game and keep my computer on all night, one eye opened as I half-sleep. But it's always the same: somehow, someone snatches up the few available appointments before me. I'm just one little pissed-off bird in an enormous flock, beating its wings against a tiny, closed window—that's what this fiasco feels like.

"You're up against *bots*," Jim tells me over dinner at his place that night. "You see this kind of cheating in fancy neighborhoods like yours."

"Not sure I get that."

"A bot is a chunk of browser code that a user parks on a website to detect a screen refresh. As soon as that happens, the bot auto-fills a form and submits it for you, or pings you that it's time to jump in. It's kind of like 'Auction Sniper' if you've ever messed around with eBay," Jim says.

"No. And that's plenty fucked up."

"What zip code do you use?"

"The one for Montrose-La Crescenta, 91202."

"No wonder. You don't have a chance. These things can pounce in a tenth of a second. It's probably tech-savvy kids feeling pressured to set this up for mommy and daddy or for mommy and daddy's friends *who just must get to Europe again this spring!*"

"Fine. So, who do I have to bribe or kill?"

"Don't worry. I think I know a workaround. How far do you want to drive?"

After dinner, Jim makes himself comfortable in front of one of three computers on his messy desk. He starts clicking. I load his dishes into the dishwasher.

"Come over here, Betty Crocker," he calls out. "Look at this area map of zip codes. I'd bet on either Compton or farther out like San Bernadino."

"But I don't live in those places, so it's cheating."

"What, are we in church? Just pick a place. You've just moved."

"Well, San Bernadino is about two hours away. Compton a little closer."

"Great. Welcome to your new home in Compton, zip code 90222."

He enters those stats on a refreshed CDC calendar, and over fifty available appointments appear in Southeast Los Angeles, three full weeks of openings at all times of day. Since today is Monday, we jump at the next appointment at 11 a.m. Tuesday morning. That's how Jim puts it: *we'll* take the next appointment, and *we'll* take the day off.

"So, you're coming with me? Don't you have to work?"

"My days are flexible. And Tuesday is a slow day, which means I get to spend tonight with you."

So, it's done. I thank him. He's disappointed that I want to return home early and won't spend the night, but I've got catch-up work to do, especially if I'm playing hooky on Monday. Plus, I want to make a few late-night phone calls to Italy for Valentine's Day, Dario being first on the list.

I begin my evening by tackling a stack of assessment skill exams I've avoided for weeks. As usual, I'll waste a month reviewing math skills already learned but forgotten over the Christmas break. My students, already falling behind in the required trajectory of graduation-oriented math, are now going backward. God help America when it realizes its contractors, accountants, bank tellers, and even cashiers have lost their ability to count.

And now there's a new crock of crazy to deal with. Principal Lovasso makes it clear that he's unhappy over news that the Los Angeles Unified School District and its teachers' union want to reopen classrooms to elementary school and high-need students. It's not the reopening that bothers him, but the vaccination recommendations—something he doesn't support. Our boss at Cavendar has outed himself as an "anti-vaxxer." Maybe I should take Loren's advice and get out while I've got the money—except that taking his advice means I'm pretty much a hypocrite since I preached fiscal tight-fistedness to my brother just a year ago. But, in just over a week, it'll be March. Three and a half years have gone by since my last Italian road trip with my periodic boyfriend Alessandro—over five years, if I add the time between meeting him in San Francisco and our first hook-up in Rome. This spring, I'll be thirty-eight years old, *forty* breathing down my neck. I'm still young enough to make a whole new future for myself, and why not? Jim's got it right: I haven't taken a vow and teaching isn't the priesthood.

Good, I've decided. Sort of. I'll be in better spirits when I chat with Dario. I have to see his house. I have to see *Dario*—go where his mind goes, enjoy the comfortableness of his body. Dario lacks the charm and sweetness of Jim, but Dario is an adventure and a visit to an exotic and sensual world. I finish my last paper, and I'm just about to make my first call when the phone buzzes. Marina.

"Marina, cara! *Buon San Valentino* to you!"

"Grazie, Mark, and to you. Now, *ascolta, per favore*—I mean, you listen to me, please?"

"Sorry—is something wrong?"

"We have a problem with our old friend Alessandro."

"What happened?"

"He has had some kind of breakdown in Basel and fell from his window early this morning. Luckily, he was not hurt badly, but broke his arm. They take him to a hospital and inform me as I am his contact."

"My god! What kind of breakdown?"

"I'm not sure. It was difficult to understand the Swiss doctors. Their Italian isn't like ours."

"Did he fall or jump?"

"This, I don't know. But the few times I have spoken to him in Basel, he seemed quite disconnected and confused. I don't think the Swiss culture suits him. Perhaps it's the death of his mom and Simone that comes back to haunt him."

"Poor Alessandro," I say. *Now this?* I think.

"Yes, poor man," Marina says. "One doctor suggests that it's a depression brought on by a previous infection with Covid. He had the virus quite bad, you know."

"I didn't know. I thought he was only positive with antibodies."

"No, he went to hospital. He didn't want you to know about it."

"Damn."

"Anyways, I call you now to say that he won't be allowed to go back to his flat when they release him from the hospital. He will be moved to another hospital for observing. I don't know how long."

"What am I supposed to do, Marina? I've pretty much lost contact with Alessandro."

"Well, I tell you one more thing and then you think about."

"Sure."

"The doctor says to me, who is this Mark he asks for? Who is this person—his partner?"

"What?"

"Yes, this is what he says. So, you think about, that's all."

I'm numb after Marina's call. I sit, staring out the window, not sure what to do, even though Marina hasn't asked me to do anything.

On Tuesday morning, Jim shows up brushed and soapy-smelling. He's carefully prepared for our journey to Compton. He's brought along snacks for the return trip, assuming we'll want to leave Southeast Los Angeles right after I'm done to spend the rest of the day relaxing at home. We give ourselves plenty of time, anticipating commuter traffic on all highways into or away from central Los Angeles. He wants to know how I've spent my evening. I tell him just a little about my phone call from Marina concerning a friend who's now having some trouble. He listens, chomping an apple. "Sounds like an Italian opera," he pronounces. Then he shares news that one of our meteorites contains yellow-green crystals of magnesium, iron, and nickel in sufficient concentrations so that portions of it qualify as peridot—a precious stone. His voice rises in excitement when he relates that, given the size and weight of the rock, even if only a tenth of it is peridot, that would mean a whopping 154 carats of the gem with a value of about nine thousand dollars. Jim tracked down someone at work who knows about these things because the guy is a fabricating engineer of rare earth silicates in the chip manufacturing division.

"I'll sell it and we can go to Italy together," Jim says, "To cheer up your buddy a little," he adds, surprising me since I offered no details about Alessandro's difficulties and didn't even mention his name.

We take the 710 Freeway South and exit onto East Compton Boulevard towards downtown. We turn south on Willowbrook Avenue, where we're greeted by a "Welcome to Compton" sign covered in graffiti. As we approach the Walmart Super Center, we see "Covid Vaccination" arrows directing us to an enormous rear parking lot that's stanchioned off with striped horses at the entrance. A few minutes later, another car pulls behind us. Two young Hispanic women appear a few yards ahead, holding clipboards. One approaches us, and the other walks to the car behind. Our young lady motions, like a traffic cop, for me to roll down my window.

"Your appointment is at eleven o'clock, sir?"

"Yes."

"Your name—?" She looks down then suddenly looks up, called away to the car behind us. After a few moments, that car turns out and begins to exit the queue, its driver gesturing at us to give him room.

She returns, looking a bit flustered, as the first check-in person returns to her station.

"Mark Anello," I continue, showing her my driver's license.

"May I see your appointment confirmation, please?"

"Fuck," I mutter under my breath.

"I have it, I have it," Jim croons, pulling it from his pocket.

Without thanking him, I hand it to her. She looks at the appointment, then back at my license. "And you live where? In Glendale?"

"Fuck," again.

Jim leans over me towards her. "We just closed on a new condo in Compton and haven't moved from our old house yet, but we should be here in a few weeks."

She studies Jim, then looks at me, then looks at Jim again, "And what's the address of your house in Compton, sir?"

"It's 310 West Magnolia Street, Unit B," Jim says smoothly.

Now, she looks up and away from us, the trace of a smile on her face. "And where do you work in Compton, Mr. Mark?"

"Whaley Middle School," I stammer, hoping I got it right. I noticed the name when we stopped at an intersection and I saw the school's letterboard. Something told me, *remember it.*

"All right," she says. "Stay in this lane and follow the cones until the end, where you'll wait until you're called to pull forward and receive your vaccination."

We drive on, leaving our check-in person with nobody else to check in. "We're coming off like two entitled jerks," I say. "You get that?"

"We need to do this and, sadly, nobody's here," Jim answers. "Anyway, quick thinking with that school name."

"How the hell did you pull that address out of your hat? *Christ!*"

"I was a Boy Scout. Always Prepared. You were on your game, too."

"Yeah, but I didn't like the Boy Scouts. I dropped out after the Navajo headdresses."

"Really? Seems you'd dig that."

We twist around for five minutes, turning this way and that, through a Walmart parking lot transformed into a prairie of orange cones—a convoluted queue for a crush of cars that never arrives. A single car suddenly appears and threads behind. In the rippling heat of the asphalt, I spot what looks like a phantom Farmers Market straight out of *Brigadoon*. More twisting and turning—towards the phantom, then away from it—until our lane straightens like a slaughter chute for cattle. Under a nest of tents, the inoculators appear, cheerful in pandemic car-hop uniforms, as if delivering fries and a Coke.

But the interrogation is short and the procedure simple enough: a swab, a jab, and a little happy dance of congratulations from the jabber as she peels the bandage. My jabber is African American, and I sense that she's disappointed in the community's poor turnout. Other than the single car in the next lane, no one is here. These conscientious vaccinators shuffle in the blue light of their tents while their allotment of vaccines bakes in the heat. We're waved to pull forward and park in a standing area where a nurse sits, prepared to treat side effects. But after ten minutes, we're cleared to pull into the lane that leads out.

We drive past an avenue of Payday Loans and decide to stop at a 7-Eleven for a Coke before heading back to the freeway. It's lunchtime. The customers inside seem cheerful, mostly African American, middle-class folks with their chips, sodas, and kids clutching candy bars.

One glances at us as we stand behind him then turns to his buddy.

"No, I won't go near that shit, and neither will my wife," he says.

"I hear you," says the pal.

Jim looks at me and puts a finger to his lips, a warning to say nothing.

"You think those guys were talking about the vaccine?" Jim asks when we're back in the car.

"Probably," I say. "People of color have reason to be suspicious with what happened to them."

"Right, that quack syphilis study in the 1930s," Jim nods.

"Tuskegee," I say. But I'm also thinking of Dario's fear of vaccinations and what happened to him.

It's early afternoon and the day is mild. We turn back onto Willowbrook Avenue towards the 710 Freeway to go home. I settle into my seat for a snooze, happy to let Jim take the wheel. But the car jerks to a stop and I bolt upright.

"Shit," Jim says, "We've got trouble."

"What?"

"Straight ahead."

And here they come, a black-and-red army of about a hundred people, their front line resembling the giant blade of a bulldozer with its curb-to-curb banner: VACCINATIONS = DEATH. Behind it, a riot of waving placards, each sign jockeying amid the others to be seen.

"*Shit*, Jim. Can't we turn off this road?"

"No. It's one way here with the island. And they've blocked the U-turn intersection."

A single car idles ahead of us, and we see the driver leap from side to side, locking doors. A few cars idle behind. The mob comes closer, barking through bullhorns.

"We're screwed!" Jim says and looks into the rear-view mirror, then: "Oh, no man—*NO!*"

The car right behind us makes a sharp turn and scrapes over the curb onto the island, in an attempt to cross to the opposite lanes. But it gets snared on an irrigation pipe that breaks off and shoots jets of water into the undercarriage. Two planks of spray fan out and flood the street.

The mob, close enough to see it all, howls with joy, and placards wave violently, looking more like weapons than signs. The front line draws close enough to see some variety among the protesters: LET YOUR BABY LIVE! goes up and down like a carousel horse while PRAY TO END ABORTION! signs swing side-to-side like some fandom club at a football game. One placard waver thrusts his battered sign above the others: a textless photo of a Native American with red circle-backslash over his face and—*here they come!* A tsunami of crazies, and we're swallowed, signs crashing against our windshield.

"*Fuck you, assholes!*" Jim screams, giving them the finger with both hands. He leans on the horn. But this inflames them even more so that several demonstrators, who'd passed and moved on to the cars behind, now double back. Two large women in Jesus bling position themselves, with folded arms, at our rear bumper. One looks down and notices the shreds of my rainbow bumper sticker. *"Perverts! Pederasts!"* she screams, attracting the attention of others, who approach to investigate. A bearded man with tattoos on his shriveled arms blocks our windshield with *YOU SHALL NOT LIE WITH A MALE AS WITH A WOMEN ITS AN ABOMMINATION;* another is more straightforward: *FAGGOTS MAKE GOOD FIRES IN HELL.* In the middle of this assault, one of the bling women comes right up to my window. "I will pray for you queers," she over-mouthes grotesquely, then giggles and moves on. Jim turns completely red and looks like he's going to have a heart attack. I grab his knee and try to comfort him, but he rips it off— *"Not here, not here!"* his voice tighter than I've ever heard it. And now a new outrage: cars across the island honk their support, some drivers even roll down their windows and cheer the demonstrators on. And we're stuck in the *fucking thick of it*, pinned in by angry and terrified people— terrified by what the world has become in their minds, angry enough to do anything to stop the "abommination." That means coming here, to East Willow Boulevard in Compton, California, to block people from returning to work from their lunch breaks or driving to appointments with doctors or dentists; that means stopping anyone who's decided, as is their right in a democracy, to get vaccinated against a disease that might kill them. A man lingers in front of us, waving a bizarre sign with a picture of Albert Einstein and the caption, UNWANTED CHILD. I don't think so. Probably he doesn't think so, either. *Thinking* just isn't happening here.

The terror goes on for another five minutes before the crowd begins to pass us. Then, someone sees something on the stuck car that attracts attention. The crowd re-gathers around the car with a new fury, pummeling it with placards. And when the placards rip off, they smash it with posts in a whole new phase of violence. *Where are the police?*

"We have to call 9-1-1!" I shout to Jim.

"Do it!" Jim shouts back.

I try, but the signal is weak. And when someone answers, I can't hear them but scream our location into the phone. A young shirtless guy jumps onto our hood, crawls over the top, then slides down, a shortcut to the action behind. Something pops in a burst of smoke—*please, no guns!* I scream to nobody in particular. But the pop and smoke come from the attacked car revving up. With a roar, the car lurches to un-snare itself—forward, back, forward again. The rioters begin to close in again when the car, in a final screeching blast of exhaust, rips free—bounces from the island into the opposite lane, where oncoming traffic honks and swerves. Six enormous jets of water shoot from the mangled pipes—an eruption of stinking "green waste" that drenches the mob. A bearded guy in fatigues tries to stop the flow, calls for help, but gives up and flees with the other protesters when the flashing red and blue lights appear. The police. In less than a minute, the boulevard clears ahead, and we blast out of Compton for the freeway.

In the aftershock of silence, I tap my phone and read aloud the feed from *The Los Angeles Times*:

> *Three protests are planned in South Los Angeles Sunday through Tuesday by a group that calls itself Informed Consent Action Network (ICAN). The group, which obtained permission from the city with a promise of peaceful and civil assembly, will target the three largest vaccination sites in the South County. It is unknown if a counter-demonstration is planned and police remain on alert.*

"So much for peaceful assembly," Jim says. "So much for the alertness of police."

"Okay?" I touch his leg. Then, still freaked out, pull it away.

"Yeah, but the Compton 7-Eleven owes me a winning Lotto ticket," Jim says, being Jim.

It takes three hours to get home with traffic. I'm tired, probably from the vaccination, and take a short nap while Jim gets on the phone to his office. At around six o'clock, I get up and turn on the news—my habit.

"Hey," Jim says. "Let's take a break from all that, okay?"

"You're right," I say. "Hungry?"

I put together a nice dinner, a simple pasta dish in a fresh tomato, onion, and zucchini sauce. It never fails, especially with some good Pecorino cheese.

"What do you call those little corkscrew things," Jim asks as I drop the pasta into boiling water. "They look like DNA."

"Rotini. The spiral shape holds the sauce. You're a left-brainer, so you should know this." I uncork a bottle of Chianti.

"You sure you should drink?"

"I'm drinking."

"Cheers to us for a day well wasted," Jim says, sitting down. He takes a healthy swallow of wine and dives into dinner. "I'm really happy you got your shot, but this was one fucked up Tuesday," he mumbles, a noodle dropping from his mouth. "That was really, really good," he says a little later when I'm clearing plates.

"A no-brainer meal," I say. "I'm sure you've had better Italian."

"I've had the best Italian."

"At your service, Mr. Hollinger."

"*Hollander*, Mark... *really?*"

"Sorry. Hollander. Good Dutch name."

"Dutch-Irish. My grandma came over from County Cork—bless her pickled heart."

That night, in bed, he pillow-talks. "I'm going to make fantastic Italian food for you every night of the week."

"What are you talking about? I just made it for you."

"Then I'll make Dutch-Irish food with a touch of Scandinavian, authentic to my mongrel lineage." He shifts closer and kisses my chest, moves up to my nipples. "I also like the tender bits," he says. Then we make love like two people in love, because—as much as I try to deny it—that's what it feels like tonight.

11

Crossroads

A distinct tension hovers above my students when I open my classroom on Wednesday morning, February 16th. They're unusually quiet and glum, except for Christy Foswell, who's constantly chattering, this time with a pink fountain of hair spouting amid her turquoise spikes. But the gloom persists. I haven't checked my email in a day, and I've probably missed something. I ask my students what's on their minds.

Star student Andy Prento volunteers. "We're freaked out by what happened, Mr. Anello."

"What happened, Andy?"

"You should probably read the email announcement, Mr. Anello."

"Okay. Short break," I say, and blank out my screen.

In a long letter, the top three paragraphs of which contain header information indicating the communication has been passed down and vetted by several levels of School District Management, we're informed that Principal John Lavosso was arrested in south Los Angeles for assaulting a policeman during an anti-vaccination demonstration. The Superintendent has terminated him, and the search for a new principal has begun. Lorraine W. Easterborough, a board member and former principal at Rolling Hills Middle School of Encino, will serve as interim principal at Cavendar.

I'm more surprised about the appointment of Easterborough of Rolling Hills, a well-to-do school vastly different from Cavendar, than about Lavosso, whose behavior had grown more erratic and eruptive in recent months. I'm sad for him, but relieved he was arrested over the weekend and not someone I might've recognized in Compton on Monday. The letter concludes with news of a mandatory meeting for all teachers and staff at 4:00 p.m. We'll meet Principal Easterborough, introduce ourselves, discuss what we value most about Cavendar, and suggest what might need changing. Questions may be submitted in advance by emailing Ms. Easterborough, who will share some of them on Thursday. It seems the interim principal will also introduce possible changes in Cavendar's charter based on the last annual report, performance rating, fiscal viability statistics, and future academic goals in light of the inevitable return of classroom instruction. I smell trouble.

"Quit," Jim says over a Chinese dinner that night. "You don't really need the money, do you?"

"Sooner or later, I'll need it," I mutter, looking down at my glassy noodles. "Besides, it's what I've done for fifteen years and do well."

He persists. "Your skills are portable. You're good at explaining things. You have patience, and you work with different cultures. I could get you a gig doing software training at my company. The pay is great for a contractor. Or, they might even consider hiring you if that's what you want."

"Training who for doing what?"

"We have a new division for educational software. Game-oriented math stuff. You know that shit. You'd ace the interview—you know why? Because *I'd be one of the interviewers,* fuck-head."

"I'd be working with you?"

"Hell, no. Completely separate divisions. Different buildings. We'd hardly see each other, which is a good thing for both the company and for us. They know what they're doing."

"Thanks. Not sure it's for me, but something to think about."

"There are plenty of same-sex couples working there. Completely out, half-out, or on the downlow. It's all good."

"So, we're officially a same-sex couple?"

"Don't freak out. I'm making a point."

We finish dinner early and I find myself alone at home, enjoying my own company less and less these days. Jim's slantways offer of employment has me a bit shaken, although, as usual, I'm charmed. But I'm also agitated and can't sleep. The bedside clock beams 1:00 a.m.

I pick up the phone and call Dario.

He answers just before I disconnect.

"Mark, dear, hello! Do I get to see your face or just hear your voice?"

"Hi, baby"— the first time I've called him that — "No, I'm in bed, and it's hard to hold the phone."

"You were holding something hard when you last held the phone, as I recall."

"Yep."

"How are you, my ghostly paramour?"

"Good."

"Jesus *divine*, such a surprise to hear from you after all these weeks," he erupts, "but I do know how life moves on."

"I sure does. I think of you, too, but I should mention—"

"And *I* should mention," he interrupts, "that I have a wonderful surprise waiting for you if and when you ever arrive at my door, which I hope will be soon now that the world has its miracle cure."

"That just it, I thought I should tell you—"

"My *god*," he interrupts again, "I've missed you."

I take a breath, then: "I've missed you too."

"My surprise will remain fresh for the next, shall we say, twenty years — about the span of time a man like me, who's about to turn fifty-five in a month, has left on this Earth."

"Sorry, I forgot about your birthday."

"No, you haven't. I just reminded you." He's quiet for a moment. "Come spend it with me," he whispers.

"I—"

"The house looks gorgeous now that it's up for sale. The pool steams at night for evening swims under an early spring moon. Satin sheets await on my bed where we'll devour every inch of each other."

"You'd make a good Romance writer, Dario."

A moment passes.

"Is something wrong, Mark? Did you need to say something?"

"No. I'll come. I promise."

"I take promises very seriously."

"I'll come. Let me arrange it."

"You'll tell me the when and where and I'll be prepared for you. And you must be prepared for me, a bit fatter for lack of exercise, and the grey continues to sprout. But come, stay with me as long as you'd like. Let's continue our adventure together."

I put off meeting Jim Thursday evening to get on the Cavendar portal and prepare my questions for Friday's introduction to the new principal. But at 5:45 p.m. I get a ping from a parent requesting a Zoom call. Dr. Sharon-Bosker Foswell, the mother of turquoise-haired Christy Foswell, a.k.a. Mandalorian Space Goddess, wishes to *discuss*. In her text invitation, Dr. Foswell informs me that she's already brought up her concerns with the interim principal, who suggested the call this evening. Fine, so my first introduction to Principal Easterborough is through a parent complaint.

"How can I help you, Dr. Foswell?" I greet the fifty-ish woman who sits before a Norman Rockwell painting of a little boy with his trousers dropped.

"Thank you for taking my call, Mr. Anello. I'm sorry to trouble you this evening, but you've upset my daughter numerous times over the past year by making insensitive and even disparaging remarks about how she chooses to wear her hair."

I take a moment to compose my reply.

"Well, my apologies to you and to Cindy for the misunderstanding because I don't believe I've ever made what you call disparaging remarks. If anything, I've complimented Christy for her creativity."

"Not according to her."

"I'm not in the habit of commenting on student attire, Dr. Foswell. It's true that we have dress codes at Cavendar, but Christy hasn't violated any of them. As I've said, if I commented at all, it was always in a positive, respectful, and affirming manner."

She takes a moment. The silence between us is brittle.

"That's an inverted form of hostility, Mr. Anello," she snaps. "You attract derisive attention to my daughter's appearance by complimenting it. You encourage other students to notice a detail of her appearance that Christy *wishes not* to draw attention to."

"As I've tried to explain—"

"My daughter is not about her hair, Mr. Anello. Christy is an intelligent young woman."

"I entirely agree."

"You have no idea how difficult it is to raise a child with chronic ADHD. I've evolved her to the point where she believes in herself but still struggles to own her power as a human being."

"Always a good thing, Dr. Foswell. Again—"

"So, I insist that you make an apology to Christy in front of the entire class tomorrow without revealing we've had this conversation. Your apology should include your admission that you have no children of your own and don't understand the developmental challenges of young women."

"I'm sorry?" I stammer, blindsided by her comment. "How do you know I have no children of my own?"

"Your public information is out there for anyone who wishes to find it. And it points to the obvious about your lifestyle."

"I think we should end this conversation, Dr. Foswell. But I appreciate your reaching out to me with your concern, and I'll consider the best way to address the situation. Thank for you taking the initiative."

"Does that mean you won't agree to—"

"Good night." And I cut her free and take a deep breath. I shut the computer and pace around the house until 9:30 p.m. when I take a sleeping pill.

Christy Foswell doesn't appear in class Friday and, agitated from my conversation with her mother last night, I didn't submit my list of concerns to Easterborough. I decide to keep a low profile at the staff meeting and watch rather than participate. At four o'clock, the new principal signs on. She appears to be in her late forties, looks stylish in oversized eyeglasses, and projects a corporate rather than den-mother vibe. She goes on about her experience teaching in private schools. She assures that, as our new principal, her "door will always remain open," but seems to ignore the spontaneous questions she invites from the thirty or so people who populate the grid of squares below her.

After a long-winded preamble during which she offhandedly mentions—to everyone's surprise—that her interim status will probably transition to permanent status, Ms. Easterborough outlines her vision for the future. Cavendar must retool for effective classroom teaching to survive. It boils down to several key points: Cavendar is still underperforming academically, which might lead to a reduction in funding. "Our school has an absentee problem," she announces, "and this may result in a reduction in funding for the remainder of 2022." In fact, every point she brings up ends with "a reduction in funding," as if she's the cheerleader for a team of fiscal conservatives in Congress who don't particularly believe in education at all.

When I call Jim late Friday night and describe the past forty-eight hours, he listens patiently, then repeats what he'd said three days ago.

"Quit. Take a break and reframe your life. We'll work this out together."

"But—"

"Why waste your best years on stupid shit? You're better than all that. Get out before fifteen years go by and you don't know where they went."

Over the weekend, I study my traveling options. February fares to Rome are discounted, but I need more time to get some clarity about my feelings for Dario. I'm nervous about launching back into the ambiguities of our relationship, so I decide to first discuss this with my mother, who, of course will discuss it with Loren. She's surprisingly mellow.

"Go and see this through with your Italian friend. You'll learn more when you're together and I know how much you love Italy. You can spend your money on things, or you can spend it exploring and finding happiness in your life," she says. My mother's cool.

"I'm planning a trip myself," she adds, "probably in the summer. Sam invited me, at last."

"That's terrific, Mom. Really."

"And Loren—Loren! He's found himself a lady friend and spends most of his time driving her around. Your brother is in Heaven."

"That rascal," I say, "of course, he wouldn't tell me. I'm glad everything is good over there."

"I guess you'll miss Easter. Do you know how long you'll stay?"

"Not sure. Not more than I have to. Just like before, I'll forward my mail to Loren. He has my signed checks and deposit slips. Give him my account number if he asks. It's fine."

"Come back for the wedding," she says, startling me. "*Joking*," she singsongs.

The following week passes easily. Christy Foswell appears in class again, her hair a surprisingly ordinary shade of brown, and I offer no apology. On Friday morning. the 25th, I'm still in my happy place until I get the email from Principal Lorraine W. Easterborough for a Zoom meeting from her office during the hour allotted for lunch. Once I tune in, her manner is all business with an over-gloss of friendliness."

"Mark," she begins, "May I call you Mark?"

"Of course," I say. "But let me begin by congratulating you on your appointment here at Cavendar. We all look forward to your leadership."

"Appreciated," she responds neutrally, fanning some papers near her face so I just see their edges at the bottom of the screen. "Mark, what sort of homework do you regularly assign your pupils to help them consolidate their math skills?"

"I go easy on them. I'm mindful of their after-school interests and short attention spans. Plus, it's always nice to assign homework and have the students actually do it."

This doesn't appear to register at all with Ms. Easterborough, who continues to shuffle papers. "Looking through your fall and winter syllabus, I see assignments such as 'Attain third-level proficiency in video game *Death Division III: The Dragon's Lair* and report back your five highest scores.' Is this an actual homework assignment?"

"Yes, DD-III is an online game that teaches the rule of division by way of creatures in fantastic worlds. The students have avatars and compete against each other to improve their computational skills."

"Do you know if these improvements are measurable?" she drones.

"Quiz scores improve, if only marginally," I drone back. "But they do improve. What really improves is the enthusiasm my students show in doing calculations, if only to get better at the game."

"And how does this address STEM requirements, which are clearly measurable?"

Easterborough has clearly put me on the spot and I sense a trap. "Well, the consensus among teachers here during the worst of the pandemic, with the support of our former principal, was that standards-based teaching should be relaxed in order to accommodate the stress students were feeling in a work-at-home environment."

"Yes, well, that was a well-intentioned but misguided solution. I'm well aware of it, but—"

Something rises up and it's time to push back. "Ms. Easterborough, or Lorraine, if I might call you that? No matter, I'll call you that..." I struggle to get a grip and stay professional. "With all due respect, Lorraine, long before getting my teaching credential, I graduated with honors from UCLA with a degree in educational epistemology. I've done the best I can do with my students here at Cavendar, and they've met me halfway. Considerably more than the students of my colleagues, I might add. And despite what you might think, this has been no small effort on my part."

"I didn't mean to suggest—"

"I'm fully prepared to resign from Cavendar and allow you to make your first new math teacher hire. I don't think you'll have applicants knocking down your door."

"Please, let me—"

"Did I say I was prepared to resign? Let me clarify: I resign, as of now. I'll give you three weeks, but no more. Now, if you'll excuse me, I want to eat my lunch."

I disconnect my conference window from hers, eat what I can of my lunch, then return to my class as if nothing happened. But as the afternoon wears on, I feel a growing sadness. Something ended this afternoon. Towards the end of the day, Easterborough texts me to ask if I'd please spend another few moments with her after class so she can clarify her concerns and express her appreciation which I didn't give her the opportunity to do earlier. I agree to meet her, but I'm still determined to leave.

She's much friendlier this time and looks a bit harried.

"First of all, I apologize," she says. "I had a lot on my plate today and didn't intend our talk to seem like an interrogation, but I might've done better to steer the conversation in a more supportive direction."

"Thank you. I also apologize, Lorraine."

"It's no picnic, taking this on, I can tell you."

"Good luck to you."

"Okay. Hear me out. You're a fine teacher, Mark. Your students like you. The few parent complaints over the years I've browsed through are ridiculous and misguided, including the latest one from Dr. Fossett, who's been, shall we say, *historically* difficult from what information I could gather about her."

"I appreciate that."

"So, in that light, please re-think your decision. Consider a half-pay leave of absence for the remainder of the school year, if need be. I believe in our continued investment in you. I believe you were born to teach. And I'll give you the time to rediscover that."

I say nothing.

"Okay?"

"Okay. Thank you. But I still want to leave in a little less than three weeks. March 16th, to be exact."

"All right, I understand," the new principal says wearily, reaching under her glasses to rub the bridge of her nose.

Friday night, Jim comes flying through my front door ecstatic and wants to celebrate. He's holding two bottles of wine.

"You played that one just right, buddy." He stretches his arms out toward me, still holding the bottles. "Look at this cocky bastard who stands before me! Quits, then gets an offer of extended leave, job guaranteed."

"Well, I don't know if the job is guaranteed."

"No matter, you're cuttin' 'em loose—*proud* of you, son," he says, banging the bottles down on the kitchen table. "These are for later. We're going out tonight."

We sit in a funky little Boho café near the Santa Monica pier munching Scotch eggs before the prime rib. Jim loves it slathered with horseradish.

"So, what's the plan now?" he says, chewing prominently.

"Not sure. I work until the middle of March."

"Then what?"

"Probably back to Italy around March 16th."

"Perfect. I get three weeks off in March. Where we going?"

I say nothing.

"Uh oh," he says amiably.

After dinner, we walk around the pier with its gaudy stalls and guitar strummers. Teenagers mope, peering down at their phones. The Pacific hisses somewhere in the dark.

Jim looks down. "So, you've decided to see your friends in Italy?"

"Pretty much."

"Friends, or ex-boyfriend friends?"

"I'll see Dario, of course. You'd like him."

"I don't think so."

"Fine."

"You'll stay with him?"

"He's got a big house, and I'm not one for wasting money on hotels."

"You'll sleep with him?"

"It's just a visit, Jim. I'll be back."

"For how long?"

"Not sure. A month, maybe. Depends on who's available and what kind of travel arrangements I can make."

We're driving home now, Jim at the wheel. The silence is thick and uncomfortable. Finally: "What are you doing, Mark? What the fuck is happening here right now?"

He's calling my shit and there's no escaping it, but I try. "I'm not doing anything you should worry about. I've been stuck in my house for years, and I have friends in Italy I haven't seen since before the pandemic—before we even *met*." I look across the flickering dark at his troubled profile. "Just relax and don't worry about it, okay?"

Nothing else is said until we pull up to the house. Jim storms through the door right behind me and heads for the bathroom. I hear a flush and he comes out with his hair all wet. Looks at me blank-faced. Bewildered.

I take a step toward him. "Do you want to stay? Do you want to spend the night?"

"Fuck, no. I'm going home."

"Can we talk about this?"

He turns to leave, then spins around to face me with an expression I've never seen before. "I don't think you like yourself, Mark."

"You're probably right," I answer. "But *you* like me, so I guess I'm likable."

His head juts toward me. "That's the sickest thing I ever heard. I mean, do you even realize how fucked up that is?"

"Tell me."

"Damn straight I will. You throw yourself into any situation where you get to take a vacation from *you*. And that means somebody here and somebody there, preferably thousands of miles away. And it has to be a whole fuck load of somebodies because it's not about the finding, it's about the *looking*."

"We all do that, don't we?"

"I don't do it. Well—not after I've found someone. And I found you."

I say it slowly, trying to be kind. "Maybe I haven't found you."

"Oh," he says, looking up at the ceiling. "I guess I'm just a dumb fuck not to see it. Well, now I see it."

We're both silent for a moment. I break it.

"I'm not sure I'm your happily ever after, Jim. I'm not sure I even believe in that."

Jim looks down as if gathering his thoughts, then looks up slowly. His eyes seem tender but frightened. "Mark. Somewhere inside, there's a solid guy—a little smashed up here and there, but a beautiful and intelligent and sensitive man—and you can't fucking find him. You need another solid guy to break through all that bullshit and love you. Me."

"You're sweet to say that, Jim."

"Right. Sweet. Obviously, I see what you don't."

Jim's face changes and knots up again. "Okay. We've talked. You're leaving for your extended play date. Goodbye."

"Unfair—"

"And here I'm thinking we've got something going, maybe even a future, and then—*guess what?*—you're off to see one of your long-distance boyfriends in Italy or Spain or wherever it is where the nights smell like toast or some such bullshit."

"You're making a big deal—"

"I'm done, Mark. I want to go home, get in bed, and jerk off wildly because, for days, I've been saving it all for you tonight. But now I'll enjoy my own company as I begin to switch off the *I love Mark Anello* algorithm in my head."

"Stop."

"No, *go,* as in *going*—" he says, "As in *I'm going now.*" He stomps to the door but stops and turns to look at me, the veins popping in his neck.

"I need to know one more thing, Mark—tell me what I see in you."

"Apparently, somebody to rescue."

"Nope. If anything, it's the other way around," Jim says, stepping out into the dark.

After a sleepless night, I crawl out of bed Saturday morning and think of calling Jim but decide it's better to let things settle down. From my side of it, I think I've been honest with Jim, more honest than I've been with Dario who knows nothing about Jim. *Christ,* what a mess. Where's Marina to help explain me to myself? But, she doesn't know about Jim, either. And Dario doesn't know about Alessandro and Marina setting us up again. Jim knew what he was talking about. I live in a tangled world of secrets. When did all of this crazy begin? For the first time in a long time, I have a heart-to-heart with my brother Loren.

"Dad screwed things up for us," he says. "More for you than me, but he screwed things up."

"You think it's about Dad, Loren?"

"Yup. All our lives, we watched Mom suffer. We got hurt by somebody hurting. It scared us."

"Maybe. Scared us because we're afraid we're like Dad and we'll hurt someone else?"

"That's part of it, but the bigger part is that we see what happens when you love somebody who leaves. And even if we take a chance with love, somewhere down the line, it turns into an abandonment of our poor, wounded mother, so we pull back."

"People get over this stuff. It's part of growing up."

"Don't believe it. Every grown-up contains a frightened kid."

"And that's your analysis."

"Fuck, yes, it's my analysis. We're scared little boys who saw what happened when Mommy loved Daddy, and Daddy disappeared—didn't die, but just walked out and closed the door like he was going to the corner for cigarettes. And we don't want to be on either side of that. We don't want to be Mom and we don't want to be Dad. So, when we like someone and tell them, we hedge our bet with someone else and tell them the same thing. It's a buffer because it keeps us from getting too close to anyone. It's obfuscation."

"Maybe. Sure."

"I think it's more complicated for you, Mark. You're older. You bonded with Dad, and I didn't. Losing Dad was harder for you and maybe you even blamed yourself. The Oedipus thing."

"Jesus Loren, did you take an online course in psychology? I never thought—"

"You never thought I might be more than just some dumb tool who dicks around with cars, right? *Surprise*, big bro.'"

"No, it's—it's just a funny theory, is all."

"That's right, a funny theory from a funny guy. My whole life, I've been a funny guy. I've got a funny disease, so I don't always talk right and my words run together if I don't concentrate. And then my funny walk.

156

You should see me struggling to get out my car. A regular barrel of laughs getting Sharon to help me."

"You're fine."

"I'm fine, but I'm not on anyone's A-list of potential husbands. And when I meet a good and patient woman like Sharon, who I like and who seems to like me, I look for the ripcord. And this is kind of happening now."

"Wow. Sorry."

"You're the same with your boyfriends, Mark. Trouble is, they're all just like you. I don't think anything works out in the gay world. Not for long."

I try to absorb these observations from my brother. "Thanks for sharing your thoughts, Loren."

"They're just my funny thoughts," he says. "I'm sure you have your own funny thoughts."

That night, I find a March 16th flight to Rome on ITA Airlines with a single-city layover. I'll leave at 4:00 p.m. Wednesday and arrive at Fiumicino airport at 2:20 p.m. local time on Thursday the 17th. I spring a few extra bucks for a flex ticket that allows me to make one schedule change in the return date, which I haven't yet decided. I save the reservation and schedule a call to Dario before I pay for it. Thank god he answers. I give him the details of my arrival and he agrees to pick me up at the airport. We figure out the best place to connect at the crowded arrival curb at Fiumicino. Dario's done this before with many guests over the years and seems to have it down.

This won't be the easy jaunt to Europe I remember from years ago. Overseas traveling now requires proof of vaccination on a CDC ID card and a phone link to a negative test no more than twenty-four hours before departure. The routine of getting a test and a negative result in only twenty-four hours is nerve-wracking. Masks are required for the duration of the flight, except when eating, and any failure to cooperate will result in an aborted flight and arrest of the offending passenger. This rule, on a budget Italian airline, is clearly aimed at Americans, who, in recent months, have outdone themselves in idiocy by refusing to mask up and even assaulting fellow passengers or flight attendants who demanded they comply—a national embarrassment.

For the next two weeks, I organize my class paperwork, finalize my end-of-year syllabus, and prepare my classes for the news of my leaving. I'm surprised at how coolly my students take it, but I suspect the lack of physical classroom time has weakened the student-teacher bond— another casualty in the Age of Zoom.

I don't call Jim, hoping he'll call me, but he doesn't. On Saturday March 12th, I tap out a simple text: *Sorry I upset you. Know that you're an amazing man and I cherish having you in my life.* I backspace over it because it sounds insincere and manipulative. *Don't be jealous...* I begin again, then wonder if that's the best way to start anything to anyone. Finally: *Jim, I'm thinking of you. I hope you'll talk to me before I leave for Rome in a week,* and send it.

Nothing.

12
Villa dei Giardini

I thought I'd suffocate on the long leg from Houston to Rome. The mask recycled my breath, so I felt chronically oxygen-deprived and dizzy. The cupped portion of my face itched like hell, and every time I slipped down the mask for a sip of water or bite of cracker, the guy chomping away in the seat behind me had a sneezing fit. No use trying to sleep with a mask; I felt like I'd been stretched on a surgeon's table waiting for anesthesia. And this: not understanding crew members, especially on an Italian airline where accents, charming as they might've been when naked-mouthed, were incomprehensible now.

When we land at the gate, I squeeze into the aisle and push my way to the exit, my arm hooked through a single strap of my carry-on bag and my suitcase zigzagging behind. Fiumicino is a crush of people under the sensory overkill of gigantic LED billboards. Most people wear masks, although more women than men, and a few proudly do not—Americans, I surmise. I fly through Customs with my passport poised and vaccination card displayed prominently on its lanyard. Dario texts me to walk forward through the exit directly opposite the English language "Ground Transportation" kiosk and wait for him at the curb under the #6-B sign. I do a last check of myself in the lavatory mirror and see a crumpled mess after my sixteen-hour flight. I smooth the creases from my clothes, exhaling vigorously to get the stench off my breath. The first kiss has to be perfect.

And there he comes—loping energetically towards me with a big smile and wearing a thin nylon jacket over a T-shirt with a print of Socrates. He looks sharp; he looks hipster. A little heavier, maybe, but I like it.

"Here you are, here you are, here you are at last!" he effuses, arms wrapped around me so tightly that I feel the friction of his jacket against my chin.

"How are you, baby?" I ask, following through with a light kiss.

"Splendid, I am; that's how I am, *splendid!* I have so much planned for us. A lovely lunch is waiting for you. And then, perhaps, a nap. Of course, that need not include sleep..."

"Take me to your castle."

"Was the flight unpleasant?"

"I could use a good wash."

Dario grows serious, takes me by the shoulders, and turns me to face him. "Time has not diminished your sexiness, you stunning man. We will no doubt catch up."

A twinge of guilt passes through me. "No doubt."

He tells me he's fit and strong and insists on carrying my luggage, but I surrender only the carry-on bag. Despite his reassurances, Dario's limp seems more pronounced, and my wobble-wheeled suitcase resists rolling in a straight line. We stumble across the parking lot to his car.

"The house is a disaster since I'm in the midst of packing. But you'll still get a good sense of it. The garden, of course, is pristine."

"I'm really looking forward to seeing it, Dario, and spending time with you."

"You'll spend as much time with me as you'd like. I want you around. I want to learn everything about you I haven't yet learned or figured out—does that scare you?"

"Maybe just a little." *Actually, a lot*, I think.

With Dario at the wheel of his Fiat, we cruise through aisles of cars toward a glassed-in booth with a striped exit bar. Two portly gatehouse sentries populate it, one eating what looks like a greasy *calzone*.

Dario rolls down his window and displays a slip of paper.

Mid-chew, the munching sentry comes forward and takes it between two fingers. "*Questo è scaduto. Devi comprarne uno nuovo ò pagare venti euro.*"

"Fuck," Dario says and looks at me sheepishly. "He's saying it expired and I have to either renew it or pay twenty euros to exit."

"No worries, I'll pay it—" But before I can reach for my billfold, he calls to the sentry: "*Prego, dove vado per rinnovare?*"

The fellow mutters something, shrugs his shoulders.

"He doesn't the fuck know where I can go to renew my monthly pass. Somewhere inside the terminal. *Asshole.*"

"I'll pay it, Dario. Let me take care of it and we're out of here."

"Okay," he says and surrenders my bill. The gate opens. "Fucking stupid fat bastard policeman," he mutters.

The town of Poreta, Dario explains, began as a sprawling collection of castles that were abandoned by a declining aristocracy and left to rot. Locals occupied the ruins, demolishing some and renovating others, and eventually, a picturesque town or *commune* developed. We approach Poreta through olive groves and wheels of sod greening in the fields. Grape-posts stretch in planar recession from the roadside to the distant walls of farmhouses. Our road climbs through thickets of ash trees, then dips, then climbs again until we reach a sideroad that snakes down to a brick-pillared gate above which an iron arch proclaims in iron lettering: *Villa dei Giardini* or "Villa of the Gardens."

"So, this is my little piece of the castle, dear man. And it opens its arms to you."

Gravel crunches underneath as we pull alongside a brick and stone house with tall windows on the ground floor and square ones above, each window framed in black-varnished shutters and pinned back by fancy bronze fasteners.

"This particular villa dates from 1725 and was occupied by an olive oil merchant," says Dario. "His ancient, fruitless groves now replaced by my garden art, poor man."

Opposite the villa and at the terminus of its driveway, a bright blue sphere rises before several orange figures in welded steel that appear to clasp each other in some indecipherable greeting.

"One of four outdoor spaces for my assemblages," Dario announces as we exit the Fiat. "Would you like to go inside immediately, or should I give you a tour of the gardens first?"

"I think the gardens. Please."

We drop my bags beside the Fiat, and he lopes ahead of me. A dog bounds behind an open window and barks ferociously as we pass. We walk against the flank of the villa under a ponderous wall lantern that leans in picturesque decrepitude, then step down to a wide terrace. I'm stunned by the panoramic view of Poreta that shimmers ahead, a view so crystal clear that you can see several other medieval towns on hillsides miles away.

Dario points, "Città Treia, that one. San Venturino, that—famous for its black celery festival every autumn. Have you ever tasted black celery?"

I shake my head *no* in wonderment of such a thing.

We step from this terrace to the first in a cascade of terraces below, each displaying a collection of colorful sculptures—here, a collection whimsical ceramic jugs stuck with branches, stones, shards of other jugs, all brightly glazed; there, a group of delicate kinetic metalworks that wave in the slightest breeze; finally, stone pieces on a patio of stone: towers of granite like the cairns I'd see when hiking the desert trails in California.

"These," says Dario, pointing to them, "Are a homage to my home in Iowa. The *Arapaho* tribes of the Great Plains used them to mark animal trails for stalking game."

Beyond the stony terrace, a pool glistens among potted trees.

"It's like the Garden of Eden, Dario. You've got your own little paradise here. And I had no idea that you worked in metal."

"Making assemblages is my preferred medium, although the physical exertion it requires can be taxing. Now and then, I hire a few boys from the village to help me with the welding."

"They're very good."

"I'm so glad you like them. Now, to your bags and a light dinner. And then, a rest for you. I have a few more errands to tend to before we go out for cocktails and meet some friends." He smiles at me, tilts his head. "If you'd like that, I mean."

"Sure."

"Then, perhaps later, I'll give a tour of my studio, the place where I paint. If not, tomorrow."

His eager Schnauzer Trixie meets us as Dario opens the door, fascinated with the scent of my luggage. Stacks of taped cardboard boxes lean in every direction, and unfolded ones are strewn about the floor, but they don't distract from the elegant interior space: bold-colored paintings, Brancusi-like tables, and artful knickknacks everywhere. Above a large woodburning fireplace, a pair of extravagant stag antlers cantilever dramatically, bleached chalk white.

"So, you've listed the house? Has anyone come to see it?"

"Well, I've procured the services of a listing agent but instructed her to suspend showings until I have more time to prepare. I have so much work to do and so very much to pack away!"

"I'm here to help."

"I wouldn't think of it. We have better ways to spend our time together."

We climb a banister-free stairway to the "first" floor—in Italy, this means the floor above the ground floor—and enter his bedroom at the end of an arched hallway. A king-sized bed sits directly under a jeweled Moroccan lantern. Beside the bed, a door opens to a small bathroom. A wall of unshaded French doors reveals a small terrace with an even higher view of the countryside.

Maybe Dario detects something in my face because he says, "I'm assuming we'll share my bed while you're here, but I've also prepared one of the guest rooms, too. Perhaps the better solution for the first few nights so you can sleep and reset your biorhythm. I do confess a bit of insomnia lately."

"That's fine, thank you."

We have lunch—rice-stuffed red peppers from the garden—with wine, which certainly begins to send me on my way. Soon, I'm upstairs, alone and unwashed, under a crisp white sheet in the guest bedroom.

It's dark when Dario comes in to wake me.

"Sweetheart, are you feeling rested? Would you still care to go out and meet a few friends for cocktails?"

I grumble through the coverlet. "Maybe some coffee first?"

"I can do that. Come down when you're ready." He stops by the door. "Have you a sweater to put on, or something? The evenings are still a bit chilly this time of year." His arm reaches out through the dark and returns with a bathrobe. "This should keep you warm."

When I roll towards his nightstand and prop myself up, I notice a text message on my cell phone—Jim. It's twelve noon in California. *Mark, I am sorry if I overreacted. What a shitty send off. Anyway, have a nice visit with Dalio.*

It would be awkward to call him now, but I'm glad he reached out. I reply with a text: *Thanks, evening here. All is fine.*"

"So, who are these night owls we're meeting for cocktails tonight?" I ask Dario, staring into the marbled foam of the most enormous cup of cappuccino I've seen in my life.

"Rhoda and Sylvano live in the town of Bevagna, about twelve kilometers away, but we'll meet them closer, in Foligno. She's South African and he's Milanese. She designs fabric and he ... just diddles. Apparently, some money there since neither of them seems to work very much. But they're interested in my pieces, so when they're in town and wish to get together, I obey."

"Smart fellow."

"And of course, I've talked about you incessantly over the years. And of course, they now want to meet you."

"Incessantly? Come on."

"Well, my mentions of you have been memorable, apparently. Therefore, I present you tonight in all of your charm."

"I'm feeling a deficit of social energy."

"You have nothing to fear. Do you think you'd like to go out with them later for dinner?"

"Later? What's later?"

"About ten-ish?"

"My God, you people do eat late."

We drive down the hill and across the valley to the town of Foligno, a city obliterated during the war because of its well-connected central train station; a city now mostly rebuilt. These days, Dario explains, the shells of Renaissance palazzos contain upscale clothing and jewelry stores, and the streets jostle with young pedestrians, even at 9:30 p.m.

Dario opens the sleek door to a glass box of a restaurant and bids me go in ahead of him. He spots his friends at a back table, far from the window, and marches forward, holding my hand. The couple, probably in their fifties, looks elegant; Rhoda sports cropped blond hair and Sylvano salt-and-pepper locks. She's thin and willowy, a younger version of Laurie Anderson; he's portly in a satin jacket, single-buttoned over a bright-patterned shirt.

Hello, hello, Hello, and hello! Everyone stands and embraces.

Dario thrusts me forward. "This is my guest of honor, dears, Mark Anello of California, who's come to keep me company for as long as he likes."

"Well!" Rhoda smiles, pecking me on each cheek. "However did you manage to scale the walls of Dario's fortress?"

"And from exotic California," Sylvano chimes in. "Look how he shows off his suntan."

"Nice to meet you both," I say. "And no, Sylvano, I'm indoors most of the time in California, so no suntan for me."

Well, well. Allora, then. Well. We settle down at our table, skip the cocktails, and decide to order a simple cold meat and cheese platter.

Dario turns to me, "Rhoda and Sylvano love this place because it's very Milano-style. Glass and stainless steel."

"Rhoda more," Sylvano corrects. "For me, it looks like a place for washing cars. But the cuisine is quite adequate."

"Interesting space," I observe. "And Dario tells me you're a fabric designer, Rhoda?"

"Yes," she says, lighting a cigarette. "I have a new line coming out for Pima cotton. A soft pattern of grey hydrangeas over which I place a tangle of black Venus flytraps. A touch of the macabre for moonlit evenings. We're hoping to interest Gabbani for his line of leisurewear."

"I love it," I say, although I'm not sure I do.

"Would you like to see?" she says, lifting her phone and swiping the screen.

"Of course," I answer, although I'm not sure I want to. But after a few swipes, I'm impressed.

Over dinner, I talk more with Rhoda than Sylvano, who's engaged in quiet conversation with Dario. Our server brings a tray of small desserts to our table, and Rhoda asks if I'd like to have a nightcap with her since *our men*—that's how she puts it—must remain sober for the drive home. I agree and we do.

"Yes, you do that, ladies—I mean, excuse me, *gentlemans*," Sylvano announces, as he and Dario rise from the table, "because Dario and I must now have a drink at the bar to discuss a new commission."

"*Prego*," Rhoda quips, sipping her Campari. "I'll keep company with this enjoyable man."

Dario winks at me as he and Sylvano get up to leave. Rhoda takes out another cigarette—pauses before lighting it. "Does my smoking bother you, dear?"

"No, but it's strange seeing so many people smoke in restaurants here."

"Most places don't allow it anymore. This one is an exception, a sanctuary for those of us who love our bad habits, not like these children with their health bars and vegetable juices."

"That's good, Rhoda. I love it."

She smiles and says nothing for a few moments, glances in the direction of Sylvano and Dario. "Sylvano is offering a big commission and wants to discuss it with Dario in private. He doesn't want me to know how much he spends on art. But I don't really care since it's his money, not mine."

"I'm sure Dario appreciates your interest in his work."

"He is a genius, you know. You should collect as much as you can, accept any gift from him, no matter how small."

I laugh. "Only if I can provide something in return," I say with a wink.

She studies me. "I'm sure you're his type. He prefers a more delicate type of masculinity for his models, and you have very sad eyes. Your wavy hair is sensuous. Are you Sicilian?"

"On my mother's side. My father was from the north."

The two men reappear, bright-eyed and buoyant. I assume they've closed the deal, although Dario says nothing about it. He does, however, pick up the tab.

The villa sits in the pitch dark of an Umbrian night as we pull up to it. Trixie leaps and whines as we enter through the kitchen lit by a single lamp.

"They're an interesting and sophisticated pair," I say as we climb the stairs. "But I could hardly keep my eyes open, especially after that last drink."

"I always enjoy them. But they're a bit intense and can wear you out. Now, we'll remove every stitch, crawl between the clean sheets of my bed, and have a good sleep. I won't touch you. I promise."

"Baby"—again, that word comes out of me— "I'm wearing twenty-four hours of travel sweat."

"That doesn't bother me at all. Would you like to take a short plunge?"

"No. Really. I'll pass for tonight and take the guest bed, if you don't mind."

"As you wish."

"Good night. And thanks for such a wonderful welcome."

"Don't hesitate to join me should you grow lonesome."

A March squall comes up in the middle of the night, pelting the windows and flashing the bedroom walls. A low rumble of thunder shakes the glassware. Something shudders and bumps outside the bedroom as if something has fallen from a shelf or bookcase. I get out of bed, quietly open the bedroom door, and step out to investigate. Dario's door is ajar, and a soft blue light spills out. Out of playful curiosity, I creep towards the light. It comes from a laptop on his empty bed, streaming porn. When I return to my room, I glance out the window to see what I can of the storm. Dario passes underneath in a soaking wet smock, holding what looks like a collapsed easel. He's illuminated in the glow of a window or open door on the ground floor, probably to his studio. It's 3:45 in the morning.

My eyes open to sunlight streaming across my pillow. I twist out of bed and walk to Dario's bedroom for a shower. It's a large, beautifully tiled shower, but has one of those hand-held mechanisms that escapes my grasp like a flapping fish and sprays water over the sliding door. I tether it back it and turn it towards me. The towel is small and rough.

I'm morning-cranky. As I dress, I hear Dario downstairs over the sound of a television or radio. When I enter the kitchen, I see him standing over the stove, his back to me, wearing open-backed slippers and what looks like the same smock I saw him in last night. "Good morning!" he beams, spinning around. He's covered head-to-toe in paint.

"My God, Dario! Did you sleep on one of your paintings, last night?"

"I slept hardly at all last night," he says cheerfully, "And I'm no worse for the wear." He strolls to me, his paint-stained hands opened for a hug, then stops. "Ah," he says, "I mustn't sully you. Not yet, anyway."

He steps back, an odd smile on his face.

"As you'll see, when inspired, I soon abandon my brushes as they devolve into mere antennae for the powerful force I feel from another dimension. I crave that connection, seek it, and when I find it, I allow it to entirely possess me so that my entire body becomes the tool of my artistic execution. It's quite an exhilarating experience. Mark!"

"Does that mean I can hang you in a gallery and make a fortune?"

"No buyers for this old man, dear." He steps forward and pecks me on the cheek. "Good morning."

I peck back. "Good morning, sweetheart."

"Wasn't the storm lovely last night?" he says, turning to the stove again.

"Yes."

He wipes his hands and has me sit down at the table, sets a bowl of cappuccino before me, and a tray of miniature pastries with jewel-like fruits on top.

"I saw you through the window last night."

"Indeed, now eat to your heart's content so I can take you down into my studio. I have no appetite myself this morning. But I want you to enjoy these delicious treats from our local *pasticceria* while I clean myself up and don something appropriate for our road trip this afternoon. The day will be lovely, so we'll drive to the birthplace of the fourteen-century artist *Giotto*—the genius who blew up Gothic iconography and replaced it with the soft-faced Madonnas of the Renaissance."

"Sounds great," I say, burning my lip with a first sip of coffee.

A half hour and five pastries later, Dario appears wearing a rough cotton shirt without a collar and looped pegs instead of buttons. There's still a trace of color between his fingers. He's wearing sunglasses.

"Ready?" he says.

"We're leaving already? I thought you'd show me your studio first."

"Oh, that's right," he groans, removing the glasses. "A bit scattered today, I am. Follow me, monsieur. *Avez-vous des valises à me faire porter?*"

"No valises and therefore no tip," I reply, playing his game.

We step into a short corridor off the kitchen that ends in a narrow staircase leading down. It opens to a large semi-basement with a span of glass doors facing north. Directly before us sits a desk. Behind it, a roll-away room divider. Two blue leather club chairs flank the desk and face each other in secret conversation.

"My reception area for clients," says Dario. "Before they view my work and hopefully buy something, I want them to relax here before they see the chaos of lies behind."

"Let's see the chaos that lies behind."

He takes my hand and pulls me forward, walks to the edge of the divider, and gives a little push so that it completely folds away to reveal what looks like a stage set of an artist's *atelier*: stretched canvases, rolled canvases, canvases hung haphazardly on the walls, canvases stacked against canvases. Six paint-encrusted easels lean under the weight of the large canvases mounted on them; some with slashes of color on naked white, others mud-thick with colors still glistening, still others with only a charcoal sketch or, as I remember Dario explaining, a *cartoon* for a future painting. Odd items of clothing lay discarded on the floor under the easels: socks, T-shirts, an odd sandal, and underwear.

"So, here you have it, dear Mark. The portal to madness. Behold this tinderbox and flee while you can." He says it with a mixture of embarrassment and pride.

"Not at all. It's incredible. The space of a man possessed by a demon-angel."

"Too kind. And so true."

"But what's with the clothes on the floor?"

"As I said, I often shuck them off in the fever of creation, wishing not to ruin them."

"I'll want a photo of that."

"We will see. Now, for the recent work."

He grabs the sleeve of my shirt and pulls me behind a high stack of paintings and a low shelf containing jars crammed with paintbrushes, piles of rags, and—thankfully—two fire extinguishers. Three easels sit side by side, perfectly spaced apart. On each, a large canvas. The work before me is bold and startling, a radical departure from what I remember of Dario's slides. Gone are the delicate glyphs and densely interwoven tendrils in complex color combinations. Gone is the precision, control, and carefully calibrated sensuality that emerged from a keen but dispassionate intelligence. These new paintings are deliberately primitive, violent, and filled with a kind of rage. They require a different kind of effort from the viewer—*demand* of the viewer: *see me, love me, save me!*

I say nothing, taking them in. Finally: "Different for you."

"Yes. Very," he replies.

"They're selling? These new ones?"

"Sylvano's commission is my first. The one on the left. He's provided instructions but has yet to view it. From his commission will come others, I hope."

"They're ... definitely a break from what came before."

"You don't like them?"

"No, it's not that. They're very powerful. But I don't understand the source of their power. It comes from something outside of you—like something has taken ahold of you, and you're struggling. Maybe it's a good struggle, I don't know..." I trail off. "I'm sorry Dario, I'm trying to be honest here."

He looks puzzled, and I strain to come up with something to soften my critique. "I mean to say—"

"No. I understand. You've sensed something different in me. Entirely correct. Perhaps the demon-angel you alluded to. Keep in mind that I trained you to recognize these contradictory dynamics when we viewed the Hieronymus Bosch together. And now my lesson comes back to me."

"You're not upset."

"Of course not," he says, brightening. "Of course! So, let's get ourselves ready to learn more about Giotto. We have a long journey ahead of us today!"

Giotto's house sits in the humid Mugello Valley, a region, Dario explains, once occupied by the proto-Roman Etruscans, who left pieces of their colosseums behind and built the first vehicular roads. In a strange twist of providence, modern Mugello hosts the *Autodromo Internazionale*, a famous car racing competition and produces a special breed of chicken we'll sample later.

The house sits on a slight rise, much of it reconstructed out of ruins. Tourists come for the small but excellent museum it contains and its view of the surrounding valley, a view that's remained much the same from the time Giotto first painted it. Mayflies buzz above the fields as we walk up the hill from the road to the entrance. A thin woman sits behind a small desk covered with brochures and asks for a donation, which Dario provides, with a little extra thrown in. He's thanked, profusely. I'm disappointed to learn that the house doesn't contain any of Giotto's original art—too valuable, and they're without the resources to protect them, the woman informs—but boasts that they've reconstructed Giotto's color laboratory, which displays materials he used to make his pigments.

After we thank the woman and begin our self-guided tour, an older woman with elaborately coiffed jet-black hair emerges from a side door, smiles, and follows us towards the laboratory. We stop to look at a few of the reproductions along the way, she standing close behind us.

"Why is she watching us?" I ask Dario. "Is she a guard?"

"I don't think so," he whispers. "I think she hopes we'll ask her for a tour, perhaps for a few coins."

We stop in front of Giotto's, *Madonna and Child*, painted between 1310 and 1315, the original of which lives in the National Gallery of Art in Washington, D.C.

"Look here, Mark," Dario begins. "If you're not familiar with Gothic religious painting, you can't really appreciate how Giotto broke away from it. This is the earliest portrait of the Madonna depicted naturalistically, as a young woman. Giotto models her face with *chiaroscuro*, an overlay of thin color, so that you see shadows on her cheeks to show the contours of flesh."

"Yes, I see that."

We move along to the next painting of note. The woman dogging behind us again.

Dario continues, "Here we have *The Celebration of Christmas at Greccio*. Look at the perspective of the pulpit over St. Francis, how the floor tilts up to create the illusion of depth. Now, look at the surrounding figures—heads behind heads behind heads—this type of three-dimensional rendering was miraculous for its time. Artists of less talent accused Giotto of sorcery."

"*Scusate, gentiluomini*," the woman interrupts, then directs her string of words to Dario. He listens patiently then translates for me.

"She says that Giotto was visited by an angel in the pasture who told him to paint the small bridge over the stream. There, he was discovered by the artist Cimabue, who was just passing by. Cimabue became Giotto's teacher and made him rich." Dario winks at me and ever-so-slightly rolls his eyes.

"Very nice story," I say.

We continue to the color laboratory, the woman now walking right beside us. Jars of brilliant pigments sit illuminated on shelves, an explanation of each below, all in Italian. Dario drifts past them, translates for me when I ask him to.

"These are the usual pigments for egg tempera," Dario says breezily, "Powdered walnuts for brown and black or arsenic mixed with wine for red. Blue was ground up lapis lazuli—too expensive, even for Giotto—but he discovered something called *mixite*, a crystalized form of copper-bismuth that emerged from certain stones after a soaking rain."

"Fascinating."

"*Scusate ancora, gentiluomini,*" the matron interrupts again. She smiles and begins a long speech in monotone, looking at each of us in turn as she goes on and on with information she seems to insist we must know. About a minute in, I make out two words that tumble from her rambling: *Apache* and *Indians*. Dario listens patiently, then looks at me weary-eyed, his expression both amused and contemptuous.

"She claims that Giotto dreamed of another angel who took him to America where he learned to mix color from the Apache Indians." Dario contains himself, but I burst out laughing.

"She can't be serious!"

"I'm afraid she is." He turns to her and begins respectfully, "*Signora, è impossibile. L'America fu scoperta da Columbo per la Spagna, oltre un secolo dopo.*"

"That's right," I add, looking at her. "By the time Columbus discovered America, Giotto was long dead."

"*No, nooo,*" she protests, drawing the words out and looking quite stunned. "*Siete entrambi ignoranti riguardo alla storia,*" she says. "You are both ignorant of history."

Dario digs in: "*Per favore, signora. Sono un artista e molto instruito.*"

I catch his drift: he's an artist and very educated in these matters. But the woman continues to disagree, now growing quite disagreeable about it, her hands flying up and down.

"Just drop it, Dario," I say.

But Dario keeps going, and his voice begins to rise. He interrupts himself to turn to me and say, very loudly, "If anyone's ignorant around here, she is!" She, of course, picks up on the word "ignorant" and flies into a rage, her whole body involved now as she steps forward, then back, then folds her hands in prayer and looks up as if asking God to give her forbearance, which he doesn't, because her tantrum picks up heat and continues. Finally, some English tumbles out of her, mostly directed at me:

"You insult me and you insult my family! I am a noble woman from Borgo San Lorenzo, now disrespected by you and your *melanzane,* your immigrant friend from Africa! Get out of here, both of you! Get out of here now or I call immigration police to put your friend back on his boat to drown in the sea!"

We leave, Dario first turning to call her, in Italian, an uneducated hag. I shrug my shoulders to her in bewilderment, but she folds her thick arms across her chest and jerks her head up and away. I find Dario outside on the path, visibly shaken, so I take his hand. He places his hand over my hand and tries to reassure me.

"This happens from time to time. I'm sorry it had to happen while we're together."

"I'm shocked. I wouldn't have expected—"

"More and more, these days. They blame immigrants for bringing Covid. I'm sure you have something similar going on the U.S."

On the way home, we stop at a *Pranzo Veloce*, or "Quick Lunch" place for some Mugello chicken. It's good, although mostly dark meat. Dario looks very tired as we make our way back to Poreta, and I wish I could take the wheel from him, but he firmly rejects even a mild suggestion of it since the habits of country drivers in Umbria are unpredictable. Back at the villa at last, he feeds Trixie and scatters treats around the rooms to keep her occupied.

"Mark, sweetheart, I'm going upstairs for a nap if you don't mind. I'm a bit worn out. Please feel free to swim, explore, read, or do whatever you'd like for an hour or so, would you, dear?"

"Sure. Can we snuggle while you nap?"

"No, I think not right now. I just need some rest, and I'm sure your heat beside me would tempt me otherwise. Forgive this old man."

"Have a good rest. Should I wake you later?"

"Yes, in about an hour," he says, with a light kiss on my cheek. "For our five o'clock cocktail."

The villa turns quiet. Schnauzer Trixie emerges from her dinner and wipes her face on the skirt of the sofa. She looks up at me, her soft brown eyes, puzzled. I'm an unfamiliar playmate. But soon, she relaxes and invites me to scratch her belly. Happy finally, she trots off to gnaw her bone.

I pass the time looking through art catalogs that fan across a low table: Uffizi, Pinocoteca, the Peggy Guggenheim Collection in Venice—all good stuff—then, feeling drowsy myself, decide to go upstairs and lie down in the guest room. Trixie follows, having decided I'm worth hanging around with, then settles into a corner. I draw the thin drape partly over the window to soften the light, stretch out on the bed, and begin to drop off.

A scraping sound from the terrace below startles me. Trixie leaps up, barking. I walk to the window and stand near enough to see out but not be seen. A young man in tight jeans with cropped hair stands on the terrace with his back to me. When he turns around, I see an exotic face, Moroccan, maybe, and muscled arms covered with tattoos. He struts around the terrace with a predatory gait, then disappears in the blind spot below the window.

I walk closer to the window and lean halfway out, call to the man and ask what he's looking for. "*Scusi, sta cercando qualcuno qui?*"

The man reappears below and looks up. "*Dove è Dario? Voglio parlargli.*"

He's looking for Dario and wants to talk to him. But he hardly looks like a friendly visitor and my gut tells me I shouldn't say that Dario is inside sleeping. "*Come ti chiami? Glielo dirò quando ritorna,*" I call out— *tell me your name and I'll tell him when he returns.* But the man sneers, spits on the ground, then saunters down the stairs towards the pool and disappears.

"I didn't know what to say to this hoodlum who cased your property," I tell Dario when he comes into the kitchen while I make myself an expresso.

"Not a hoodlum, sweetheart," he says nonchalantly, rubbing his eyes. "Probably Jabari, my Egyptian,"

"Does Jabari have tattoos covering both arms?"

"Probably Jabari," he repeats mechanically. "I owe him some money." He tears a piece of bread from a loaf on the shelf and chews. "What do you say about meeting another friend for dinner sometime during the next two weeks? His name is Niccola Sisto and he's a professor from Foggia."

"Odd name."

"Niccola comes up every now and then to soak in the thermal pools. He left me a delightful message and would love to meet you."

"After ten again, I assume?"

"I'll suggest we make it sooner on your behalf, my delicate early bird."

A week goes by peacefully. As the weather grows warmer, I watch Dario doing calisthenics in his garden and ignore his waves to join in. During the early afternoons, he disappears into his studio where I leave him alone, passing the time exploring his art, inside and out, or lying across one of the plush recliners on the terrace to take in the magnificent, ever-changing colors of the Umbrian valley.

One late morning, before stepping downstairs, he hands me a box of charcoals and a sketchpad.

"I don't allow visitors to remain here for long unless they develop their drawing skills. The house demands it."

"So, I have to earn my keep?"

"Draw what excites you."

"Does that include Dario Soole in his birthday suit?"

"That depends on your progress."

"I'll get right to it," I say, waving him away.

Dinner, on a mild April evening of the following week, happens in the leafy yard of a *ristorante rustico* in Poreta's centrale, or downtown. We sit at a table under a string of bare bulbs and dine on *cinguale ragu*, or wild boar in tomato sauce over tagliatelle.

After some small talk during which I try to place the accent of this well-dressed stranger, I finally ask, "So, what do you teach, Niccola?"

"I teach philosophy at the University of Foggia, near Bari," Niccola answers. "But I was born in Macedonia fifty-three years ago and received my early education there."

"Macedonia," I say, "is a place I know nothing about, and philosophy is a subject I know next to nothing about."

Niccola smiles. "Philosophy is a discipline sadly neglected but badly in need of revival among young people nowadays, especially in Italy."

Dario beams, apparently proud of his friend. I dip my bread into *ragu* throughout the evening as Dario and Niccola go on to entertain me with stories of their friendship over the years, although neither of them can provide a distinct memory of the circumstances that brought them together.

"And what do you teach, Mark?" asks Niccola, dipping a biscuit into his wine.

"I teach, or *taught* mathematics to middle school students in California. I guess you'd say *scuola media* here."

"If your teaching included calculus, we'd say *scuola secondaria* for the grade level that precedes *Scuola Superiore*, or High School, for you."

"No calculus, thank God."

He leans towards me. "Did you ever try introducing aesthetic philosophy in your mathematics? Fibonacci, the Golden Mean, those sorts of disciplines?"

"No, that would be over the heads of most of my students. But I'm no longer concerned with their heads because I'm done with teaching and look forward to doing something else."

"Have you a large fortune, then?" Niccola asks, casually and apparently without reservations about asking.

"Just enough to allow me some freedom." I take a last sip of wine.

Coffee is ordered to fuel this period of post-dinner conversation. Dario seems wide awake, his eyes bright and beaming.

"So, how were the pools today, Niccola? Some pretty boys?"

"Yes, several handsome specimens today and the day before. The waters were miraculous, and the aches in my back have subsided. You must take Mark there, Dario. You must both have a good soak. If I could stay longer, I'd soak with you."

"I'm uncomfortable in public pools," Dario says. "People stare."

"Yes," Niccola says. "A pity how Italians can be so narrow-minded sometimes, I suppose, like Americans."

"Not all Americans are narrow-minded," I counter.

"Of course not," Niccola reassures. "Americans are quite important to me, I've made quite a lucrative business catering to their needs..." he begins, trailing off.

"Niccola studied in New York before returning to Foggia to become the esteemed Professor Sisto," Dario says.

"Columbia College," Niccola adds. "My Ph.D. or what we call *Dottorato di Ricerca* in Italy. However, Mark, my experience with the educational environment at Columbia was an education apart from my education."

"How so?" I ask.

"Early on, it became very clear to me that American universities were pressured to teach ideologies of the corporate and ruling classes, rather than the usual canon as defined by educational research guidelines. I see that lawsuits are now being filed about this in America, several by professors with whom I was affiliated at Columbia."

"That's correct," I say, impressed with how informed he is on the issue, "Curricula intrusion is getting a lot of press these days. But it's also being challenged in the courts, as you've pointed out."

Niccola continues. "But the trouble occurs when the governing boards of each state have final say about who is hired without having to justify their decisions."

"To some degree, maybe."

"To all degrees. I present the big picture to you now, Mark: in America, academic rigor is bullied by forces that consolidate power at the top, and—" he points one finger at me and the other at Dario as if aiming two pistols— "you Americans *accept* this. The absurd expense of a college education as an example."

"I agree with you, Niccola," I say, "but we also agree that this kind of interference has attracted scrutiny from the appropriate agencies. We're not all as stupid as you might think."

"Yes, you scrutinize, but in the meantime, you *pay*. I know of what I speak. I put three of my own children through good colleges in America, more so for the prestige of the college than the quality of the education it offered. In fact, I'm sure that my own hiring at a first-rate university in Foggia was in large part due to my second-rate degree from Columbia. Can anything be more absurd?"

"Status has always mattered in higher education. That's true everywhere."

"Indeed," Niccola says, leaning forward, his elbows on the table, "but *status* is very expensive and creates enormous economic pressure, even on those of us who see ourselves as professionals. For me, the pursuit of it has necessitated the establishment of multiple streams of income."

He locks his eyes to mine in what seems like a challenge. I look away, breaking his stare. "Not unusual these days," I say.

He doubles-down. "*Multiple streams of income*, Mark. And just as corporate forces operate within the grey areas of the law, my business dealings sometimes operate within the grey areas of commerce."

I say nothing and try to absorb what Niccola seems on the verge of confessing. Finally,

"Grey areas? I'm not sure I understand."

"You don't understand, and I shall say no more about it for now," he concludes, tapping a cigarette from a silver box.

"Good Heavens, Niccola," Dario says, "Have you channeled Karl Marx this evening?"

We share a good laugh about this. A fresh wind blows away the unsettling tension that had begun to gather over our table.

"So sorry, gentlemen," Niccola demurs. "I do get a bit impassioned about such things, as you can see. But I must thank you both for an altogether refreshing evening. And for me, some much-needed intellectual stimulation."

We drive home slowly, the road through the valley dark and overhung with trees. Now and then, a scooter buzzes past us like an enormous sputtering insect.

"Thank you for introducing me to Niccola," I say to Dario, "but did you agree with his takedown of the American educational system?"

"I'm afraid so."

"Really. I'm disappointed."

"Why?"

"Because it means you'll never go back."

"Why would I go back? What happens in America doesn't concern me anymore. And if I lived in America again, I would continue to ignore most of America."

"I'm not sure that's possible."

"I make my own world, Mark, as we all should."

He turns to me as we pull up to the villa. I can barely see his face in the dim light. "I knew our minds would take flight this evening."

"Yes."

"Now, I look forward to relaxing in my bed. I hope tonight, if you're not too tired."

"I'm not. But I need a swim to freshen up."

"The pool is still chilly. And the pool light doesn't work."

"We have moonlight. Let's be brave," I say, placing my hand inside his thigh. "Let's be clean."

I strip nude in his bedroom and walk out to retrieve my robe. When I return, Dario is wearing his robe. Together, we carefully step down through the terraces, Dario with a flashlight. The pool ripples mysteriously; its surface flutters in the light of a tawny full moon. Dario explains that a shadowed alcove at the pool's edge encloses a collection of metal figures he specifically designed for this setting, and the large pots surrounding the pool contain Sicilian lemon and lime trees.

In the dim light, he throws off his robe and jumps in, sinks down to his neck, and bounces around from the shock of cold. He splashes me to join him. I follow, flapping my arms against my chest. Dario comes up behind me and wraps his strong arms around my belly. He pushes against me, so I feel his hardness. He reaches down and starts to probe, then goes under. I feel his tongue down there. The erotic energy between us is incandescent and powerful. He swims through my legs and, in an eruption of water, emerges in front of me—his eyes gleaming and fierce.

He pulls my head to him and kisses me hard, moves to the sides of my neck, and goes lower. He tries to lift me up to the coping, but I stop him.

"Stop. You'll hurt yourself."

"I want to open you wide," he says.

"Let's go back inside," I say.

Robed, we climb the terraces then up the stairs to his dark bedroom where he drops my robe about my feet and gently dries me, guides me into his bed, then disappears into the bathroom. He comes out wearing a long-sleeved cotton shirt.

"What's this?" I say.

"My chest gets chilled at night, sweetheart."

"I'll keep you warm."

"Yes, I know you will," he says, crawling into bed, the shirt still on.

The night passes in lovemaking tender and aggressive, sensual and brutish, a commiseration and competition. But Dario resists all attempts I make to remove his shirt. In the light of early morning, his sleeved arm droops across the coverlet. He opens his eyes, smiles at me, then places the arm beneath the sheets and hooks it around me. I begin to doze off again until the bed jolts as Dario jumps up, rushes into the bathroom, and vomits.

"What's wrong?" I say, getting up to follow him. But he shuts the half-opened door and mumbles he'll be out in a minute. He tells me to go downstairs and make expressos for both of us. Ten minutes later, he comes into the kitchen dressed, sits down, and sips his coffee. The blood seems to have drained from his face.

"The magic of our connection returned last night," he says with a thin smile. "Sorry, I'm just a little nauseous this morning. Nothing to be concerned about."

"What's going on, Dario? You would tell me if something's going on, wouldn't you?"

"Yes."

"You don't look well. Please say it isn't Covid or HIV. You wouldn't keep something like that from me, would you?"

"Of course not," he says, finishing his coffee and standing up.

We spend the day relaxing and his strength returns.

In the weeks that follow, something feels different. Without a word, and often before I'm even awake, Dario disappears to work on his commission. I never intrude, and he doesn't invite me down. When he emerges, we spend late afternoons on the wide terrace, lying next to each other on lounge chairs. Sometimes, he seems curious about the sketches I've done during the day and wants to see them. Other days—and oddly, when I tell him I'm really pleased with a sketch—he shows no interest at all.

On a particularly clear and lovely afternoon in early May, we watch a flock of starlings change shape over the distant cities.

"It's called *murmuration*," I say, without Dario having asked.

"Why do they do it?"

"For safety. The flocking protects the birds inside, with the inside and outside birds changing places."

"It's like a conjuring. A secret message."

"Could be."

A distant church bell peals, echoed by another. A warm breeze rustles the garden..

"Mark?"

"Yes."

"What are your dreams? Where would you like your life to go from here?"

I squirm. I'm not in the mood to speculate about the rest of my life. "I'm not sure..." I begin. I look at him looking at me, then watch the starlings. "I've enjoyed teaching, but I'm not sure how much it matters anymore. The world is changing, and I'm trying to figure out how to change with it."

"So true."

"I'd like to convince my family to be happier, independent of what I do or don't do. I guess the only way for that to happen is to just keep doing what I'm doing."

"So wise."

"And I want to write down all that's happened over the past few years to remind myself who I was when I'm no longer who I am. In case anyone is interested after I'm gone."

A chill goes through me. My voice, what I've said, reminds me of my father's letter.

"I like your answers," Dario says softly. "But tell me, does Dario Soole fit into any of this?"

"If you'd like."

"I see," he says, sounding not entirely convinced.

I make a frittata for supper, and we sit in the dim light of the kitchen, watch Trixie scratch herself against the edge of the pantry door. Dario surprises me with a bowl of black figs soaked in rum and *mascarpone* cheese for dessert.

"I hope my answers to your question didn't upset you," I say as we lie in bed together that night, he in his shirt.

"Not really, sweetheart. I appreciate your honesty."

"I do feel safe with you right now."

"I'm glad, but I wouldn't dare wish that you stay with me forever."

I say nothing and turn my head to kiss him. He shifts to his side and runs his hand gently over me, his voice a low whisper in my ear. *"This is your chest—but who will lie on it?"* He squirrels his hand down to my groin. *"This is your cock—where will it go?"* He slides his hand up and over my breastbone. *"This is your heart— who will cherish it?"* Then, he removes his hand and rolls on his back. *"I shall never know."*

13

A Black Dog

Dario continues his long mornings of painting that now stretch into the afternoons. Soon, an entire day passes before he comes upstairs, and then several days go by when I don't see him at all—that is, until he tumbles into bed, waking me. I notice he's sleeping poorly and sometimes gets up in the dead of night to go back to his studio, emerging at daybreak looking exhausted. I nickname him "Nosferatu." He counters with a rambling lecture about cultivating patience; that when the demon angel calls, the devoted artist drops everything and follows it to a reward, in this case, Sylvano's commission. "Can I at least see your progress?" I ask, but Dario's response is to walk away, so I stop asking.

It's been a month and a half since I left Jim in Los Angeles. During this first week of May, Dario's garden blooms riotously, and chittering birds make their roosts in the chinks of the villa's walls. Our lovemaking, while still frequent, begins to change. Dario lately prefers it rough. What was once an erotically tender *quid pro quo* becomes a take-down match. Still, romantic moments survive, more so early in the morning than at night. Now and then, I sense a wistfulness in Dario, as if he wants to recapture our happy afternoons of casual nudity at Plaza de Chueca, but he seems on edge and still refuses to remove his long-sleeved shirt. This shirt thing begins to get on my nerves. One morning, hearing me in the shower, he got out of bed to join me under the spray *in his fucking shirt.* I said nothing, closed my eyes and let him use the soap creatively.

When I'm alone on long afternoons, I busy myself unfolding and taping together cardboard boxes. Dario's attention to packing his belongings has evaporated. Every day, I point out the latest stack I've put together for him, but the boxes remain empty. When I'm not taping, I scroll around on my phone. One morning, I notice a *WhatsApp* notification from Jim sent the night before, but the message text was deleted. Marina also calls, twice, leaving no voicemails. I message her to ask for an update on Alessandro, but she doesn't reply.

I'm beginning to feel isolated here at Villa dei Giardini and wonder where this strangeness with Dario will lead. I consider that maybe the pandemic didn't so much interrupt as simply end whatever future I might've had with Dario. I wonder how much time it'll take me to figure that out.

By the middle of May, Dario notices my restlessness and allows me to drive the Fiat for short runs to the *supermercato* to buy groceries for dinner each night. Dario's crazy schedule doesn't accommodate going out anymore, so I learn to enjoy these almost daily trips, chatting with the grocers, buying chunks of cheese, bunches of garlic, and sheets of sliced meats. I sometimes take the long way back to the villa, growing more comfortable with the car on the larger roads with their roundabouts and cryptic signage. I even brave the autostrada, a surprisingly easy and pleasant drive compared to the 110 Freeway in Los Angeles.

I'm about to set out one late afternoon and get as far as the kitchen door when I stop—*him again*, the hoodlum with crewcut and tattoos, lurking on the patio. This time, I shout through the locked grate.

"What are you doing here? Leave the property or I'll call the police!"

I get a good look at him now—a rough character with a leering smile, just a few teeth behind it.

"*Bring daht black dog Dario out here, I need to have a talking with him,*" he says, arms straight down and clenched fists at the ends of them. He says it bending towards me, his body in the shape of a gun.

"Get out of here—*vai, subito*—or I call the police." I repeat the word loudly and slowly, "The p-o-l-i-c-e."

He thrusts one arm up and slaps its bicep with the hand of his other arm, a gesture of *up yours*. Then, he picks up one of Dario's brightly glazed pots, holds it above his head, and smashes it to the ground. Trixie comes galloping down the stairs, barking wildly, and lunges against the door so violently that the latch gives way and the door swings open. I cry out to her, but she sets off after the man and nips his heels until he kicks her hard before leaping down the terrace stairs and vanishing. Trixie turns, limp-tailed, and walks back to me just as Dario comes down from the bedroom, naked from the waist down.

"What's going on?"

"Your crazy friend Jabari came back. I chased him off, but he smashed one of your pieces."

Dario glances through the door. "Oh, dear. My yellow oxide. Such a brute."

"Trixie got away and went after him. He kicked her pretty hard."

"My poor girl!" he says, stooping down to examine her. She returns a mild wag. "She's fine."

"What's this all about, Dario?"

"I haven't settled with Jabari. I'll call him and drive downtown to pay."

"This is the guy who worked for you and lived in your house? Someone who comes over and breaks your stuff?"

"Well, I suppose he's quite upset with me."

"About what?"

"About you."

I'm stunned. "Oh, *fuck!* Now I have a jealous ex-boyfriend to deal with. Why didn't you level with me?"

"No matter."

"How much do you owe?"

"About eighty euros. To him, a fortune."

"Do you need the money?"

"Of course not. I'll shower and go see him. Dinner would be nice when I return if you can manage it."

"Should I come with you?"

"I said, dinner would be nice—"

"Yes, yes! All right. Just keep this guy away from here!"

Dario takes the car and disappears for a long time. Without the car, I look through his kitchen cupboards and make do with what's there. I find three waxed cartons of chicken soup, a bag of tricolor pasta, and a half loaf of bread. I also discover a box of what I assume, after some difficulty, is chocolate cake mix and perform the miracle of baking in his sixty-year-old oven. Finally, a bottle of prosecco lurks in the corner, so I tuck it into the refrigerator.

I put everything together and wait for him—this day being May 18th, my birthday, which I'd mentioned to Dario several times throughout the week. Two hours later, Trixie whines and looks up at me hungrily with her runny brown eyes, but I don't remember where Dario keeps her dog food, so I spoon her a plate of soup. By nine o'clock, I'm worried. I wish I knew someone to call. At around ten, the Fiat putters outside. Dario walks through the door with an odd, vacant expression on his face.

"All settled," he says cheerlessly.

"Sit down and we'll eat," I say. "I won't ask what happened tonight."

"I want to take a short trip, Mark. Maybe to Bevagna to visit Sylvano and Rhoda at home, my patrons we dined with when you first arrived. I need a break from all this."

"From all what?"

"The stress of taking on Sylvano's very challenging commission."

"Of course. Eat."

He sits down and eats with gusto. "Have some bread," I say. "It's still fresh."

"Good god, I'm living with an Italian mamma," he grumbles, only half to himself.

"Sorry," I say softly, after which I say nothing and watch him eat. Finally: "Did you remember that today is my birthday? I made a chocolate cake and found some prosecco. Would you like to celebrate with me?"

He glances up, his spoon poised. "Oh dear. I'm sure I had that written down somewhere."

"It's not important," I say.

"I'll pass on the cake and prosecco, thanks, but Happy Birthday."

"It's hard to believe that I'm thirty-eight as of eleven-fifteen this evening, accounting for the time difference."

"Consider yourself fortunate," Dario says. "If we were in China, you would've turned thirty-eight on New Year's Day, February 10th, regardless of your birth month." He places his hand over my wrist. "You're still a sweet and adorable child."

In bed, I pull down the coverlet and offer a massage to relax him. He lays on his belly and allows me to pull his T-shirt to the top of his back. Progress.

"When do you want to go to Bevagna?" I ask, "In a week or so?"

"Yes. That gives me time to finish my commission within the three-month deadline and deliver it to Sylvano. I'll ask him to wire me an advance tomorrow. He'll give us the balance when we visit."

"I'll gladly give you eighty euros, Dario."

"No, no, that's been taken care of," he says, rolling onto his side and pulling my arm around him. "But you're sweet to offer."

That night, as usual, he's up and gone. The next day, he sleeps. This graveyard shift routine persists, and I don't expect to see much of Dario until the very end of the week. But on Friday morning, May 20th, the quiet house is interrupted by a gentle tapping on the grate over the kitchen door.

"Scusi? Dario? Hello? *È Jabari."*

I enter the kitchen to see a slight, olive-skinned man with curly black hair holding a loaf of bread. He flashes a friendly smile.

"Oh, hello, Signore. You must be the Mister Marco from California. I have a gift from my mother to Dario. I am his friend Jabari from Cairo. How do you do?"

I take the bread and tell Jabari that Dario isn't feeling well. He lingers, and we exchange pleasantries as I try to hide the shock of finally meeting Jabari, who's not the tattoo-covered intruder whom I now fear even more.

Dario comes down a few hours later to say that he's not very hungry and won't have dinner. He steps into the kitchen for a moment and notices the bread.

"Ah, you went to the market?"

"Yes, we're out of bread."

"Very good, mamma," he says, tearing a piece from the loaf and returning upstairs.

That night, he's unusually restless and even cries out once in his sleep. I try to comfort myself by putting my hand around his body, but he jumps away and wrestles with the pillow before settling down again. Hours later in the pitch dark, I pat the mattress beside me to find him gone.

This time, I've had enough. I slide from bed and walk to the guest room window, where I see light spilling from the studio below. Tonight, I'll pay Dario a visit. I walk across the kitchen, open the door to the stairway, and step down towards the blazing light of his studio. When I reach the bottom, I nudge the folded wall aside and see a completely naked Dario, his back to me, twisting grotesquely before a large canvas that he slashes with paint. He jumps to a second canvas, turns it sideways, stabs it with a brush. He leaps to a third canvas, flips it over to its *unfinished side,* and smears paint with his hands. He talks, sings and laughs to himself, throwing both arms above his head in a little dance—a scene so bizarre that I start to back away. But he hears me, turns around wild-eyed, paint brushes in his fists and a canvas knife in his mouth. His chest, arms, and belly are completely covered in colored pigments, although his face is clean. He spits the knife from his mouth, drops the brushes, and approaches. His prick is painted red and fully erect. He grabs it to draw my attention.

"Mark!" he sings in a warbling trill, "Welcome to the *Garden of Earthly Delights!* Tonight, Dionysus and Jesus wrestle for my soul—and Buddha sucks my cock! Come drink from my holy pipe and save me!"

I'm scared shitless, offer a ridiculous little wave, and back my way up the stairs. As I reach the kitchen, I hear a crash outside and peer through the grate to see another of Dario's magnificent ceramic pots smashed, this one right in front of the door. Something wedged in the rubble juts out, a piece of cardboard with some crude writing on it.

I force open the door and bring the cardboard inside, examine its ominous-looking warning scrawled in an Italian dialect I can't decipher—except for a few words: *droghe, dovuto,* and *per l'eroina*—"drugs," "owed," and "for the heroine."

I take the message to Dario's bedroom and place it, face down, on his dresser next to a decorative apothecary jar. Then, I steel myself, go back downstairs to make coffee, and wait for daybreak.

Dario appears wearing his sleeved T-shirt inside out and stumbles through the kitchen, pressing his hands against the wall for balance. I intercept and guide him up the stairs to his bedroom. He's cleaned much of the paint from his lower body, but he won't remove his shirt, so I strip the sheets from the bed and ease him down to the bare mattress. I leave the door open and sit in the guest room.

After a few moments, I hear the shower running. Then, suddenly, a crash. I race to the bathroom to find Dario collapsed, crumpled nude in the shower stall. The hot water runs over him, melting much of the remaining paint away, and now I can see them: the tracks and jabs and scars and ruptured veins, all in an ugly purple tangle covering both arms. I lift his body and notice deep punctures between his toes and below his ankle bones. He begs me to take him to bed, where he pulls me close and points towards his dresser at the apothecary jar, the one where I'd placed the cardboard message earlier. When I approach with the jar, he grabs it from me, struggles, then gestures for me to open it. His fingers tremble as he removes a syringe and vial, a thick rubber tourniquet, and cotton swabs. He fills the syringe then uses his teeth to knot the rubber around his forearm. He jabs a crusted needle not once, but three times into an old puncture so that it bleeds and oozes while the heroine empties into him. A calm comes over his face as the drug races through his body and brain.

He opens his eyes to look at me with a soporific smile. "My angel," he mumbles.

"Fucking hell, Dario—I knew something was wrong, but never *this*."

"I love you."

"Shut up."

"But I do..."

"How much money do they want?"

"More than you have."

"Tell me."

He scrunches his face in concentration. "Fifteen thousand euros. By next Saturday."

"That's May 28th. We have time,"

"I asked him for a few extra days." He looks away and struggles to say it: "Yazid agreed but demanded a favor." Looks at me again, "The beast with the tattoos."

"A favor?"

He turns his head to the side to avoid looking at me, "I had to let him..."

I wait. "So now you're a *whore?*"

"Please, Mark," he whimpers, the tears rolling across his face.

"No wonder you didn't want cake on my birthday."

"Please..." he says, now in full blubber.

I take a moment, wipe his face. "How much do you have in your account? What's left of that sixty thousand you made in Madrid?"

He composes himself, turns to me, and blinks hard several times.

"Your account, Dario?"

The words come slowly. "It's an expensive recreation, sweetheart, and it's gone on for years."

"Jesus."

"Please, let me sleep a little. I'll call Sylvano later and ask him to wire a three thousand advance into my account on Monday. We'll collect the balance later in the week when we deliver his painting—how about Thursday? That gives us time to put together all the cash we need for Yazid's lovely visit."

"What's the total amount Sylvano owes?"

"Ten thousand euros."

"So, with Sylvano's advance and the seven thousand you'll collect from him when you deliver the painting, you'll still be short five thousand euros, won't you?"

"Yes, I suppose."

"You *suppose?* Do the fucking math!" I close my eyes and take a deep breath. "Okay. I'll transfer five thousand dollars from my account in the States into your account here to cover you. Let's get these gangsters off your back. When you feel better, look on your dresser and read the friendly note they left outside your door this morning. I couldn't understand it."

"All right. Let me sleep."

"Not until you tell me what happens when this shit wears off."

He strokes my arm. "I have my familiar little blue pills to bring me round, my Adderalls. I got them from—" he waves his hand, "No matter."

I look away from him. "Right. Your phony vitamins".

"Let me sleep, Mark. Please. Just let me sleep."

I leave him to go downstairs. Three hours later, he appears more himself.

"Sylvano's wiring three thousand euros first thing Monday, and the money will be in my account before noon. He's excited that we'll deliver his painting next week. Thank God I finished it. Now, it can dry for a few days before I wrap it."

I reheat some soup for dinner, but Dario tells me he can't keep food down. Night comes quickly, and we lie beside each other in the dark. Trixie creeps into the room and comes up to the bed. She looks at Dario with sad, puzzled eyes. He reaches out to scratch behind her ears. Satisfied, she settles down in her favorite corner.

"My sweetest girl, Trixie. My beautiful black girl with the sad eyes," Dario whispers. Looks at me, "My beautiful white man with even sadder eyes."

"How did this start, Dario?"

"How does anything start?"

"Were you using in Spain when we first met?"

"Not the hard stuff. My addies, mostly. They gave me the energy I needed to work."

"Where did you get them?"

He shifts away, his bare leg no longer against mine. "I really don't want to go into all that now. Covid made it much worse. The isolation. Then Jabari came with his hashish and kept me company. It passed the time." He turns his head to me. "I wouldn't blame you if you hated me and wanted to leave. But you were the answer, I thought, when we were together in Madrid, as I thought I was the answer for you... but it seemed all of that had ended, despite our telephonic flirtations."

Sunday morning, we shower together. I take each of his bruised arms in my hands and soap them gently. He winces in pain. The suds turn pink with blood. "Can I rest assured you've been tested for HIV?" I ask.

"Yes, a week before you came to Poreta. Negative." He takes me by the shoulders and turns me to face him. Water streams over us, curls of grey hair droop against his forehead. "There's been no one else, Mark. Only you. I've waited over two years."

Two bathrobes hang beside the shower, and we each take one. Dario has me sit on the bed and places a chair directly in front of me. He stands before me looking vaguely excited, folds his arms.

"Well, are you ready?"

"Ready for what?"

He goes to his closet and pulls out a large rectangular object wrapped in brown butcher paper.

"Do you remember our phone call when I invited you to visit and told you I had a surprise?"

"Yes."

"Well, here's the surprise, inspired by that sketch I did of your lovely body in Madrid." He lifts the object to the seat of the chair, unwraps the butcher paper, and jerks it away with a flourish. A portrait. I recognize myself against the moonlit window in Dario's hotel room in Vallecas. But now I'm rendered in rich, painterly colors, my body luminous, my eyes looking straight out of the canvas as if searching for anyone who might be searching for me. I'm also strewn with flowers, a cluster of them covering my privates.

Dario beams. "I've titled it, 'Mark with Moonlight in Window.'" He flashes a broad smile at me and looks like he wants me to say something. "Do you like it? Maybe it sounds better in Spanish, but I don't how to say that."

"You've sprinkled me with flowers?"

"Yes, you were a little shy, as I remember. But also because you read Boccaccio's flower poem so beautifully that day in the park. I wanted to add a visual reminder of what was a very tender moment between us—at least for me."

"I like it, Dario. It's more in the style of your earlier work, the stuff you showed me in your hotel room that night."

He pulls me over to him. "A nice surprise, then, yes?"

"Yes."

"My gift to you. Am I foolish to hope it hangs in Italy rather than California?"

I don't answer.

"Well, at least I didn't hear *no*," he says as he rewraps the painting and puts it back in his closet.

On Sunday evening, we go over our plan to visit Sylvano on Thursday and how to ensure things go smoothly when Dario's dealers arrive on Saturday. I learn that Yazid and his goons will appear at the villa at 3 p.m. expecting their cash. Dario tells me he keeps five hundred euros hidden in the house for an emergency and suggests that the emergency, in this case, may be another fix to get him through the week. I tell him that *this will not happen* and that the extra cash will cover any unexpected complications, like a fluctuating currency rate between euros and American dollars that could short us.

I ask Dario if he can contact these people to make an early drop-off somewhere and keep them away from the house.

"No, Mark," he says. "You don't contact these people. They come to you."

Dario sleeps in on Monday. When he's finally up and dressed, we rush to the bank for the wiring information my bank needs to expedite the emergency transfer. As we stand at the service window with Dario translating, I learn that five thousand dollars is the maximum amount that can be transferred within a twenty-four hour period to discourage money laundering. I also learn that it takes up to twelve hours for the transfer to complete after it's initiated at the source end. The *cassiere di banca,* or bank teller, reminds me that it's the middle of the night in California, too early for his bank to contact my bank, and that I must initiate the transfer from an American bank when it opens by faxing paperwork that an Italian bank requires—including a copy of my passport—paperwork that he, the *cassiere*, will request from his *direttore,* or manager, when the manager returns from his pastry and expresso break.

We find lunch and wait for the direttore. Dario seems edgy, but at least he's communicative. The Adderalls, he tells me, make the heroine cravings manageable, at least for a week.

"Fine, but you're going to the hospital when this is over," I say.

He looks down. "I can see that you despise me."

"I wouldn't be here if I despised you."

"You never expected this, and now you're stuck."

"I'll help you work this out. Beyond that, I don't know." I take his hand and hold it for a moment. "But I'm here to help you work this out."

We return to the bank and pick up the required paperwork from the manager, who, for some reason, shakes my hand. Dario asks a favor. If I complete the paperwork within the hour, will the manager fax it to California before closing? The manager agrees and asks for my passport so he can make a copy of my photo to include with the fax. He shows us to a small desk, where I begin deciphering this complicated form that requires long strings of numbers penciled into little squares.

Forty minutes later, I'm finished and push the paperwork through the teller window. The manager now reminds me that, because of the great time difference between Italy and California, I shouldn't expect the cash to appear in Dario's account until late Tuesday or even Wednesday and that any additional requests for cash must wait twenty-four hours after the arrival of the first request. None of this information cheers us.

"We're cutting it very close," I say as we drive home.

"Don't worry, sweetheart," Dario says, "We'll make it."

Dario's tremors increase Monday night but vanish towards morning. As the sky lightens, we touch each other softly, explore the warm and secret places of each other's body. Mild arousals come and go. Lying on our backs, I take Dario's hand in mine and fall asleep.

We wake up close to noon, Tuesday. Dario phones the bank to confirm that Sylvano's advance has arrived, but my transfer is still pending. The cassiere consults his computer to check the initiation-to-delivery timeline and predicts the transfer will arrive later that afternoon and clear for withdrawal by Wednesday morning. But on Wednesday afternoon, it still hasn't arrived, and the cassiere reminds us that Thursday is a bank holiday, so we'll have to wait until Friday. To complicate matters, Sylvano phones Dario to say that he and Rhoda will be out of town Thursday and Friday and asks Dario to deliver the painting early Saturday—the same day of our three o'clock deadline in what has now become a nerve-wracking fiasco.

We race back to the bank early Friday. The direttore greets us and stands before a computer. He confirms that five thousand American dollars have been transferred into Dario's account, but with the exchange rate being what it is, and the reduction of twenty-five euros for the transfer fee, only £4,668 euros may be withdrawn as cash. We're short 332 euros. For that, we'll use Dario's emergency money.

Several more forms have to be filled out to make the large withdrawal before the direttore wraps the cash in bundles and places it in a zipper bag. It's clear that he regrets so large a withdrawal from his small bank, but he's gentlemanly about it. I'm pretty sure he sniffs something shady in the whole affair, but we've played by the rules, and he doesn't ask questions.

Back in the villa, Dario goes downstairs to his studio and calls up for me to join him. He's finished wrapping Sylvano's large painting in butcher paper and twine, so not an inch of it shows. We carry it up to the kitchen and lean it against the door. On Saturday, we'll carry the painting to the Fiat and slide it into back seat area, where it just fits.

Dario looks drawn; tells me the stress of the week has brought on the agitation of withdrawal. He goes to bed early while I linger downstairs to make some phone calls. Over the past two weeks, three messages from Jim appeared, then disappeared moments after he sent them. I wonder why he's ghosting me like this, so I check the local time: early morning there. I tap in his number and he answers on the first ring.

"So, how's it going, Marco Polo? It's been almost three months. I thought maybe you fell into Vesuvius."

"We're nowhere near it," I say.

"Montaña Pico?" He tries again.

"No, that's in Portugal."

"I never was any good at geography. So, where the hell are you?"

"Still in Poreta with Dario."

"Enjoying your honeymoon?"

"Jim..."

"Mark."

"I apologize for not calling," I say.

"I apologize for sending messages I deleted," he answers.

"Yeah, what was that all about?"

"Wouldn't you like to know." He takes a breath. "Just, to say I missed you."

"You deleted *that*?"

"Wasn't sure you wanted to hear it. It's been a while. I thought maybe you were cooking rotini for some Italian porn star now."

"Nope."

"Good. You're turning me on. Can I touch myself?"

"Hold off a bit."

"Not gonna happen, dude."

"Anyway, Jim... I've missed you, too."

"Anyway, Mark, I've also missed you, too."

"Lots of drama in *Bella Italia* this time around."

"What did you expect in the land of Verdi and Lucrezia Borgia?"

"Tell me about it."

"Come back. It's time." Jim says it softly.

"I will. Being far away for so long makes me miss our crummy neighborhood."

"Isn't that a quote from 'The Wizard of Oz?'"

"There's no place like home," I play along.

"Not so fast, I want to be far away with you. I haven't seen shit."

"Good. We'll fix that."

"I've got you on record."

"All right."

"So, get your ass back here so we can plan a trip, scout meteorites, and discuss classic literature. Naked."

"Always the jokester."

"Maybe even schedule a romantic getaway for a booster shot. You in?"

"Bye."

"Wait. Seriously."

"Waiting."

"I miss you, Mark. For real. There it is, no deletion."

"Same here."

"And I'm not giving up talking to you about an opportunity here I think is perfect for you."

"Okay," I say. "Later."

We blink off, and I sit back to savor the afterglow of our conversation. Then, I turn out the light and creep upstairs in the dark. Standing in the hallway, I suddenly feel a strange uneasiness that I think began when Dario revealed his beautiful portrait of me. Without quite knowing what I'm doing or why I'm doing it, I slip into a snoring Dario's bedroom, open his closet, and remove the wrapped portrait. I take it down to the kitchen, find the keys to the Fiat, and place the portrait into the trunk, where it easily fits and can't be seen. That night, I sleep in the guest room.

Saturday morning, Dario comes down in a long-sleeved shirt, freshly showered. We skip breakfast to get an early start to Bevagna. Dario asks why I didn't join him in bed, and I tell him that, considering the importance of the day, I thought we'd sleep more soundly apart. Dario fills Trixie's water bowl and leaves biscuits scattered about the house to keep her busy. She knows we'll be gone for a while and isn't happy. He lifts her head to his face and gives her a big kiss before we climb into the Fiat.

He's still shaking a bit, so asks me to take the wheel. For thirty minutes, we wind south through the valley along a narrow road before we turn onto the autostrada for the rest of the journey. An hour later, we enter the commune of Bevagna, with its medieval castle and surrounding suburbs. We turn into the stone driveway of Sylvano and Rhoda's sleek modern house just as Rhoda looks up from her garden. She sees us, smiles, and wipes her hands on her apron.

"Such a lovely morning!" she calls out and walks to us.

"Hello, dearest," Dario returns. "The garden thrives with your ministrations. What have you got there?"

"Ah, these," she chirps, offering her cheek to each of us. "These are white mulberries." She lifts a few of the yellow fruits from the pocket of her apron and invites us to taste them. "The unexpected bounty of a rogue volunteer that would not surrender to pruning."

"Scrumptious!" Dario gushes.

"Aren't they?" Rhoda says. "The rogue now rewards me for sparing its life. We'll have a tart for breakfast."

Dario motions for me to help him remove the large, wrapped canvas from the back seat. "We have your commissioned painting, as promised."

"We're delighted, especially Sylvano. He's cleared several walls for it. You'll help him decide."

We enter the house, and Sylvano emerges from the kitchen barefoot and shirtless, wearing baggy slacks. He's a large man, but nicely built. "Greetings, friends!" he says, as we stumble into the living room with the painting, "So huge it is! I'd forgotten! Just lean there against the wall for now and come sit."

We place the wrapped painting against a wall directly opposite the table.

"You're looking quite healthy, Sylvano," Dario observes. "You enjoyed your little trip?"

"For god's sake, Sylvano," says Rhoda, "Put something on. Nobody wants to see what you look like when you get out of bed."

Dario looks at me, then looks, in turn, at Rhoda and Sylvano. "We have no problem with it," he shrugs.

Sylvano gives us the thumbs-up and answers Dario's question. "Yes, we took a drive to Florence to see some friends of Rhoda's who are well-connected in the field of textile design."

Rhoda adds, "My dear friend Lucia's obsession is architecture." She places cappuccinos and a tray of mulberry pastries before us. "Her patterns feature the black and white stonework of *Santa Maria del Fiore*. She's also put together some accessory designs inspired by its famous porthole."

We enjoy our breakfast quietly. Sylvano and Rhoda look at each other affectionately. Sylvano smiles. "Ah, married life," he says. "When Rhoda studied figure drawing in San Severino, she enjoyed sketching me in all my glory as well as the other beautiful men. Now I bore her."

"So untrue," Rhoda says, sipping her cappuccino.

Comfortable and relaxed, the morning passes as we enjoy our *colazione* in the large room's ample light and exchange more stories and gossip. But, I watch the time. Sylvano notices me glance at my watch.

"Are you in a hurry, friends? Is there anything else we can do for you?"

"No," says Dario. "You've been too kind."

"Then, shall we see what you've created for us?" Sylvano repositions his chair as Rhoda finishes clearing the plates.

"We shall," says Dario, walking to the wrapped painting and waving me to help him.

We lift the canvas and bring it closer, directly opposite Sylvano and the now-seated, Rhoda. I hold the canvas upright as Dario unfastens the twine, then pulls away the thick butcher paper with a flourish. I'm standing beside the painting, so I can't see what it looks like; I see only the expression on Sylvano's face.

"Dario. What is this?"

"The work I've made for you," Dario effuses, a trace of strain in his voice. "What you've paid me to create."

"No. This is not..." Sylvano turns to Rhoda. Silence.

"Dario," she says, folding her hands, "This is not at all what we expected. We loved your other work—your slides, what hangs in your home, some of the canvases in your studio."

"But this is bold and fresh!" Dario announces. "A completely new direction for me. You're the first to experience it!"

I begin to feel uncomfortable, so I shift the weight of the painting to Dario and walk around to see it. It's the same canvas Dario slashed and stabbed and buried in thick blobs of enamel the night of his hallucinatory collapse—a dreary, bloody mess. *Oh my god,* I mutter to myself.

"I can't accept this from you, my friend," Sylvano says, getting up. "No, this is unsatisfactory. I trusted, from our consultation over dinner, that you clearly understood what I wanted based on what we'd seen of your work."

"But, Sylvano... *Signore...*" The color drains from Dario's face.

Sylvano approaches, his voice rising. "You should not have experimented without informing me. You should've invited me to see the progress of my commission so I could correct you before it was too late."

"Does that mean—"

"No! I will not pay for this terrible, ugly painting. It even frightens me. What's come over you?"

"Sylvano..." Rhoda begins in a conciliatory tone, but says no more.

"But you must pay me! You *must!*—" Dario starts to shake.

"Dario, calm down!" I whisper.

Sylvano's eruption subsides, replaced by an expression of pity and weariness. "Dario, I leave you the three thousand euros advance as payment for your effort. But this—this disturbing mess—I do not want in our home."

Dario stands, releasing the painting, which crashes, finished side down, to the floor. He lowers his head. I can see that he's crying.

I walk towards the couple and spread my arms to them in surrender. They glance at me, offer a brief smile, then look away.

"Sylvano. Rhoda. Dario has misjudged and I'm partly to blame. I turned down his invitations to view the painting's progress because I was too busy with my own concerns."

"Don't blame yourself, Mark," Rhoda offers.

I feel around in my pocket for the keys to the Fiat. "We'll make good. Dario will either repair this work to your liking or create something entirely new. You have our promise."

Sylvano looks at me, folds his arms. "Why should I pay for something I haven't seen when I'm disappointed in what I've seen already?"

"Maybe there's another alternative," I say. "Give me a minute." I walk out the front door to the driveway, open the trunk of the Fiat, and remove Dario's wrapped portrait of me.

"What are you doing?" Dario says when I return and place the canvas on its edge before his customers. "No, Mark—" he says, beginning to understand, *"You can't—"*

But I *can*. I untie the twine and unwrap the portrait. In the bright light of the room, the colors erupt, and the painting comes to life.

"Oh! Rhoda exclaims, "Now, that's something. Is it you?"

"Yes, in Madrid."

"It is—" she looks at her husband, "Quite stunning."

"A gift from Dario to me, and now I offer it to you."

"Of course." Sylvano huffs. "For how much?"

"As I said, Dario's gift to me, and now my gift to you—"

"Gift?"

"Yes, that is, if you agree to pay Dario the balance of the commission with the understanding that he'll either rework the original painting to your liking or do something entirely new. And this includes a promise that he'll share his progress at all stages of execution."

Dario, his face still wet, looks up and manages a weak smile. "Mark is my most excellent new agent. As you can see, I badly need one."

"This is satisfactory for us," Rhoda says, looking at her husband, who returns a brusque nod. She turns to Dario and smiles. "I'm very sorry for all of this distress. But you've both made good with the gift of this masterpiece. Truly. I've never seen such a tender, loving depiction of a man by another man. So many layers. Such sensuality and mystery and sadness. The colors and composition remind me of Gauguin's Tahitian portraits. What have you named it, Dario?"

He brightens up. "Mark with Moonlight in Window."

"Better in French, I think: *Marc avec la Lune à la Fenêtre.*"

"Very classy, Rhoda," I say.

"Yes, it suits."

"Since the banks are closed today. Is it possible for you to pay us cash?" I say it plainly to disguise how tightly my stomach knots.

"Ah," says Sylvano, "A good agent indeed."

He returns from another room with a packet of wrapped bills. Then, with light hugs and perfunctory kisses, they bid us a warm but cordial goodbye.

We're covered in sweat as we bump down this hill in the Fiat. The sky is flat, white, and featureless.

"Jesus, it's nearly one o'clock," I say. "Do we have everything?"

"Yes," Dario says, his hands shaking. "I put the cash into the bank bag with your deposit. It's in the glove compartment. There's also the house money in there to cover any shortages and whatever else may come up, as you said. But I'm scared."

"So am I."

"I'm scared at what might come down. You don't know these people."

"Don't think about it. We wait for them. Give them their money. They count it and they go. Maybe they smash something on the way out. Good fucking riddance."

"Three o'clock deadline," Dario says. He says it again. Then again, asking me if I heard him the first two times.

"It'll be over soon, Dario."

The autostrada slows soon after we join it. Then, traffic stops altogether.

"Holiday travelers," I say.

"Three o'clock," he repeats.

By two o'clock, we've hardy moved. Smoke billows over the autostrada some distance away. An accident.

"Is there a way I can get off and around this, Dario?"

"Don't you think everybody would be doing that? We're goddamn *stuck*, Mark!"

It's nearly two-thirty before the traffic loosens up, and we crawl past a mangled truck, charred to cinders. Six blue cars containing *Polizia Stradale* surround it.

Dario begins to shake violently. He's slick with sweat, talks rapidly. "You don't know these people, Mark. You don't know what they'll do if they don't find us there. You don't—"

"Stop it, Dario. They're stupid thugs who just want their money."

"Yes, but they're also very evil men. You don't know them, Mark. This morning, I read everything they wrote on the cardboard you left in my room. I understood the horrible words that you couldn't understand."

"What words?"

"Words like *blood* and *pain* and *burn*. Words like *torture*. And then these words: *A black dog dies with a black dog.*"

"Meaning?"

"A Sicilian proverb."

"Meaning?"

"Think about it. I'm a black dog to them. Who's the other?"

A chill moves up my spine. "Trixie."

"They tell me what they'll do to Trixie. They are very sick men, Mark."

I roar ahead, now exceeding the speed limit, but it's clear that we won't be back at the villa by 3 p.m.

"Is there any way you can reach somebody, Dario? That tattooed Moroccan guy on your terrace?"

"Yazid."

"That's his name?"

"He works for an Albanian branch of the Mafia that operates out of Foligno."

"Can you get a message to him?"

"I told you that you don't contact these people," he says, picking up his phone all the same.

Shaking, he punches in some numbers, swearing as he misdials.

"Dario—" I begin.

He waves me quiet, cups the phone. "Ciao, Niccola! *Stai bene?*"

His voice is strained and overloud. I listen and soon figure out that he's talking to the Niccola we had dinner with a few weeks ago. I understand little, but I hear the name *Yazid* over and over as if each half of the conversation strains to establish some important connection.

After a minute of this, some mutual recognition seems to occur, and Dario's voice loses its tone of alarm. Something said on the other side seems to calm him.

He ends the call and looks at me. "Niccola says he'll try."

"Niccola Risto, the philosophy professor?"

"The same."

"He'll try what?"

"He has connections to these people. I didn't want to mention this to you when we met for dinner, although it seemed he was about to."

Dario goes on to explain that Niccola, for all his decrying of capitalist corruption, has managed to climb the ranks in the underworld of drug trafficking and is now quite the kingpin. Through Dario's desperate description, Niccola eventually recognized Yazid as one of the low-level henchmen in the Albanian distribution cell. Niccola knows Yazid's boss and how to reach him. He'll ask for more time.

"How much more time?"

"He'll call soon and tell me."

It's now 2:45 p.m. The phone rings and Dario fumbles to answer it, dropping the phone and missing the call. "Fuck!" he screams and pounds the dashboard.

The phone rings again. This time, he connects.

"*Si... si...*" he says, and "*Grazie mille.*" He disconnects and takes a deep breath. "We have until 3:30 p.m. "After that, nothing is guaranteed."

"We'll make it," I assure him.

We turn towards Poreta and descend into the valley.

"You and your friends are full of surprises, Dario."

"Niccola tried to talk me out of getting involved with these people. But I had no choice because I was hooked on addies and they made me crazy. Heroin took the edge off and smoothed things out. All during Covid, of course."

"Shit."

"Niccola warned me about these people. But the cocktail worked. On a good day, I felt like a twenty-year-old. On a bad day, I was truly out of my mind. Eventually, the bad days took over." Dario brushes his fingers against my cheek. "Or should I say, *bad nights.*"

"Did Niccola start you on the Adderall?"

"No, it happened before. I needed something to keep me sharp so I could score some big commissions, especially the ones I was angling for in Madrid."

"Madrid. Where we met."

"Yes. My initiation into the world of amphetamines was by way of a conversation with our mutual acquaintance—" He moves his hand to my knee as if to steady my driving, "Our dear friend *Carlos Pineda.*"

We turn into the villa's driveway. Four gangly men lounge about, all smoking amid freshly smashed ceramics. They've shattered the glass of two kitchen windows and ripped the kitchen door from its hinges so that the doorway gapes open. The men toss their cigarettes and approach the Fiat even before we've shut the engine. One opens the driver-side door, grabs my arm, and pulls me out. Another grabs Dario, who loses his balance and tumbles to the ground.

The man who assaulted Dario bends down and screams into his face. "*Dove sono i nostri soldi, testa di cazzo?*" ... *Where is our money, dick-head?*

Dario struggles to his feet. "*Un momento...* Give me the bag, Mark."

I pull the bag from the glove compartment but hold it tight against my chest. "Dario, tell these guys to find Yazid. I won't give the money to anyone but Yazid."

Dario translates, but the thug laughs and grips my arm again. He drags me away from the Fiat to the edge of the terrace. One of the others shouts to him, then another, and an argument erupts and gathers heat. The thug swears, releases my arm, then pushes his battered face so close I can smell his stinking breath. He screams his answer to Dario into my face.

"*Yazid goes inside to burn alive the black dog!*"

"Get the fuck away," I say, and break from him to run through the doorway into the kitchen. I step over smashed furniture and glassware before I see Yazid, who stands, knife in hand. A blowtorch flickers beside him on the floor. Laid out next to it like a tray of surgeon's tools, more knives, a poker, a hacksaw, and duct tape. Trixie is taped to the floor, her mouth wrapped shut so tightly she struggles to breathe. A red-hot screwdriver leans against another, only inches from her eyes.

Yazid sneers, his front teeth black. Even his fingers have tattoos. He wears a bling-worthy Greek Orthodox cross around his neck. "Just in time, fag," he rasps, "now I don't have pleasure to carve up bitch dog to feed my pigs."

"I have your cash. Go outside and count it in front of the others."

"Give to me now."

"No, the others say you keep it for yourself. They say you steal from them."

The trick works. "Beh! Pieces of shit *Šiptarji* scum," he grumbles and pushes past me, waves to follow.

Outside, with all gathered around, I hand Yazid the bag and watch as he counts it, then counts it again. My eyes count it with him, and both times, he pauses when he reaches twelve thousand euros, momentarily puzzled by the additional 168 euros of house cash. He separates it out, waves it at Dario and me, and smiles. "Good. Something a little extra for my overtime," he says, tucking it under his shirt.

The others yawn, light each other's cigarettes, and scratch their groins as they mount their motorcycles. Yazid pushes the bag under his belt, climbs onto his fancy bike, and rolls over to us. He grins his rotten grin. *"Arrivederci, succhiatore di cazzi!"* he sneers, and revs up his engine. *"So long, cocksuckers!"* he shouts and roars away with his middle finger in the air.

14

Vagabond Amid Stars

The crisis over, Dario plummets into full-blown withdrawal by the first of June. He shakes all night and heaves violently, complains the sheets burn his skin, and bread tastes rotten. He soils the bed at least once a day but refuses to shower and crawls under clean linen in the guest room until I threaten to pour a bucket of cold water on him.

I scan the internet for local treatment, go down rabbit hole websites that serve up pop-up ads for health drinks and facial cremes. Finally, I ask Dario for Niccola's phone number, but he refuses to give it to me because, according to the way these things work he explains, Niccola is *not* the person to contact when a "customer" develops a medical problem. "He's a drug dealer, not a drug store," Dario rasps.

On Thursday morning, after two days of watching him suffer, I have no choice but to call Marina. It's the second day of June. Marina will probably feel slighted by my concern for Dario and apparent disregard for Alessandro, but I'll deal with that. I check the time to make sure it's the private hour when Marina is supposed to be alone and taking phone calls and I punch her in.

"*Pronto,*" she answers cheerfully.

"*Questo è Mark*, Marina. How is everything?"

"More or less the same. You are still in Poreta?"

"Yes, but first tell me about Alessandro."

"No, first tell me about you. I hear already some trouble in your voice."

"Dario is..." I begin to choke up, fumbling the phone in my hand.

"Mark, tell me! My goodness!"

"He's in a bad way, Marina. Dario got into heroin and now he's hooked, and he's run out, and he's suffering and screaming. I don't know how to help him."

"Dario is heroin addict? I can't *believe!*"

"It all started in Spain with Carlos, from what I could make of the story."

"That horrible, horrible man! You must get Dario to *ospedale* where they give the Naloxone—right away!"

"To where?"

"The *Centro di Intervento*, or 'Intervention Center' at the local hospital where they give the Naloxone injections for antidote."

"I can't get him out of bed."

"No, no. You call *ambulanza* and explain situation. They know how to do."

"How do I—"

"Here, I call for you. What is the address there?"

I stumble through the kitchen and living room throwing papers aside, looking for an addressed envelope. I find one and read aloud the incomprehensible series of letters and numbers.

"Good. I call now. You will wait outside."

"What do I pay them?"

"We don't pay for these things in Italy. I will explain to them. You let them in, and they take care of everything, okay? And do not warn Dario!"

"Thank you, Marina. I love you."

"Oh my god about Dario! Tomorrow, we speak and I tell you the news here. Too much to explain tonight. You must rest and get some sleep. I care very much for you, Mark. I do wish you happiness, Mark. You are a good man, and you deserve peace."

I wait, a nervous Trixie on her leash beside me. After ten minutes, a flashing blue light appears at the far end of the driveway, and a box-shaped ambulance approaches. Two young men in white scrubs jump out, nod to me, then go directly to work: they swing open the double doors in back and pull out a fenced stretcher with straps. Trixie stands watching them, tail between her legs. I begin to walk ahead of the paramedics thinking that I should maybe warn Dario, but they call me back and caution me to stay calm and guide them to Dario's room. One hands me a card with the name of the hospital and a paper to sign.

When we enter the bedroom, Dario turns his head to the side and screams, "OH, BLOODY HELL, MARK!" but they immediately set to work: they pull off the sheet and wrap Dario in a hospital gown, slide up the stretcher fence to keep him from rolling out. One of them leans down and says something to Dario, who shakes his head "no." Satisfied, they leave him unstrapped as they lift the stretcher and carry him away. I sign the paper and follow them to the back of the ambulance, where they hook Dario up to an I-V. The cuter of the two—pale blue eyes—looks at me and gives me the thumbs-up. He says, "*Naloxone, un farmaco miracoloso,*" pulling the door closed. The other jumps behind the wheel, starts the engine, and the ambulance creeps away.

I stare down the empty road. Gusts of dry leaves swirl in the garden. Dario's sculptures, some of which were kicked over by the thugs, look sad and abandoned. Trixie's whimper brings me back to myself, and for the rest of the afternoon and into the night, she lies by the kitchen door, listening... waiting for Dario to come home.

The following Friday morning, I call Marina to follow up. She's relieved and asks if I'm all right.

"I'm very sad, Marina. The house is so big and empty now. His bed... no one's there."

"You have saved his life, Mark."

"Tell me about you, then about poor Alessandro."

"For me, the same. I am stuck in an unhappy marriage. Luciano does not touch me but now threatens to beat me if I don't follow every command. He wishes something for dinner which I prepare, then changes his mind and will not eat what I've made, sometimes throwing on the floor and frightening the children."

"I'm so sorry."

"But I can handle him. The bigger problem is Alessandro, who is still in Basel but cannot take care of himself as they fill him with so many pharmaceutical drugs for depression he can hardly function."

"Does he still work?"

"Yes, but he can't do his job well, and they cannot fire him and so everyone is unfriendly to him."

"Poor Alessandro. What the fuck is happening to everybody, Marina?"

"I will fly to Basel tomorrow to see him and determine the situation. Do you want to join me in Basel? We will see if we can stay at his house. If not, we go to a small hotel together, just for a few days."

"Maybe, at least for a little while. I have to follow through here with Dario and see what happens next."

"I tell you what happens next because the hospital calls and tells me, as I was the first contact. They will keep him there until he is through the crisis, and then he stays for observation. Depending on prognosis, the doctors either release him to go home or recommend a rehabilitation center with social supports and therapy. In other words, a halfway house for at least a year."

"I have to go see him."

"Did you sign a paper?"

"Yes."

"Good. I tell hospital you wish to replace me as first contact. If Dario agrees, then they allow you, but you must be very careful what you say because he is quite unstable and still in danger of falling back into self-destructive behaviors."

"I'm well aware."

"Yes, now the difficult part. The separation as he recovers."

"He thinks I betrayed him."

"No, I don't believe. But is still best if you join me in Basel to get away and allow Dario to find the help he needs without emotional complications."

"I'll have to arrange to have the house and Trixie looked after."

"I understand. Ciao for now."

I discover Dario's phone book while gathering clothes I think he'll need at the hospital, although I may only be allowed to drop them off. I find the number for Dario's former housemate Jabari and consider asking him to stay at the villa again. If he isn't keen on the idea, I'll offer to pay him. I'll even extend the invitation to his mother who would surely enjoy Dario's beautiful kitchen for her bread baking. Trixie probably remembers Jabari, too.

I make the call, and after some confusion about who I am, Jabari gladly agrees. He tells me Dario has been like a father to him, and that once he'd hoped he might match up Dario with his mother, who badly needs a husband. But yes, he'd be delighted to stay in the villa, although he's now working in a neighboring commune doing a tree trimming job, so won't be able to come for another week.

That evening, I watch Trixie puzzle from room to room looking for Dario and try to dispel my gloom by studying Google Maps for the best way to cross the Alps into Switzerland. I decide it would be too risky to drive the Fiat and remember the Flixbus option that took me from Pivonnia to the airport in Rome four years ago. I buy a ticket online for Saturday, June 11th, six days before my ninety-day Italian visa expires. I download the ticket to my phone, which conveniently includes a navigational link to the nearest Flixbus pick-up station.

I've just signed off when my phone jumps to life again. Dario. I connect, but find I can't even manage a "hello."

"Mark?" he says, his voice coarse and rasping. "Sweetheart, are you there?"

"Dario... I'm *so sorry*—"

"Stop. They'll allow me one visitor before they shut me in here for who-knows-how-long, so please come soon. We'll talk then."

"I plan to. Should I bring extra clothes for you?"

"And a few other things, if you don't mind, sketch pad and pencils. I have them in a slate box on the table in my studio. Also, my watercolors and brushes on that table. My nail clipper, too. Same table. And then, something else."

"Yes?"

"My porn, tucked under the statue of St. Lidwina-the-Frozen in the rose garden."

"I'm not sure where that is—"

"Joking, sweetheart."

"Ah. You're feeling better."

"I've been detoxified by the perennial drip of Naloxone, a nectar for the chemically interrupted."

"So, I've learned."

"The real 'something else' is a photo of you. Take one out of your wallet if need be, or have Jabari take one of you and print it for me."

"Sure."

"Come visit tomorrow, if possible. Before they move me."

"They're moving you?"

"Who knows? People have been known to disappear in the dead of night. It's like Stalin's Russia."

Saturday afternoon, I drive to Poreta Centrale and find *Ospedale Santa Maria Nuova* in a small suburb just south of the city. Nuns in white sailboat hats glide through the modest lobby, which features an up-lit statue of the Virgin standing in a small pool vibrating with bubblers. I'm directed to a lift that goes to the top floor only, the floor that contains patients with a tendency to self-harm who must be monitored.

Dario occupies a corner room by himself. His hair seems whiter and his face looks drawn. But his smile beams and I'm so very happy to see him. I put down my bag and hug what I can reach of him under the I-V tubes.

"We mustn't be too effusive," he says. "This is a Catholic institution."

"It's so good to see you."

We look at each other. He sighs. "Quite the adventure we've been through together, wouldn't you agree?"

"We're here, no worse for the wear."

"Says you."

"Says me."

"Such indefatigable positivism. I could swallow you whole." He glances around in exaggerated paranoia. "Not the best way to put it."

"Where do you want your stuff?"

"Where is my photo?"

"The only one I could find was smashed into my wallet behind my car insurance card. I had to tear someone out of it." I hand him a photo of me and ex Allen Riesler, minus ex Allen Riesler. "You still want it?"

"Yes."

"Enjoy yourself."

Dario studies it for a moment. "You gorgeous man, you."

"You liar," I say.

"Compliments are difficult for you, aren't they? Too bad we won't have the opportunity to analyze this in more detail."

"Too bad," I say.

"As for my stuff, just drop it where you're standing. The sisters have their own ways of pinching—I mean, *organizing* things here."

I pull up a chair and reach across the bed rail to hold his hand. "What happens now? What should I do? Marina suggests I follow her to Basel for a little while. She's there to look after Alessandro."

"Yes," he sighs. "Seems like we men are all delicate creatures these days and require women to look after us." He studies me with a vague smile. "I sense that you've already decided what to do, and I encourage you to follow through."

"You mean, go to Basel?"

"If that fits into the bigger plan. What I mean is that you should live your life, Mark. Since I'm in for a long journey ahead, I'm afraid."

I'm silent for a moment and look at him. "You're telling me to leave you?"

"I'm telling you to live your life. And I hope that life will still have some room for your friend Dario Soole, who, I know now, fell in love with you the day we met."

"Dario—don't say any more now. Please."

Dario says nothing, retracts nothing, but he smiles and squeezes my hand. A very old man with a walker stops by the open door and looks in, seeming confused. A nun appears to gently lead him away.

"This isn't the conversation I was expecting," I say.

"No?"

"No."

"Things change," he answers.

"Change? They *fall apart*, and I'm not sure what to do anymore."

"You have your home in California, where your family waits for you—the family you wish to heal. And you have your true friends in Italy, if ever you choose to come back and see us."

"Of course, I'll come back, I'll—"

He places his hand on my face to quiet me. "But I have no family and no country, Mark. I'm a black man, I'm a homosexual man, I'm an old man, and now I'm a sick man. I'm despised in America and misunderstood here. If I have a country at all, it's the *sky*." He gazes up, his eyes gleaming and trancelike. He lifts his arms and spreads his fingers as if to touch something. "I'm a vagabond who wanders the night sky amid the stars, Mark, and my beggar's tin cup shines to make another star."

"Dario..." I say, softy.

"We'll all be stars up there, eventually, especially the lost ones among us..." He points to something imaginary on the ceiling and traces it with his finger, "Most of us won't even have names. But we'll keep company with the billions of other stars, and together, we'll look down and remember how beautiful this Earth once was." He looks at me sweetly, his eyes wide and wet. "And so, I asked you to come so I could say to you, Mark—my sweetheart, my most enticing model, and my wonderful adventure—*goodbye*, or at least farewell."

He touches my face again, but I break away and stand up. I glance around the room bewildered before I take a breath, gather myself, and walk to the door. I don't look back—but then I do. Just once.

I don't hear from Dario the following week and resist calling him. When Jabari arrives at noon the following Saturday, I'm all packed and ready for him to drop me off at the Flixbus station. He thanks me again for the use of Dario's house, says he knows it quite well, and tells me how much he looks forward to his mom arriving in a few days to cook for him. He's already found workers to clear up the smashed pottery and replace the broken doors and window of the kitchen, he assures, patting my shoulder. Trixie sniffs his bare knees, then cozies up to him. For me, she stretches her neck luxuriously as an invitation for one last scratch.

I have no idea what to expect in Basel, Switzerland, a city I know nothing about in a country I've never visited. But I'll have seven hours to scroll my phone and find out—that is, once we leave the tedious autostrada and plunge into the epic panorama of the Alps: a Wagnerian opera become manifest with its cloud-shredding peaks that glisten like daggers over the valleys. The enormous Flixbus pivots along the serpentine *Gotthardstrasse*, taking curves so precipitous that, from where I sit, it feels like the whole side of it cantilevers out from the road and hangs purely in mid-air. We pass a deep-green forest that struggles up the side of a mountain until it ascends too high, where the atmosphere turns thin and dry, and the leafy crowns shrivel to brambles.

At eight o'clock in the evening on June 11th, we arrive at Basel's *Bahnhof*, the multi-level train and bus station on *Centralbahnstrasse*, at the City Center. Buses and cars circle around a pavilion for the intra-urban electric trams. Following Marina's directions, I consult a map, purchase my ticket at a kiosk, and climb onto one of seven articulated tram cars painted grasshopper green, each dotted with photographs of Basel citizens claimed by Covid. The tram jerks forward, then clacks softly as it glides beneath its catenary, first travelling north over the Rhine River, then following the river west along Klybeckstrasse to Müllheimerstrasse and Alessandro's flat. I find the four-story mansion-turned-apartment-house, buzz in, and exit on the third floor to see Marina waiting for me in the flat's doorway, directly opposite the lift.

"Welcome, welcome," she says, pecking me on the cheek. "Alessandro is having a smoke on the balcony by the kitchen now. The cast is recently off his arm and he feels well. He'll join us directly."

The flat is large and plain and, depending on where you look, either immaculate or filthy. Mops lean against the walls, dusters occupy tables and desks, and a plastic bucket of cleaning products sits just outside the toilet.

"Since coming here a week ago, I have helped Alessandro tidy up. You have no idea the state of this place. Truly *un disastro*. But we say no more about it now," she says her voice lowering, as Alessandro comes into the room.

"Ciao, Mark!" he says, coming over to hug me, the reek of tobacco on his clothes and in his long greasy hair. "You look a bit thin now. You want something to eat now? I have also chocolate cakes."

"Talk about *thin*—my god, Alessandro, it's amazing how much weight you've lost. You look ten years younger!"

"Eh, is the fucking medicines. I don't eat as I like. And I have no energies because I am still depressing. But now you are here with Marina, and you both enjoy *città di Basilea* while I work on my stupid job."

Marina says, "Mark, my bedroom is down the hall, and there is another spare bedroom. Or if you wish..." she hesitates, "You and Alessandro."

"The spare room is fine," I say.

Alessandro says, "I have a lot of passes for museums, but I never go. I save you a lot of money if you take these passes tomorrow when I am working for my bitch of a boss."

"Thanks, we might do that," I say.

Alessandro walks off to pee noisily and doesn't bother to shut the door. Coming back out, he farts. Marina covers her mouth and giggles.

"Oops! I make a bit of gas. Fucking medicines."

"Definitely the spare room," I say.

Alessandro, now apparently tired of the welcoming chitchat, settles in front of the television to watch his favorite show, the Italian equivalent of "America's Got Talent." A parade of Italian wannabees parade before a panel of garishly costumed judges, two of whom are clearly transvestites with ballooning hair. Alessandro munches from a bowl of cheese crackers and pulls a short blanket over his legs. It seems he's completely blotted us out. Marina shrugs and tells me she'll go to bed. Leads me to my room and points out an adjoining bathroom.

She says before she bids me goodnight, "He stays up half the night with the television very loud. If you need the earplugs, I give to you."

"No, I remember a little of this from before. As long as he's in the other room."

"Good. So, already with you here, I can see how his mood improves. It was quite difficult for the first day. I hope you can stay a little while after I leave to help settle him. He needs your company since he makes no friends here."

"I'll do what I can, but it's awkward, Marina. I mean, after what happened with Alessandro and now Dario and everything else."

"I understand, but very good you get away from Dario for a while. Maybe you still have some affectionate feelings for Alessandro and you can be a friend to him. I think with the right doctor he will be cured."

"When are you leaving?"

"In about a week. I have concerns about Luciano and need to be near my children. We will talk more about this tomorrow. Good night now."

The following morning, June 13th, I'm rattled in my narrow bed by the 8 a.m. peals of Saint Matthew Church, or Matthäuskirche, as I learn from my Basel navigation app. My bare window looks over a large communal yard banked by the grimy backsides of houses similar to this one. Over their rooftops, the bell tower looms.

I come into the kitchen to see Alessandro on the balcony in his bathrobe, his back to me, plumes of white smoke billow from the side of him. As he turns to face me, I remember that posture: right arm wrapped around his chest in a self-hug, hand nestled in his armpit, the other hand holding, at some distance from his face, a rolled cigarette with a long ash. He smiles, blows a plume, then stubs out the butt on the railing and comes inside.

"Buongiorno," he says, "Marina still tired. You have a nice sleep?"

"*Ovviamente,*" I answer, "*Sempre dormo bene dopo un viaggio.*"

"Eh, your Italian is not so good anymore. You don't practice."

"When was it ever good?"

"With me, it was better. Now, already I hear mistakes."

"Fine."

"I make expresso. You want?"

"Sure."

He clatters through a sink overflowing with dirty dishes, fishes out an expresso cup from the depths, and gives it a rinse. He pours what's mostly sludge into the cup and places it, without a saucer, on the table between us. Again, I notice Alessandro's state of dishevelment: his hair is greasy and unwashed. He hasn't shaved for days.

"I get dressed, take my bicycle to work now."

"You might..." I begin.

"What?"

"Nothing."

"I come home at four o'clock and bring pastry. Then I make soup later to eat for us. You take Marina someplace to cheer her up. She has the problems with the *stronzo* husband."

"I know."

"Maybe you should marry Marina," he says. A familiar trope.

"Have a good day," I say.

A gloom hangs over Basel in the early morning hours. Behind the banked houses to the southeast, the high glass towers of the Pharmaceuticals catch the yellow-white of the early sun, their tops edged in blinking beacons. The blended hums of the electric trams rise in pitch like the prayers of a muezzin from his mosque; here and there, sparks flash from their catenaries.

Marina emerges, dressed in long slacks and a flowered blouse. I'm embarrassed to greet her in my sweats and flip-flops.

"How do you do, Mark?" she says, in a playful mood. "Has our odd friend left for the day?"

"He looked terrible. And he didn't shower."

"I know, I know," she says, waving it away. "I've tried to make him aware, but he ignores. I believe it's the drugs." She goes to the kitchen table, pushes aside papers upon papers, uncovers the plastic tray. "*Guarda.* Look here..."

At least fifty boxes of medications pack the tray, most of them torn open and their pill-sheets half out. Underneath a layer of packer bottles without caps, hundreds of stray pills cover the bottom of the tray with no markings to identify what they are and what they do. The boxes have names like *Olazanpina, Fluoxetine,* and *Zoloft*; *Doxepin, Tofranil,* and *Pamelor*.

"My god. He takes all of these? Every day?"

"I don't know. They are very strong *triciclici* for the depression."

"Tricyclics. Yes. Harsh stuff."

"Basel is the best place for drugs. The doctors give out like sweets he tells me. I just hope they know what they are doing to him."

We decide to skip the museums as the day turns pleasant and walk to the *Unterer Rheinweg*, or promenade, along the river. Basel is known to be one of the most pedestrian-friendly cities in all of Europe, and the wide walkway ambles from the Muttenz neighborhood in the south all the way up to the Dreiländereck peninsula in the north, where Switzerland touches Germany and France. Linden trees shade the way, and fancy coffee stalls steam under them. Swans float at the river's edge and happily shit on the narrow concrete piers that look like they've been designed for that very purpose. On the opposite shore, the panorama of Old Basel shimmers: the limestone spires of Evangelisch-Reformierte Kirche rocket above the Rittergasse neighborhood. A delicate Ferris wheel rests quietly nearby.

At this hour, young women wheel prams or strollers, and the children tucked inside are well-behaved and smartly dressed, like their moms. Wealth is evident here—a quiet and dignified affluence and rows of elegant townhouses line the Rheinweg with Bentleys in their driveways.

Marina seems happier now, or at least momentarily happy within a general melancholy that I noticed the first day I met her, four years ago. She tells me that Luciano is, in turn, tender and cruel and still very suspicious of her weeks in Spain, especially since she'd discouraged him from joining her there. He jokes and plays with the children enthusiastically and then ignores or even punishes them over minor annoyances. She feels his sudden shifts in mood have begun to damage them.

"Does he drink or use drugs, Marina? It sounds like a substance abuse problem."

"If so, he hides it very well," she says. "But no, I don't think so."

"And—dare I bring this up again: Carlos?"

"I told you some of the story. Carlos was completely false with me. I don't know what he wanted. If money, I made clear I had very little of it. So, this is the piece of the puzzle I cannot fit together."

I could say so much more, I think, but I'm silent.

"I suppose I could track him down if I really wanted," Marina says. "That is, if Carlos Pineda is his real name. He mentioned quite a few of his business associations over dinner that night, remember?"

"Yes."

She sighs and looks out over the river. "But what is the purpose?"

"Let sleeping dogs lie," I say, smiling.

"You Americans very much like dogs," she says. "My father told me that once, during the war, he ate one."

"Never, *ever* mention that if you come to the States."

"As Alessandro says, *I make a little joke.*"

"Such a joke will cost you your life in places like Portland, Oregon."

"You make me laugh, Mark, and I don't laugh very much anymore. Alessandro, he makes me sad and even gives me a bit of the creeps."

Late in the afternoon, we stroll along Müllheimerstrasse towards Alessandro's apartment house just as Alessandro cruises past us on his bicycle. He seems to see us but doesn't stop or even wave. As we approach, he locks his bike to the grate, opens the door and goes in, slamming it behind. Ten seconds later, we're standing in the exact same spot, Marina fumbling with her keys.

"Why did he do that?" I ask Marina. "Does he resent us staying with him?"

"No, he wants us here—at least he wants you here. Me, I'm not so sure. But he is an odd man, and I am not so sure of anything about him anymore."

Alessandro comes bounding out of the toilet as we enter the flat. "Sorry, I had to take a good shit," he announces. "I think the medicine."

"You are forgiven," I say.

"Now I put out some cakes."

Marina jumps in: "Oh no, Alessandro! Mark and I had too many sweets today, so we'll just wait for dinner."

Alessandro shrugs, lights the gas for coffee, and finishes off the cakes by himself.

At eight o'clock, after a plain dinner of pasta and egg soup, I expect Alessandro to settle down with his television and ignore us, but he seems to want to chat.

"Do you mind if I have a smoke in the kitchen?" he asks us while rolling a cigarette.

Marina says, "This is your home, of course, but maybe you could smoke out on the balcony as we discussed?"

He sighs. "*Va bene*, I do this to protect your delicate lungs." He looks at me. "Italian women have very delicate lungs, and Italian men are put on Earth to protect the delicate lungs of Italian women."

Marina stiffens. "*Scusami*, Alessandro. "What does it mean what you've said?"

"I say that men are your protective angels of the lungs because you women are all *tutte delicate*."

Now, she's clearly rankled. "And I say that, under the circumstances, Mark and I are *your* protective angels."

"Eh..." Alessandro muses, lights his cigarette, "Maybe Mark, but not so much you."

"*What?* How dare you say this to me, Alessandro!"

"Why so upset? I make a little joke."

"What kind of *stupido* joke? What's wrong with you, Alessandro?"

"Nothing," he says, turning to step onto the balcony.

I follow Marina to her bedroom. She's crying, looks up at me. "I don't know if I can stay here one more day with him. I work and clean his house like a slave and not even a *grazie* comes out of him. I think I will leave tomorrow."

"Sleep, and you'll feel better in the morning," I say. "We'll go to a museum."

"He's just—I don't know what you ever saw in him." She anticipates my response. "But I, if anyone, should understand how these things happen."

"Shit happens, Marina. Another quaint American expression."

The evening is clearly over for Marina, and she stays in her room. I go back to the kitchen and wait for Alessandro to finish his smoke. He comes in and only glances at me.

"I do the dishes now. Sorry for the *disordine* of my house, but I have no energies."

I pick up a soiled dish towel and stand beside him. "You should be kinder to Marina. She's your friend."

"I just make a little joke. She has no sense of humor."

"A mean joke."

"Oh, bravo. So, you also torture me now?"

"I'm trying to figure you out. I've never been able to figure you out."

"Stop trying. And Marina is no Madonna. She likes the sex. She even tells me when we were together that she wants you to fuck her on the beach in San Vita Lo Capo."

"That's very flattering, but it means nothing. She's a good person."

"Eh, sì. You win. I apologize to her in the morning. Now I go watch my program. Tomorrow, you take free pass and visit Pharmaceutical Museum. They have a good collection of dildos."

I return to my bedroom and scroll on my phone, pin the location of the *Pharmaziemuseum der Universität Basel* on my nav map so I can find it tomorrow. I message Marina to ask if it's something she'd be interested in doing. If so, I'll buy us a nice breakfast in Café Flora on Klybeckstrasse Avenue, a twenty-four hour jazz venue that everyone raves about on the Swiss equivalent of Yelp. She doesn't answer, so I give her space and turn out the light. But the June evenings are hot in Basel, and I can't sleep. I open my window and crack my door for a breeze, nod off again, but wake up a few hours later for no apparent reason. The flat is dark and quiet. Even the windows of the courtyard are black. I drift back to sleep and open my eyes as the light comes up. Something rattles in the kitchen. I go to walk out but trip over the shoulder straps of my carry-on bag, which seems to have been moved, its zipper half opened. I conclude that maybe it just toppled from its chair in the middle of the night, startling me.

I catch Alessandro as he's headed out the door.

"I go to work early today," he says. "Big meeting on June the fourteen with the moron boss."

"Were you looking for something in my carry-on bag last night?"

"Are you crazy? You think I steal from you?"

"Somebody moved it. Or maybe it just fell off the chair."

"I don't touch anything," he sniffs.

"Okay, sorry. Where's Marina, still sleeping?"

"No, she has gone home already. I apologize like you wanted, but she says she must catch her flight back and to say goodbye to you."

"What?"

"She didn't want me to wake you. I must leave now. You go to museum."

After he's gone, I text Marina to tell her I wish she would've stayed at least another day—after all, it was she who invited me to join her—but she doesn't answer. So, now, on my own in Basel, I decide to make the best of it. I shower, dress, and set out for the day.

The Pharmaceutical Museum is a six-kilometer walk south along the *Rheinweg Unterer* to *Mittlere Brücke* pedestrian bridge that crosses to the western half of the city. The museum sits amid a cluster of buildings on the campus of the Basel University and offers a collection—not for the squeamish—of eighteenth-century curatives and surgical instruments, including ground-up meteorites for weight loss (which I photograph for Jim), and smoke-filled enema pumps for reviving persons nearly drowned. Mummification was apparently all the rage among rich doctors who wanted their remains preserved after death, and a gallery of large vitrines contains heads, livers, genitals, and other keepsakes for loved ones to cherish. At two o'clock, having lost my appetite for lunch, I text Alessandro and tell him I'm close to the Italian Ministry of Education and suggest we meet and walk home together. He agrees, but cautions he'll be later than his usual hour. Texting Alessandro triggers a memory of four summers ago when we'd traveled together, and his phone constantly buzzed with messages. Now, Alessandro's phone hardly rings at all.

He meets me in front of the embassy, looking disheveled as ever, dark circles around his eyes. "A very fucked up day," is his greeting.

We walk home quietly, but on the way, I'm curious about the little boathouse under a pulley-driven cable. The cable stretches across the river to another boathouse on the opposite shore, Alessandro's neighborhood.

"How much is the ferry, Alessandro?"

"Who knows. I never use."

I take his arm, walk towards it, and tell him I'll pay. A covered wooden skiff draws close, and the boatman stands on its prow, gripping a post that hooks to the moving cable and drags the ferry in. To dock, he unhooks the ferry from the cable, which continues to scroll. When we pay our fare and settle in, he hooks up to the cable again and we hitch a ride back. It's simple and fun, but Alessandro seems bored and lights a cigarette.

Back in his flat, he makes coffee and breaks open a box of biscuits. We sit quietly in the late afternoon light.

"I am sorry about Marina," he says, "And I thank you for coming to stay with me."

"That's what friends are for."

"Grazie."

"I care very much about you, Alessandro," I say.

"We had many good times. And now I have no one."

"I was sorry to hear about your mama and your brother, but I'm glad you're well."

"Not so well."

"This is temporary. You make friends easily. You always had a lot of friends in Italy. I'm sure you can make friends here."

"I am glad you still like me."

"Yes, but I live very far away from you, and I'll be going back to California soon."

"Maybe you can spend more time here, as you once said."

"I don't think so. I have my family in the States and my mom to look after."

"You are a good son to your mother."

"I hope so." I think about saying something else, then say it. "I've also made a new friend in California."

"A new friend?"

"Yes."

Alessandro tells me he's tired and wants to nap, after which he'll make dinner. I offer to take us out.

"No," he says. "Food in Basel very expensive and I want to save money. So tonight, we cook ourselves for enjoyment."

I restrain myself from correcting him. He salutes and retires to his room, adding: "You wake me up at seven o'clock so I can wash up."

Thirty minutes later, Marina texts me to say that she's sorry for leaving so suddenly but that she missed her children terribly and was afraid, if we'd talked, she'd change her mind. I text her back with assurances that I'll keep her posted about Alessandro, but she doesn't answer. At seven o'clock, I knock on Alessandro's door and wait. I knock again, then slowly push it open. He's sprawled on his bed, naked and fully aroused. He half sits up and smiles at me.

"*Vieni qui*, Mark. Now that Marina is gone, we have sex."

"What? No."

"*Veni qui subito* Mark. Come here to me."

"I'm not having sex with you, Alessandro. Stop it."

"Why not?"

"Do you want me to leave?"

"No, no. Please don't leave." He sits up, deflated. "The drugs they give me make me horny, I think."

"I would think just the opposite."

"Eh, not for me. Okay, okay. I will have a shower now and then I cook a nice pasta for dinner. I am sorry for the embarrassment."

"It's okay."

"I thought that maybe you wanted to get off a bit."

"I'm good."

Over dinner, I'm surprised that he initiates additional conversation about this, but I engage cautiously.

"I remember all our good times together," he says.

"Yes, you took me to many places."

"Did I make a nice tour for you?" He looks at me seriously until his face cracks to show he's replaying an old joke.

"Yes. You could've charged a lot of money," I say, playing along.

"Tomorrow, I work, but the next day, I take off so we can explore together. We go to a museum for clocks that I am curious about."

"That sounds fun. You want me to do anything here while you're gone?"

"No, I clean the house a little at a time, if you don't mind. For now, I concentrate on cleaning myself as I am feeling a bit better. So, Mark, I ask you this now: sometime later, do you care to come with me to a bathhouse?"

"A spa? For bathing?"

"Well, you get clean, and then you get dirty, and then you get clean again."

"Definitely feeling better, you."

"Maybe on my day off we go there. But first, we go to see the clocks."

"And then we get our clocks cleaned?"

"What means, that?"

"Nothing. It's an American expression," I say, getting up to rub his shoulders. Soon, his body relaxes, and he taps my hand to stop.

15
Strange Connection

On our way to the clock museum, we stroll Elizabethenstrasse to visit the Church of Saint Elizabeth, draped in rainbow banners. A banner in English announces that the church welcomes all faiths, races, genders, and orientations. We seem to have gone out of our way to see this church, and it's late morning before we arrive at the pink Neoclassical mansion of Johann Rudolph Burckhardt, an eighteenth-century manufacturer of silk ribbons for ladies and occasional benefactor of Mozart.

Alessandro tells me that Johann's son Ludwig loved to dress up as a maharani and parade around town wrapped in his father's fancy threads. Cross-dressing Ludwig also amassed one of the most extensive collections of mechanical clocks in Europe. But here I experience my first altercation with an overly fastidious Swiss admission woman who refuses to recognize my American vaccination card.

"What is this?" she sniffs after I unclip the card from its lanyard and slide it over the counter to her.

"A record of my vaccinations in the United States, issued by the Centers for Disease Control."

"We don't recognize such cards in Switzerland."

"Excuse me, madam, but you're the first person to question it. I've been to the Pharmaceutical Museum using this same card."

"We are not they," she says and pushes it back to me.

"But *they* are in Basel, Switzerland, just as you are."

She opens a drawer and pulls out a card with tiny black squares on it, waves it before me. "You need to have a code of this design that we scan for authentication of your vaccination."

Maybe I should've been prepared for this complication, but this is the first time I've run into it. "If you please, madam," I begin, "in America, we use a different system than yours. We use the American QR code to access online information, and you use the Swiss QR Bill code. This is why I have a vaccination *card*."

Alessandro, who's stood behind me during this exchange, comes closer, fidgeting nervously.

"Unacceptable," the woman pronounces, "other Americans with the correct documentation have been admitted with no complexities."

"Maybe other Americans had a different ticket taker. May I speak to your—?"

Alessandro grabs my elbow. "Don't make a big stink Mark, we go someplace else."

I turn to him, "Yes, I will make a stink. She has no right to keep me out."

He gently guides me away from the counter and whispers, "This *stronza* is a problem. We go and come back later when somebody else in here. There are other nice things to do today."

I surrender. The woman looks away and jerks her chin in the air.

Back outside, Alessandro explains that museum volunteers are often well-to-do people of the neighborhood and can be difficult; that they are often older people who sometimes have a bias against foreigners. "So now you understand what I put up with these goddamn people of Basel," he says.

"So, what now?" I speak to the air.

"We go to Münsterplatz to see ninth-century Basler Münster church and the house of Erasmus. Also, they have good waffles there."

A comfortable tram ride winds north to the rosy spires of the Romanesque Adalberto Cathedral, which the Protestants renamed *Basler Münster* four hundred years ago. It's one of Basel's great landmarks and a point of reference for navigating around the city. The church rises over the stone-grey Münsterplatz square; beyond its spires, a view of the Rhine glitters. Smart coffee shops offer tables at the edge of the square, and a tree-shaded garden provides a place for meditation and prayer.

We buy our waffles with cream from a stall and sit on benches close to a tour guide who directs his customers' attention to a mansion at the end of a crooked street. He's a tall, blond, eccentrically dressed young man I take to be about twenty-five who sports a goatee, wears a beret, and looks very much like an American beatnik.

"In this neighborhood, called Rittergasse," he trumpets, "and over there in that green house at the end of the street, the great Dutch writer Erasmus hid out to avoid becoming barbeque fuel for the Italian Inquisition..." He pauses for timid laughter. "Erasmus got the heck out of Rome after he published a book that pissed off a lot of folks. That book, enticingly titled 'In Praise of Folly,' poked fun at the Catholic Church for selling indulgences to illiterate peasants all over Europe, but especially here in Switzerland." The beatnik blond stops and regards the upturned faces that surround him. "Does everyone know what an *indulgence* is?" He scans his audience expectantly. A few hands half-raise, and one man mutters something unintelligible. "Now, now, let's keep it clean..." the beatnik jokes, "... *anyone?* He gives up. "Okay, for those of you who don't know, an indulgence is kind of like paying off a parking ticket. You gave some money to a priest who handed you a contract saying that God forgave you for the sin you just committed. This meant you wouldn't lose your Business Class seat in Heaven." More shy laughter from his listeners, but most begin to peel away. He presses on "—Anyway, thanks to Gutenberg, 'In Praise of Folly' became a best seller, and bad-boy Erasmus brought us into *The Age of Reason* which eventually produced actuary tables, focus groups, Darwinian capitalism, and ALEXA." He bows in a parody of effusive politeness and removes his beret for donations.

The three people left in his audience applaud lightly, appearing confused by this odd delivery. Only one drops an offering into the sad little cap.

"Poor guy," I say. "Too much the hipster for that stuffy audience."

"I have seen before," Alessandro replies. "A student at the University. There are many making such entertainments this time of year."

I pull out my billfold. "I think he deserves more than a few coins."

"No, save your money, Mark."

"Why? He's a poor student working a tough crowd to make ends meet. An American, for sure, although I can't make out the accent."

"Not poor at all. From Boston area."

"You know him?"

"A bit."

As the young man begins to pack up, we approach. I'm about to introduce myself but he recognizes Alessandro and greets him first.

"How are you doing, Mr. Pugliacci?"

"Hello, Prentis. Here is another creature from your country."

"Oh, yeah?"

"My dear friend Mark from California."

"Hey, California." He reaches out and we shake hands awkwardly.

"I enjoyed your Erasmus rap," I say. "Where are you from?"

"Massachusetts. I'm doing a two-year extension study at Universität Basel, the Alma Mater of Erasmus, my current obsession."

"Good for you." I notice that his hipster vibe has vanished, replaced by the broad tones of an American blueblood. "From what school in the States?"

"Harvard. Actually, I began my undergraduate work on religious hucksterism at Yale, where I formulated my thesis on hucksterism throughout the Renaissance and its debunking in the seventeenth century."

"Wow," Alessandro says.

"I'm now writing a second thesis on proto-Christian iconography and polytheism among the ancient people of North Africa and how it entered the West through Spain."

I turn to Alessandro. "I'd like to invite this young man to dinner. How about it?" I direct that last question to both of them.

"Oh, sorry," Prentis responds, "I couldn't today."

"You come Friday, then—" Alessandro insists, "You come this Friday to dinner at my house. I make the nice veal and funghi you like very much and then you have nice intellectual conversations with my American creature." Alessandro looks at me, then back at Prentis. "Mark is a teacher of California. I think he misses a bit talking to other American creatures."

"That would be lovely," Prentis says cordially. "Thanks very much, Alessandro."

The day getting on, we stroll away from Munsterplatz to get a closer look at the Erasmus' house before leaving Rittergasse. As we walk down the hill towards the river, we stop at another stall for a delicious sausage on a soft, warm roll.

"So, you know this Prentis?" I ask.

"Not really. I see him making the speeches one or two times and we talk so he practices his Italian."

"Is he family?"

"Whose family?"

"Does he like men?"

"Oh. Not sure. Once I invite him for dinner, but nothing happens."

By late afternoon, the streets of the city grow dark while the spires of the churches redden with the setting sun.

"Where are we going?" I ask Alessandro as he pushes ahead, turning this way and that, without an explanation.

"I take you now for a bit of fun and some refreshment. You will enjoy."

"You mean—"

"It is the first bathhouse to open in many years. Lots of Italians go there. The Swiss queens think they are better than us."

"Seems I have no say in this decision," I grumble, but I'm secretly relieved that at least Alessandro will emerge smelling better.

"You see just for the architecture, an old gymnasium in the Art Deco style."

"Fine, but I'm not participating. If you find someone you like, just tell me, and I'll go back to Müllheimerstrasse and wait for you." I can hardly believe I'm saying this to Alessandro, a man who, years ago, almost broke my heart by merely chatting with a hotel housekeeper. How far away that all seems now.

The bathhouse, tucked in a blind corner of one of the old marketplaces, is a masterpiece of heroic brutalism. Its Babylonian-styled entrance displays an enormous bronze of St. George, nude on a horse, slaying a serpent. Behind it sits a huge sandstone frieze where naked Aryan supermen wrestle, toss javelins, and lug boulders on their backs.

"You like?" says Alessandro.

We enter the vestibule and pay for our passes, gather our towels and locker keys, and come into a chamber of marble and tile, a sea-green pool at the center, and corridors going off in every direction. Men, in robes, towels, or nothing at all (except their eyeglasses) wander about exchanging hard looks.

In the locker room, Alessandro strips and wraps himself around the waist, "And you? Will you be a nun this evening?"

"Probably," I say. "I'll take off my clothes and explore a little. You were right about the architecture."

We no sooner leave the locker room when a thin man in a towel, a large scar down his breastbone, appears from the darkness and slap-steps towards us.

"*Mannaggia,* Aldo! *Dove diavolo sei stato?*"

"*Ciao, Giulio! Sto bene, e tu?*" Alessandro turns to me. "I speak English so you understand us," he says, then back to the towel. "It has been a long time since we practice our English together, Giulio."

"We practice many things together, Alessandro!"

"*Sì*, but now you make an embarrassment in front of my friend."

"So, now the baths are open, and you come to celebrate your one year in Basel. What do you do during *la quarantena?*"

"I have been sick but now feeling better."

"And who is this new friend?" asks the towel. "What happened to the old friend?"

"This is Marco, from America."

"*Eh*, America," the towel laughs. "Say hello to Trump for me."

Alessandro says, "Giulio, what old friend are you talking about? The Moroccan*?*"

"*Sì*, the one with the big cock," towel replies.

"Eh, that one in jail now. I find out from the boyfriend of his husband."

"Mamma Mia, such a pity to put such a cock in jail! But maybe it is happier there now."

The towel turns to me, unsmiling. Looks me over. "So, tell me, what does the American cock look like? Red, white, and blue?"

"You'll never know, pal," I say.

Alessandro, seeming unsettled, takes my arm and we begin to walk away. "You have a lovely evening, Giulio, we will go now. Good-bye." Still holding my arm, he leads the way. "We soak in the thermal pool to relax and then shortly we go home, yes?"

"Please."

The pool sits at the end of a long faux cavern and is gotten into by climbing over an arrangement of fake boulders so that naked men must crouch, bend, and crawl in full close-up view of one other to reach the water. But once there, the gentle foam, lit blue from beneath, feels soft as silk. Settled, I soon feel hands exploring me. It's not unpleasant, but I'm not aroused and guide them away. Alessandro, sitting opposite me, kisses an older man whose legs entwine his, their forearms hidden in the foamy water and extended towards each other. This continues for some time, and I make an effort to look away, as if privacy were an issue in a place like this. Eventually, the older man's head disappears underwater, and Alessandro's face turns blissful. He winks at me. Again, I'm astonished that I feel not the slightest tinge of jealousy—but Alessandro does! To my amazement, he complains and whines after we've showered and begun dressing.

"I didn't like the man next to you. He was very good looking, but an annoyance to me. How he secretly touched you."

"It was no secret, and he didn't turn me on at all."

"I don't believe."

"You're jealous of *me*? The way *you* carried on in there?"

"Is allowed."

"Oh, is that so? Excuse me, mister macho Italian."

"I excuse you."

"And what about this Moroccan guy your friend in the towel mentioned? Who's that?"

Alessandro lights a cigarette. "I tell you to be honest. Someone I meet at a secret orgy at Giulio's house during pandemic, only for vaccinated men. Because I had the Covid already."

"Figures."

"To be honest, now and then maybe you hear of several men I meet during those years when we don't speak. But now, no one because not much interest. And I don't get hard easily."

During the tram ride home, I'm annoyed with myself. This last conversation sounded too much like the arguments I'd had with Alessandro in the old days. Maybe I fool myself by pretending I have no residual feelings of jealousy, but the stronger feeling is more aggravation than jealousy, this constant confusion with Alessandro's disconnected behavior.

Back at the flat, he serves up some fried leftover pasta and settles in front of the television, as usual. I retreat to my room thinking I'll read to learn more about Basel and probably turn in early. But the T.V. switches off and Alessandro appears in the doorway.

"We had a good day today. Thank you for cheering me up."

"You just need to go out once in a while."

"I don't like going out alone."

"Make some friends."

He stands there, looks at me, then down at his shuffling foot. "I mean, tonight would you like... I won't get very hard."

"No, thank you."

"Va bene," he says. "Buona notte."

I sleep in on Friday morning. Alessandro has left for work by the time I enter the kitchen. He's left plates, cups, and dirty silverware strewn everywhere, so I make it my morning project to clean things up, especially since we're having a guest this evening. Around noon, he calls.

"Ciao, lazy man."

"You wouldn't call me lazy if you saw how I've cleaned this place up."

"I appreciate."

"Busy today?"

"No, I am the only one here in the office. The disgusting boss takes Friday off sometimes, and the *stronza* whore who works in the afternoon calls in sick today. I want to leave early but now I have to close up everything."

"Would you like me to go shopping for our guest tonight?"

"You know where is store?"

"Yes. On Klybeckstrasse."

"Bravo. You become familiar with neighborhood now. Yes, buy the funghi and a half-kilo of veal, cut thin. You can speak bad Italian to them and they will answer in even worse Italian. Or you can speak English. But do not try to speak German as they do not care for that."

"Got it."

I take my time shopping, then stroll back along a shady street, dodging chestnuts that fall from the trees. The golden, late-summer afternoon stretches ahead, and I begin to feel nostalgic about my months in Italy. I also begin to understand Alessandro's alienation from the culture of the Swiss. Most neighborhoods are eerily quiet all day, except for early mornings and late afternoons, when the school children skip home with their leather bags. And Müllheimerstrasse sits deep within a neighborhood of families. From what I can tell, few places exist in Basel where eccentrics can gather to keep each other company. Alessandro, in his odd shabbiness, must appear strange to these well-dressed young women and men, who stroll with their well-dressed and perfectly behaved children, eating perfectly shaped ice cream cones. It's easy to feel the outsider here; smiles offered are returned timidly if returned at all; walkers approaching from the opposite direction expect a foreigner—whom they quickly recognize—to give way to them, as I often do. When I don't, some mutter of reproach often follows, but only after they're well behind me.

My spirits lift when I hear strains of jazz as I near a new intersection. The sign above says *Café Flora*, and tables in bistro style, occupied by bearded and sandaled men, cluster under a striped canopy. A lone saxophonist wails on a patio surrounded by potted geraniums. I enter the place and take my table; several men look up from their newspapers to nod at me. The women, too, seem to at least acknowledge my existence and smile.

I order a cappuccino in Italian from a French waiter who immediately pegs me for an American and asks if I've ever met Lady Gaga. He welcomes me and explains that, ever since April of 2022, Americans have been congregating at *Flora* on Friday evenings to hear good jazz and that Basel has, in fact, a sizeable American expat community of college professors and executives from the American drug companies. He encourages me to come "visit Flora" if I'm ever lonely for Americans and adds, "But, why would you be lonely for Americans when you have all of these delightful Swiss to fall in love with?" The roll of his eyes signals just the opposite.

When I arrive back at the flat and unpack Alessandro's groceries, my thoughts return to Marina. Maybe she's embarrassed to call rather than text because of her sneaking out. I don't want to risk phoning her since the situation with Luciano seems volatile, so I finish my chores and settle down to text her on *WhatsApp*:

I'm sitting here in Alessandro's kitchen and missing you. I hope all is manageable over there. It's very hot here this summer, but Alessandro seems a little better lately and has cleaned himself up. Tonight, we're even entertaining an American student for dinner. Anyway, I forgive you for abandoning us, but please send some news of YOU when you get a chance. Love, Mark.

My message remains unread. At least the little blue checkmark never appears beside it to show that she's even opened it.

Alessandro flies through the door at five o'clock, sweat dripping down his face. "Oh my god," he says, "So much to do."

"Relax," I say. "Everything we need is here. You have plenty of time."

"I don't have dinner guests here for many months. I forget how to cook."

"He's a college student," Alessandro. "He probably eats ramen noodles all week."

"What is?"

"Japanese pasta."

At eight o'clock, the flat disinfected and the dishes sparkling, a calmer Alessandro prepares his *vitello con funghi*, adding a bit of white wine for a smokey flourish. Prentis buzzes at 7:59 p.m. and bounds up the stairwell holding a small bouquet of tulips. Alessandro accepts them effusively, sticking his nose deep into the bunch as if there were something to smell. When he comes up for air, pollen dusts his nostrils.

"So sweet! But why you don't take the elevator?" he croons, tapping the tip of Prentis's nose and looking a bit ridiculous in his candy-striped apron.

"I climb the stairs whenever possible, thanks."

Alessandro has set the table impeccably, with tucked napkins and clean, if mismatched, wine glasses. An empty marmalade jar with a few springs of flowering rosemary serves as a centerpiece until the tulips replace them. It's an entirely new fuss-about-the-kitchen side of Alessandro I've never seen before, and he's good at it. The veal is seared, forked, and plated beside a tangle of mushroomed pasta. Prentis attacks it with relish, folding a large piece of meat onto his fork and stuffing it into his mouth.

"*Mannaggia*," Alessandro says, "The poor man starves."

"Not at all," Prentis answers, looking up mid-chew. "It's just that I don't cook and don't care much for Swiss food. But *this*—" He sweeps his fork like a wand over the table, "This is *amazing!*"

This, of course, makes Alessandro very happy, and his face glows like a pumpkin. He refills our guest's wine glass.

"Now, Prentis," he says, "you will drink more wine and explain for us your many interesting ideas. But mostly to Mark, because I am not so educated as Mark, and your words sometimes make puzzles to me. Americans speak a strange language that sounds to me very rude."

"I hear you, Alessandro," Prentis says, chomping. "Americans seem direct because they're accustomed to the transactional exchanges that occur in a highly capitalist society. So yes, to Europeans, Americans might sound rude."

Alessandro looks at me. "You see what I mean?"

The *vitello* finished, Alessandro clears the table and serves dessert: frozen tiramisu amped up with a dollop of fresh cream and Frangelico liqueur. We lean back in our chairs, happy and relaxed, Alessandro sprawls in his chair like a pasha, the shreds of a napkin tucked under his chin.

"Do you have a girlfriend in Basel, Prentis?" he asks.

"No girlfriend," Prentis says neutrally, diving into his dessert.

"Nobody to keep you warm on the cold nights?"

"Nope."

"Alessandro," I interrupt, "Why don't you take out some prosecco and let Prentis tell us more about his studies at Yale."

Prentis looks around. "Don't get me started," he says. "I'd love to, but it might make zombies out of both of you."

"Not at all," I say as Alessandro brings out the fluted glasses and uncorks the bottle.

Through the opened balcony door, accordion music comes up from the courtyard, and a woman sings. It's pleasant, and we listen, enjoying our prosecco, until the 11 p.m. chimes of Matthäuskirche begin—the last hour before matins at six in the morning.

Prentis raises his glass to eye level, and looks through the bubbling prosecco as if hypnotized. He begins slowly. "So, as I've said, this Erasmus stuff is just a side interest. My original thesis was inspired by my undergraduate studies of religious fraud and its debunking in the seventeenth century."

"Bravo for that," mutters Alessandro.

"Not so fast," Prentis says, revived. "It came roaring back in the nineteenth century with European immigration to America. Now, we see the fusion of religious fraud with free-market economics in the twentieth and twenty-first centuries and how it encourages worldwide fascism."

I sip my prosecco. "Explain that connection."

Prentis smiles and leans across the table. "Are you ready for this? It's all in my thesis, *Polytheism: Instigator of Authoritarianism*. It examines how the ancient systems of religious pluralism threatened the totalitarian rulers of world who plotted to replace pluralism with monotheism—a single, all-powerful God on whom they placed their own likenesses."

"This sounds familiar," I muse, trying to connect it with something I'd heard before.

"Drink more prosecco, Prentis," says Alessandro.

"Thanks," says Prentis, and he swallows thoughtfully. "To the ancient autocrats, polytheism meant decadence, and this association persisted through history and transformed into our recent contempt for democracy. Think about it. Today, poly-*anything* is considered subversive and dangerous: polyamorous, polyglot, polygamist—all problematic to the power-hungry."

"I have a headache now," Alessandro says, getting up from the table. But Prentis is just warming up.

"All the same," he pushes on, "polytheism thrived all over the world for six thousand years, long before the monotheist religions of Islam, Christianity, and Judaism took hold. But at a certain point in time, the belief in multiple gods was violently suppressed. The methods of its suppression documented in writings that are collectively known as the *Gàndar Exegesis*, named after the cave where they were first discovered."

Alessandro stands near the balcony and lights a cigarette, uninterested. But as Prentis continues to explain, I feel a distinct *déjà vu,* and a shiver moves up my spine.

"And where is this cave, Prentis?"

"Of all places, the Canary Islands of Spain."

"And how do you know all this, Prentis?"

"Through a contact I made with an archeologist who'd worked to preserve *Gàndar* and similar sites."

"What was his name, Prentis?"

Prentis suddenly seems uncomfortable. He looks nervously at Alessandro.

"Why?"

I don't answer.

"Sebastiàn Vollaro," he says, finally. "Or just *Vollaro*, as he called himself."

"Sebastiàn Vollaro," I repeat.

"Yes," Prentis says, "Sebastiàn Vollaro..."

The room grows still. Alessandro puffs his cigarette thoughtfully. Prentis's eyes dart about the kitchen. He puts down his prosecco and looks down. "Who, I suppose I should mention, is currently in prison for murdering his pregnant wife and two other women."

"Of course. It all makes sense now," I say, mostly to myself.

"But that doesn't diminish the brilliance of his research, and I'm sorry he's no longer a contact. I guess the guy turned out to be some psycho drug addict with a twisted thing for young mothers."

"Sì, a *psicopatico* Spaniard," Alessandro calls out, stepping closer. "I read something about him on internet once, but not the same name."

"Yes," Prentis says, "Vollaro was the professional name he went by. His real name was Carlos. Carlos Pineda."

For the rest of the evening, I'm quiet, weighed down with this new knowledge and wondering how much of it, if any, to share with Marina—if it's even possible to reach her.

"Well, friends," Prentis says, rising from the sofa we'd all settled into, "Time to get some sleep so I can pull off my tour tomorrow—one of my favorites, at Spalentor Gate in the old city."

"Is that something I should see?" I ask.

"Don't get him started," Alessandro grumbles, half asleep.

I rise with our guest and see him to the door. "Pay no attention to Alessandro tonight, Prentis. He worked hard preparing something special for you, and I'm proud of him."

"Of course. Alessandro's a cool guy. But a real enigma of a person."

Alessandro grunts himself upright and makes a noise about Prentis spending the night, but Prentis assures us that Basel is a safe city with reliable trams, and this is hardly the latest evening he's ever parted company with someone.

"Ah, to be so young again," I say as we watch our guest bound back down the stairs to the street.

After Alessandro goes to bed, I search for some information about Carlos Pineda late into the night. I find only one small article in a Spanish-language newspaper. But the article has been scanned from newsprint and posted with such poor resolution that it's almost impossible to decipher. The small photo, too—a likeness, but nothing definitive. Another hour of searching brings up vague mentions of Vollaro on more reputable sites, like UNESCO's, but all in the broader context of the Gàndar cave and the battle to save it from developers, which apparently has succeeded. I also find, to my surprise, a mention of one Harvard undergraduate student, Prentis Langley, of the *Langley Foundation for Historic Preservation* of Beacon Hill, Boston. The scarcity of digital information about Carlos begins to make sense and suggests the maneuverings of a wealthy foundation to disassociate itself from scandal by doing what wealthy foundations do, employ 'reputation defender' services to close down the negative information streams on the internet. Prentis was discreet but relaxed enough to reveal something important, the significance of which he'll never know. I'm thankful Alessandro plied him with prosecco.

The next morning, I wake up to the sound of Alessandro shouting and find him in the living room leaning over the computer and holding his phone. He shouts and sobs to someone on the other end, his voice rising to panic. He turns and sees me, waves me to go away. I go into the kitchen but he follows, so I step out to the balcony where I can still hear him. I see a woman in the courtyard looking up. She calls up to me and I don't understand a word, but her tone suggests, *is everything all right?* I give her a perfunctory wave of reassurance then hear a crash, followed by silence. I wait a moment and go back inside.

Alessandro leans against a wall, sobbing. He's kicked over a small table. He turns to look at me, his face knotted and red.

"My boss called because I leave door unlocked at work and forget to set alarm. Now someone breaks in and has stealed from us."

"Oh, shit."

"I have to go into office today, Saturday, and right away because boss is there and police are waiting also."

"Do you want me to come with you?"

"No. He was very angry. Maybe he fires me today, so I am no longer working."

"Go and talk to him. He knows your situation with the medication and all."

"Sì, I must go right now!"

"Please take a shower first."

"Right now, I go to him!"

He throws on his clothes and tumbles out the door looking like someone still recovering from a bender. I stand there bewildered. What seemed like a mild Saturday morning that smelled fresh and clean—a day to relax—has turned into a day of crisis. *Figures.*

16
The Unravelling

As July turns to August, the sun sets earlier behind the mountains to the west, and the scorching blue afternoons of Basel's summer turn milder. Towards evening, the air holds a hint of mountain laurel. Mornings, the peals of church bells sound crisper in the cool. In just over five months, the old year will pass and 2023 begins.

On this particular morning, I rise from our bed and collect Alessandro's pills in a paper cup. I fill another cup with half water and half apricot juice, and take it to him. He props himself up on an elbow and swallows the pills in one gulp. Then, he goes back to sleep.

In an hour or so, he'll awaken—the most dangerous time when I stay close to him. Twice last week, I came out of the toilet to find him leaning over the balcony and staring down at the concrete below. I gently guided him, trembling, back into the kitchen, held him up when it seemed he would collapse, and tried to get some food into him before he left for work.

After the June 17th theft of six computers containing confidential information about the Italian Ministry of Education and its employees, Alessandro was removed from his desk and assigned the job of label-typist for outgoing mail. He works part-time, six days a week, and on a schedule that makes it almost impossible to use the time off productively. But Alessandro seems to have little interest in using his time off for anything other than watching television, although I've managed to talk him into a weekly visit to the spa where we soak and he emerges clean.

The visits to his psychologist have increased, and so have his medications. But he struggles with the side effects, so I suggested he seek the advice of another psychologist. On this, he refuses to budge. I would consult Marina if I could, but my *WhatsApp* message to her months ago remains unread. So, I'm on my own, caretaking a sick and isolated man.

Alessandro's mother is dead; his brother Simone also lost to Covid. Here, in Basel, no one calls, and few come to visit.

As the pandemic appears to retreat and masks become optional, people venture out again, and Müllheimerstrasse is lively with groups of young people. Light-strung boats of tourists trawl the Rhine. I recognize Prentis as we stroll through Münsterplatz one evening and wave to him. He waves back but keeps walking. No wonder: Alessandro shuffles beside me, slouched and unresponsive.

After those few additional weeks in Basel, it became clear that my extended stay would calm Alessandro. This gives me both a sense of pride and a growing alarm. After his breakdown in June, he begged me to share his bed, and I capitulated. Sex is out of the question, and I'm glad for that, although I'm glad for the warmth of his body as the nights grow cooler. But, I'm beginning to feel uneasy about neglecting communication with my family. Switzerland and California share opposite sides of the same day, so mid-morning—the best time to reach my mother—means a late-night shout into an unreliable phone connection. Since Alessandro goes to bed earlier now, I do my best to not wake him and trigger his anxiety.

Bad days often follow good days. I've learned that Saturdays are triggers. Today is Friday, August 12th, and tomorrow will be Saturday, the eighth Saturday since the burglary—still fresh in his mind, it seems. I phone his work to check up on him.

"*Pronto, posta*," he answers, his voice flat.

"I'll come meet you after work today and we can go shopping. I have nothing to make for dinner tonight."

"I am not hungry."

"Well, I am. And we need to eat."

"Go to Madis *supermercato* and buy lasagna from the woman selling cheese. She makes dinner plates for us."

"So, you won't come with me?"

"You go and practice your bad Italian with Swiss cheese woman who speaks even worse Italian. I go home to sleep as usual."

It's not an unpleasant walk down busy Klybeckstrasse to the market. I pass Café Flora, and the French waiter recognizes me and waves me enter, but I salute and move on. The trams hum in every direction and gently assert their right-of-way. Cars and pedestrians pause patiently. The late afternoon deepens with a quiet urgency as men and women return from work with little of the aggressive thrusting forward that you see in a city like Los Angeles or New York.

I'm glad Alessandro hasn't joined me. Time spent walking alone makes me feel alive and glad to be alive. And when I return to Alessandro refreshed and happy, it seems to rub off on him, although I'm not sure why.

He's already asleep when I enter the flat. I place two lasagnas with their salads into the small refrigerator and enter the bedroom to lie next to him. He snores like a lion until he shifts slightly, and in that moment of quiet, I fall asleep, too.

I wake up in the near dark to see just one light burning at the front of the flat. I leave the bedroom to find Alessandro in the living room, bracing himself against the back of a chair and shaking so violently that the chair scrapes forward against the floor.

"Hey—what's happening now?"

He half turns, and I see only his profile. Sweat drips from the tip of his nose.

"Tomorrow, Saturday. I have the panic attack again."

"Nothing can hurt you anymore. Just breathe and relax."

I walk closer to him. The look on his face is one of pure terror—his eyes blinded with tears and his complexion so white it seems the blood has drained from his body.

"Did you take all your medication today?"

"I think so."

"You're not sure? Maybe we should keep a record."

He stares at me and stretches his mouth without talking, a sudden flush of red on his face. His body stiffens and his hands turn into fists.

"Medicine isn't helping. I am in hell, Mark. You don't understand how I am tortured by devils because I am in hell. Please hold me, Mark!"

I wrap my arms around him and pull him into me tightly, pressing his body against mine so there's no room for these so-called devils to squeeze between us. He bawls hotly into my shoulder, his hands pressing my back. The stiffness subsides, although his look of terror doesn't. I take him by the shoulders and gently back him away from me.

"Watch me now, Alessandro…" I take a step back and make a sweeping movement with my arms as if pulling something out of him and gathering it to myself. "I'm dragging these devils out of you and holding them here against my chest—do you see them? No? It doesn't matter. *I see them.*"

"Va bene."

I stagger in a play-act struggle to hold a heavy bundle as I stumble to the window and swing it open. With a great flourish, I heave the pretend bundle out the window and into the street.

"I've thrown them out, Alessandro! I've thrown these fucking devils out of this house and into the gutter!"

A smile sparks on his face. "*Si?*"

"Yes. Did I miss one? Should I do it again?"

He trembles and nods.

So, I repeat the pantomime, even more elaborately than before, drawing the devils out of him and gathering them in a bundle against me, then thrusting the bundle from his fourth-floor window and locking it shut.

"Grazie, Mark. You are a shaman."

"When the devils come again, we'll practice this Alessandro. So you'll remember how to do it when I'm not here."

"You are going someplace?"

In the lamplit kitchen, we settle down to enjoy our lasagna quietly. Across the courtyard, the chimes peal eight o'clock. I'm still eating when he abruptly gets up from the table, leaves his plate and utensils behind, and goes into the living room to watch his programs. By the time I finish the dishes and set up the small expresso pot for the next morning, he's already in bed. I pour myself a glass of wine to relax, then softly creep in beside him. He sleeps soundly through the night and on Saturday morning, he seems calm. I watch groggily as he grooms and dresses. He glances at me once before leaving the bedroom, the door of the flat clicking shut.

With Alessandro gone, I feel more relaxed and plan my day. Intrigued by Prentis' mention of the Spalentor Gate months ago, I finally decide to seek it out and take some photos. I'm gathering my things to leave when the phone buzzes in my trousers. I recognize the prefix as Italian but don't know the number. I click to connect, hoping it's Marina.

"My goodness, my goodness, my goodness, I've captured you at last," croons a familiar voice.

"*Dario?* I didn't expect to hear from you."

"'Goodbye' sounds so final in English. This is also true in Italian where in Tuscany, for example, 'addio' means we shall never see each other again. This is not the case with us, dear man."

"How are you, Dario?"

"Holding up. I'm sorry to have upset you so with my dramatic monologue."

"I'm in Basel now, with Alessandro."

"Yes, I encouraged you to go."

"You're okay there?"

"Yes. Still getting clean, as they say. But I have some hopeful news that leads me to believe that this won't be the end of the line for me."

"Tell me."

"You remember, of course, Sylvano and Rhoda, my embarrassing dressing down at their home and your generous gift to them of *Marc Avec la lune à la Fenêtre?*"

"I still feel bad about that"

"No need to smooth it over. Sylvano and Rhoda have proven themselves true friends again, having gotten wind of this unfortunate and institutional turn in my life."

"They're good people," I say.

"Yes, ever the optimist, you. Anyway, Rhoda, with her success in textile design, has her feelers pointing in every direction with many good connections at the ends of them. Apparently, she made some phone calls to people who know people and all that sort of thing, and just yesterday, I've been informed that I'll soon be leaving this place."

"You're going home?"

"Not quite. I won't be back home painting for some time. But I've been accepted into an eighteen-month program at a place called San Patrignano, up north in Rimini, near the coast."

"A whole year and a half? What is this place?"

"It's a retreat, sweetheart, a sort of sanitarium for artists in recovery that encourages artistic expression as part of their therapy. They believe addiction is best treated when the addict joins a community of like-minded people in recovery. I check in next Saturday, August 20th."

"This sounds good, Dario."

"It's not perfect. They have no painting facilities there, so my entry is by way of design— *textile design*, exactly what Rhoda does. They seem to have quite a few textile artists in programs at 'SanPa,' as they call it there, and a small retail shop where patients can sell their creations. I suppose I'll learn something new."

"Textiles? Like making pictures on cloth?"

"Exactly. A cozy little colony of ink-tweaking weavers getting clean. Do you suppose it's because 'thread' rhymes with 'pill-head'?"

"Absolutely."

"Now. About you."

"Does this 'SanPa' place allow visitors?"

"Only those I approve of. Anyone even remotely associated with my using is forbidden. Fortunately, none of these people are close friends."

"Good."

"I must reluctantly add Niccola to this list, although Trixie owes her life to him."

"Jabari is staying at your place to look after her."

"Yes, I know. Well done."

"Basel is no picnic. I'm dealing with Alessandro's mood swings."

"How long do you plan to stay there?"

"Not too much longer. My ninety-day Swiss visa runs out on Monday, September 12th. But I fear he's grown dependent on me."

"Escape while you can."

"It's complicated."

"It is not."

I hold the phone away from me for a moment because I think I hear something in the flat, then continue. "I recently learned some bizarre news about Carlos—Marina's Carlos. Have you heard from Marina at all?"

"No, she hasn't called which isn't unusual, especially when she's having problems with Luciano. What is your news?"

"It's nuts, Dario. Carlos Pineda—this gorgeous guy from the Canary Islands, this goddam *love of her life*, as Marina told it—turns out to be a psychopathic killer who's serving time in La Palmas prison for the murder of three women, the last one his pregnant wife, who burned to death."

"Oh, dear."

"That's what you say? *Oh, dear?*"

"Where did you learn this?"

"Long story, but through a connection with an American student here in Basel who'd corresponded with Carlos while researching his dissertation."

Dario says nothing.

"I've confirmed the story, Dario. There's stuff about Carlos on the internet, although not much. They picked up his DNA from a gasoline can under the charred body, and it connected him to the deaths of the other women, all young mothers."

"My god. My god."

"Looks like he was about to play out this sick shit with Marina. Good thing she left."

Dario breathes hard into the phone, starts to say something, then stops. "What was his having sex on Hortaleza Street all about?"

"Obviously he had a thing for men, too. Who knows? Maybe he wanted to switch things around a little and *you* were next on his list."

I can hear Dario thinking. "But it doesn't make sense. Why pursue a woman like Marina who lived thousands of miles from him? There must've been another reason."

"Like what?"

Dario pauses as if considering how best to put it to me. "Maybe, just maybe, he loved Marina. He was truly a madman, but he loved Marina, and the distance kept her safe."

"A generous theory for a killer, Dario."

"This affair with a married woman in Madrid he cared for became dangerous for her, so he decided to end it with some grand deceit."

"Grand deceit?"

"A proposal of marriage. He inflames her with his proposal, then cuts her off, hoping that the hurt would be deep enough to keep Marina from ever looking for him again, and save her life."

"Carlos the saint."

"Don't be ridiculous, Mark—of course, I'm not suggesting such a thing. However, living in a place like this does make you see a bit of the saint in everyone, as well as the demon. A lesson I hope you'll learn one day—minus the incarceration, of course."

"Noted."

Dario sighs, "I'm distressed by this terrible revelation. Of course, you'll say nothing of what you've learned to Marina. Time will pass, and eventually, she'll find out. Let that happen as it will happen."

"So good to talk to you again, Dario."

"And to you, dear friend. Until the next time."

He disconnects. I stand for a moment, looking out the window, trying to recall what I was about to do before this conversation. A footfall from behind startles me. I turn to see Alessandro, his face very close to mine.

"What are you saying about Marina? I can hardly *believe!*"

"You're back already?"

"I forget my phone and call you from the office to bring it, but you don't answer, so I come for it. What is this fantastic story of this crazy man I read about on the internet who tries to kill Marina, Mark? Who are you telling this to and why do you hide it from me?"

He asks again, and I don't answer. He glowers at me for a moment, then turns, grabs his phone and leaves, slamming the door.

Try as I might in the days that follow, I'm unable to plausibly justify why I haven't told Alessandro about Marina and her secret Spanish lover. He doesn't buy it when I say, "She didn't want to upset you," and throws back in my face that he's known Marina since they were children. He fumes that if anyone should know about her difficulties, it should be him, not some *Joey-come-lately-*—his words—from America. I tell him I understand his anger but that it just doesn't work that way. Choosing a confidant is a personal matter. Maybe it's *because* I'm a relative stranger that Marina felt free to unburden herself to me rather than to Alessandro who she feared would judge her.

"She cheats on Luciano who is the father of her children," he mutters, half to himself, and half to me every morning as he dresses for work. And every evening, as we clear the dishes after dinner, he says it again. "She cheats on her husband like a *stronza* whore after Luciano supports her for fifteen years."

"Don't talk about her like that. Stop thinking about this now."

"She cheats with a *omosessuale* who is also a murderer. Very smart, Marina!" he fumes.

"Stop it, Alessandro," I say, finally, as we undress for bed. "We're not going to discuss this until you've settled down."

"I wonder what Luciano will say when I call and tell him what his wife does in Spain with Mark the American?"

"Alessandro—" I look him squarely in the eyes, "Luciano must never, *ever* know."

It's the last conversation we have about Marina.

17
Reunion

On Wednesday, August 17th, Alessandro returns from work to tell me that the Ministry of Education wants to break his contract. As an incentive to resign, his supervisor offered him severance, a small pension, and a good recommendation should he decide to work again. I'm surprised at how calmly he delivers this news, asking only if I believe the offer, two thousand euros to start, followed by a monthly pension of four hundred euros until he reaches early retirement age, at sixty-three, seems reasonable.

"That's twenty-five years from now. Can you live on that?"

"I can get another job if I need. The pension continues if I work or not."

"Then, I think it's a pretty good deal."

"First thing I do is get out of fucking Basel."

"And go back to Pivonnia?"

"I am not sure. Maybe America."

I'm taken aback. "That kind of income wouldn't go very far there. Besides, I thought you didn't like America."

"But California is a good place."

"What are you saying, Alessandro? You want to come back with me?"

"California has many Mexicans. I like the Mexicans very much."

"You like the Mexicans."

"Sì. They are a friendly people."

"Then, why don't you go to Mexico?"

He seems to think about it. "Because I have been already. With Braxton once. The time before I meet you in San Francisco."

"What are you talking about, Alessandro?"

This is the wrong thing to say. The color drains from Alessandro's face, and he begins shaking again.

"*What—?* What's happening now?"

"I have no one, Mark. I am confused and alone."

"Stop it. Get ahold of yourself."

"I want to die, Mark."

"What time did you take your medication?"

"Fuck my medication! It does nothing! It makes me crazier! It makes me stink! And now I lose my job and I am ashamed!"

"Come into the bedroom and sit down."

"And now, even you—my best friend, keeps secrets."

"This again."

"You disrespect me in my own house, Mark."

"Come into the bedroom."

He lunges at me, then deflects to the kitchen table, sweeping everything off it, including the plastic tray of medication. The tray tumbles across the floor to the balcony where it breaks open, spilling boxes, vials, and pills everywhere. He drops to his hands and knees, picks up fistfuls of drugs, and scoops them into his mouth.

I straddle him, force him to the floor on his belly, his head sideways, and pry open his mouth. I reach in to scoop out the sticky mass of pink and white as he gags and tries to bite. "You think you have problems now? Spit this shit out!" I hoist myself up from a straddle and drive my knees into his lower back—*once, twice*—until he heaves up another mass of pink. He stops struggling as the puke pools away from his face. I'm shocked at how much he'd already swallowed.

I help him up from the floor, wipe his face, and guide him to bed. In the low light, I sit on the bed beside him, both of us breathing heavily. A church bell peals across the river. Alessandro looks up at me, eyes glistening.

"We were together once, and then I make mistake. I am sorry, Mark. Do not go away from me now because I have no one."

"Alessandro..."

"I can't be without anyone."

"What about Braxton? I thought you two were getting back together."

"Braxton? The Australian?"

"Of course, Braxton the Australian. Your ex-partner. You don't know who I'm talking about?"

"Braxton came for a while and stayed with me in Pivonnia. But then I think about it and decide *no*."

"You never saw the flowers in Budapest?"

"*Mamma mia,* such a memory you have. Braxton wanted to, but I decide no and ask him to go away. So, I hurt him, not the other way around as in the old days."

"Why did you change your mind?"

"Because I didn't need him anymore. And he was boring. And he had the cancer and complained about it all the time."

"That's very sad."

"And now I am boring. And he is cured, but I have devils inside."

"You'll be okay."

"You said once that Braxton was the devil I knew and better than the devil I didn't know. And you were right. This new devil is much worse than Braxton." Alessandro takes my hand. "You see, Mark, I broke Braxton's heart back then and I am sorry for it. He has a strange heart, but I broke it and sent him away."

I stay on the bed beside Alessandro until he grows tired and crawls under the covers. After he drops off to sleep, I go into the kitchen, take his phone from the charging station, and find Braxton's number. I begin to tap it into my phone, then pause to consider the possible consequences of making this call—decide to connect, anyway. God knows what time it is over there, and I don't care. While I listen to the peculiar ring on the other end, I step out onto the balcony, where I'm sure Alessandro can't hear and wait for someone to answer.

As August draws to a close, Alessandro's mood improves. But when he realizes he's trashed much of his medication and begins to run out, he requests refills sooner than he's entitled to them. His doctor asks him to explain the short. When the details of the earlier incident come out, the doctor suggests that he check himself into a hospital on Tuesday, August 30th, for one week. While there, the doctor can observe his behavior and perhaps decrease or change the medication. Alessandro discusses it with me and asks if I think he should follow the doctor's advice. I do, and he consents.

Two days before he's admitted, he shops, cooks, and cleans the house—for me, he says. He's easier to be around. Instead of his usual bland expression, real emotions appear on his face. He sleeps soundly at night, all probably due to the lower levels of tricyclics cooking his brain.

On Monday evening, after spending a last day together, Alessandro goes to bed early. I join him after sorting out the cheapest flight options back to Los Angeles and the best way to get from Alessandro's neighborhood to EuroAirport at Mulhouse Freiburg. He snores softly as I drop off to a welcome sleep, but I wake up in the dead of night to feel a pressure against me. He's removed his clothes and he's amorous. He places his hand on my chest and drapes his bare leg over mine, rubs his hand and leg against me. His soft touch brings back our early intimate encounters—*the glide of his skin*—those first days of lovemaking in the hotel room in Rome. His touch brings back Ischia, too, when the moon's eclipse made a ruby ring above the sea. His touch, his soft and tender touch—*the electric glide of his skin*—I roll to him and kiss him. When he pushes his large, warm hand under the elastic of my shorts, I flash on the memory of two silver rings in my pocket that never saw the light of day.

NO.

I tell him I'm thirsty and need a glass of water, but once out of bed, I stay there and begin to sort my things.

At the first light, he's up and in the shower. He dresses in clean clothes and comes into the kitchen for an expresso and toast. We don't talk much. He says nothing about my leaving his bed during the night but quietly packs a small suitcase and waits in the hall for the bell to ring announcing his ride.

It's hard not to feel sad watching Alessandro as he stands there. He tells me to stay in the flat as long as I like and encourages me to use his bicycle. He makes sure I have our student friend Prentis's phone number for intellectual conversation and reminds me that veal funghi is his favorite dish. He doesn't catch that I might be leaving soon and leaves me cash to pay bills. He tells me where he keeps his condoms should I wish to entertain a guest. Then, the buzzer sounds, and with a small wave, he's gone.

I have a lot to do in the days remaining before my visa expires. Switzerland requires a negative Covid test no more than twenty-four hours before departure. It's one of only a few European countries that still enforces strict travel restrictions, although worldwide vaccination efforts have weakened the deadliness of the virus. Per regulations, the test must be of a specific antigen-measuring sort that comes from a certified pharmacist. I need to schedule an appointment, get swabbed at a certified location, sign into a test results portal, and wait for my hopefully negative results to appear, after which I can copy and display them on my phone. It's a throwback to the old days.

I book my Air France flight for 6 a.m. on Tuesday, September 6th, one week from today. Then, I locate a pharmacist on Klybeckstrasse and make my appointment for opening time at 9 a.m. Monday, September 5th, cutting my twenty-four-hour window to twenty-one hours. I plot out my tram route to the airport and calculate commuting time, but completely overlook that the trams don't run after midnight. This means that I'll either have to find a cab, or spend the night at the airport terminal, waiting.

I start to pack. As usual, I'll take my two pieces of luggage into the cabin—my suitcase overhead and my strapped carry-on bag beneath my seat—to avoid checking them. And there's no denying it, I want to see Alessandro again, but I'm not sure what to say to him because he doesn't know I'm leaving. I call the hospital and a man answers, speaking Swiss, of course. I ask for Alessandro by name in English, but the answerer doesn't understand English. I reboot my Italian and spew it out, hoping for the best as I prepare to exit this crazy country with its fixation on rules.

"*Pronto!*" Alessandro answers brightly.

"Hi, it's Mark. I want to come see you."

"So, come see me."

"Can I come over the weekend?"

He cups the phone. I hear muffled conversation.

"Yes, come Saturday afternoon," he says. "I also have a guest you meet while he's here."

I catch a southbound tram to the hospital. I'm admitted, after the usual complications, with my CDC vaccination card. I take the elevator to the top floor and approach Alessandro's room, the door stubbed open with a cart of medicines. When I enter, the first thing I see is a bouquet of flowers. And then I see Braxton—older and gaunter—sitting next to Alessandro on the bed.

"Nice flowers," I say.

"Who is this criminal? Who let him in?" Alessandro pipes, sitting up. He's fully dressed.

Braxton walks to me, takes my hand, and draws me close, "Not just any flowers," he whispers, "but purple kalanchoe, the kind they grow in Budapest."

"Thank you," I whisper. "Have you told him—?"

"Of course."

"So, Mark," Alessandro squawks, "are you here to steal paintings from the wall? Maybe they give to you if you ask."

"Hi, Alessandro."

"Maybe you can marry a *psichiatra*. They have some sexy ones here."

"You doing okay?"

He smiles in a way I haven't seen him smile in years. "How you arrange this—this man to come find me? Now Braxton wants to stay, and I can't get rid of him." He motions for me to sit on the bed beside him.

"I'm just stopping by. My flight leaves this Tuesday, and I need to do the whole Covid test business before I go through the gate. I wanted to check up on you."

"Go for test on Leutengasse. Cheap there."

"I made an appointment at Klybeckstrasse."

"Poor you."

"Why?"

He shrugs.

"Anyway," I continue, "Thanks so much for everything, Alessandro. I'll always remember our adventures together. But now it's time to go back to California and pick things up where I left them."

"Good. Braxton a better cook than you, anyway."

"Now, now, Alessandro!" Braxton scolds, "Don't be a bitch." Turns to me, "I do wish you could stay and visit us for a while, but I understand your urgency. Traveling is so tedious these days."

"No worries. Give me a year or two and I'll be back."

"How American! So optimistic!" He comes over to me and takes my hand. "But do have a marvelous journey back home, whatever the future. We'll try to work things out here for as long as we can put up with one another."

"That means three days," Alessandro snipes.

"We're going to quit smoking together," Braxton adds.

"Two days," Alessandro snipes again.

"I'm very glad to hear that," I say. "Well, goodbye then, you two."

"*Arrivederci,*" Braxton says.

"*Arrivederci,*" Alessandro says.

"*Arrivederci,*" they say, more or less together.

I sleep poorly the next two nights because the apartment feels strange without Alessandro. I also worry about possible delays during my trip to the airport and missing my plane. Private car service to Mulhouse Freiburg in the morning means traffic. It's also expensive and, judging from the one-star ratings of most of the car services here, unreliable. I decide to take the tram the night before and spend the night in the Air France terminal, waiting for my morning flight and for my negative test results to post.

On Monday morning, I walk to the Klybeckstrasse pharmacy and stand outside until it opens. At 9:15 a.m., a polite young pharmacist lets me in but explains in perfect English that the nurse dispensing the tests won't arrive for an hour. When the nurse arrives at 10:30, she smiles stiffly, enters a glassed room, and turns on a fluorescent light. Another half hour goes by before she motions me to walk down a corridor and sit at a table behind a medical screen. Fifteen minutes later, she sits opposite me, asks for my passport, and hands me a sign-in sheet where I scratch my name, my phone number, and a password for the pharmacy's website, where my results will be posted within twenty-four hours after she submits my sample to the lab—in Colberg, France! All of this is communicated in English, so heavily accented in Swiss, that the young pharmacist stands next to me and provides clarification when necessary, which is *always*. The swabbing finished, the sample is capped and stuffed into an envelope. I'm provided a card with the website address.

"The password is your first and last name hyphenated," the young pharmacist translates. "And don't worry, we courier to Colberg this afternoon and your results will post sometime during the night. You'll receive a notification of the posting on your phone."

Back at the flat, I'm disorganized, having packed, unpacked, and repacked so many times. I look forward to the return of everyday conveniences like finding a pair of clean socks in the same place and only *my* shoes tucked under the bed. It'll also be nice to have large built-in closets again instead of impossible wardrobe cabinets with their inscrutable doors. I carefully sort clothes, documents, toiletries, and museum brochures into my bag. In the end, I'm stuffing things wherever I have room for them, taking care to keep the important stuff—cash, medicines, duplicate vaccination records, phone chargers, and itinerary sheets—bundled together in my strapped carry-on bag where I can reach them.

It's 4 p.m. by the time I'm done, and I plan to take the 11 p.m. tram to the airport to shorten my overnight wait. I splash cold water on my face, fix myself a gouda cheese sandwich, then lie down for a short nap with my phone beside me should my results buzz in. But nearly two hours later, I wake up to find nothing.

At dusk, the air chills. Smoke rises from chimneys across the yard. The blinking red lights of the Novartis tower begin their evening semaphores, and a veil of clouds covers a pale moon. I open the door to the balcony to breathe it all in, and in the half-light, a tiny pink pill rolls towards me from under the railing. The familiar kitchen and its balcony feel lonely now, and I can't shake away the gloom that I'll never step out to see this view again.

It's late morning in California, so I pick up the phone and call my mother. The ring on the other side crackles with static.

"Just a minute," she answers, breathlessly. Then, "I had to put down something heavy before I could speak. Hi, Mark! Where are you?"

"Hi Mom, I'm waiting for my flight at the Basel airport."

"Where to next? Borneo to pick breadfruit?"

"Don't faint. Los Angeles."

"You mean you're coming home? *That's* different."

"I need you to be nice. What heavy thing were you putting down?"

"My suitcase. Can you believe I'm just getting around to storing it after my trip in July?"

"Your trip? Oh, right! To see Sam."

"To see Sam."

"So?"

"So. What airline did you say you were taking, and when?"

"It's Air France from here to Boston then Delta Airlines to LAX. I'll get in at ten in the morning on Tuesday, the same day I leave Basel."

"You pick up a day. Wonderful."

"Yep."

"What else is happening with you?"

"I'm just done here. I miss you and Loren."

"Anything else?"

"Why do you ask?"

"Talk to me."

"I'll talk when I'm back. I'm sorry I haven't kept in touch."

"We give you your space. Besides, we've been busy."

"Busy with what?"

"Well, with Loren, for one thing."

"Uh oh."

"No, it's good."

"Spill the beans."

"Too much to explain over the phone, Mark."

"Okay. Let's do some explaining off the phone when I'm back."

"Anyone meeting you?"

"I'll take an Uber, probably, after I go through customs and all that stuff, although that may happen in Boston."

"Uber," she repeats. "is that something like Zoom…? *Joking!*" she quips. "Have a safe trip, Mark. My amazing son, Mark—"

"Wait. Mom."

"Yes, honey?"

I take a breath and close my eyes. "Has it ended there yet? This Covid nightmare?"

She also takes a moment. "It's better, that's all I can say. Much better."

To kill time, I turn on the television—just for the sound of human voices. At 10:30 p.m., wrapped in a sweater for my overnight stay at the airport, I leave Alessandro's key on his kitchen table, turn out the lights, and quietly close the door behind me. I walk, for the last time, down Müllheimerstrasse and catch the airport tram at an intersection almost directly opposite Café Flora. The café jumps with music and laughter this Friday night. Under the covered terrace aglow with heat lamps, a man plays the accordion beside two women in scarves, stumming guitars. Their voices warble up through the chilly air:

Bye, bye, Miss American Pie….

18
Something Hidden

The main terminal of Basel's EuroAirport feels like an abandoned warehouse late at night. Plastic bucket seats line both sides of a wide aisle where a team of women push brooms. With only the women and their brooms for company, I settle myself across several seats near an information screen and find a charging outlet for my phone. I hate these seats; their edges rise up in sharp ridges just high enough to make snoozing across them impossible. I also discover that I've camped near a group of carnival rides for children. Rocket ships, sports cars, and magic ponies pulse with garish lights, and a cartoon voice in a continual loop invites, in four languages, anyone within fifty feet to *come to Playland and meet my magical friends!*

Midnight comes and goes with nothing from the pharmacy. A long, cold night stretches ahead. I close my eyes to the torture of cartoon voices and try to nap, but four hours later, I find myself slouched sideways, my back aching, my dropped phone buzzing from the floor.

My test results have been posted. Half-awake and all thumbs, I fumble my first connection to the Klybeckstrasse portal, then screw it up a second time. On the third try, the portal freezes. When it finally responds, it takes fifteen minutes to figure out where the results live and where to enter my password. Eventually, the password field appears. I tap in my hyphenated name and wait:

PASSWORD INCORRECT.

I try again and again. Once more. I don't exist. I've *never* existed, either as "Mark-Anello," or "Marc-Anello," or "Marco-Anello." In a flash of insight about how badly designed web portals can be, I try "Anello-Mark" and its many variations. Still nothing. I get up and start to pace. How do I fix this? I have a fucking plane to catch! And, if I weren't crazed enough already, I'm continually serenaded by a cartoon-happy *welcome to Playland* to meet magical friends. Then, I remember the fractured English of the pharmacy nurse and think to try foreign language misspellings—"Markus-Anello," "Marcke-Anello," "Manheim-Anello," "Anello-Manheim," "Manheim-Steamroller—" STOP. I close my eyes and take a breath. Open them and type carefully: Mark-VANELLO. *The heavens open!* I'm negative. I'm clean. I'm glorious.

I gather my stuff and pull out three crumpled boarding passes from my carry-on bag—Air France from Basel to Paris, Air France from Paris to Boston, and then Delta from Boston to Los Angeles. I recheck the Basel to Paris flight number and stuff the two connecting flight passes back into my bag. The information screen wakes up and glitters, and I find my assigned departure gate. I stagger forward, one foot half-asleep, pushing my wobble-wheeled suitcase until I'm safely out of earshot of that torturous invitation to meet magical friends. I idle in the security queue while removing my belt, shoes, wallet, change from my pocket, and any other alarm-setters, then enter the green-lit booth where a revolving X-ray camera scans my body and broadcasts naked pictures of me to security personnel throughout Western Europe. I settle into another uncomfortable bucket seat until called to board, then bolt ahead like a marathon runner, nab my overhead space, wedge my carry-on under me, and lay claim to my seat. I mutter a prayer of thanks that I'm on the aisle and relax.

I've never felt so tired in my life. While others around me laugh and chatter in a variety of languages, I'm ready for some sleep—at 6:30 in the morning, local time. After my seatmates arrive, stepping on more feet than I thought I had, I drop into that sleep, hoping my companions for the two-hour flight to Paris will prove themselves compassionate human beings and settle down. They seem to, and I feel the roughness of our acceleration diminish until I know we're airborne.

The cheerful voice of the captain rouses me, and I wake up, nose pressed to the window, as the Eiffel Tower wheels below. Soon we're down and I'm marching with my luggage toward my connecting flight to Boston. I have an hour, buy a croissant, and settle in.

Twenty minutes before boarding, I pull out my two remaining boarding passes, tuck the one I'll need into my passport, and stuff the other back into my carry-on. I find my window seat and momentarily displace two elderly French ladies who rise with genial annoyance. I try to apologize and make small talk in French before I notice that this truly annoys them. No matter. I've begun the longest leg of my trip, I'm dead tired, and I don't really want to talk to anybody. I start to doze during the life jacket demonstration.

I'm jolted awake almost six hours later by the bump of the snack cart, the two seats next to me now empty. Across the empty space, a cycloptic blue window glows.

"Was I snoring?" I ask the blond server who offers waffle cookies.

"No, two aisle seats opened up in the back and *les madames* wanted to sit closer to the rear lavatory."

"I see."

"Your row will stay empty for the rest of your flight."

When she moves on, I lift the handrests and slide to the window. We're over the Atlantic, blue below and above—featureless blue-on-blue with small balloon-clouds breaking the sweep of it. Only a sliver of moon distinguishes up from down. In my lingering dreaminess, the blue reminds me of the Tyrrhenian Sea off the coast of Ischia that afternoon nearly four years ago when Alessandro and I argued over a lunch of bland fish. The empty seats beside me trigger a memory of my agonizing and fevered flight home from Madrid. The shapes of the clouds bring back images of my Alpine journey to Basel... places and faces, movies in my head, already a little fuzzy around the edges.

Dinner, with a commotion of carts, follows: a tasty pot-au-feu with tender beef and vegetables. A new round of commotion begins as pairs of blue-gloved attendants march down the aisle collecting trash. I feel the plane pitch as we start our descent into Boston's Logan Airport. Eight hours of flying time have been completely swallowed by the time change; it's now 6:30 in the morning here, too. An announcement crackles through the cabin listing the gates for connecting flights, although my Delta flight to Los Angeles isn't mentioned. No worries; I have a two-hour layover and look forward to stretching my legs.

The shabbiness of Boston's Logan Airport next to Basel's EuroAirport hits me like blast of foul air when I exit. I drag my wonky suitcase and hoist my carry-on through corridor after corridor on the way to U.S. Customs, a gymnasium-sized room with stanchioned queues packed with returning travelers. It takes nearly forty minutes before I can even see my officer, who seems to have issues admitting nearly everyone who stands before him. But I'm one of the lucky ones, and with a glance and a stamp, he returns my passport and I pass through. I find the departing terminal and gate for my flight to L.A. and settle into a ketchup-stained seat. I'm early, so the waiting area has only a few people.

It's high time I called Jim and too late to avoid the guilt of not calling sooner. It's probably a chilly morning in L.A., and Jim might be sleeping. I click through his number anyway, worried that the longer I wait, the more that announcing I'm back will come off like a last-minute invitation to a party where the guests have already arrived.

He answers after the fifth ring, sounding groggy.

"You."

"Jim?"

"Jim."

Confused, I stammer, "This is Mark, Jim."

"This is Jim, Mark."

At least we've begun a conversation. "What are you doing, Jim?"

"Testing Newton's first law."

"What?"

"A body at rest remains at rest... I'm in bed, jerkoff. It's not even six o'clock."

"Oh. Sorry."

"Does this mean I have to get up and do pushups?"

"Pushups? For what?"

"For you. Thanks for keeping me informed."

"Sorry, again."

"I mean—*six fucking months*, Mark?"

"I know. But I'm on my way back."

"So I've heard. I bought some ribbed condoms. I don't do that for just anybody."

"How did you find out?"

"*Phone Search Online.* I assumed Frances Anello and Loren Anello of Glendale were distant relatives."

"You called my mother?"

"Your brother. Great guy. I like him. He was happy to share what he knew, that is, practically *nothing...* but we had a nice chat. He called me when he learned you were coming back today. He found out from your mother after she found out from you."

"Who did you say you were?"

"A loan shark with a box razor. What did you want me to say?"

I don't answer.

"'I'm your brother's friend,' I said, dumbass. But Loren knows what's going on."

"You think?"

"Yeah. Because I threw in, 'and his favorite cocksucker.'"

I look around a waiting area that's grown busier, my ears beginning to burn from this conversation. "I'm sorry, Jim. Lots of last-minute decisions here."

"Let's practice making some long-term decisions. What do you say?"

"Not sure what you mean."

"I mean, I'd like you to stick the fuck around for a while, at least until I can get back the spare socks and underwear I left in your dresser."

"Okay, I can promise that."

"Promises, promises."

"Don't be pissed."

"I'm never pissed. I just mix poison martinis. Fix you one later?"

"Later?"

"Later. I'll meet you in the arriving flights area in front of the Delta terminal."

After the *twenty-minute-until-boarding* announcement, I gather my stuff but resist launching out of my seat to join impatient passengers, already standing and pressed against each other. When it's time to board, I heave myself up and join a shorter line.

I reach the gate attendant, feel inside the pocket of my carry-on for the Delta boarding pass—my *last* boarding pass—but my hand slides back and forth in an empty space. I jump my hand to a neighboring pocket. Nothing. I drop both bags, stretch open the carry-on, and hold it to the light. Nope.

I step away from the line and pat myself down furiously, checking every back pocket, inner pocket, and zipped pocket. I'm now the only person left in the boarding area, and of course, the attendant asks in her most cloying of cloying attendant voices, "Having a problem, sir?" while probably thinking, *another idiot who doesn't have his shit together.* Without answering, I tear into my carry-on again, plunging my hand back into the original pocket to see if, by some miracle, I've missed something.

I have. The tips of my fingers find a tear in the lining that I hadn't noticed before and where, in my haste, I'd stuffed the boarding pass before leaving Paris. I reach deep through the tear and coax out the crumpled pass along with something else—a small pink envelope addressed only to "Mark" in Marina's careful handwriting. With blood roaring in my ears, I surrender the boarding pass and take my seat, pinching the envelope tightly between my fingers.

I find my aisle seat. As soon as I sit down, I examine the secret space where I found the letter. The slit through the lining is straight and clean, as if someone sliced it with a razor or sharp knife. It's hardly an accidental tear, but a deliberate cut, camouflaged rather than hidden. Very clever, Marina—to sneak into my bedroom and tuck something into my carry-on where it wouldn't be discovered right away, but soon enough.

As the engines whine to life and the flight attendants mime their safety routines, I slide my finger under the flap of Marina's envelope and draw out a single sheet.

Caro Mark,

I write this letter to you the night before I return to Italy and leave you alone with Alessandro in Basel. I came into your bedroom while you slept and hid it well because I don't want you to read it until I am safely away. It will be the last

*communication from me, and I must sadly say that you will
never see or hear from me again.*

*All night I think about my life and decide to take the children
and hide where I cannot be found or contacted. By the time
you read this letter, it is done. I will keep the children until
they are old enough to decide whether to remain with me.
But, for now, I know that they feel happy and safe in my
company and wish to escape. They say they have many things
to tell me about Luciano that I am not sure I want to hear.*

*I tell you now that you are an exceptionale man and anyone
who finds you will be very lucky. If Alessandro was different
he would see this and if Dario gets better he will see this. But
you also must see this and move on in your life. I know that
you understand these things but forget. I am the same. But it
is not too late for the future. It is never too late for the future.*

With love, Marina.

The plane rumbles, smooths, alights, then tacks west over the
backyards of Boston. Beyond them, the glass towers of downtown glitter.
I catch a glimpse of all this when I crane my neck to see around the young
woman sitting by the window. But the view ends when she closes the
shade.

19
Return of the Nomad

In the half-light of the cabin with the drone of engines in my ears, I close my eyes. I open them to a different light: the light of our long-ago kitchen in the apartment on East 84th Street.

I'm five years old and sit in my pajamas at the kitchen table next to an open window.

A Sunday morning breeze sweeps in. My dad stands at the stove frying eggs. He's young and handsome and my mother is beautiful. She stands over the table folding napkins. Dad sings as he scrambles our eggs and slides them onto Mom's favorite breakfast plates, the yellow ones with dandelions and fiddleheads. We sit together and butter toast until Mom jumps up to follow the squeals of a baby in the next room. She returns with Loren, pink and spittle-faced, pointing in every direction and kicking his strong legs. Outside, the hanging white undershirts wave like a row of little white clouds. Behind them, the distant city looks like a watercolor: blue and forever.

Six hours later, the midday sun beams and shades go up. Snacks are served and cleared, and we prepare to land. The familiar tangles of freeways pass below and grow closer until there's nothing but pavement and we bounce back to Earth. On the way to the terminal exit, I go to the men's room to splash water on my face and smooth my hair. My face looks drawn and tired, and in the full-length mirror, I see that I've gained weight. I'll meet Jim looking pretty shabby, I'm afraid, so do what I can, and relax. I text him and make my way to the arriving passengers curb just outside the Air France terminal. Jim is there already, wearing a stylish blue blazer and craning his neck to find me. He looks very handsome.

"Hey nomad," he says, walking up and staring at me, "where's your tent?"

"Oh shit," I say, "I'll have to go back."

He doesn't smile but hugs me and gives me a quick kiss.

"Thanks for meeting me," I mumble, walking to his car.

"No problem," he says, paying the parking attendant and crossing the gate.

I'm back—back amid the blandishments of Los Angeles with its shabby palm trees, inelegant storefronts, and dingbat apartment houses in pink and turquoise. Layers of parked cars range on both sides of us as we flow through light traffic.

"So," I say, nesting my hand between his legs.

"So," he responds.

A moment passes. He glances at me. "I have news to report, and I want to get your reaction."

"Oh yeah"?

"In July, my company opened a position in San Diego. I applied for it."

"What's in San Diego?"

"Nice weather. Beaches. PETCO Park."

"What's that?"

"Never mind. Anyway, I interviewed and got it. A promotion with more money and an annual bonus. I start on October third."

"So, now *you're* leaving."

"That's where the discussion comes in."

"Congratulations, Jim. Great news."

"And...?"

I struggle to put my thoughts together. "At some point pretty soon, I'll have to go back to work because teaching is all I know. I'm not sure my sabbatical from Cavendar still stands, but I'll find out."

"Cavendar closed at the end of June. Everybody got split up between two schools in La Canada and Flintwood."

"What?"

"I read it in the paper."

"Shit."

"Sorry."

"I'd better pay a visit to principal Easterborough."

"So, about this news. Does it sound like something you might...?"

"Let me think about it."

"You do that. You should also call your mother. Or we can drop by."

"So, my mother knows about you?"

"Yes, *she knows about me*," he says, looking bewildered. "Your brother spread the word."

"I'm not quite ready to visit family yet. Let's just go home."

"Okay, boss."

We turn onto Montrose and pull into the driveway of my house, the ever-present Mrs. Sandoval still pruning her hibiscus bushes, which, in all the years I've watched her, never look pruned. As usual, she looks up, then down again. Jim takes the lead by grabbing my luggage and heading for the front door. He waits for me to tease out my keys. Mrs. Sandoval stops her pruning and looks up.

Once we're inside, the stale air of my house fills my nose. Jim goes to the sink, blows into an empty glass, and fills it with tap water. Then, he settles down on my couch and pats the cushion beside him. He strokes the side of my face with his curled fingers.

"You want to mess around? Six months is a long time."

"How about you let me clean myself up, call my mom, and then you come back for dinner later?"

"You're killing me."

"You can hold off... I mean, can't you?"

He stares, says nothing.

"I mean, *haven't* you?"

"Haven't I what? Relieved myself fourteen times a day or messed around?"

"Yeah."

"Yeah? That's your answer?" He stops his stroking and sighs. "Yes to the first, no to the second. Call me an idiot, but I still think you're worth waiting for. But the clock is ticking. My motorcycle mechanic wants me to enroll in naked *Qi Jong*."

He gets up and cracks his back. "Okay, we're on for dinner, but this place smells like someone used your carpets for cake batter. Come to my house so I can show off my culinary skills. I promise a most elegant repast of meatloaf with mashed potatoes."

"Exactly what I'm in the mood for."

"Good. Call your mom, floss your fangs, douche your dumper—whatever. I'll call you later."

A quick peck and he's out the door.

I want to talk to someone. Mom answers after the first ring, breathless again.

"So, tell me more about this new fella," she says after the requisite snarkiness about my not having told her sooner.

"I met him at the community pool right before I left for Italy again."

"And he's not from Belarus or anything, right?"

"No. Burbank."

"When can you bring him over to meet everyone?"

"I need to unpack, and then he's making dinner tonight. I'd like to get a nap in there somewhere. How about early next week or even next weekend?"

"What's his preference?'

"Excuse me?"

"Foodwise."

"Oh. He's easy. Basic Italian."

"Perfect."

"And since we're truth-sharing, you never told me about your trip to Chicago to see Sam Derwitz."

"We had a lovely time. He's a perfect gentleman. But I could never live in Chicago."

"Why would you even think about living in Chicago?"

"Call me when you'd like to come over with Jim," she says.

By mid-afternoon, I finish unpacking and do a load of wash. I'd love to take a nap before I shower, but my mind fixates on news of Cavendar's closing, so I jump online and find an old article about it in the *Los Angeles Times*. It seems that on May 15th, Mayor Garcetti pressured the Los Angeles Panel for Education Policy to shut down five public schools because of funding shortages and poor academic performance. The Mayor proposed consolidation to address under-performance in districts that faced higher costs per pupil. Cavandar would close to students for three days at the end of June while the staff prepared. Classes would resume in two new locations on July 1st. The article ends with a list of phone numbers for up-to-date recorded information about the consolidation. One number I recognize is that of Cavendar's main office, so I call it. To my surprise, a woman with a familiar voice answers.

"Lorraine here. May I help you?"

"Principal Easterborough? Is that you?"

"Who is this, please?"

"Mark Anello, your math teacher on leave."

"Oh, yes! Hello."

"Hello, well, I'm just back from Europe and so sorry to hear about Cavendar."

"Yes..." she says in a tone that suggests there's been much grief and anger about the closure, now mostly subsided. "Quite a few changes."

"It seems so."

"You know that I can't offer your position back."

"Understood."

"But I assume you enjoyed your time away."

"Very much."

"Good." She sighs. "So, there you were, visiting all of these wonderful places, and here I am, in the office of an abandoned school, collecting my things. Anyway, you're a welcome distraction."

"I live fairly close. Might I stop by briefly to see the school one more time and say hello?"

"Of course."

Principal Easterborough opens the doors and admits me to her former office. We sit at opposite sides of the desk, just as before, but each of us in a vastly different space. "Thanks for coming," she says, "Travelling makes you happy I can see."

"Yes, but after so many months... well, it's good to settle down again."

She divides a large stack of papers into two stacks and moves one across her desk. "I wish I could say the same."

"So, which of the two schools have you moved to?"

"Neither. I'm returning to New Mexico. A few years ago, I assisted in the organization of a Navajo Nation school on the reservation and found it rewarding."

"Wonderful."

"Everything's changed here, Mark. We've lost some of our best students, although I'm confident that most of them will eventually succeed somewhere else. But I worry about the others—the ones who were just beginning to push through and take off. It'll be a long time before they come back, if they come back at all."

"I know. It's very sad."

"Did you know that the city plans to demolish Cavendar? We presented a proposal to turn it into a community center, but it went nowhere." She looks around the room. "Soon, where we sit will probably be the lobby of some boutique hotel."

"I can't believe it—"

"We were the standard-bearers, you and me. I could see that bond almost immediately, despite our getting off on the wrong foot. And I believe that tension between us was all about sharing the frustration, even the *anger*, that came from trying to make a difference."

"I appreciate your saying that."

"I didn't have a solution, with the situation being what it was. It's difficult to insist on excellence when everyone seems set against it."

"You'll make a difference wherever you go, Lorraine."

"Thank you." She rises. "Would you like to see your old classroom?"

"No, thank you."

"Well, then. Such a pleasant surprise to see you. I believe the same for you—you'll thrive somewhere and succeed brilliantly. It's written all over you."

"That's very kind."

"So, let me finish here and go home."

"Best of luck, Lorraine."

"And to you Mark," she says with a downcast smile, locking the door when I step back outside.

At six o'clock my phone buzzes, waking me from a catnap. Jim is taking the rest of the week off and asks if I can be at his place in an hour. I shower, shave, and pick through the rack of clothes in my closet, clothes I haven't seen for months. I select a shirt and trouser pair that's miraculously free of wrinkles, grab my sunglasses and wallet, and I'm about to head out the door when I remember something else: my toothbrush. Just in case Jim no longer has the one he'd put aside for me.

His condo is immaculate: the office is cleared of papers and crusted coffee cups, and his kitchen sparkles where an oven-timer ticks. On his kidney-shaped coffee table, I see one of our meteors displayed under a pin spotlight he's strategically positioned above it.

"Where's the other one?" I ask, even before I've settled down.

"Not sure," he says, "Probably under the bed."

"Hello," I say, going over to him.

"How' you?" he says, giving me a peck and solid hug. "Sit your ass down and relax. Want a cocktail?"

"You do cocktails?"

"I do cocktails. I also do cocks." He places his hand over his mouth in a pretend faux pas.

"You've had a cocktail."

"I've had a cocktail."

"Sure, I'll have a cocktail. As long as it's not a poisoned martini."

Two negronis later, we move to his small dining table, which he's decorated beautifully, including wine glasses with cloth napkins tucked in.

"This is crazy-fancy, Jim."

"The food isn't, so don't expect much."

But the food *is*—he sets down a perfectly squared block of ground beef with a dark red glaze across the top and three strips of bacon for an extra flourish. He follows with a swirl of horseradish-laced mashed potatoes and a long plate of seared French green beans with shallots.

"Jesus," I say, "you're a closet chef."

"All for you, baby," he says—purely, sweetly, without a trace of snarkiness. "Welcome home."

Dessert is gelato. Pistachio.

We're slouched on the sofa with our shoes off, not quite sleepy but relaxed. He takes my foot and rubs it. Then he sits up and looks at me. I sit up and look back,

He leans forward across his knees, looking down at the floor. "Mark," he begins solemnly, "as I mentioned before, there's the possibility of a position for you at my company, if you're interested. I'd be on the interview and selection committee."

"We talked about that, Jim. Thing is—I just don't think tech training is something I could take to. I like working with people."

"Okay, well hear me out. Right after you called me from Basel, I got wind that we've started a new initiative for software development called *Social Data Models.* That means building new tools to track the vectors of disease, pockets of crime, child poverty, housing discrimination—that kind of stuff. People stuff. Making things better stuff."

"Cool."

"In San Diego."

"Even cooler."

"So, this is where you fit in: they'll need someone with teaching skills to train these geeks because the field of social metrics is, like, way out of their wheelhouse. It's really good pay, Mark. Say you're interested and I'll put you in for it. I'll do the interview and deal with any new candidate issues that might come up."

"Like what? Like I'm an entitled homosexual?"

He rolls his eyes. "Like you've never worked in tech before. But the thing is, you *teach*. And *math*, no less."

"Would you let on that we know each other?"

"Sure. Seriously, it'll be fine after a year or two. People couple up all the time at the firm. I won't be your boss, and you'll work in a department separate from mine, probably on another floor or even in another building. The campus is huge. And here's a perk—they have an Olympic-sized swimming pool."

"Are you kidding?"

"San Diego, man." He jostles me, "Fucking San Diego!"

"I'll think about it."

He throws up his hands in exaggerated annoyance. "Always thinking about it! What am I gonna do with you?"

"All right. I'll sleep on it. Better?"

He scoots closer, leans us back, his arm across my legs.

"Listen..." he says, sitting back up again, turning to me, and holding his hands apart as if carrying an invisible box. It's a gesture he uses when he makes an important pitch.

"Listening."

"I'm really sorry I went off on you after our date in Santa Monica. I was crazy-jealous."

"I know, Jim. And I was a total prick."

"So, I need to tell you... how can I say it? I mean, I've thought about it a lot since that night because I still see us as a hand-in-glove combination. That is, if you think about it the way I do, which maybe you don't."

"Trying to follow here, Jim."

"Okay. First of all, I think you're hot. Italians turn me on, but not if they live in Italy. You—well, maybe you need to back off from Italians a little.

"For sure."

"What else... your mind goes to cool places and mine doesn't. You're a deep well, I'm a parking lot. You're a Sudoku game, I'm a grocery store coupon."

"Please. Stop."

"Anyway, here's the most important part, and it's something you should know even if you decide you don't want to be with me, which I can live with, assuming I have enough alcohol and drugs…"

"Not funny, Jim."

"I know, I know. Sorry."

"So, what's the most important part?"

He looks up as if exasperated. "*Jesus,*" he says to the light fixture, then looks me straight in the eye. He says the words slowly. "You have the glow of *family*, Mark. It's a little fucked up, to be sure, but it's still there. Maybe it takes someone like me to point out your cluelessness about this, because I've never had family the way you have it—never."

"My family can be a pain in the ass."

"I get that, but I mean, just talking to your brother… you have a family who supports you and protects you and totally loves you man, for fuck's sake. *Own it!*"

I look down and try to pull myself together, but my voice cracks. "You're right. You're so fucking right."

"So, promise me you'll remember that, even if Jim and Mark are history a year from now."

"I'll try."

"Because I'm right, *right?*"

"Right."

It's a dark, cool night, but Jim's sheets smell like a summer day as we crawl into bed. We lie on our backs, close together. A car cruises by on the street and makes ghosts against the wall. Jim takes my hand, strokes it, then rolls on his side to me, his eyes gleaming. His breath smells like meatloaf, vodka, and wine—as I'm sure mine does—despite the brushing. He pulls me on top of him for what we both want: that amazing sensation of body against body, flesh against flesh, the smooth and the rough, the warm and the cool, the dry and moist of a friction both erotic and mystical. The sheets tangle around our feet as we break out in a sweat and fall into that final rhythm that leads to release and collapse and the aura of afterward.

"I love you, you bastard," he says softly, although it seems to boom in the quiet stillness of the room.

And finally, I say it: "I love you, too."

He moves, just a little.

"But what's love got to do with it?" I throw in.

"I'm sleeping with Tina Turner," he deadpans, rolling over.

A night of deep, moist sleep seems to pass in a moment, and morning light warms the room. I'm on my side, facing the center of the bed. I open my eyes to see Jim, also on his side, eyes open and looking at me. He almost smiles.

"Yes," I say.

"Yes what?"

"Let's do this."

He blinks a few times, then sits up. Stares straight ahead for a moment, then looks at me. "You mean, San Diego, yes? Like, yes?"

"Yes."

"Yes! Yes! Well, if it's yes!—" he leaps out of bed in his beautiful altogether and struggles into a threadbare robe. "Throw something on and wait for me to call you. When I do, get your butt into the living room."

He calls and I follow. A bouquet of wilted flowers sits in a drinking glass on the coffee table. Next to it, a small velvet box wrapped with a narrow gold ribbon. I sit beside him.

"Sorry about the flowers. I had to hide them until it was the right time, if it would ever be the right time—I mean, I didn't know the timeline or how to keep the flowers fresh, even though I changed the water twice and—"

"They're nice. It's nice."

"Oh, okay." He's suddenly awkward and nervous. He reaches for the box and extends it to me listlessly. "So... here."

I hold it in my palm. It's heavier than I expected. "Earbuds? Snoring cancellation devices?"

"Pull the damn ribbon and flip the top before I grab it back and run for my life."

I hold the box between us and slip off the ribbon that twists to the floor. The hinged lid opens smoothly. Inside, two rings sit side-by-side on their pillow; identical silver rings, each with a brilliant, polished oval of yellow-green.

"Peridot," Jim says, removing one of the rings, "from our meteorite. The one missing from my coffee table." He takes my hand and slides the ring on my finger. Then he removes the other ring and puts it on his own finger. "I used my own finger to size yours. Does it fit?"

I twist the ring and it fits perfectly, but say nothing, because the words don't come easily. Finally, with great effort, just one utterance: "Wow."

"Wow?"

"So, what do these mean, exactly?"

Jim scrunches up his face. "I'm not sure, exactly. But they're better than a handshake."

"I'll give you that," I say, blinded by wet eyes.

20
The View From Up Here

I'm tearing around the house like a maniac, looking for my passport. Jim appears, approaches calmly, and hands it to me.

"It was on the floor next to the toilet. Reading material?"

"Thank God."

"You don't really need your passport, Mark. We're going to Chicago, not Beijing."

"I know, I know. I just get nervous trying to pull my driver's license out of my wallet."

"Maybe you need a bigger wallet. Or one that doesn't contain the Oxford English Dictionary." He looks at me, winks. "That was a compliment."

Jim stands in front of the largest window of our condo, the one facing San Diego Harbor. Far below, the sun catches the tips of sailboats.

"Hey, Mr. Nervous," he says, "do you want a cocktail before we go downstairs and wait for the car? We've still got some vodka."

"Thanks, but I'll save my drinking for the wedding," I say.

Jim fixes himself a Smoky Martini. "Your mama did well, sonny. Sam's a solid guy."

"He is, I just wish they would've settled here instead of there."

"Give the lady some space, if you please. You've hardly been at her side with all your bumming around."

"You're right."

"See? You've finally learned to learn from me."

For the past eighteen months, we've lived on the eleventh floor of a harbor-view condominium Jim discovered while strolling around during his afternoon lunch break. It sits among lower buildings on India Street, the un-eponymous name for a street in the heart of San Diego's "Little Italy," replete with expresso and pastry shops, Italian cuisine plain and fancy, and tourists from all over the world, including—*can you imagine!*—Italy.

We closed on the condo in November of 2022. Soon after, I talked Jim into taking a basic Italian class at the Cultural Center on Thursday evenings. He refused at first, because he felt my proficiency was far above his, so I enrolled too—just for fun and moral support. But it was less fun when, one month later, Jim equaled and then bested me in conversational Italian, having taken to the language and mastered even some of its most exasperating irregular verb forms. "It's my programming skills," he explained. "Language is about the foundational logic of grammar, and once you get that, you pretty much get the key to the kingdom..." and on and on he goes about it, every time we study together, this damn husband of mine, Jim *Hollander*-Anello, a name, he brags, that sounds like a Formula One race car driver.

Two days from today, on May 18th, 2024, we'll dance as a couple when my mother weds Sam Derwitz, a decent guy who offers her a life both familiar and new. Five months ago, she moved into his lake view condo in Edgewood, Chicago, where they enjoy the theatre, concerts, eating out—all the things senior adults do when regrets and disappointments fade away, and it's time to enjoy the time left ahead. At Sam's advice, Mom kept her Glendale house so that Loren and Sharon could move in with their twin boys. They do Thanksgiving; we do Christmas. Next Christmas will be a fine one. They'll all be fine ones.

The news of old friends trickles in, except for Marina, who never resumed contact. A story about Carlos Pineda appears on page thirty-two of *People Magazine*, then explodes as a reporter picks it up, making it a featured investigation on an internationally syndicated version of *Sixty Minutes*. The angle is novel: the irony of a serial murderer who nonetheless managed to preserve one of the most valuable architectural discoveries in over a hundred years. Marina, wherever she is, might know all this by now. If she does, I hope it gives her some closure.

Alessandro and Braxton returned to Italy, and after finding a doctor who stabilized his medication, Alessandro reclaimed his former position at the Ministry of Education. The happy couple sent an animated "Welcome to Your New Home" card the day we moved in and arranged a Zoom call so I could give them a virtual tour. Alessandro's hangdog expression seemed less hangdog, although Braxton did most of the talking. They were thrilled to find a new bathhouse in a nearby city that featured "sexy Moroccans" who offered perfumed rubdowns with happy endings. They've invited Jim and me to join them on one of these escapades one summer.

And then Dario, who brings back the most vivid memories, as I know he will for many years. We kept in touch, more or less, long enough for him to share that his almost year-and-a-half in the San Patrignano Community inspired first-rate work in a medium he knew nothing about before his breakdown: textiles. Soon, Dario's creations, some woven into fabric and others printed on silk, were displayed in the Community's retail store and snapped up. Word spread. The big break came in early 2023 when SanPa's executive manager summoned Dario into this office to discuss negotiating a contract with fashion giants *Dolce & Gabbana, Salvatore Ferragamo, and Lucio Fontana*—all of whom had approached the Community to commission original designs. With the help of a fellow patient who'd been a lawyer, Dario drew up a contract that split his fees with the Community with an option to renegotiate after his graduation on February 20th, 2024. Dario—the savvy dealmaker at last!

Overnight, Dario's textile designs appeared everywhere. Milan's high-fashion magazine *Abitare* regularly featured them on Milan's hottest models, male and female; *Oggi Italia* and *Vogue Italia* followed with cover shoots, and American *Vogue* included a profile of Dario and his astonishing rise. It was all the heady stuff of dreams as Jim and I followed Dario's career closely—Jim having finally heard all the details of my time in Madrid and Poreta and pronouncing them worthy of a Romance Novel.

But the excitement of Dario's success, the *realness* of it, didn't hit home until just last December when Jim and I chased around Bloomingdales with our Christmas list. Jim saw it first, draped over a fancy rack on a counter guarded by two young clerks. He carefully removed and unfolded the long silk scarf and held it towards me by its corners—and there I was: stark naked on a bed and strewn with flowers, a moon rising in the window—*Marc avec la Lune à la Fenêtre,* the colors of his original painting reproduced brilliantly; "Mark with Moonlight in the Window"—it said so right underneath in a kind of caption, along with: "Designed by Dario Soole, Vallecas, Madrid."

It's comforting to know that Dario finally secured a steady income while also rewarding the place that nurtured him and teased out his gift. He looked forward to renting a large new studio after his upcoming release from San Patrignano. But, in early February of 2024, a new strain of Covid swept through Rimini, and Dario, with his lifelong aversion to vaccinations, fell ill. He soldiered on in the Community's infirmary but developed pneumonia and was moved to the respiratory intensive care unit of Rimini's *Ospedale G. Marconi.* He died on February 16th, three days before his graduation and on the first anniversary of our wedding day at the Universalist Church in San Diego. We learned about his death in a late-night prowl on the internet.

We later learned that what remained of Dario's estate (after providing for Jabari and Trixie) went to the Global Polio Eradication Initiative, a charitable trust for the eradication of the poliomyelitis virus worldwide. A man who'd avoided vaccines his entire life left almost everything he owned to an organization that expanded access to vaccines. I suddenly understood Dario better than I ever had before—*he* was the true optimist; Dario harbored hope for the world, even as he sensed his own fate.

"Okay, let's skedaddle," Jim says, lifting both of our suitcases. He's already watered the plants and set the alarm. We exit to its gentle warning blips and walk down the hallway to the elevator. The door opens, and we join a couple we vaguely recognize from the floor above.

"Going on vacation?" The woman asks, her arm looped around her husband's arm.

"Yep," I say, "to Chicago for a wedding."

"Chicago," the man scoffs. "Too hot and dirty. Why would anyone go there?"

"We like it," says Jim, holding back on the *asshole* word, although it's clearly in his tone.

"Have a *blessed* trip," they say together, pronouncing it BLESS-ed. Then, they get off only two floors below where they got on.

Three hours later, we're somewhere over the shadowed heartland where winding roads glitter with the lights of long hauls. I resist the urge to nap because I'm filled with a strange exhilaration that feels like—although I'm not exactly sure—*happiness*. I rest my forehead against the cool window and look out. The view from up here is amazing—thirty thousand feet above everything, so you can take it all in at once: the houses and cars and parks and schools... and *I'm* part of that crazy mess. I feel like I'm closer to figuring out my life than ever before—if figuring it out even matters, and I'm not sure it does anymore because everything sorts out sooner or later. Just look out the window. Somehow, it all makes sense from up here in a way it doesn't when you're in the thick of it. Suddenly, from up here, what you see below looks like a puzzle where every little piece finds its place. But I wonder if you can still say "up here," as in *the view from up here looks great,* when you're not "up here" anymore, but in an entirely different space. I mean, did the astronauts say it when they walked on the moon and looked back at the Earth? Do Martians say it if Martians exist and watch us through their telescopes? And what about some alien life-form hitching a ride on a meteor where there's no *up here* because the view constantly changes—what would it say if it could say anything?

I share this woolgathering with Jim, who sits quietly in the middle seat studying his Italian grammar. He looks straight ahead, listens, and seems to think about it. Then, he turns and looks at me, smiles.

"The view up here looks pretty good to me," he says.

"What view? You're not even by the window."

"You're getting better, but you still fail to see the obvious."

"You say that all the time, Jim, and I still don't know what it means."

"Work on it."

"Work on what?"

"Exactly," Jim says, opening his book again. "Thank God I'm a patient man."

Palm Desert, CA, December 25, 2023

Acknowledgments

A short thank you to the many people who generously contributed their time and energy to reading, critiquing, encouraging, and cheering me on to the finish line. First and foremost, my publisher and editor, Ian Henzel, who believed in *Bread* enough to put it between two covers. Close behind him are author-editors, Georgia Ann Hughes, Emily Dwass, Sara Marchant, Zoe Ghahremani, Patrick McMahon, Joseph McCormack, and Omar Gonzales. Poets Craig Marin Getz and Sue Burge added their poetic sensibilities to the prose; screenwriter Donata Lewandowski Guerra, director Vince Maynard, screenwriter-filmmakers Eduardo Santiago and Richard Kilroy added their cinematic sensibilities, and translators *par excellence* Jill Earick Ananyi and Ada Ramirez were pressed into service despite their busy schedules. Finally, I'm greatly indebted to my foundational critique groups and close friends who've listened to me read too many drafts for too long: Jan Parker, Karen Sleeth, and Trish Sheppard from the Wildacres Retreat of North Carolina; Lily Berman, Ken White, Bill Rodgers, Judith Lieber of Palm Springs, and Glenn Schwartz of Write Out Loud, Los Angeles. My brilliant friends and "fellow" creatives Patrice la Mariana, Stephen Sturk, and Mike Vaugn all contributed their considerable skills and gifted me with their infinite patience through this amazing journey—I owe them big-time.

About the Author

Glen Peters, also writing under the name of Glen Vecchione, is the author of science, math, and history books that have been translated into several languages and distributed throughout the world. His poetry and short stories appear in *Missouri Review, ZYZZYVA, Cincinnati Review, Comstock Review, Timberline Review*, and *Main Street Rag*. Glen won the Editor's Choice Award in *The Last Stanza Poetry Journal* and was the featured poet in *Sequestrum's* "Wonder" issue of January 2024. He was also nominated for the 2022 and 2023 Pushcart Prizes and named a Finalist in the 2022 *Sewanee Review* poetry competition. Glen wrote the music and lyrics to the Jazz Ballet *The Legend of Frankie and Johnny*, produced by the Nat Horne Theatre on Broadway in 1980. His play-in-verse, *Cowboy BO and the Train Whistle* was produced at the Lyceum Theatre in San Diego in 2011. *Where the Nights Smell Like Bread* is his first novel.

Made in the USA
Las Vegas, NV
22 April 2025

21232806R00177